JULIET

ANNE

FORTIER

...

Juliet

a novel

BALLANTINE BOOKS

NEW YORK

Published in the United States by Ballantine Books,
an imprint of The Random House Publishing Group,
a division of Random House, Inc., New York.

BALLANTINE and colophon are registered
trademarks of Random House, Inc.

LIBRARY OF CONGRESS CATALOGING-IN-PUBLICATION DATA
Fortier, Anne.
Juliet: a novel / Anne Fortier.

p. cm.
ISBN 978-0-345-51610-7
eBook ISBN 978-0-345-51977-1
1. Family secrets—Fiction.   2. Siena (Italy)—Fiction.   I. Title.
PS3606.O7487J85 2010
813'.6—dc22   2010002093

Printed in the United States of America
on acid-free paper

www.ballantinebooks.com

2 4 6 8 9 7 5 3 1

FIRST EDITION

Book design by Barbara M. Bachman

To my beloved mother,
Birgit Malling Eriksen,
whose magnanimity and herculean research
made this book possible

Go hence to have more talk of these sad things.
Some shall be pardon'd, and some punished,
For never was a story of more woe
Than this of Juliet and her Romeo.

—SHAKESPEARE

JULIET

THE PROLOGUE

. . .

*T*HEY SAY I DIED.

My heart stopped, and I was not breathing—in the eyes of the world I was really dead. Some say I was gone for three minutes, some say four; personally, I am beginning to think death is mostly a matter of opinion.

Being Juliet, I suppose I should have seen it coming. But I so wanted to believe that, this time around, it would not be the same old lamentable tragedy all over. This time, we would be together forever, Romeo and I, and our love would never again be suspended by dark centuries of banishment and death.

But you can't fool the Bard. And so I died as I must, when my lines ran out, and fell back into the well of creation.

O happy pen. This is thy sheet.

There ink, and let me begin.

Alack, alack, what blood is this which stains
The stony entrance of this sepulchre?

...

IT HAS TAKEN ME A while to figure out where to start. You could argue that my story began more than six hundred years ago, with a highway robbery in medieval Tuscany. Or, more recently, with a dance and a kiss at Castello Salimbeni, when my parents met for the first time. But I would never have come to know any of this without the event that changed my life overnight and forced me to travel to Italy in search of the past. That event was the death of my great-aunt Rose.

It took Umberto three days to find me and tell me the sad news. Considering my virtuosity in the art of disappearing, I am amazed he succeeded at all. But then, Umberto always had an uncanny ability to read my mind and predict my movements, and besides, there were only so many Shakespeare summer camps in Virginia.

How long he stood there, watching the theater performance from the back of the room, I do not know. I was backstage as always, too absorbed in the kids, their lines and props to notice anything else around me until the curtain fell. After the dress rehearsal that afternoon, someone had misplaced the vial of poison, and for lack of better, Romeo would have to commit suicide by eating Tic Tacs.

"But they give me heartburn!" the boy had complained, with all the accusatory anxiety of a fourteen-year-old.

"Excellent!" I had said, resisting a motherly urge to adjust the velvet hat on his head. "That'll help you stay in character."

Only when the lights came on afterwards, and the kids dragged me on-stage to bombard me with gratitude, did I notice the familiar figure loom-ing near the exit, contemplating me through the applause. Stern and statuesque in his dark suit and tie, Umberto stood out like a lone reed of civilization in a primordial swamp. He always had. For as long as I could remember, he had never worn a single piece of clothing that could be con-sidered casual. Khaki shorts and golf shirts, to Umberto, were the gar-ments of men who have no virtues left, not even shame.

Later, when the onslaught of grateful parents subsided and I could fi-nally walk off the stage, I was stopped briefly by the program director, who took me by the shoulders and shook me heartily—he knew me too well to attempt a hug. "Good job with the youngsters, Julie!" he gushed. "I can count on you again next summer, can't I?"

"Absolutely," I lied, walking on. "I'll be around."

Approaching Umberto at last, I looked in vain for that little happiness at the corner of his eyes that was usually there when he saw me again after some time away. But there was no smile, not even a trace, and I now un-derstood why he had come. Stepping silently into his embrace, I wished I had the power to flip reality upside down like an hourglass, and that life was not a finite affair, but rather a perpetually recurring passage through a little hole in time.

"Don't cry, principessa," he said into my hair, "she wouldn't have liked it. We can't all live forever. She was eighty-two."

"I know. But—" I stood back and wiped my eyes. "Was Janice there?"

Umberto's eyes narrowed as they always did when my twin sister was mentioned. "What do you think?" Only then, up close, did I see that he looked bruised and bitter, as if he had spent the last few nights drinking himself to sleep. But perhaps it had been a natural thing to do. Without Aunt Rose what would become of Umberto? For as long as I could re-member, the two of them had been yoked together in a necessary partner-ship of money and muscle—she had played the withering belle, he the patient butler—and despite their differences, clearly neither of them had ever been willing to attempt life without the other.

The Lincoln was parked discreetly over by the fire pit, and no one saw Umberto placing my old pack in the trunk before opening the back door for me with measured ceremony.

"I want to sit in front. Please?"

He shook his head in disapproval and opened the passenger door instead. "I knew it would all come apart."

But it had never been Aunt Rose who insisted on the formality. Although Umberto was her employee, she had always treated him like family. The gesture, however, was never returned. Whenever Aunt Rose would invite Umberto to join us at the dinner table, he would merely look at her with bemused forbearance, as if it was an ongoing wonder to him why she kept asking and just somehow didn't get it. He ate all his meals in the kitchen, always had, always would, and not even the name of sweet Jesus—spoken in rising exasperation—could persuade him to come and sit down with us, even at Thanksgiving.

Aunt Rose used to dismiss Umberto's peculiarity as a European thing and smoothly segue into a lecture about tyranny, liberty, and independence that would inevitably culminate in her pointing a fork at us and snorting, "and that is why we are *not* going to Europe on vacation. Especially Italy. End of story." Personally, I was fairly certain that Umberto preferred to eat alone simply because he considered his own company vastly superior to what we had to offer. There he was, serene in the kitchen, with his opera, his wine, and his perfectly ripened block of Parmesan cheese, while we—Aunt Rose, me, and Janice—bickered and shivered in the drafty dining room. Given the option, I would have lived every minute of every day in the kitchen, too.

As we drove through the dark Shenandoah Valley that night, Umberto told me about Aunt Rose's last hours. She had died peacefully, in her sleep, after an evening of listening to all her favorite Fred Astaire songs, one crackling record after another. Once the last chord of the last piece had died out, she had stood up and opened the French doors to the garden outside, perhaps wanting to breathe in the honeysuckle one more time. As she stood there, eyes closed, Umberto told me, the long lace curtains had fluttered round her spindly body without a sound, as if she was already a ghost.

"Did I do the right thing?" she had asked, quietly.

"Of course you did," had been his diplomatic answer.

IT WAS MIDNIGHT by the time we rolled into Aunt Rose's driveway. Umberto had already warned me that Janice had arrived from Florida that afternoon with a calculator and a bottle of champagne. That did not, however, explain the second jock-mobile parked right in front of the entrance.

"I sincerely hope," I said, taking my pack out of the trunk before Umberto could get to it, "that is *not* the undertaker." No sooner had I said the words than I winced at my own flippancy. It was completely unlike me to talk like that, and it only ever happened when I came within earshot of my sister.

Casting but a glance at the mystery car, Umberto adjusted his jacket the way one does a bulletproof vest before combat. "I fear there are many kinds of undertaking."

As soon as we stepped through the front door of the house, I saw what he meant. All the large portraits in the hallway had been taken down and were now standing with their backs to the wall like delinquents before a firing squad. And the Venetian vase that had always stood on the round table beneath the chandelier was already gone.

"Hello?" I yelled, feeling a surge of rage that I had not felt since my last visit. "Anyone still alive?"

My voice echoed through the quiet house, but as soon as the noise died down I heard running feet in the corridor upstairs. Yet despite her guilty rush, Janice had to make her usual slow-motion appearance on the broad staircase, her flimsy summer dress emphasizing her sumptuous curves far better than had she worn nothing at all. Pausing for the world press, she tossed back her long hair with languid self-satisfaction and sent me a supercilious smile before commencing her descent. "Lo and behold," she observed, her voice sweetly chilled, "the virgitarian has landed." Only then did I notice the male flavor-of-the-week trailing right behind her, looking as disheveled and bloodshot as one does after time alone with my sister.

"Sorry to disappoint," I said, dropping my backpack on the floor with a thud. "Can I help you strip the house of valuables, or do you prefer to work alone?"

Janice's laughter was like a little wind chime on your neighbor's porch, put there exclusively to annoy you. "This is Archie," she informed me, in her business-casual way, "he is going to give us twenty grand for all this junk."

I looked at them both with disgust as they came towards me. "How generous of him. He obviously has a passion for trash."

Janice shot me an icy glare, but quickly checked herself. She knew very well that I could not care less about her good opinion, and that her anger just amused me.

I was born four minutes before her. No matter what she did, or said, I would always be four minutes older. Even if—in Janice's own mind—she was the hypersonic hare and I the plodding turtle, we both knew she could run cocky circles around me all she liked, but that she would never actually catch up and close that tiny gap between us.

"Well," said Archie, eyeing the open door, "I'm gonna take off. Nice to meet you, Julie—it's Julie, isn't it? Janice told me all about you—" He laughed nervously. "Keep up the good work! Make peace not love, as they say."

Janice waved sweetly as Archie walked out, letting the screen door slam behind him. But as soon as he was out of hearing range, her angelic face turned demonic, like a Halloween hologram. "Don't you dare look at me like that!" she sneered. "I'm trying to make us some money. It's not as if you're making any, is it now?"

"But then I don't have your kind of . . . expenses." I nodded at her latest upgrades, eminently visible under the clingy dress. "Tell me, Janice, how *do* they get all that stuff in there? Through the navel?"

"Tell me, Julie," mimicked Janice. "How does it feel to get nothing stuffed in there? Ever!"

"Excuse me, ladies," said Umberto, stepping politely between us the way he had done so many times before, "but may I suggest we move this riveting exchange to the library?"

Once we caught up with Janice, she had already draped herself over Aunt Rose's favorite armchair, a gin and tonic nestling on the foxhunt-motif cushion I had cross-stitched as a senior in high school while my sister had been out on the prowl for upright prey.

"What?" She looked at us with ill-concealed loathing. "You don't think she left half the booze for me?"

It was vintage Janice to be angling for a fight over someone's dead body, and I turned my back to her and walked over to the French doors. On the terrace outside, Aunt Rose's beloved terra-cotta pots sat like a row of mourners, flower heads hanging beyond consolation. It was an unusual sight. Umberto always kept the garden in perfect order, but perhaps he found no pleasure in his work now that his employer and grateful audience was no more.

"I am surprised," said Janice, swirling her drink, "that you are still here, Birdie. If I were you I would have been in Vegas by now. With the silver."

Umberto did not reply. He had stopped talking directly to Janice years ago. Instead, he looked at me. "The funeral is tomorrow."

"I can't believe," said Janice, one leg dangling from the armrest, "you planned all that without asking us."

"It was what she wanted."

"Anything else we should know?" Janice freed herself from the embrace of the chair and straightened out her dress. "I assume we're all getting our share? She didn't fall in love with some weird pet foundation or something, did she?"

"Do you mind?" I croaked, and for a second or two, Janice actually looked chastened. Then she shrugged it off as she always did, and reached once more for the gin bottle.

I did not even bother to look at her as she feigned clumsiness, raising her perfectly groomed eyebrows in astonishment to let us know that she certainly had not intended to pour quite so much. As the sun slowly melted into the horizon, so would Janice soon melt into a chaise longue, leaving the great questions of life for others to answer as long as they kept the liquor coming.

She had been like that for as long as I remembered: insatiable. When we were children, Aunt Rose used to laugh delightedly and exclaim, "That girl, she could eat her way out of a gingerbread prison," as if Janice's greediness was something to be proud of. But then, Aunt Rose was at the top of the food chain and had—unlike me—nothing to fear. For as long as I could remember, Janice had been able to sniff out my secret candy no matter where I hid it, and Easter mornings in our family were nasty, brutish, and short. They would inevitably climax with Umberto chastising her for stealing my share of the Easter eggs, and Janice—teeth dripping with chocolate—hissing from underneath her bed that he wasn't her daddy and couldn't tell her what to do.

The frustrating thing was that she didn't look her part. Her skin stubbornly refused to give away its secrets; it was as smooth as the satin icing on a wedding cake, her features as delicately crafted as the little marzipan fruits and flowers in the hands of a master confectioner. Neither gin nor coffee nor shame nor remorse had been able to crack that glazed façade; it was as if she had a perennial spring of life inside her, as if she rose every morning rejuvenated from the well of eternity, not a day older, not an ounce heavier, and still ravenously hungry for the world.

Unfortunately, we were not identical twins. Once, in the schoolyard, I had overheard someone referring to me as Bambi-on-stilts, and although Umberto laughed and said it was a compliment, it didn't feel that way. Even when I was past my most clumsy age, I knew I still looked lanky and anemic next to Janice; no matter where we went or what we did, she was as dark and effusive as I was pale and reserved.

Whenever we entered a room together, all spotlights would immediately turn to my sister, and although I was standing there right beside her, I became just another head in the audience. As time went on, however, I grew comfortable with my role. I never had to worry about finishing my sentences, for Janice would inevitably finish them for me. And on the rare occasions when someone asked about my hopes and dreams—usually over a polite cup of tea with one of Aunt Rose's neighbors—Janice would pull me away to the piano, where she would attempt to play while I turned the sheets for her. Even now, at twenty-five, I would still squirm and grind to a halt in conversations with strangers, hoping desperately to be interrupted before I had to commit my verb to an object.

WE BURIED AUNT ROSE in the pouring rain. As I stood there by her grave, heavy drops of water fell from my hair to blend with the tears running down my cheeks; the paper tissues I had brought from home had long since turned to mush in my pockets.

Although I had been crying all night, I was hardly prepared for the sense of sad finality I felt as the coffin was lowered crookedly into the earth. Such a big coffin for Aunt Rose's spindly frame . . . now I suddenly regretted not having asked to see the body, even if it would have made no difference to her. Or maybe it would? Perhaps she was watching us from somewhere far away, wishing she could let us know that she had arrived safely. It was a consoling idea, a welcome distraction from reality, and I wished I could believe it.

The only one who did not look like a drowned rodent by the end of the funeral was Janice, who wore plastic boots with five-inch heels and a black hat that signaled anything but mourning. In contrast, I was wearing what Umberto had once labeled my Attila-the-Nun outfit; if Janice's boots and neckline said *come hither,* my clunky shoes and buttoned-up dress most certainly said *get lost.*

Half a handful of people showed up at the grave, but only Mr. Gallagher, our family lawyer, stayed to talk. Neither Janice nor I had ever met him, but Aunt Rose had talked about him so often and so fondly that the man himself could only be a disappointment.

"I understand you are a pacifist?" he said to me, as we walked away from the cemetery together.

"Jules loves to fight," observed Janice, walking happily in the middle, oblivious to the fact that the brim of her hat was funneling water on both of us, "and throw stuff at people. Did you hear what she did to the Little Mermaid—?"

"That's enough," I said, trying to find a dry spot on my sleeve to wipe my eyes one last time.

"Oh, don't be so modest! You were on the front page!"

"And I hear your business is going very well?" Mr. Gallagher looked at Janice, attempting a smile. "It must be a challenge to make everyone happy?"

"Happy? Eek!" Janice narrowly avoided stepping in a puddle. "Happiness is the worst threat to my business. Dreams are what it's all about. Frustrations. Fantasies that never come true. Men that don't exist. Women you can never have. That's where the money is, date after date after date—"

Janice kept talking, but I stopped listening. It was one of the world's great ironies that my sister was into professional matchmaking, for she was probably the least romantic person I had ever known. Notwithstanding her urge to flirt with every one of them, she saw men as little more than noisy power tools that you plugged in when you needed them and unplugged as soon as the job was done.

Oddly enough, when we were children, Janice had had an obsession with arranging everything in pairs, two teddy bears, two cushions, two hairbrushes . . . even on days when we had been fighting, she would put both our dolls next to each other on the shelf overnight, sometimes even with their arms around each other. In that respect it was perhaps not strange that she would choose to make a career out of matchmaking, seeing that she was a genuine Noah at putting people in pairs. The only problem was that, unlike the old patriarch, she had long since forgotten why she did it.

It was hard to say when things had changed. At some point in high school she had made it her mission to burst every dream I might ever have had about love. Running through boyfriends like economy pantyhose, Janice had taken a peculiar pleasure in grossing me out by describing everybody and everything in a dismissive slang that made me wonder why women consorted with men at all.

"So," she had said, rolling pink curlers into my hair on the night before our prom, "this is your last chance."

I had looked at her in the mirror, puzzled by her ultimatum but prevented from responding by one of her mint-green mud masks that had dried to a crust on my face.

"You know"—she had grimaced impatiently—"your last chance to pop the cherry. That's what prom's all about. Why do you think the guys dress up? Because they like to dance? Puh-*leez*!" She had glanced at me in the mirror, checking her progress. "If you don't do it at prom, you know what they say. You're a prude. Nobody likes a prude."

The next morning, I had complained about a stomachache, and as the prom came closer, my pains grew worse. In the end, Aunt Rose had to call the neighbors and tell them that their son had better find himself another date for the evening; meanwhile, Janice was picked up by an athlete called Troy and disappeared in a smoke of squealing tires.

After listening to my moans all afternoon, Aunt Rose began insisting we go to the emergency room in case it was appendicitis, but Umberto had calmed her down and said that I did not have a fever, and that he was certain it was nothing serious. As he stood there next to my bed later in the evening, looking at me peeking out from underneath my blanket, I could see that he knew exactly what was going on, and that, in some strange way, he was pleased with my scam. We both knew there was nothing wrong with the neighbors' son as such, it was just that he did not fit the description of the man I had envisioned as my lover. And if I could not get what I wanted, I would rather miss the prom.

"Dick," Janice now said, stroking Mr. Gallagher with a satin smile, "why don't we just cut to the chase. How much?"

I did not even try to intervene. After all, as soon as Janice got her money, she would be off to the eternal hunting grounds of the bushytailed wannabe, and I would never have to set eyes on her again.

"Well," said Mr. Gallagher, stopping awkwardly in the parking lot, right next to Umberto and the Lincoln, "I'm afraid the fortune is almost entirely tied up in the estate."

"Look," said Janice, "we all know it's fifty-fifty down to the last nickel, okay, so let's cut the crap. She wants us to draw a white line down the middle of the house? Fair enough, we can do that. Or"—she shrugged as if it was all the same to her—"we simply sell the place and split the money. How much?"

"The reality is that in the end"—Mr. Gallagher looked at me with some regret—"Mrs. Jacobs changed her mind and decided to leave everything to Miss Janice."

"What?" I looked from Janice to Mr. Gallagher to Umberto, but found no support at all.

"Holy shit!" Janice flared up in a broad smile. "The old lady had a sense of humor after all!"

"Of course," Mr. Gallagher went on, more sternly, "there is a sum put aside for Mister—for Umberto, and there is a mention of certain framed photographs that your great-aunt wanted Miss Julie to have."

"Hey," said Janice, opening her arms, "I'm feeling generous."

"Wait a minute—" I took a step back, struggling to process the news. "This doesn't make any sense."

For as long as I could remember, Aunt Rose had gone through hell and high water to treat us equally; for heaven's sake, I had even caught her counting the number of pecans in our morning muesli to make sure one of us didn't get more than the other. And she had always talked about the house as something that we—at some point in the future—would own together. "You girls," she used to say, "really need to learn how to get along. I won't live forever, you know. And when I am gone, you are going to share this house."

"I understand your disappointment—" said Mr. Gallagher.

"Disappointment?" I felt like grabbing him by the collar, but stuck my hands in my pockets instead, as deep as they could go. "Don't think I'm buying this. I want to see the will." Looking him straight in the eye I saw him squirming under my gaze. "There's something going on here behind my back—"

"You were always a sore loser," Janice broke in, savoring my fury with a catty smile, "that's what's going on."

"Here—" Mr. Gallagher clicked open his briefcase with shaky hands and handed me a document. "This is your copy of the will. I'm afraid there's not much room for dispute."

UMBERTO FOUND ME in the garden, crouched under the arbor he had once built for us when Aunt Rose was in bed with pneumonia. Sitting down next to me on the wet bench, he did not comment on my childish disappearing act, just handed me an immaculately ironed handkerchief and observed me as I blew my nose.

"It's not the money," I said, defensively. "Did you see her smirk? Did you hear what she said? She doesn't care about Aunt Rose. She never did. It's not fair!"

"Who told you life was fair?" Umberto looked at me with raised eyebrows. "Not me."

"I know! I just don't understand—but it's my own fault. I always thought she was serious about treating us equally. I borrowed money—" I clutched my face to avoid his stare. "Don't say it!"

"Are you finished?"

I shook my head. "You have no idea how finished I am."

"Good." He opened his jacket and took out a dry but slightly bent manila envelope. "Because she wanted you to have this. It's a big secret. Gallagher doesn't know. Janice doesn't know. It's for you only."

I was immediately suspicious. It was very unlike Aunt Rose to give me something behind Janice's back, but then, it was also very unlike her to write me out of her will. Clearly, I had not known my mother's aunt as well as I thought I did, nor had I fully known myself until now. To think that I could sit here—today of all days—and cry over money. Although she had been in her late fifties when she adopted us, Aunt Rose had been like a mother to us, and I ought to be ashamed of myself for wanting anything more from her.

When I finally opened it, the envelope turned out to contain three things: a letter, a passport, and a key.

"This is my passport!" I exclaimed. "How did she—?" I looked at the picture page again. It was my photo all right, and my date of birth, but the name was not mine. "Giulietta? Giulietta Tolomei?"

"That is your real name. Your aunt changed it when she brought you here from Italy. She changed Janice's name, too."

I was stunned. "But *why*? . . . How long have you known?"

He looked down. "Why don't you read the letter?"

I unfolded the two sheets of paper. "You wrote this?"

"She dictated it to me." Umberto smiled sadly. "She wanted to make sure you could read it."

The letter read as follows:

My dearest Julie,

I have asked Umberto to give you this letter after my funeral, so I suppose that means I am dead. Anyway, I know you are still angry that I never took you girls to Italy, but believe me when I say that it was for your own good. How could I ever forgive myself if something happened to you? But now you are older. And there is something there, in Siena, that your mother left for you. You alone. I don't know why, but that is Diane for you, bless her soul. She found something, and supposedly it is still there. By the sound of it, it was much more valuable than anything I have ever owned. And that is why I decided to do it this way, and give the house to Janice. I was hoping we could avoid all this and forget about Italy, but now I am beginning to think that it would be wrong of me if I never told you.

Here is what you must do. Take this key and go to the bank in Palazzo Tolomei. In Siena. I think it is for a safety-deposit box. Your mother had it in her purse when she died. She had a financial advisor there, a man called Francesco Maconi. Find him and tell him that you are Diane Tolomei's daughter. Oh, and that is another thing. I changed your names. Your real name is Giulietta Tolomei. But this is America. I thought Julie Jacobs made more sense, but no one can spell that either. What is the world coming to? No, I have had a good life. Thanks to you. Oh, and another thing: Umberto is going to get you a passport with your real name. I have no idea how you do these things, but never mind, we will leave that to him.

I am not going to say goodbye. We will see each other again in Heaven, God willing. But I wanted to make sure you get what is rightly yours. Just be careful over there. Look what happened to your mother. Italy can be a very strange place. Your great-grandmother was born there, of course, but I'll tell you, you couldn't have dragged her back there for all the money in the world. Anyway, don't tell anyone what I have told you. And try to smile more. You have such a beautiful smile, when you use it.

Much love & God bless,
Auntie

It took me a while to recover from the letter. Reading it, I could almost hear Aunt Rose dictating it, just as wonderfully scatterbrained in death as she had been when she was still alive. By the time I was finished with Umberto's handkerchief, he did not want it back. Instead, he told me to take it with me to Italy, so that I would remember him when I found my big treasure.

"Come on!" I blew my nose one final time. "We both know there's no treasure!"

He picked up the key. "Are you not curious? Your aunt was convinced that your mother had found something of tremendous value."

"Then why didn't she tell me earlier? Why wait until she's—" I threw up my arms. "It doesn't make sense."

Umberto squinted. "She wanted to. But you were never around."

I rubbed my face, mostly to avoid his accusatory stare. "Even if she was right, you know I can't go back to Italy. They'd lock me up so fast. You know they told me—"

Actually, they—the Italian police—had told me significantly more than I had ever passed on to Umberto. But he knew the gist of it. He knew that I had once been arrested in Rome during an antiwar demonstration, and spent a very unrecommendable night in a local prison before being tossed out of the country at daybreak and told never to come back. He also knew that it hadn't been my fault. I had been eighteen, and all I had wanted was to go to Italy and see the place where I was born.

Pining in front of my college's bulletin boards with their gaudy ads for study trips and expensive language courses in Florence, I had come across a small poster denouncing the war in Iraq and all the countries that took part in it. One of those countries, I was excited to discover, was Italy. At the bottom of the page was a list of dates and destinations; anyone interested in the cause was welcome to join in. One week in Rome—travel included—would cost me no more than four hundred dollars, which was precisely what I had left in my bank account. Little did I know that the low fare was made possible by the fact that we were almost guaranteed to *not* stay the whole week, and that the tab for our return flights and last night's lodgings would—if all went according to plan—be picked up by the Italian authorities, that is, the Italian taxpayers.

And so, understanding very little about the purpose of the trip, I circled back to the poster several times before finally signing up. That night, however, tossing around in my bed, I knew I had done the wrong thing and that I would have to undo it as soon as possible. But when I told Janice the next morning, she just rolled her eyes and said, "Here lies Jules, who didn't have much of a life, but who *almost* went to Italy once."

Obviously, I had to go.

When the first rocks started flying in front of the Italian Parliament—thrown by two of my fellow travelers, Sam and Greg—I would have loved nothing more than to be back in my dorm room, pillow over my head. But I was trapped in the crowd like everyone else, and once the Roman police had had enough of our rocks and Molotov cocktails, we were all baptized by tear gas.

It was the first time in my life I found myself thinking, *I could die now.* Falling down on the asphalt and seeing the world—legs, arms, vomit—through a haze of pain and disbelief, I completely forgot who I was and where I was going with my life. Perhaps like the martyrs of old, I discovered another place; somewhere that was neither life nor death. But then the pain came back, and the panic, too, and after a moment it stopped feeling like a religious experience.

Months later, I kept wondering if I had ever fully recovered from the events in Rome. When I forced myself to think about it, I got this nagging feeling that I was still forgetting something crucial about who I was—something that had been spilled on the Italian asphalt and never come back.

"True." Umberto opened the passport and scrutinized my photo. "They told Julie Jacobs she can't return to Italy. But what about Giulietta Tolomei?"

I did a double take. Here was Umberto, who still scolded me for dressing like a flower child, urging me to break the law. "Are you suggesting—?"

"Why do you think I had this made? It was your aunt's last wish that you go to Italy. Don't break my heart, principessa."

Seeing the sincerity in his eyes, I struggled once more against the tears. "But what about you?" I said gruffly. "Why don't you come with me? We could find the treasure together. And if we don't, to hell with it! We'll become pirates. We'll scour the seas—"

Umberto reached out and touched my cheek very gently, as if he knew that, once I was gone, I would never come back. And should we ever meet again, it would not be like this, sitting together in a child's hideaway, our backs turned to the world outside. "There are some things," he said softly, "that a princess has to do alone. Do you remember what I told you . . . one day you will find your kingdom?"

"That was just a story. Life isn't like that."

"Everything we say is a story. But nothing we say is *just* a story."

I threw my arms around him, not yet ready to let go. "What about you? You're not staying here, are you?"

Umberto squinted up at the dripping woodwork. "I think Janice is right. It's time for old Birdie to retire. I should steal the silver and go to Vegas. It will last me about a week, I think, with my luck. So make sure to call me when you find your treasure."

I leaned my head against his shoulder. "You'll be the first to know."

Draw thy tool—here comes of
the house of Montagues

· · ·

A s far back as I could remember, Aunt Rose had done everything in her power to prevent Janice and me from going to Italy. "How
many times do I have to tell you," she used to say, "that it is not a place for
nice girls?" Later on, realizing that her strategy had to change, she would
shake her head whenever anyone would broach the subject, and clasp her
heart as if the very thought of the place put her at death's door. "Trust
me," she would wheeze, "Italy is nothing but a big disappointment, and
Italian men are pigs!"

I had always resented her inexplicable prejudice against the country
where I was born, but after my experience in Rome I ended up more or
less agreeing with her: Italy was a disappointment, and the Italians—at
least the uniformed variety—made pigs look pretty good.

Similarly, whenever we would ask her about our parents, Aunt Rose
would cut us off by reciting the same old story. "How many times do I
have to tell you," she would grunt, frustrated at being interrupted in the
middle of reading the newspaper wearing her little cotton gloves that kept
the ink off her hands, "that your parents died in a car accident in Tuscany
when you were three years old?" Fortunately for Janice and me—or so the
story continued—Aunt Rose and poor Uncle Jim—bless his soul—had
been able to adopt us immediately after the tragedy, and it was our good
luck that they had never been able to have children of their own. We ought
to be grateful that we had not ended up in an Italian orphanage eating

spaghetti every day. Look at us! Here we were, living on an estate in Virginia, spoiled rotten; the very least we could do in return was to stop plaguing Aunt Rose with questions she didn't know how to answer. And could someone please fix her another mint julep, seeing that her joints were aching something fierce from our incessant nagging.

As I sat on the plane to Europe, staring out into the Atlantic night and reliving conflicts past, it struck me that I missed everything about Aunt Rose, not just the good bits. How happy I would have been to spend another hour with her, even if she were to spend that hour ranting. Now that she was gone, it was hard to believe she could ever have made me slam doors and stomp upstairs, and hard to accept that I had wasted so many precious hours in stubborn silence, locked in my room.

I angrily wiped a tear rolling down my cheek with the flimsy airline napkin and told myself that regrets were a waste of time. Yes, I should have written more letters to her, and yes, I should have called more often and told her I loved her, but that was all too late now; I could not undo the sins of the past.

On top of my grief there was also another sensation gnawing at my spine. Was it foreboding? Not necessarily. Foreboding implies that something bad will happen; my problem was that I didn't know if anything would happen at all. It was entirely possible that the whole trip would end in disappointment. But I also knew that there was only one person I could rightfully blame for the squeeze I was in, and that person was me.

I had grown up believing I would inherit half of Aunt Rose's fortune, and therefore had not even tried to make one of my own. While other girls my age had climbed up the slippery career pole with carefully manicured nails, I had only worked jobs I liked—such as teaching at Shakespeare camps—knowing that sooner or later, my inheritance from Aunt Rose would take care of my growing credit-card debt. As a result, I had little to fall back on now but an elusive heirloom left behind in a faraway land by a mother I could barely remember.

Ever since dropping out of grad school I had lived nowhere in particular, couch-surfing with friends from the antiwar movement, and moving out whenever I got a Shakespeare teaching gig. For some reason, the Bard's plays were all that had ever stuck in my head, and no matter how hard I tried, I could never get tired of *Romeo and Juliet.*

I occasionally taught adults, but much preferred kids—maybe because I was fairly sure they liked me. My first clue was that they would always refer to the grown-ups as if I weren't one of them. It made me happy that they accepted me as one of their own, although I knew it was not actually a compliment. It simply meant that they suspected I had never really grown up either, and that, even at twenty-five, I still came across as an awkward tween struggling to articulate—or, more often, conceal—the poetry raging in my soul.

It didn't help my career path that I was at a complete loss to envision my future. When people asked me what I would like to do with my life, I had no idea what to say, and when I tried to visualize myself five years down the road, all I saw was a big, black pothole. In gloomy moments I interpreted this impending darkness as a sign that I would die young, and concluded that the reason I could not envision my future was that I had none. My mother had died young, and so had my grandmother—Aunt Rose's younger sister. For some reason, fate was on our case, and whenever I found myself contemplating a long-term commitment, whether it was work or housing, I always bowed out at the last minute, haunted by the idea that I would not be around to see it to completion.

Every time I came home for Christmas or a summer holiday, Aunt Rose would discreetly beg me to stay with her rather than continue my aimless existence. "You know, Julie," she would say, while picking dead leaves off a houseplant or decorating the Christmas tree one angel at a time, "you could always come back here for a while, and think about what you would like to do with yourself."

But even if I was tempted, I knew I couldn't do that. Janice was out there on her own, making money on matchmaking and renting a two-bedroom apartment with a view over a fake lake; for me to move back home would be to acknowledge that she had won.

Now, of course, everything had changed. Moving back in with Aunt Rose was no longer an option. The world as I knew it belonged to Janice, and I was left with nothing more than the contents of a manila envelope. As I sat there on the plane, rereading Aunt Rose's letter over a plastic cup of sour wine, it suddenly occurred to me how thoroughly alone I was now, with her gone and only Umberto left in the world.

Growing up, I had never been good at making friends. In contrast,

Janice would have had a hard time squeezing her closest and dearest into a double-decker bus. Whenever she would go out with her giggling throng at night, Aunt Rose would circle around me nervously for a while, pretending to look for the magnifying glass or her dedicated crossword pencil. Eventually, she would sit down next to me on the sofa, seemingly interested in the book I was reading. But I knew she wasn't.

"You know, Julie," she would say, picking specks of lint from my pajama bottoms, "I can easily entertain myself. If you want to go out with your friends—"

The suggestion would hang in the air for a while, until I had concocted a suitable reply. The truth was that I did not stay at home because I felt sorry for Aunt Rose, but because I had no interest in going out. Whenever I let people drag me along to some bar I always ended up surrounded by meatheads and pencil necks, who all seemed to think we were acting out a fairy tale in which—before the night was over—I would have to choose one of them.

The memory of Aunt Rose sitting next to me and in her own sweet way telling me to get a life sent another pang through my heart. Staring glumly through the greasy little airplane window into the void outside, I found myself wondering if perhaps this whole trip was meant as some kind of punishment for how I had treated her. Perhaps God was going to make the plane crash, just to show me. Or perhaps he would allow me to actually get to Siena, and *then* let me discover that someone else had already snagged the family treasure.

In fact, the more I thought about it, the more I began to suspect that the real reason Aunt Rose had never broached the issue while she was still alive was that it was all baloney. Perhaps she had simply lost it in the end, in which case the alleged treasure might well turn out to be nothing but wishful thinking. And even if, against all odds, there really had been something of value still kicking around in Siena after we left some twenty-plus years ago, what were the chances it was still there? Considering the population density of Europe, and the ingenuity of mankind in general, I would be very surprised if there was any cheese left in the center of the maze once—and if—I ever got there.

The only thought that was to cheer me through the long sleepless flight was that every miniature drink handed out by the smiling flight attendants took me farther away from Janice. There she was, dancing around in a house that was all hers, laughing at my misfortune. She had no idea I was going to Italy, no idea that poor old Aunt Rose had sent me on a golden-goose chase, and at least I could be glad about that. For if my trip failed to result in the recovery of something meaningful, I would rather she was not around to crow.

WE LANDED IN FRANKFURT in something resembling sunshine, and I shuffled off the plane in my flip-flops, puffy-eyed and with a chunk of apple strudel still stuck in my throat. My connecting flight to Florence was more than two hours away, and as soon as I arrived at the gate, I stretched out across three chairs and closed my eyes, head on my macramé handbag, too tired to care if anyone ran away with the rest.

Somewhere between asleep and awake I felt a hand stroking my arm.

"Ahi, ahi—" said a voice that was a blend of coffee and smoke, "mi scusi!"

I opened my eyes to see the woman sitting next to me frantically brushing crumbs off my sleeve. While I had been napping, the gate had filled up around me, and people were glancing at me the way you glance at a homeless person—with a mix of disdain and sympathy.

"Don't worry," I said, sitting up, "I'm a mess anyway."

"Here!" She offered me half her croissant, perhaps as some kind of compensation, "You must be hungry."

I looked at her, surprised at her kindness. "Thanks."

Calling the woman elegant would be a gross understatement. Everything about her was perfectly matched; not just the color of her lipstick and nail polish, but also the golden beetles perched on her shoes, her handbag, and on the perky little hat sitting atop her immaculately dyed hair. I highly suspected—and her teasing smile more than confirmed—that this woman had every reason to be content with herself. Probably worth a fortune—or at least married to one—she looked as if she did not have a care in the world save to mask her seasoned soul with a carefully preserved body.

"You are going to Florence?" she inquired, in a strong, utterly charming accent. "To see all the so-called artworks?"

"Siena, actually," I said, my mouth full. "I was born there. But I've never been back since."

"How wonderful!" she exclaimed. "But how strange! Why not?"

"It's a long story."

"Tell me. You must tell me all about it." When she saw me hesitating, she held out her hand. "I am sorry. I am very nosy. I am Eva Maria Salimbeni."

"Julie—Giulietta Tolomei."

She nearly fell off her chair. "Tolomei? Your name is *Tolomei*? No, I don't believe it! It is impossible! Wait . . . what seat are you in? Yes, on the flight. Let me see—" She took one look at my boarding pass, then plucked it right out of my hand. "One moment! Stay here!"

I watched her as she strode up to the counter, wondering whether this was an ordinary day in Eva Maria Salimbeni's life. I figured she was trying to change the seating so we could sit together during the flight, and judging by her smile when she returned, she was successful. "E voilà!" She handed me a new boarding pass, and as soon as I looked at it, I had to suppress a giggle of delight. Of course, for us to continue our conversation, I would have to be upgraded to first class.

Once we were airborne, it did not take Eva Maria long to extract my story. The only elements I left out were my double identity and my mother's maybe-treasure.

"So," she finally said, head to one side, "you are going to Siena to . . . see the Palio?"

"The what?"

My question made her gasp. "The Palio! The horse race. Siena is famous for the Palio horse race. Did your aunt's housekeeper—this clever Alberto—never tell you about it?"

"Umberto," I corrected her. "Yes, I guess he did. But I didn't realize it's still taking place. Whenever he talked about it, it sounded like a medieval thing, with knights in shining armor and all that."

"The history of the Palio," nodded Eva Maria, "reaches into the very"—she had to search for the right English word—"*obscurity* of the Middle Ages. Nowadays the race takes place in the Campo in front of City Hall, and the riders are professional jockeys. But in the earliest times, it is believed that the riders were noblemen on their battle horses, and that they would ride all the way from the countryside and into the city to end up in front of the Siena Cathedral."

"Sounds dramatic," I said, still puzzled by her effusive kindness. But maybe she just saw it as her duty to educate strangers about Siena.

"Oh!" Eva Maria rolled her eyes. "It is the greatest drama of our lives. For months and months, the people of Siena can talk of nothing but horses and rivals and deals with this and that jockey." She shook her head lovingly. "It's what we call a dolce pazzia . . . a sweet madness. Once you feel it, you will never want to leave."

"Umberto always says that you can't explain Siena," I said, suddenly wishing he was with me, listening to this fascinating woman. "You have to be there and hear the drums to understand."

Eva Maria smiled graciously, like a queen receiving a compliment. "He is right. You have to feel it"—she reached out and touched a hand to my chest—"in here." Coming from anyone else, the gesture would have seemed wildly inappropriate, but Eva Maria was the kind of person who could pull it off.

While the flight attendant poured us both another glass of champagne, my new friend told me more about Siena, "so you don't get yourself into trouble," she winked. "Tourists always get themselves into trouble. They don't realize that Siena is not just Siena, but seventeen different neighborhoods—or, contrade—within the city that all have their own territory, their own magistrates, and their own coat of arms." Eva Maria touched her glass to mine, conspiratorially. "If you are in doubt, you can always look up at the corners of the houses. The little porcelain signs will tell you what contrada you are in. Now, your own family, the Tolomeis, belong in the contrada of the Owl and your allies are the Eagle and the Porcupine and . . . I forget the others. To the people of Siena, these contrade, these neighborhoods, are what life is all about; they are your friends, your community, your allies, and also your rivals. Every day of the year."

"So, my contrada is the Owl," I said, amused because Umberto had occasionally called me a scowly owl when I was being moody. "What is your own contrada?"

For the first time since we had begun our long conversation, Eva Maria looked away, distressed by my question. "I do not have one," she said, dismissively. "My family was banished from Siena many hundred years ago."

...

LONG BEFORE WE LANDED in Florence, Eva Maria began insisting on giving me a ride to Siena. It was right on the way to her home in Val d'Orcia, she explained, and really no trouble at all. I told her that I did not mind taking the bus, but she was clearly not someone who believed in public transportation. "Dio santo!" she exclaimed, when I kept declining her kind offer, "why do you want to wait for a bus that never shows up, when you can come with me and have a very comfortable ride in my god-son's new car?" Seeing that she almost had me, she smiled charmingly and leaned in for the clincher. "Giulietta, I will be so disappointed if we cannot continue our lovely conversation a bit longer."

And so we walked through customs arm in arm; while the officer barely looked at my passport, he did look twice at Eva Maria's cleavage. Later, when I was filling out a sheaf of candy-colored forms to report my luggage missing, Eva Maria stood next to me, tapping the floor with her Gucci pump until the baggage clerk had sworn an oath that he would per-sonally recover my two suitcases from wherever they had gone in the world, and—regardless of the hour—drive directly to Siena to deliver them at Hotel Chiusarelli, the address of which Eva Maria all but wrote out in lipstick and tucked into his pocket.

"You see, Giulietta," she explained as we walked out of the airport to-gether, bringing with us nothing but her minuscule carry-on, "it is fifty percent what they *see,* and fifty percent what they *think* they see. Ah—!" She waved excitedly at a black sedan idling in the fire lane. "There he is! Nice car, no?" She elbowed me with a wink. "It is the new model."

"Oh, really?" I said politely. Cars had never been a passion of mine, primarily because they usually came with a guy attached. Undoubtedly, Janice could have told me the exact name and model of the vehicle in question, and that it was on her to-do list to make love to the owner of one while parked on a scenic spot along the Amalfi Coast. Needless to say, her to-do list was radically different from mine.

Not too offended by my lack of enthusiasm, Eva Maria pulled me even closer to whisper into my ear, "Don't say anything, I want this to be a sur-prise! Oh, look . . . isn't he handsome?" She giggled delightedly and steered us both towards the man getting out of the car. "Ciao, Sandro!"

The man came around the car to greet us. "Ciao, Madrina!" He kissed his godmother on both cheeks and did not seem to mind her running an admiring claw through his dark hair. "Bentornata."

Eva Maria was right. Not only was her godson sinfully easy on the eyes, he was also dressed to kill, and although I was hardly an authority on female behavior, I suspected he never lacked willing victims.

"Alessandro, I want you to meet someone." Eva Maria had a hard time curbing her excitement. "This is my new friend. We met on the plane. Her name is Giulietta *Tolomei*. Can you believe it?"

Alessandro turned to look at me with eyes the color of dried rosemary, eyes that would have made Janice rumba through the house in her underwear, crooning into a hairbrush microphone.

"Ciao!" I said, wondering if he was going to kiss me, too.

But he wasn't. Alessandro looked at my braids, my baggy shorts, and my flip-flops, before he finally wrung out a smile and said something in Italian that I didn't understand.

"I'm sorry," I said, "but I don't—"

As soon as he realized that, on top of my frumpy appearance I did not even speak Italian, Eva Maria's godson lost all interest in me. Rather than translating what he had said, he merely asked, "No luggage?"

"Tons. But apparently, it all went to Verona."

Moments later I was sitting in the backseat of his car next to Eva Maria, fast-forwarding through the splendors of Florence. As soon as I had convinced myself that Alessandro's brooding silence was nothing but a consequence of poor English skills—but why should I even care?—I felt a new kind of excitement bubble up inside me. Here I was, back in the country that had spat me out twice, successfully infiltrating the happening class. I couldn't wait to call Umberto and tell him all about it.

"So, Giulietta," said Eva Maria, at last leaning back in comfort, "I would be careful and not tell . . . too many people who you are."

"Me?" I nearly laughed. "But I am nobody!"

"Nobody? You are a Tolomei!"

"You just told me that the Tolomeis lived a long time ago."

Eva Maria touched an index finger to my nose. "Don't underestimate the power of events that happened a long time ago. That is the tragic flaw of modern man. I advise you, as someone from the New World: Listen more, and speak less. This is where your soul was born. Believe me, Giulietta, there will be people here to whom you are someone."

I glanced at the rearview mirror to find Alessandro looking at me with narrow eyes. English skills or no, he clearly did not share his godmother's fascination with my person, but was too disciplined to voice his own thoughts. And so he tolerated my presence in his car for as long as I did not step outside the proper boundaries of humility and gratitude.

"Your family, the Tolomeis," Eva Maria went on, oblivious to the bad vibes, "was one of the richest, most powerful families in all of Siena history. They were private bankers, you see, and they were always at war with us, the Salimbenis, to prove who had more influence in the city. Their feud was so bad that they burnt down each other's houses— and killed each other's children in their beds—back in the Middle Ages."

"They were enemies?" I asked, stupidly.

"Oh yes! The worst kind! Do you believe in destiny?" Eva Maria put a hand on top of mine and gave it a squeeze. "I do. Our two households, the Tolomeis and the Salimbenis, had an ancient grudge, a bloody grudge . . . If we were in the Middle Ages, we would be at each other's throats. Like the Capulets and the Montagues in *Romeo and Juliet.*" She looked at me meaningfully. "Two households, both alike in dignity, in fair *Siena,* where we lay our scene—do you know that play?" When I merely nodded, too overwhelmed to speak, she patted my hand reassuringly. "Don't worry, I am confident that you and I, with our new friendship, will at last bury their strife. And this is why"—she turned abruptly in her seat—"Sandro! I am counting on you to make sure Giulietta is safe in Siena. Did you hear me?"

"Miss Tolomei," replied Alessandro, looking at the road ahead, "will never be safe anywhere. From anyone."

"What kind of talk is that?" scolded Eva Maria. "She is a Tolomei; it is our duty to protect her."

Alessandro glanced at me in the mirror, and I got the impression that he could see far more of me than I could see of him. "Maybe she doesn't want our protection." From the way he said it I knew it was a challenge, and I also knew that—despite his accent—he was eminently at home in my language. Which meant that he had other reasons for being monosyllabic with me.

"I sure appreciate this ride," I said, deploying my cutest smile. "But I am sure Siena is very safe."

He acknowledged the compliment with a slight nod. "What brings you over here? Business or pleasure?"

"Well . . . pleasure, I suppose."

Eva Maria clapped her hands excitedly. "Then we will have to make sure you are not disappointed! Alessandro knows all the secrets of Siena. Don't you, caro? He will show you places, wonderful places that you would never find on your own. Oh, you will have fun!"

I opened my mouth, but had no idea what to say. So I closed it again. It was quite evident from his frown that showing me around Siena would rank very low on Alessandro's agenda for the week.

"Sandro!" Eva Maria went on, her voice turning sharp. "You will make sure Giulietta has fun, no?"

"I can imagine no greater felicity," replied Alessandro, turning on the car radio.

"See?" Eva Maria pinched my flushed cheek. "What did Shakespeare know? Now we are friends."

Outside, the world was a vineyard, and the sky was suspended over the landscape like a protective blue cape. It was where I was born, and yet I suddenly felt like a stranger—an intruder—who had snuck in through the back door to find and claim something that had never belonged to me.

IT WAS A RELIEF when we finally pulled up in front of Hotel Chiusarelli. Eva Maria had been more than kind throughout the trip, telling me this and that about Siena, but you can only make so much polite conversation after losing a night's sleep and all your luggage in one fell swoop.

Everything I owned had been in those two suitcases. I had basically packed up my entire childhood right after Aunt Rose's funeral, and had left the house in a taxi around midnight with Janice's triumphant laughter still ringing in my ears. There had been all sorts of clothes, books, and silly knickknacks, but now they were in Verona, and I was here, stuck in Siena with little more than a toothbrush, half a granola bar, and a pair of earplugs.

After pulling up at the curb in front of the hotel and dutifully opening the car door for me, Alessandro escorted me all the way into the vestibule. He obviously didn't want to, and I obviously didn't appreciate the gesture, but Eva Maria was watching us both from the backseat of the car, and by now I knew that she was a woman who was used to having things her way.

"Please," said Alessandro, holding the door open. "After you."

There was nothing else to do but enter Hotel Chiusarelli. The building greeted me with cool serenity, its ceiling held high by marble columns, and only very faintly, from somewhere below us, could I discern the sound of people singing while throwing pots and pans around.

"Buongiorno!" An august man in a three-piece suit rose behind the reception counter, a brass nametag informing me that his name was Direttor Rossini. "Benvenu—ah!" He interrupted himself when he saw Alessandro. "Benvenuto, Capitano."

I put my hands flat on the green marble with what I hoped was a winning smile. "Hi. I am Giulietta Tolomei. I have a reservation. Excuse me for a second—" I turned towards Alessandro. "So, this is it. I am safely here."

"I am very sorry, Signorina," said Direttor Rossini, "but I do not have a reservation in your name."

"Oh! I was sure—is that a problem?"

"It is the Palio!" He threw up his arms in exasperation. "The hotel is complete! But"—he tapped at the computer screen—"I have here a credit card number with the name Julie Jacobs. Reservation for one person for one week. To arrive today from America. Can this be you?"

I glanced at Alessandro. He returned my stare with perfect indifference. "Yes, that's me," I said.

Direttor Rossini looked surprised. "You are Julie Jacobs? *And* Giulietta Tolomei?"

"Well . . . yes."

"But—" Direttor Rossini took a little side step to better see Alessandro, his eyebrows describing a polite question mark. "C'è un problema?"

"Nessun problema," replied Alessandro, looking at us both with what could only be a deliberate non-expression. "Miss Jacobs. Enjoy your stay in Siena."

Within the blink of an eye Eva Maria's godson was gone, and I was left with Direttor Rossini and an uncomfortable silence. Only when I had filled out every single form he put in front of me did the hotel director finally allow himself to smile. "So . . . you are a friend of Captain Santini?"

I looked behind me. "You mean, the man who was just here? No, we're not friends. Is that his name? Santini?"

Direttor Rossini clearly found me lacking in understanding. "His name is *Captain* Santini. He is the—what do you say—Head of Security at Monte dei Paschi. In Palazzo Salimbeni."

I must have looked stricken, because Direttor Rossini hastened to comfort me. "Don't worry, we don't have criminals in Siena. She is a very peaceful city. Once there was a criminal here"—he chuckled to himself as he rang for the bellboy—"but we took care of him!"

For hours I had looked forward to collapsing on a bed. But now, when I finally could, rather than lying down I found myself pacing up and down the floor of my hotel room, chewing on the possibility that Alessandro Santini would run a search on my name and truffle out my dark past. The very last thing I needed now was for someone in Siena to pull up the old Julie Jacobs file, discover my Roman debacle, and put an untimely end to my treasure hunt.

A bit later, when I called Umberto to tell him I had arrived safely, he must have heard it in my voice, because he instantly knew something had gone wrong.

"Oh, it's nothing," I said. "Just some Armani stiff who discovered I have two names."

"But he is an Italian," was Umberto's sensible reply. "He doesn't care if you break some law a little bit, as long as you wear beautiful shoes. Are you wearing beautiful shoes? Are you wearing the shoes I gave you? . . . Principessa?"

I looked down at my flip-flops. "I guess I'm toast."

CRAWLING INTO BED that night, I slipped right into a recurring dream that I had not had for several months, but which had been a part of my life since childhood. The dream had me walking through a magnificent castle with mosaic floors and cathedral ceilings held up by massive marble pillars, pushing open one gilded door after the other and wondering where everyone was. The only light came from narrow stained-glass windows high, high over my head, and the colored beams did little to illuminate the dark corners around me.

As I walked through those vast rooms, I felt like a child lost in the woods, and it frustrated me that I could sense the presence of others, but that they never showed themselves to me. When I stood still, I could hear them whispering and fluttering about like ghosts, but if they were indeed ethereal beings, they were still trapped just like me, looking for a way out.

Only when I read the play in high school had I discovered that what these invisible demons were whispering were fragments from Shakespeare's *Romeo and Juliet*—not the way actors would recite the lines onstage, but mumbled with quiet intensity, like a spell. Or a curse.

*Within this three hours
will fair Juliet wake*

. . .

IT TOOK THE BELLS OF the basilica across the piazza to finally stir
me from sleep. Two minutes later Direttor Rossini knocked on my door
as if he knew I could not possibly have slept through the racket. "Excuse
me!" Without waiting for an invitation, he lugged a large suitcase into my
room and placed it on the empty baggage stand. "This came for you last
night."

"Wait!" I let go of the door and gathered the hotel bathrobe around me
as tightly as I could. "That is not my suitcase."

"I know." He pulled the foulard from his breast pocket and wiped a
bead of sweat from his forehead. "It is from Contessa Salimbeni. Here,
she left a note for you."

I took the note. "What exactly is a contessa?"

"Normally," said Direttor Rossini with some dignity, "I do not carry
luggage. But since it was Contessa Salimbeni—"

"She is lending me her clothes?" I stared at Eva Maria's brief handwritten note in disbelief. "And shoes?"

"Until your own luggage arrives. It is now in Frittoli."

In her exquisite handwriting, Eva Maria anticipated that her clothes
might not fit me perfectly. But, she concluded, it was better than running
around naked.

As I examined the specimens in the suitcase one by one, I was happy
Janice could not see me. Our childhood home had not been big enough
for two fashionistas, and so I—much to Umberto's chagrin—had em-

barked upon a career of being everything but. In school, Janice got her compliments from friends whose lives were headlined by designer names, while any admiration I got came from girls who had bummed a ride to the charity store, but who hadn't had the vision to buy what I bought, or the courage to put it together. It was not that I disliked fancy clothes, it was just that I wouldn't give Janice the satisfaction of appearing to care about my looks. For no matter what I did to myself, she could always outdo me.

By the time we left college, I had become my own image: a dandelion in the flower bed of society. Kinda cute, but still a weed. When Aunt Rose had put our graduation photos side by side on the grand piano, she had smiled sadly and observed that, of all those many classes I had taken, I seemed to have graduated with the best results as the perfect anti-Janice.

Eva Maria's designer clothes were, in other words, definitely not my style. But what were my options? Following my telephone conversation with Umberto the night before, I had decided to retire my flip-flops for the time being and pay a little more attention to my bella figura. After all, the last thing I needed now was for Francesco Maconi, my mother's financial advisor, to think I was someone not to be trusted.

And so I tried on Eva Maria's outfits one by one, turning this way and that before the wardrobe mirror, until I found the least outrageous one—a foxy little skirt and jacket, fire-engine red with big black polka dots—that made me look as if I had just emerged from a Jaguar with four pieces of perfectly matched luggage and a small dog called Bijou. But most important, it made me look as if I ate hidden heirlooms—and financial advisors—for breakfast.

And by the way, it had matching shoes.

IN ORDER TO GET to Palazzo Tolomei, Direttor Rossini had explained, I must choose to either go up Via del Paradiso or down Via della Sapienza. They were both practically closed to traffic—as were most streets in downtown Siena—but Sapienza, he advised, could be a bit of a challenge, and all in all, Paradiso was probably the safer route.

As I walked down Via della Sapienza the façades of ancient houses closed in on me from all sides, and I was soon trapped in a labyrinth of centuries past, following the logic of an earlier way of life. Above me a ribbon of blue sky was crisscrossed by banners, their bold colors strangely vivid among the medieval brick, but apart from that—and the odd pair of jeans drying from a window—there was almost nothing that committed this place to modernity.

The world had developed around it, but Siena didn't care. Direttor Rossini had told me that, for the Sienese, the golden age had been the late Middle Ages, and as I walked, I could see that he was right; the city clung to its medieval self with a stubborn disregard for the attractions of progress. There were touches of the Renaissance here and there, but overall, the hotel director had sniggered, Siena had been too wise to be seduced by the charms of history's playboys, those so-called masters, who turned houses into layer cakes.

As a result, the most beautiful thing about Siena was her integrity; even now, in a world that had stopped caring, she was still Sena Vetus Civitas Virginis, or, in my own language, Old Siena, City of the Virgin. And for that reason alone, Direttor Rossini had concluded, all fingers planted on the green marble counter, it was the only place on the planet worth living in.

"So, where else have you lived?" I had asked him, innocently.

"I was in Rome for two days," he had replied with dignity. "Who needs to see more? When you take a bite of a bad apple, do you keep eating?"

From my immersion in the silent alleys I eventually surfaced in a bustling, pedestrian street. According to my directions it was called the Corso, and Direttor Rossini had explained that it was famous for the many old banks that used to serve foreigners traveling the old pilgrim route, which had gone straight through town. Over the centuries, millions of people had journeyed through Siena, and many foreign treasures and currencies had changed hands. The steady stream of modern-day tourists, in other words, was nothing but the continuation of an old, profitable tradition.

That was how my family, the Tolomeis, had grown rich, Direttor Rossini had pointed out, and how their rivals, the Salimbenis, had grown even richer. They had been tradesmen and bankers, and their fortified palazzos had flanked this very road—Siena's main thoroughfare—with impossibly tall towers that had kept growing and growing until, at last, they had both come crashing down.

As I walked past Palazzo Salimbeni I looked in vain for remnants of the old tower. It was still an impressive building with quite the Draculean front door, but it was no longer the fortification it had once been. Somewhere in that building, I thought as I scurried by, collar up, Eva Maria's godson, Alessandro, had his office. Hopefully he was not—just now—scrolling through some crime register to find the dark secret behind Julie Jacobs.

Farther down the road, but not much, stood Palazzo Tolomei, the ancient dwelling of my own ancestors. Looking up at the splendid medieval façade, I suddenly felt proud to be connected to the people who had once lived in this remarkable building. As far as I could see, not much had changed since the fourteenth century; the only thing suggesting that the mighty Tolomeis had moved out and a modern bank had moved in were the marketing posters hanging in the deep-set windows, their colorful promises sliced by iron bars.

The inside of the building was no less stern than the outside. A security guard stepped forward to hold the door for me as I entered, as gallantly as the semiautomatic rifle in his arms would allow, but I was too busy looking around to be bothered by his uniformed attention. Six titanic pillars in red brick held the ceiling high, high above mankind, and although there were counters and chairs and people walking around on the vast stone floor, these took up so little of the room that the white lion heads protruding from the ancient walls seemed entirely unaware that humans were present.

"Sì?" The teller looked at me over the rim of glasses so fashionably slim they could not possibly transmit more than a wafer-thin slice of reality.

I leaned forward a bit, in the interest of privacy. "Would it be possible to talk to Signor Francesco Maconi?"

The teller actually managed to focus on me through her glasses, but she did not appear convinced by what she saw. "There is no Signor Francesco here," she said firmly, in a very heavy accent.

"No Francesco Maconi?"

At this point, the teller found it necessary to take off her glasses entirely, fold them carefully on the counter, and look at me with that supremely kind smile people fix on you just before they stick a syringe in your neck. "No."

"But I know he used to work here—" I did not get any further before the woman's colleague from the booth next door leaned in on the conversation, whispering something in Italian. At first, my unfriendly teller dismissed the other with an angry wave, but after a while she began to reconsider.

"Excuse me," she said eventually, leaning forward to get my attention, "but do you mean *Presidente* Maconi?"

I felt a jolt of excitement. "Did he work here twenty years ago?"

She looked horrified. "Presidente Maconi was always here!"

"And would it be possible to speak with him?" I smiled sweetly, although she did not deserve it. "He is an old friend of my mother's, Diane Tolomei. I am Giulietta Tolomei."

Both women stared at me as if I were a spirit conjured up before their very eyes. Without another word, the teller who had originally dismissed me now fumbled her glasses back on her nose, made a phone call, and had a brief conversation in humble, underdog Italian. When it was over she put down the receiver reverently, and turned towards me with something akin to a smile. "He will see you right after lunch, at three o'clock."

I HAD MY FIRST MEAL since arriving in Siena at a bustling pizzeria called Cavallino Bianco. While I sat there pretending to read the Italian dictionary I had just bought, I began to realize that it would take more than just a borrowed suit and a few handy phrases to level with the locals. These women around me, I suspected, sneaking peeks at their smiles and exuberant gestures as they bantered with the handsome waiter Giulio, possessed something I had never had, some ability I could not put my finger on, but which must be a crucial element in that elusive state of mind, happiness.

Strolling on, feeling more klutzy and displaced than ever, I had a stand-up espresso in a bar in Piazza Postierla and asked the buxom barista if she could recommend a cheap clothes store in the neighborhood. After all, Eva Maria's suitcase had—fortunately—not contained any underwear. Completely ignoring her other customers the barista looked me over skeptically and said, "You want everything new, no? New hair, new clothes?"

"Well—"

"Don't worry, my cousin is the best hairdresser in Siena—maybe in the world. He will make you beautiful. Come!"

After taking me by the arm and insisting that I call her Malèna, the barista walked me down to see her cousin Luigi right away, even though it was clearly coffee rush hour, and customers were yelling after her in exasperation as we went. She just shrugged and laughed, knowing full well that they would all still fawn over her when she came back, maybe even a little bit more than before, now that they had tasted life without her.

Luigi was sweeping up hair from the floor when we entered his salon. He was no older than me, but had the penetrating eye of a Michelangelo. When he fixed that eye on me, however, he was not impressed.

"Ciao, caro," said Malèna and gave him a drive-thru peck on both cheeks, "this is Giulietta. She needs un makeover totale."

"Just the ends, actually," I interjected. "A couple inches."

It took a major argument in Italian—which I was more than relieved to not understand—before Malèna had persuaded Luigi to take on my sorry case. But once he did, he took the challenge very seriously. As soon as Malèna had left the salon, he sat me down on a barber chair and looked at my reflection in the mirror, turning me this way and that to check all the angles. Then he pulled the elastic bands from my braids and threw them directly into the trash bin with an expression of disgust.

"Bene . . ." he finally said, fluffing up my hair and looking at me once again in the mirror, a little less critically than before. "Not too bad, no?"

WHEN I WALKED BACK to Palazzo Tolomei two hours later, I had sunk myself further into debt, but it was worth every nonexistent penny. Eva Maria's red-and-black suit lay neatly folded on the bottom of a shopping bag, matching shoes on top, and I was wearing one of five new outfits that had all been approved by Luigi and his uncle, Paolo, who happened to own a clothes store just around the corner. Uncle Paolo—who did not speak a word of English, but who knew everything there was to know about fashion—had knocked 30 percent off my entire purchase as long as I promised never to wear my ladybug costume again.

I had protested at first, explaining that my luggage was due to arrive any moment, but in the end the temptation had been too great. So what if my suitcases were waiting for me when I returned to the hotel? There was nothing in them I could ever wear in Siena anyway, perhaps with the exception of the shoes Umberto had given me for Christmas, and which I had never even tried on.

As I walked away from the store, I glanced at myself in every shopwindow I passed. Why had I never done this before? Ever since high school I had cut my own hair—just the ends—with a pair of kitchen scissors every two years or so. It took me about five minutes, and, honestly, I thought, who could tell the difference? Well, I could certainly see the difference now. Somehow, Luigi had managed to bring my boring old hair to life, and it was already thriving in its new freedom, flowing in the breeze as I walked and framing my face as if it was a face worth framing.

When I was a child, Aunt Rose had taken me to the village barber whenever it occurred to her. But she had been wise enough never to take Janice and me at the same time. Only once did we end up in the salon chairs side by side, and as we sat there, pulling faces at each other in the big mirrors, the old barber had held up our ponytails and said, "Look! This one has bear-hair and the other has princess-hair."

Aunt Rose had not replied. She had just sat there, silently, and waited for him to finish. Once he was finished, she had paid him and thanked him in that clipped voice of hers. Then she had hauled us both out the door as if it were we, and not the barber, who had misbehaved. Ever since that day, Janice had never missed an opportunity to compliment me on my beary, beary lovely hair.

The memory nearly made me cry. Here I was, all dolled up, while Aunt Rose was in a place where she could no longer appreciate that I had finally stepped out of my macramé cocoon. It would have made her so happy to see me like this—just once—but I had been too busy making sure Janice never did.

PRESIDENTE MACONI WAS a courtly man in his sixties, dressed in a subdued suit and tie and astoundingly successful in combing the long hairs from one side of his head across the crown to the other. As a result, he carried himself with rigid dignity, but there was genuine warmth in his eyes that instantly annulled the ridiculous.

"Miss Tolomei?" He came across the floor of the bank to shake my hand heartily, as if we were old friends. "This is an unexpected delight."

As we walked together up the stairs, Presidente Maconi went on to apologize in flawless English for the uneven walls and warped floors. Even the most modern interior design, he explained with a smile, was helpless against a building that was almost eight hundred years old.

After a day of constant language malfunctions it was a relief to finally meet someone fluent in my own tongue. A touch of a British accent suggested that Presidente Maconi had lived in England for a while—perhaps he had gone to school there—which might explain why my mother had chosen him as her financial advisor in the first place.

His office was on the top floor, and from the mullioned windows he had a perfect view of the church of San Cristoforo and several other spectacular buildings in the neighborhood. Stepping forward, however, I nearly stumbled over a plastic bucket sitting in the middle of a large Persian rug, and after ensuring that my health was intact, Presidente Maconi very carefully placed the bucket precisely where it had stood before I kicked it.

"There is a leak in the roof," he explained, looking up at the cracked plaster ceiling, "but we cannot find it. It is very strange—even when it is not raining, water comes dripping down." He shrugged and motioned for me to sit down on one of two artfully carved mahogany chairs facing his desk. "The old president used to say that the building was crying. He knew your father, by the way."

Sitting down behind the desk, Presidente Maconi leaned back as far as the leather chair would allow and put his fingertips together. "So, Miss Tolomei, how may I help you?"

For some reason, the question took me by surprise. I had been so focused on getting here in the first place, I had given little thought to the next step. I suppose the Francesco Maconi who had—until now—lived quite comfortably in my imagination knew very well that I had come for my mother's treasure, and he had been waiting impatiently these many, many years to finally hand it off to its rightful heir.

The real Francesco Maconi, however, was not that accommodating. I started explaining why I had come, and he listened to me in silence, nodding occasionally. When I eventually stopped talking, he looked at me pensively, his face betraying no conclusion either way.

"And so I was wondering," I went on, realizing that I had forgotten the most important part, "if you could take me to her safety-deposit box?"

I took the key out of my handbag and put it on his desk, but Presidente Maconi merely glanced at it. After a moment's awkward silence he got up and walked over to a window, hands behind his back, and looked out over the roofs of Siena with a frown.

"Your mother," he finally said, "was a wise woman. And when God takes the wise to heaven, he leaves their wisdom behind, for us on earth. Their spirits live on, flying around us silently, like owls, with eyes that see in the night, when you and I see only darkness." He paused to test a leaded pane that was coming loose. "In some ways, the owl would be a fitting symbol for all of Siena, not just for our contrada."

"Because . . . all people in Siena are wise?" I proposed, not entirely sure what he was getting at.

"Because the owl has an ancient ancestor. To the Greeks, she was the goddess Athena. A virgin, but also a warrior. The Romans called her Minerva. In Roman times, there was a temple for her here in Siena. This is why it was always in our hearts to love the Virgin Mary, even in the ancient times, before Christ was born. To us, she was always here."

"Presidente Maconi—"

"Miss Tolomei." He turned to face me at last. "I am trying to figure out what your mother would have liked me to do. You are asking me to give you something that caused her a lot of grief. Would she really want me to let you have it?" He attempted a smile. "But then, it is not my decision, is it? She left it here—she did not destroy it—so she must have wanted me to pass it on to you, or to someone. The question is: Are you sure you want it?"

In the silence following his words, we both heard it clearly: the sound of a drop of water falling into the plastic bucket on a perfectly sunny day.

AFTER SUMMONING A second key-holder, the somber Signor Virgilio, Presidente Maconi took me down a separate staircase—a spiral of ancient stone that must have been there since the palazzo was first built— into the deepest caverns of the bank. Now for the first time I became aware that there was a whole other world underneath Siena, a world of caves and shadows that stood in sharp contrast to the world of light above.

"Welcome to the Bottini," said Presidente Maconi as we walked through a grottolike passageway. "This is the old, underground aqueduct that was built a thousand years ago to lead water into the city of Siena. This is all sandstone, and even with the primitive tools they had back then, Sienese engineers were able to dig a vast network of tunnels that led fresh water to public fountains and even into the basement of some private houses. Now, of course, it is no longer used."

"But people go down here anyway?" I asked, touching the rough sandstone wall.

"Oh, no!" Presidente Maconi was amused by my naïveté. "It is a dangerous place to be. You can easily get lost. Nobody knows all the Bottini. There are stories, many stories, about secret tunnels from here to there, but we don't want people running around exploring them. The sandstone is porous, you see. It crumbles. And all of Siena is sitting on top."

I pulled back my hand. "But this wall is . . . fortified?"

Presidente Maconi looked a bit sheepish. "No."

"But it's a bank. That seems . . . dangerous."

"Once," he replied, eyebrows up in disapproval, "someone tried to break in. Once. They dug a tunnel. It took them months."

"Did they succeed?"

Presidente Maconi pointed at a security camera mounted high in an obscure corner. "When the alarm went off, they escaped through the tunnel, but at least they didn't steal anything."

"Who were they?" I asked. "Did you ever find out?"

He shrugged. "Some gangsters from Napoli. They never came back."

When we finally arrived at the vault, Presidente Maconi and Signor Virgilio both had to swipe their key cards for the massive door to open.

"See?"—Presidente Maconi was proud of the feature—"not even the president can open this vault on his own. As they say, absolute power corrupts absolutely."

Inside the vault, safety-deposit boxes covered every wall from floor to ceiling. Most of them were small, but some were large enough to serve as a luggage locker at an airport. My mother's box, as it turned out, was somewhere in between, and as soon as Presidente Maconi had pointed it out to me and helped me insert the key, he and Signor Virgilio politely left the room. When, moments later, I heard a couple of matches striking, I knew they had seized the opportunity to take a smoking break in the corridor outside.

Since I first read Aunt Rose's letter, I had entertained many different ideas of what my mother's treasure might be, and had done my best to temper my expectations in order to avoid disappointment. But in my most unchecked fantasies I would find a magnificent golden box, locked and full of promise, not unlike the treasure chests that pirates dig up on desert islands.

My mother had left me just such a thing. It was a wooden box with golden ornamentation, and while it was not actually locked—there *was* no lock—the clasp was rusted shut, preventing me from doing much more than merely shaking it gently to try and determine its contents. It was about the size of a small toaster-oven, but surprisingly light, which immediately ruled out the possibility of gold and jewelry. But then, fortunes come in many substances and forms, and I was certainly not one to scoff at the prospect of three-digit paper money.

As we said goodbye, Presidente Maconi kept insisting on calling a taxi for me. But I told him I did not need one; the box fitted very nicely in one of my shopping bags, and Hotel Chiusarelli was, after all, nearby.

"I would be careful," he said, "walking around with that. Your mother was always careful."

"But who knows I'm here? And that I've got this?"

He shrugged. "The Salimbenis—"

I stared at him, not sure if he was really serious. "Don't tell me the old family feud is still going on!"

Presidente Maconi looked away, uncomfortable with the subject. "A Salimbeni will always be a Salimbeni."

Walking away from Palazzo Tolomei, I repeated that sentence to myself several times, wondering precisely what it meant. In the end I decided it was nothing more than what I ought to expect in this place; judging by Eva Maria's stories about the fierce contrade rivalries in the modern Palio, the old family feuds from the Middle Ages were still going strong, even if the weapons had changed.

Mindful of my own Tolomei heritage, I put a little swagger in my gait as I walked past Palazzo Salimbeni for the second time that day, just to let

Alessandro know—should he happen to look out the window at that exact moment—that there was a new sheriff in town.

Just then, as I glanced over my shoulder to see if I had made myself absolutely clear, I noticed a man walking behind me. Somehow he didn't fit the picture; the street was full of chirping tourists, mothers with strollers, and people in business suits, talking loudly into their cell phones at some invisible other. This man, by contrast, was wearing a mangy tracksuit and a pair of mirrored sunglasses that did nothing to conceal the fact that he had been looking straight at my bags.

Or was I imagining things? Had Presidente Maconi's parting words ruffled my nerves? I paused in front of a shopwindow, hoping very much the man would pass me and continue on his way. But he didn't. As soon as I stood still, he paused, too, pretending to look at a poster on a wall.

Now for the first time, I felt the little fleabites of fear, as Janice used to call them, and ran through my options in a couple of deep breaths. But there was really only one thing to do. If I kept walking, chances were he would eventually sidle up to me and snatch the bags right out of my hands, or, even worse, follow me to see where I was staying, and pay me a visit later.

Humming to myself I entered the store, and as soon as I was inside, I ran up to the clerk and asked if I could leave through the back entrance. Barely looking up from his motorcycle magazine, he simply pointed at a door at the other end of the room.

Ten seconds later I came shooting out into a narrow alley to nearly overturn a row of Vespas parked side by side. I had no idea where I was, but that didn't matter. The important thing was that I still had my bags.

WHEN THE TAXI DROPPED me off back at Hotel Chiusarelli, I would have happily paid anything for the trip. But when I overtipped the driver, he shook his head in protest and gave back most of it.

"Miss Tolomei!" Direttor Rossini came towards me with some alarm as soon as I entered the vestibule. "Where have you been? Captain Santini was just here. In uniform! What is going on?"

"Oh!" I tried to smile. "Maybe he came to invite me out for coffee?"

Direttor Rossini glared at me, his eyebrows suspended in a pointed arc of disapproval. "I do not think the captain was here with carnal intentions, Miss Tolomei. I very much suggest you call him. Here—" He handed me a business card as if it was a holy wafer. "This is the number of his telephone, there, written on the back side, do you see? I suggest"—Direttor Rossini raised his voice as I continued past him down the hall—"you call him right now!"

It took me about an hour—and several trips to the hotel reception desk—to open my mother's box. After trying every tool I had, such as the hotel key, my toothbrush, and the telephone receiver, I ran downstairs to borrow tweezers, then nail clippers, then a needle, and finally a screwdriver, only too aware that Direttor Rossini looked less and less friendly every time he saw me.

What finally did the trick was not actually opening the rusty clasp, but unscrewing the entire closing mechanism, which took me quite a while, since the screwdriver I had borrowed was too small. But I was fairly sure Direttor Rossini would explode if I showed up at his reception desk one more time.

Through all those efforts, my hopes and expectations for the contents of the box had grown steadily more wild, and once I was able to open the lid, I could barely breathe with anticipation. Seeing that it was so light, I had become convinced there was a fragile—and very costly—item in the box, but when I finally looked inside, I realized my mistake.

There was nothing fragile in the box; in fact, there was barely anything at all except paper. Boring paper at that. Not money or stocks or deeds or any other kind of securities, but letters in envelopes and different kinds of texts typed out on sheets that were either stapled together or rolled up with rotting rubber bands. The only actual objects in the box were a notebook with scribbles and doodles, a cheap paperback copy of Shakespeare's *Romeo and Juliet,* and an old crucifix on a silver chain.

I inspected the crucifix for a while, wondering if perhaps it was extremely old and somehow valuable. But I doubted it. Even if it was an antique, it was still just made of silver, and as far as I could see, there was nothing special about it.

Same story with the paperback volume of *Romeo and Juliet.* I flipped through it several times, determined to see its value, but there was nothing about the book that struck me as the least bit promising, not even a single pencil-note in the margin.

The notebook, on the other hand, had some interesting drawings that could—with a bit of goodwill—be interpreted as having to do with a treasure hunt. Or maybe they were just sketches from trips to museums and sculpture gardens. One sculpture in particular had caught my mother's eye—if indeed this was her notebook, and these her drawings—and I could see why. It represented a man and a woman; the man was kneeling, holding a woman in his arms, and had her eyes not been open, I would have guessed she was asleep or even dead. There were at least twenty different drawings of this sculpture in the notebook, but many of them dwelled on details, such as facial features, and in all honesty, none of them made me any wiser as to why my mother had been so obsessed with it in the first place.

There were also sixteen private letters in the box, sitting on the bottom. Five were from Aunt Rose, begging my mother to give up her "silly ideas" and return home; four were also from Aunt Rose, but they were sent later, and my mother had never opened them. The rest were in Italian, sent to my mother from people I did not know.

At this point, there was nothing left in the box except the many typewritten texts. Some were creased and faded, others were newer and more crisp; most were in English, but one was in Italian. None of them appeared to be original texts, they were all—except the Italian one—translations that must have been typed out sometime within the last hundred years or so.

As I looked through the bunch, it gradually became clear to me that, in fact, there was rhyme and reason in the seeming madness, and once I had acknowledged as much, it did not take me long to spread out the texts on my bed in some kind of chronological order:

Maestro Ambrogio's Journal (1340)
Giulietta's Letters to Giannozza (1340)
The Confessions of Friar Lorenzo (1340)
La Maledizione sul Muro (1370)
Masuccio Salernitano's *Thirty-Third Story* (1476)
Luigi da Porto's *Romeo & Juliet* (1530)
Matteo Bandello's *Romeo & Juliet* (1554)
Arthur Brooke's *Romeus & Juliet* (1562)
William Shakespeare's *Romeo & Juliet* (1597)
Giulietta and Giannozza Family Tree

Once I had them laid out before me, however, it took me somewhat longer to make sense of the collection. The first four texts—all from the fourteenth century—were mysterious and often fragmented, while the later texts were clearer. But most important, the later texts had one thing in common; they were all versions of the story of Romeo and Juliet, culminating in the one that most people knew: Shakespeare's *Most Excellent and Lamentable Tragedy of Romeo and Juliet.*

Although I had always considered myself a bit of an expert on that play, it came as a complete surprise to me to discover that the Bard had not, in fact, invented the story, but had merely piggybacked on previous writers. Granted, Shakespeare was a genius with words, and if he had not run the whole thing through his pentameter machine, it is doubtful whether it would ever have become widely known. But even so, it looked—in my humble opinion—as if it had already been a darn good story when it first landed on his desk. And interestingly enough, the earliest version of it—the one written by Masuccio Salernitano in 1476—was not set in Verona at all, but right here, in Siena.

This literary discovery very nearly distracted me from the fact that I was, quite frankly, uncovering a pretty hefty, personal disappointment. There was nothing in my mother's box that had any monetary value whatsoever, nor was there—among all the papers I had looked at so far—the slightest suggestion of family valuables hidden elsewhere.

Perhaps I should have been ashamed of myself for thinking like this; perhaps I should have shown more appreciation for the fact that I was finally holding something in my hands that had belonged to my mother.

But I was too confused to be rational. What on earth had made Aunt Rose believe there was something tremendously valuable at stake—something worth a trip to what was, in her mind, the most dangerous of places, namely Italy? And why had my mother kept this box of paper in the belly of a bank? I felt silly now, especially thinking of the guy in the tracksuit. Of course he had not been following me. That, too, must have been a figment of my all too fertile imagination.

I started leafing through the earlier texts without enthusiasm. Two of them, "The Confessions of Friar Lorenzo" and "Giulietta's Letters to Giannozza," were nothing more than collections of fragmented phrases, such as, "I swear by the Virgin that I have acted in accordance with the will of Heaven" and "all the way to Siena in a coffin for fear of the Salimbeni bandits."

"Maestro Ambrogio's Journal" was more readable, but when I began leafing through it, I almost wished it wasn't. Whoever this Maestro was, he had had a bad case of verbal diarrhea and had kept a journal about every single triviality that had happened to him—and, by the look of it, his friends, too—in the year 1340. As far as I could tell, it had nothing to do with me or with anything else in my mother's box, for that matter.

That was when my eyes suddenly fell on a name in the middle of the Maestro's text.

Giulietta Tolomei.

I frantically scrutinized the page under the bedside lamp. But no, I had not been mistaken; after some initial musings on the hardships of painting the perfect rose, the verbose Maestro Ambrogio had written page after page after page about a young woman who happened to have a name identical to mine. Coincidence?

Leaning back in my bed, I started reading from the beginning of the journal, occasionally checking the other fragmented texts for cross-reference. And so began my journey back to Siena in the year 1340, and my kinship with the woman who had shared my name.

And in this borrow'd likeness of shrunk death
Thou shalt continue two and forty hours

...

Siena, A.D. 1340

O<small>H, THEY WERE FORTUNE'S FOOLS!</small>

They had been on the road for three days, playing hide-and-seek with disaster and living on bread as hard as rock. Now, finally, on the hottest, most miserable day of summer, they were so close to their journey's end that Friar Lorenzo could see the towers of Siena sprouting bewitchingly on the horizon ahead. And here, sadly, was where his rosary ran out of protective power.

Sitting on his horse cart, rocking wearily along behind his six mounted travel companions—all monks like himself—the young friar had just begun to envision the sizzling beef and soothing wine awaiting them at their destination when a dozen sinister-looking horsemen came galloping out of a vineyard in a cloud of dust to surround the small traveling party and block the road to all sides, swords drawn.

"Greetings, strangers!" bellowed their captain, toothless and grimy but lavishly dressed, no doubt in the clothes of previous victims. "Who trespasses on Salimbeni territory?"

Friar Lorenzo yanked on the reins of his cart to stop the horses, while his travel companions did their utmost to position themselves between the cart and the bandits.

"As you can see," replied the most senior of the monks, holding out his shoddy cowl as proof, "we are but humble brothers from Florence, noble friend."

"Huh." The brigand leader looked around at the alleged monks, his eyes narrow. Eventually, his gaze settled on Friar Lorenzo's frightened face. "What treasure on the cart back there?"

"Nothing of value to you," responded the senior monk, backing up his horse a bit to better block the bandit's access to the cart. "Please allow us passage. We are holy men and pose no threat to you or your kinsmen."

"This is a Salimbeni road," the captain pointed out, underlining his words with his blade—a signal for his comrades to move closer. "If you wish to use it, you must pay a toll. For your own safety."

"We have paid five Salimbeni tolls already."

The villain shrugged. "Protection is expensive."

"But who," argued the other with stubborn calm, "would attack a group of holy men bound for Rome?"

"Who? The worthless dogs of Tolomei!" The captain spat twice on the ground for good measure, and his men were quick to do the same. "Those thieving, raping, murdering bastards!"

"This is why," observed the monk, "we should rather like to reach the city of Siena before dark."

"She is not far," nodded the brigand, "but her gates close early nowadays, on account of the grievous disruptions caused by the rabid dogs of Tolomei to the general disturbance of the fine and industrious people of Siena and even more so, I might add, to the grand and benevolent house of Salimbeni—in which dwells my noble master—in particular."

The captain's speech was received with supportive grunts from his gang.

"So, as you can surely appreciate," he continued, "we do, in all humbleness of course, rule this road and most other roads in the general vicinity of this proud republic—of Siena, that is—and so my insightful advice to you, as a friend to another friend, is to hurry up and pay that toll now, so you can get on your way and slip inside the city before she closes, after which point innocent travelers like yourselves are likely to fall prey to the scoundrelous gangs of Tolomeis that come out to pillage and such—as shall not be specified in the face of holy men—after nightfall."

There was a deep silence after the villain had spoken. Crouched on the cart behind his companions, holding the reins slack, Friar Lorenzo felt his heart hopping around inside his chest as if it was looking for a place to hide, and for a moment he thought he was going to faint. It had been one of those days—a scorching sun and not the slightest breeze—that reminded one of the horrors of Hell. And it did not help that they had run out of water many hours ago. If Friar Lorenzo had been in charge of the moneybag, he would readily have paid the villains anything in order to move on.

"Very well, then," said the senior monk, as if he had felt Friar Lorenzo's silent plea, "how much, then, for your protection?"

"Depends." The villain grinned. "What do you have on that cart, and what is it worth to you?"

"It is a coffin, noble friend, and it contains the victim of a dreadful plague."

Most of the brigands drew back at this news, but their captain was not so easily put off. "Well," he said, his grin broadening, "let's have a look, shall we."

"I do not recommend it!" said the monk. "The coffin must remain sealed—those are our orders."

"Orders?" exclaimed the captain. "Since when did humble monks get *orders*? And since when"—he paused for effect, nursing a smirk—"did they begin to ride horses bred in Lipicia?"

In the silence that followed his words, Friar Lorenzo felt his fortitude plunging like a lead weight to the very bottom of his soul, threatening to come out the other end.

"And look at that!" the brigand went on, mostly to amuse his comrades. "Did you ever see humble monks wear such splendiferous footwear? Now there"—he pointed his sword at Friar Lorenzo's gaping sandals—"is what you should *all* have worn, my careless friends, if your intent was to avoid taxation. As far as I can tell, the only humble brother here is the mute fella on the cart; as for the rest of you, I'll bet my balls you are in the service of some munificent patron other than God, and I am confident that the value of that coffin—to him—far exceeds the miserable five florins I am going to charge you for its release."

"You are mistaken," replied the senior monk, "if you think us capable of such expense. Two florins are all we can spare. It reflects ill on your patron to thwart the Church by such disproportionate greed."

The bandit relished the insult. "Greed, you call it? Nay, my fault is curiosity. Pay the five florins or I shall know how to act. The cart and coffin stay here, under my protection, until your patron claims them in person. For I should dearly love to see the rich bastard who sent you."

"Soon, you will be protecting nothing but the stench of death."

The captain laughed dismissively. "The smell of gold, my friend, overcomes all such odor."

"No mountain of gold," retorted the monk, casting aside his humility at last, "could suitably cover yours."

Hearing the insult, Friar Lorenzo bit his lip and began looking for an escape. He knew his travel companions well enough to predict the outcome of the spat, and he wanted no part in it.

The brigand leader was not unimpressed with the audacity of his victim. "You are determined, then," he said, head to one side, "to die on my blade?"

"I am determined," said the monk, "to accomplish my mission. And no rusty blade of yours can sever me from my goal."

"Your mission?" the bandit crowed. "Look, cousins, here is a monk who thinks God has made him a knight!"

All the brigands laughed, more or less aware of the reason, and their captain nodded towards the cart. "Now get rid of these fools and take the horses and the cart to Salimbeni—"

"I have a better idea," sneered the monk, and tore off his cowl to reveal the uniform underneath. "Why don't we go see my master Tolomei instead, with your head on a pole?"

Friar Lorenzo groaned inwardly as his fears were fulfilled. With no further attempts at concealment, his travel companions—all of them Tolomei knights in disguise—drew their swords and daggers from cloaks and saddlebags, and the mere sound of the roused iron made the brigands pull away in astonishment, if only to instantly throw themselves and their horses forward again in a screaming, headlong attack.

The sudden clamor made Friar Lorenzo's horses coil on their haunches and erupt in a frenzied gallop, pulling the cart along as they went, and there was little he could do but tear at the useless reins and plead for reason and moderation in two animals that had never studied philosophy. After three days on the road they showed remarkable spirit as they pulled their load away from the turmoil and up the bumpy road towards Siena, wheels wailing and the coffin bouncing this way and that, threatening to fall off the cart and break into splinters.

Failing all dialogue with the horses, Friar Lorenzo turned to the coffin for an easier opponent. Employing both hands and feet, he tried to hold it steady, but while he struggled for a good grip on the unwieldy thing, a motion on the road behind him made him look up and realize that the comfort of the coffin should be the very least of his concerns.

For he was being followed by two of the brigands, galloping apace to reclaim their treasure. Scrambling to prepare his defense, Friar Lorenzo found only a whip and his rosary, and he watched with trepidation as one of the bandits caught up with the cart—knife between his toothless gums—and reached out to grasp the wooden siding. Finding the necessary fierceness within his clement self, Friar Lorenzo swung the whip at the boarding pirate and heard him yelp with pain as the oxtail drew blood. One cut, however, was enough for the villain, and when Friar Lorenzo struck again, the other got hold of the whiplash and jerked the handle right out of his grip. With no more than the rosary and its dangling crucifix left for self-protection, Friar Lorenzo took to throwing bits of leftover lunch at his opponent. But despite the hardness of the bread, he was unable to prevent him from finally climbing on board.

Seeing that the friar was out of munition, the brigand rose to his feet in gleeful triumph, took the knife from his mouth, and demonstrated the length of the blade to its trembling target.

"Stop in the name of Christ!" exclaimed Friar Lorenzo, holding up his rosary. "I have friends in Heaven who will strike you dead!"

"Oh really? I don't see them anywhere!"

Just then did the lid of the coffin swing open, and its tenant—a young woman whose wild hair and flaming eyes made her look like an angel of venegeance—sat up with all signs of consternation. The mere sight of her was enough to make the bandit drop his knife in horror and turn completely ashen. Without hesitation the angel leaned out of the coffin, picked up the knife, and thrust it immediately back into the flesh of its owner, as high up his thigh as her anger could reach.

Screaming with anguish, the wounded man lost his balance and tumbled off the end of the cart to even greater injury. Her cheeks glowing with excitement, the girl turned to grin at Friar Lorenzo, and she would have climbed out of the coffin had he not prevented her.

"No, Giulietta!" he insisted, pushing her back down. "In the name of Jesus, stay there and be quiet!"

Slamming the lid over her indignant face, Friar Lorenzo looked around to see what had become of the other horseman. Alas, this one was less of a madcap than his mate and had no intention of boarding the rumbling wagon at its current speed. Instead, he galloped ahead to seize the harness and slow the horses, and much to Friar Lorenzo's distress, the measure soon began to take effect. Within another quarter mile the horses were gradually forced into cantering, then trotting, and finally to a complete standstill.

Only then did the villain approach the cart, and as he rode towards it, Friar Lorenzo saw that it was none other than the lavishly clad captain of the brigands, still smirking and seemingly untouched by the bloodshed. The setting sun gave the man a halo of bronze that was utterly undeserved, and Friar Lorenzo was struck by the contrast between the luminous beauty of the countryside and the sheer viciousness of its dwellers.

"How about this, Friar," began the villain, with uncanny gentility. "I grant you your life—in fact, you can even take this fine cart and these noble horses, no tolls paid—in exchange for that girl?"

"I thank you for the generous offer," replied Friar Lorenzo, squinting against the sunset, "but I am the sworn protector of this noble lady, and I cannot let you have her. If I did, we would both go to Hell."

"Bah!" The brigand had heard it all before. "That girl is no more of a lady than you or I. In fact, I strongly suspect she is a Tolomei whore!"

An indignant shriek was heard from inside the coffin, and Friar Lorenzo quickly put his foot on top of the lid to hold it closed.

"The lady is of great consequence to Messer Tolomei, that is true," he said, "and any man that lays a hand on her will bring a war upon his own kin. Surely your master, Salimbeni, desires no such feud."

"Ah, you monks and your sermons!" The bandit rode right up to the cart, and only then did his halo fade. "Do not threaten me with war, little preacher. It is what I do best."

"I beg you to let us go!" urged Friar Lorenzo, holding up his quivering rosary and hoping it would catch the sun's last rays. "Or I swear upon these holy beads and the wounds of sweet Jesus that cherubs will come down from Heaven and strike your children dead in their beds!"

"They shall be welcome!" The villain drew his sword anew. "I have too many to feed as it is." He swung his leg across the head of his horse to jump aboard the cart with the ease of a dancer. Seeing the other backing away in terror, he laughed. "Why so surprised? Did you really think I would let you live?"

The brigand's sword withdrew to strike, and Friar Lorenzo sank to his knees in submission, clutching the rosary and waiting for the slash that would cut short his prayer. To die at nineteen was cruel, particularly when no one was looking on to witness his martyrdom, except his divine Father in Heaven, who was not exactly known for running to the rescue of dying sons.

Nay sit, nay sit, good cousin Capulet,
For you and I are past our dancing days

...

I CANNOT REMEMBER HOW FAR I got in the story that night, but the birds had started chirping outside when I finally drifted off on a sea of papers. I now understood the connection between the many different texts in my mother's box; they were all—in each their way—pre-Shakespearean versions of *Romeo and Juliet*. Even better, the texts from 1340 were not just fiction, they were genuine eyewitness accounts of the events that had led to the creation of the famous story.

Although he had not yet made an appearance in his own journal, the mysterious Maestro Ambrogio, it seemed, had personally known the real human beings behind some of literature's most star-crossed characters. I had to admit that so far none of his writing offered much overlap with Shakespeare's tragedy, but then, more than two and a half centuries had passed between the actual events and the Bard's play, and the story must have traveled through many different hands along the way.

Bursting to share my new knowledge with someone who would appreciate it—not everyone would find it funny that, through the ages, millions of tourists had flocked to the wrong city to see Juliet's balcony and grave—I called Umberto on his cell phone as soon as I got out of my morning shower.

"Congratulations!" he exclaimed, when I told him that I had successfully charmed Presidente Maconi into giving me my mother's box. "So, how rich are you now?"

"Uh," I said, glancing at the mess on my bed. "I don't think the treasure is in the box. If there even *is* a treasure."

"Of course there's a treasure," Umberto countered, "why else would your mother put it in a bank safe? Look more carefully."

"There's something else—" I paused briefly, trying to find a way of saying it without sounding silly. "I think I'm somehow related to Shakespeare's Juliet."

I suppose I couldn't blame Umberto for laughing, but it annoyed me all the same. "I know it sounds weird," I went on, cutting through his chuckle, "but why else would we have the same name, *Giulietta Tolomei*?"

"You mean, Juliet Capulet?" Umberto corrected me. "I hate to break it to you, principessa, but I'm not sure she was a real person—"

"Of course not!" I shot back, wishing I had never told him about it, "But it looks like the story was inspired by real people . . . Oh, never mind! How's life at your end?"

After hanging up, I started paging through the Italian letters my mother had received more than twenty years ago. Surely there was someone still alive in Siena who had known my parents, and who could answer all the questions Aunt Rose had so consistently brushed aside. But without knowing any Italian it was hard to tell which letters were written by friends or family; my only clue was that one of them began with the words "Carissima Diana—" and that the sender's name was Pia Tolomei.

Unfolding the city map I had bought the day before, together with the dictionary, I spent some time searching for the address that was scribbled on the back of the envelope, and finally managed to pinpoint it in a minuscule piazza called Piazzetta del Castellare in downtown Siena. It was located in the heart of the Owl contrada, my home turf, not far from Palazzo Tolomei where I had met Presidente Maconi the day before.

If I were lucky, Pia Tolomei—whoever she was—would still be living there, eager to speak with Diane Tolomei's daughter and lucid enough to remember why.

PIAZZETTA DEL CASTELLARE was like a small fortress within the city, and not that easy to find. After walking right past it several times, I finally discovered that I had to enter through a covered alleyway, which I had first assumed was the entrance to a private yard. Once inside the piazzetta, I was trapped between tall, silent buildings, and as I looked up at all the closed shutters on the walls around me, it was almost conceivable that they had been drawn shut sometime in the Middle Ages and never opened since.

In fact, had there not been a couple of Vespas parked in a corner, a tabby cat with a shiny black collar poised on a doorstep, and music playing from a single open window, I would have guessed that the buildings had long since been abandoned and left to rats and ghosts.

I took out the envelope I had found in my mother's box and looked at the address once more. According to my map I was in the right place, but when I did a tour of the doors I could not find the name *Tolomei* on any of the doorbells, nor could I find a number that corresponded to the house number on my letter. To become a mailman in a place like this, I thought, clairvoyance must be a prerequisite.

Not knowing what else to do, I started ringing doorbells, one at a time. Just as I was about to press the fourth one, a woman opened a pair of shutters way above me, and yelled something in Italian.

In response, I waved the letter. "Pia Tolomei?"

"Tolomei?"

"Yes! Do you know where she lives? Does she still live here?"

The woman pointed at a door across the piazzetta and said something that could only mean, "Try in there."

Only now did I notice a more contemporary kind of door in the far wall; it had an artsy, black-and-white door handle, and when I tried it, it opened. I paused briefly, unsure of the proper etiquette for entering private homes in Siena; meanwhile, the woman in the window behind me kept urging me to go inside—she clearly found me uncommonly dull—and so I did.

"Hello?" I took a timid step across the threshold and stared into the cool darkness. Once my eyes adjusted, I saw that I was standing in an entrance hall with a very high ceiling, surrounded by tapestries, paintings, and antique artifacts on display in glass cabinets. I let go of the door and called out, "Anybody home? Mrs. Tolomei?" But all I heard was the door closing with a sigh behind me.

Not entirely sure how to proceed, I started down the hallway, looking at the antiques on the way. Among them was a collection of long, vertical banners with images of horses, towers, and women that all looked very much like the Virgin Mary. A few were very old and faded, others were modern and quite garish; only when I got to the end of the row did it dawn on me that this was no private home, but some kind of museum or public building.

Now, finally, I heard the sound of uneven footsteps and a deep voice calling out impatiently, "Salvatore?"

I spun around to face my unwitting host as he emerged from a neighboring room, leaning on a crutch. He was an older man, definitely past seventy, and his frown made him look older still. "Salva—?" He stopped on the spot when he saw me, and said something else that did not sound particularly welcoming.

"Ciao!" I said, in a bushy-tailed sort of way, and held up the letter as one does a crucifix in front of Transylvanian nobility, just in case, "I am looking for Pia Tolomei. She knew my parents." I pointed at myself. "Giulietta Tolomei. To-lo-mei."

The man walked up to me, leaning heavily on his crutch, and plucked the letter right out of my hand. He looked suspiciously at the envelope and turned it over several times to reread the addresses of both the recipient and the sender. "My wife sent this letter," he finally said, in surprisingly smooth English, "many years ago. To Diana Tolomei. She was my . . . hmm . . . aunt. Where did you find it?"

"Diane was my mother," I said, my voice sounding oddly mousy in the big room. "I am Giulietta, the oldest of her twins. I wanted to come and see Siena—see where she lived. Do you . . . remember her?"

The old man did not speak right away. He looked at my face with eyes full of wonder, then reached out and touched a hand to my cheek to make sure I was real. "Little Giulietta?" he finally said. "Come here!" He grabbed my shoulders and pulled me into an embrace. "I am Peppo Tolomei, your godfather."

I barely knew what to do. Normally I was not someone who ran around hugging people—I left that to Janice—but even I didn't mind it from this endearing old man.

"I'm sorry to barge in—" I started, then stopped, not sure what to say next.

"No-no-no-no-no!" Peppo brushed it all aside. "I am so happy you are here! Come, let me show you the museum! This is the museum for the contrada of the Owl—" He barely knew where to start and hopped around on his cane, looking for something impressive to show me. But when he saw my expression, he stopped himself. "No! You don't want to see the museum! You want to talk! Yes, we must talk!" He threw up his arms and nearly knocked over a sculpture with the crutch. "I must hear everything. My wife—we must go see my wife. She will be so happy. She is at the house—*Salvatore!* . . . Oh, where *is* he?"

Five minutes later I came shooting out of Piazzetta del Castellare straddling the rear end of a red-and-black scooter. Peppo Tolomei had helped me into the saddle with the gallantry of a magician helping a lovely young assistant into a box he intends to saw in half, and as soon as I had a secure grip on his suspenders, we zoomed out through the covered alleyway, breaking for no one.

Peppo had insisted on closing up the museum right away and taking me home with him, so that I could meet his wife, Pia, and whoever else happened to be around. I had gladly accepted the invitation, assuming that the home to which he was referring was just around the corner. Only now, as we flew up the Corso past Palazzo Tolomei, did I realize my mistake.

"Is it far?" I yelled, hanging on as best I could.

"No-no-no!" replied Peppo, narrowly missing a nun pushing an old man in a wheelchair. "Don't worry, we will call everyone and have a big family reunion!" Excited at the prospect, he began describing all the family members I would soon be meeting, though I could barely hear him in the wind. He was too distracted to notice that, as we passed Palazzo Salimbeni, we went right through a handful of security guards, forcing them all to jump aside.

"Whoa!" I exclaimed, wondering if Peppo was aware that we might be having our big family reunion in the slammer. But the guards made no moves to stop us, merely watched us go past the way dogs on a tight leash watch a fluffy squirrel strut across the road. Unfortunately, one of them was Eva Maria's godson, Alessandro, and I was almost certain he recognized me, for he did a double take at the sight of my dangling legs, perhaps wondering what had happened to my flip-flops.

"Peppo!" I yelled, pulling at my cousin's suspenders, "I really don't want to be arrested, okay?"

"Don't worry!" Peppo turned a corner and accelerated as he spoke. "I go too fast for police!" Moments later we shot through an ancient city gate like a poodle through a hoop, and flew right into the artwork of a full-blown Tuscan summer.

As I sat there, looking at the landscape over his shoulder, I wanted so much to be filled with a sense of familiarity, of finally returning home. But everything around me was new; the warm wafts of weeds and spices, the lazily rolling fields—even Peppo's cologne had a foreign component that was absurdly attractive.

But how much do we really remember from the first three years of our lives? Sometimes I could conjure a memory of hugging a pair of bare legs that were definitely not Aunt Rose's, and Janice and I were both sure we remembered a large glass bowl filled with wine corks, but apart from that, it was hard to tell which fragments belonged where. When we occasionally managed to uncover memories of ourselves as toddlers, we always ended up confused. "I'm *sure* the wobbly chess table was in Tuscany," Janice would always insist. "Where else could it have been? Aunt Rose has never had one."

"Then how," I would inevitably counter, "do you explain that it was Umberto who slapped you when you pushed it over?"

But Janice couldn't explain it. In the end, she would merely mumble, "Well, maybe it was someone else. When you're two years old, all men look the same." Then she'd snort, "Hell, they still do."

As a teenager I used to fantasize about returning to Siena and suddenly remembering everything about my childhood; now that I was finally here, hurtling down narrow roads without recognizing anything, I began to wonder if living away from this place for most of my life had somehow withered away an essential part of my soul.

PIA AND PEPPO TOLOMEI lived on a farm in a small valley, surrounded by vineyards and olive groves. Gentle hills rose around their property on all sides, and the comfort of peaceful seclusion more than made up for the lack of extended views. The house was by no means grand; its yellow walls had weeds growing in the cracks, the green shutters needed so much more than just a paint job, and the terra-cotta roof looked as if the next storm—or maybe just someone sneezing inside—

would make all the tiles come rattling down. And yet the many trailing vines and strategically placed flowerpots somehow complemented the decay and made the place utterly irresistible.

After parking the scooter and grabbing a crutch leaning against the wall, Peppo took me directly into the garden. Back here, in the shade of the house, his wife, Pia, sat on a stool amongst her grandchildren and great-grandchildren like an ageless harvest goddess surrounded by nymphs, teaching them how to make braids out of fresh garlic. It took several attempts before Peppo was able to make her understand who I was and why he had brought me there, but once Pia finally dared to trust her ears, she stuck her feet into her slippers, got up with the aid of her entourage, and enfolded me in a tearful embrace. "Giulietta!" she exclaimed, pressing me to her chest and kissing me on the forehead all at once. "Che meraviglia! It is a miracle!"

Her joy in seeing me was so genuine that I almost felt ashamed of myself. I had not gone to the Owl Museum this morning in search of my long-lost godparents, nor had it occurred to me before this moment that I even *had* godparents, and that they would be this happy to see me alive and well. Yet here they were, and their kindness made me realize that—until now—I had never felt truly welcome anywhere, not even in my own home. At least not when Janice was around.

Within an hour the house and garden filled with people and food. It was as if everybody had been waiting just around the corner, local delicacy in hand, desperate for an excuse to celebrate. Some were family, some friends and neighbors, and they all claimed to have known my parents and to have wondered what ever happened to their twin daughters. No one said anything explicit, but I sensed that, back then, Aunt Rose had swooped in and claimed Janice and me against the wishes of the Tolomei family—thanks to Uncle Jim she still had connections in the State Department—and that we had vanished without a trace, much to the frustration of Pia and Peppo, who were, after all, our godparents.

"But that is all in the past," Peppo kept saying, patting me on the back, "for now you are here, and we can finally talk." But it was hard to know where to begin; there were so many years that must be accounted for, and so many questions that needed answers, including the reason for my sister's mysterious absence.

"She was too busy to come along," I said, looking away. "But I'm sure she'll visit you soon."

It did not help that only a handful of the guests spoke English, and that every answer to every inquiry had to first be understood and interpreted by a third party. Still, everyone was so friendly and warm that even I, after a while, began to relax and enjoy myself. It didn't really matter that we couldn't understand each other, what mattered were those little smiles and nods that said so much more than words.

At one point, Pia came out on the terrace with a photo album and sat down to show me pictures from my parents' wedding. As soon as she opened the album, other women clustered around us, eager to follow along and help turn the pages.

"There!" Pia pointed at a large wedding picture. "Your mother is wearing the dress I wore at my wedding. Oh, aren't they a handsome couple? . . . And here, this is your cousin Francesco—"

"Wait!" I tried to prevent her from turning the page, but in vain. She probably did not realize that I had never seen a picture of my father before, and that the only grown-up photo of my mother I had ever known was her high-school graduation portrait on Aunt Rose's piano.

Pia's album came as a surprise to me. Not so much because my mother was visibly pregnant underneath the wedding gown, but because my father looked as if he was a hundred years old. Obviously, he was not, but standing next to my mother—a college dropout vixen with dimples in her smile—he looked like old man Abraham in my illustrated children's Bible.

Even so, they appeared to be happy together, and although there were no shots of them kissing, most of the photos showed my mother clinging to her husband's elbow and looking at him with great admiration. And so after a while I shrugged off my astonishment and decided to accept the possibility that here, in this bright and blissful place, concepts like time and age had very little bearing on people's lives.

The women around me confirmed my theory; none of them seemed to find the union in any way extraordinary. As far as I could understand, their chirping commentary—all in Italian—was primarily about my mother's dress, her veil, and the complex genealogical relationship of every single wedding guest to my father and to themselves.

After the wedding photos came a few pages dedicated to our baptism, but my parents were barely in them. The pictures showed Pia holding a baby that could have been either Janice or me—it was impossible to tell which one, and Pia could not remember—and Peppo proudly holding the other. There appeared to have been two different ceremonies—one inside a church, and one outside in the sunshine, by the baptismal font of the contrada of the Owl.

"That was a good day," said Pia, smiling sadly. "You and your sister became little civettini, little owls. It was too bad—" She did not finish the sentence, but closed the album very tenderly. "It is such a long time ago. Sometimes I wonder if time really heals—" She was interrupted by a sudden commotion inside the house, and by a voice impatiently calling her name. "Come!" Pia got up, suddenly anxious. "That must be our Nonna!"

Old Granny Tolomei, whom everyone referred to as Nonna, lived with one of her granddaughters in downtown Siena, but had been summoned to the farm this afternoon in order to meet me—an arrangement that clearly did not fit her personal schedule. She was standing in the hallway, irritably arranging her black lace with one hand while leaning heavily on her granddaughter with the other. Had I been as uncharitable as Janice, I would have instantly proclaimed her the picture-perfect fairy-tale witch. All that was missing was the crow on her shoulder.

Pia rushed forward to greet the old lady, who grudgingly allowed herself to be kissed on both cheeks and escorted into a particularly favored chair in the living room. Some minutes were spent making Nonna comfortable; cushions fetched, placed, and moved around, and special lemonade brought in from the kitchen, immediately sent back, and brought in anew, this time with a slice of lemon perched on the rim.

"Nonna is our aunt," Peppo whispered in my ear, "and your father's youngest sister. Come, I will introduce you." He pulled me along to stand at attention in front of the old lady and eagerly explained the situation to her in Italian, clearly expecting to see some sign of joy on her face.

But Nonna refused to smile. No matter how much Peppo urged her— even begged her—to rejoice with the rest of us, she could not be persuaded to take any kind of pleasure in my presence. He even had me step forward so that she could see me more clearly, but what she saw only gave her further reason to scowl, and before Peppo managed to pull me out of range, she leaned forward and snarled something I did not understand, but which made everyone gasp with embarrassment.

Pia and Peppo practically evacuated me from the living room, apologizing all the way. "I am so sorry!" Peppo kept saying, over and over, too mortified to even look me in the eye. "I don't know what is wrong with her! I think she is going crazy!"

"Don't worry," I said, too stunned to feel anything, "I don't blame her for not believing it. It's all so new, even for me."

"Let us go for a little walk," said Peppo, still flustered, "and come back later. It is time I show you their graves."

THE VILLAGE CEMETERY was a welcoming, sleepy oasis, and very different from any other graveyard I had ever seen. The whole place was a maze of white, freestanding walls with no roof, and the walls themselves were a mosaic of graves from top to bottom. Names, dates, and photos identified the individuals dwelling behind the marble slabs, and brass sconces held—on behalf of the temporarily incapacitated host—flowers brought by visitors.

"Here—" Peppo had a hand on my shoulder for support, but that did not prevent him from gallantly opening a squeaky iron gate and letting us both into a small shrine off the main drag. "This is part of the old Tolomei . . . hmm . . . sepulchre. Most of it is underground, and we don't go down there anymore. Up here is better."

"It is beautiful." I stepped into the small room and looked around at the many marble plates and the bouquet of fresh flowers standing on the altar. A candle was burning steadily in a red glass bowl that seemed vaguely familiar to me, indicating that the Tolomei sepulchre was a place carefully maintained by the family. I suddenly felt a stab of guilt that I was here alone, without Janice, but I quickly shook it off. If she had been here, she would most likely have ruined the moment with a snarky comment.

"This is your father," pointed Peppo, "and your mother right next to him." He paused to muse on a distant memory. "She was so young. I thought she would be alive long after I was gone."

I looked at the two marble plates that were all that was left of Professor Patrizio Scipione Tolomei and his wife, Diane Lloyd Tolomei, and felt my heart flutter. For as long as I could remember, my parents had been little more than distant shadows in a daydream, and I had never imagined I would one day find myself as close to them—at least physically—as this. Even when fantasizing about traveling to Italy, for some reason it had never occurred to me that my first duty upon arrival must be to find their graves, and I felt a warm wave of gratitude towards Peppo for helping me do the right thing.

"Thank you," I said quietly, squeezing his hand, which was still resting on my shoulder.

"It was a great tragedy the way they died," he said, shaking his head, "and that all Patrizio's work was lost in the fire. He had a beautiful farm in Malamerenda—all gone. After the funeral your mother bought a little house near Montepulciano and lived there alone with the twins—with you and your sister—but she was never the same. She came to put flowers on his grave every Sunday, but"—he paused to pull a handkerchief from his pocket—"she was never happy again."

"Wait a minute—" I stared at the dates on my parents' graves. "My father died before my mother? I always thought they died together—" But even as I spoke, I could see that the dates confirmed the new truth; my father had died more than two years before my mother. "What fire?"

"Someone—no, I shouldn't say that—" Peppo frowned at himself. "There was a fire, a terrible fire. Your father's farm burned down. Your mother was lucky; she was in Siena, shopping, with you girls. It was a great, great tragedy. I would have said that God held his hand over her, but then two years later—"

"The car accident," I muttered.

"Well—" Peppo dug the toe of his shoe into the ground. "I don't know the truth. Nobody knows the truth. But"—he finally met my eyes—"I always suspected that the Salimbenis had a hand in it."

I didn't know what to say to this. I pictured Eva Maria and her suitcase full of clothes sitting in my hotel room. She had been so kind to me, so eager to make friends.

"There was a young man," Peppo went on, "Luciano Salimbeni. He was a troublemaker. There were rumors. I don't want to—" Peppo glanced at me nervously. "The fire. The fire that killed your father. They say it was not an accident. They say someone wanted to murder him and destroy his research. It was terrible. Such a beautiful house. But you know, I think your mother saved something from the house. Something important. Documents. She was afraid to talk about it, but after the fire, she began to ask strange questions about . . . things."

"What kind of things?"

"All kinds. I didn't know the answers. She asked me about the Salimbenis. About secret tunnels underground. She wanted to find a grave. It was something to do with the Plague."

"The . . . bubonic plague?"

"Yes, the big one. In 1348." Peppo cleared his throat, not comfortable with the subject. "You see, your mother believed that there is an old curse that is still haunting the Tolomeis and the Salimbenis. And she was trying to find out how to stop it. She was obsessed with this idea. I wanted to believe her, but—" He pulled at his shirt collar as if he suddenly felt hot. "She was so determined. She was convinced that we were all cursed. Death. Destruction. Accidents. 'A plague on both our houses' . . . that is what she used to say." He sighed deeply, reliving the pain of the past. "She always quoted Shakespeare. She took it very seriously . . . *Romeo and Juliet*. She thought that it had happened right here, in Siena. She had a theory—" Peppo shook his head dismissively. "She was obsessed with it. I don't know. I am not a professor. All I know is that there was a man, Luciano Salimbeni, who wanted to find a treasure—"

I could not help myself, I had to ask, "What kind of treasure?"

"Who knows?" Peppo threw up his arms. "Your father spent all his time researching old legends. He was always talking about lost treasures. But your mother told me about something once—oh, what did she call it?—I think she called it Juliet's Eyes. I don't know what she meant, but I think it was very valuable, and I think it was what Luciano Salimbeni was after."

I was dying to know more, but by now Peppo was looking very distressed, almost ill, and he swayed and grabbed my arm for balance. "If I were you," he went on, "I would be very, very careful. And I would not trust anyone with the name of Salimbeni." Seeing my expression, he frowned. "You think I am pazzo . . . crazy? Here we are, standing by the grave of a young woman who died before her time. She was your mother. Who am I to tell you who did this to her, and why?" His grip tightened. "She is dead. Your father is dead. That is all I know. But my old Tolomei heart tells me that you must be careful."

WHEN WE WERE SENIORS in high school, Janice and I had both volunteered for the annual play—as it so happened, it was *Romeo and Juliet.* After the tryouts Janice was cast as Juliet, while my role was to be a tree in the Capulet orchard. She, of course, spent more time on her nails than on memorizing the dialogue, and whenever we rehearsed the balcony scene, I would be the one to whisper the first words of her lines to her, being, after all, conveniently located onstage with branches for arms.

On opening night, however, she was particularly horrible to me— when we sat in makeup, she kept laughing at my brown face and pulling the leaves out of my hair, while she was being dolled up with blond braids and rosy cheeks—and by the time the balcony scene rolled around, I was in no mood to cover for her. In fact, I did quite the opposite. When Romeo said, "what shall I swear by?" I whispered, "three words!"

And Janice immediately said, "three words, dear Romeo, and good night indeed!" which threw Romeo off completely, and had the scene end in confusion.

Later, when I was posing as a candelabrum in Juliet's bedroom, I made Janice wake up next to Romeo and say right off the bat, "hie hence, begone, away!" which did not set a very good tone for the rest of their tender scene. Needless to say, Janice was so furious she chased me through the entire school afterwards, swearing that she was going to shave off my eyebrows. It had been fun at first, but when, in the end, she locked herself in the school bathroom and cried for an hour, even I stopped laughing.

Long after midnight, when I sat in the living room talking with Aunt Rose, afraid of going to bed and submitting myself to sleep and Janice's razor, Umberto came in with a glass of vin santo for us both. He did not say anything, just handed us the glasses, and Aunt Rose did not utter a word about my being too young to drink.

"You like that play?" she said instead. "You seem to know it by heart."

"I don't really like it a whole lot," I confessed, shrugging and sipping my drink at the same time. "It's just . . . *there,* stuck in my head."

Aunt Rose nodded slowly, savoring the vin santo. "Your mother was the same way. She knew it by heart. It was . . . an obsession."

I held my breath, not wanting to break her train of thought. I waited for another glimpse of my mother, but it never came. Aunt Rose just looked up, frowning, to clear her throat and take another sip of wine. And that was it. That was one of the only things she ever told me about my mother without being prompted, and I never passed it on to Janice. Our mutual obsession with Shakespeare's play was a little secret I shared with my mother and no one else, just like I never told anyone about my growing fear that, because my mother had died at twenty-five, I would, too.

AS SOON AS PEPPO dropped me off in front of Hotel Chiusarelli, I went straight to the nearest Internet café and Googled *Luciano Salimbeni.* But it took me several verbal acrobatics to come up with a search combination that yielded anything remotely useful. Only after at least an hour and many, many frustrations with the Italian language, I was fairly confident of the following conclusions:

One: Luciano Salimbeni was dead.

Two: Luciano Salimbeni had been a bad guy, possibly even a mass murderer.

Three: Luciano and Eva Maria Salimbeni were somehow related.

Four: There had been something fishy about the car accident that had killed my mother, and Luciano Salimbeni had been wanted for questioning.

I printed out all the pages so that I could reread them later, in the company of my dictionary. This search had yielded little more than Peppo Tolomei had just told me this afternoon, but at least now I knew my elderly cousin had not merely invented the story; there really had been a dangerous Luciano Salimbeni at large in Siena some twenty years ago or so.

But the good news was that he was dead. In other words, he definitely could not be the tracksuit charmer who—maybe, maybe not—had stalked me the day before, after I left the bank in Palazzo Tolomei with my mother's box.

As an afterthought, I Googled *Juliet's Eyes.* Not surprisingly, none of the search results had anything to do with legendary treasures. Almost all were semischolarly discussions about the significance of eyes in Shakespeare's *Romeo and Juliet,* and I dutifully read through a couple of passages from the play, trying to spot a secret message. One of them read:

Alack, there lies more peril in thine eye
Than twenty of their swords.

Well, I thought to myself, if this evil Luciano Salimbeni had really killed my mother over a treasure called Juliet's Eyes, then Romeo's statement was true; whatever the nature of those mysterious eyes, they were potentially more dangerous than weapons, simple as that. In contrast, the second passage was a bit more complex than your average pickup line:

Two of the fairest stars in all the heaven,
Having some business, do entreat her eyes
To twinkle in their spheres till they return.
What if her eyes were there, they in her head?

I mulled over the lines all the way down Via del Paradiso. Romeo was clearly trying to compliment Juliet by saying that her eyes were like sparkling stars, but he sure had a funny way of phrasing it. It was, in my opinion, not particularly smooth to woo a girl by envisioning what she would look like with her eyes gouged out.

But really, this poetry was a welcome diversion from the other facts I had learned that day. Both my parents had died in a terrible way, separately, and possibly even at the hands of a murderer. Even though I had left the cemetery hours ago, I was still struggling to process this horrendous discovery. On top of my shock and sorrow I also felt the little fleabites of fear, just as I had the day before, when I thought I was being followed after leaving the bank. But had Peppo been right in warning me? Could I possibly be in danger now, so many years later? If so, I could presumably pull myself back out of danger by going home to Virginia. But then, what if there really was a treasure? What if—somewhere in my mother's box—there was a clue to finding Juliet's Eyes, whatever they were.

Lost in speculation, I strolled into a secluded cloister garden off Piazza San Domenico. By now day was turning dusk, and I stood for a moment in the portico of a loggia, drinking in the last rays of sunshine while the evening shadows slowly crawled up my legs. I did not feel like going back to the hotel just yet, where Maestro Ambrogio's journal was waiting to sweep me through another sleepless night in the year 1340.

As I stood there, absorbed in the twilight, my thoughts circling around my parents, I saw him for the first time—

The Maestro.

He was walking through the shadows of the opposite loggia, carrying an easel and several other items that kept slipping from his grip, forcing him to stop and redistribute the weight. At first I simply stared at him. It was impossible not to. He was unlike any other Italian I had ever met, with his long, gray hair, sagging cardigan, and open sandals; in fact, he looked most of all like a time traveler from Woodstock shuffling around in a world taken over by runway models.

He did not see me at first, and when I caught up with him and handed him a paintbrush he had dropped, he jumped with fear.

"Scusi," I said, "but I think this is yours."

He looked at the brush without recognition, and when he finally took it, he held it awkwardly, as if its purpose completely escaped him. Then he looked at me, still perplexed, and said, "Do I know you?"

Before I could answer, a smile spread over his face, and he exclaimed, "Of course I do! I remember you. You are—oh! Remind me . . . who are you?"

"Giulietta. Tolomei? But I don't think—"

"Sì-sì-sì! Of course! Where have you been?"

"I . . . just arrived."

He grimaced at his own stupidity. "Of course you did! Never mind me. You just arrived. And here you are. Giulietta Tolomei. More beautiful than ever." He smiled and shook his head. "I never understood this thing, time."

"Well," I said, somewhat weirded out, "are you gonna be okay?"

"Me? Oh! Yes, thank you. But . . . you must come and see me. I want to show you something. Do you know my workshop? It is in Via Santa Caterina. The blue door. You don't have to knock, just come in."

Only then did it occur to me that he had me pegged for a tourist and wanted to sell some souvenirs. *Yeah right, buddy,* I thought, *I'll get right on that.*

WHEN I CALLED UMBERTO later that night, he was deeply disturbed by my new insights into my parents' deaths. "But are you sure?" he kept saying, "are you sure this is true?" I told him that I was. Not only did everything point to the fact that there had been dark forces at play twenty years ago, but as far as I could see, those forces might still be lingering and on the prowl.

"Are you sure he was following you?" Umberto objected. "Maybe—"

"Umberto," I interrupted him, "he was wearing a tracksuit."

We both knew that in Umberto's universe only a black-hearted villain would walk down a fashionable street dressed in sportswear.

"Well," said Umberto, "maybe he just wanted to pick your pocket. He saw you leaving the bank, and he figured you had taken out money—"

"Yes, maybe. I sure don't see why someone would steal this box. I can't find anything in it to do with Juliet's Eyes—"

"Juliet's Eyes?"

"Yeah, that's what Peppo said." I sighed and threw myself down on the bed. "Apparently, that's the treasure. But if you ask me, I think it's all a big scam. I think Mom and Aunt Rose are sitting up in heaven, having a really good laugh right now. Anyway . . . what are you up to?"

We talked for at least another five minutes before I discovered that Umberto was no longer in Aunt Rose's house, but at a hotel in New York, looking for work, whatever that meant. I had a hard time imagining him waiting tables in Manhattan, grating Parmesan cheese over other people's pasta. He probably shared my sentiments, for he sounded tired and out of spirits, and I wanted so much to be able to tell him that I was on track to land a major fortune. But we both knew that, despite recovering my mother's box, I had barely figured out where to start.

Death that hath suck'd the honey of thy breath
Hath had no power yet upon thy beauty

Siena, A.D. 1340

. . .

THE LETHAL STRIKE NEVER CAME.

Instead, Friar Lorenzo—still kneeling in prayer before the brigand—heard a brief, frightful wheeze, followed by a tremor that rocked the whole cart, and the sound of a body tumbling to the ground. And then . . . silence. A brief glance with a half-open eye confirmed that, indeed, his intended killer was no longer looming over him, sword drawn, and Friar Lorenzo stretched nervously to see where the villain had disappeared so suddenly.

There he lay, broken and bloody on the bank of the ditch, the man who had—moments ago—been the cocksure captain of a band of highwaymen. How frail and human he looked now, thought Friar Lorenzo, with the point of a knife protruding from his chest, and with blood trickling from his demonic mouth and into an ear that had heard many sobbing prayers but never taken pity on a single one.

"Heavenly Mother!" The monk uplifted his folded hands to the sky above. "Thank you, O sacred Virgin, for saving your humble servant!"

"You are welcome, Friar, but I am no virgin."

Hearing the ghostly voice and realizing that the speaker was very near and rather dreadful-looking with plumed helmet, breastplate, and lance in hand, Friar Lorenzo sprang to his feet.

"Noble Saint Michael!" he cried, at once exalted and terrified. "You have saved my life! That man, there, that rascal, was just about to kill me!"

Saint Michael raised his visor to reveal a youthful face. "Yes," he said, his voice human now, "I had surmised as much. But I must add to your disappointment: I am no saint either."

"Whatever your description, noblest knight," exclaimed Friar Lorenzo, "your advent is in truth a miracle, and I am confident that the holy Virgin will reward such kind actions in Heaven!"

"I thank you, Friar," replied the knight, his eyes full of mischief, "but when you talk to her next, could you tell her that I will happily settle for a reward here on earth. Another horse, perhaps? For this one is sure to land me with the pig at the Palio." ·

Friar Lorenzo blinked once, maybe twice, as he began to realize that his savior had spoken the truth; he was indeed no saint. And judging by the way the young man had spoken of the Virgin Mary—with impertinent familiarity—he was certainly no pious soul either.

There was no mistaking the faint creaking of the coffin lid as its tenant tried to steal a glance at her bold savior, and Friar Lorenzo quickly sat down on top of it to hold it closed, his gut telling him that here were two young people who must never know each other. "Ahem," he said, determined to be polite, "whereabouts is your battle, noble knight? Or are you off to defend the Holy Land?"

The other looked incredulous. "Where are you from, funny friar? Surely a man so connected to God knows that the time of crusades has passed." He threw out his arm in the direction of Siena. "These hills, those towers ... this is my Holy Land."

"Then I am truly glad," said Friar Lorenzo hastily, "that I have not come hither with evil intent!"

The knight was not convinced. "May I ask," he said, squinting, "what errand you have in Siena, Friar? And what do you have in that coffin?"

"Nothing!"

"Nothing?" The other glanced at the dead body on the ground. "It is very unlike the Salimbenis to bleed for nothing. Surely you have something desirable with you?"

"Not at all!" insisted Friar Lorenzo, still too shaken to put faith in yet another stranger with demonstrated killing skills. "In this coffin lies one of my poor brothers, grotesquely disfigured by a fall from our windy bell tower three days ago. I must deliver him to Messer—um . . . to his family in Siena this very evening."

Much to Friar Lorenzo's relief, the expression on the other's face now changed from rising hostility into compassion, and he asked no more about the coffin. Instead, he turned his head and looked impatiently down the road. Following his gaze, Friar Lorenzo saw nothing but the setting sun, but the sight reminded him that it was thanks to this young man, heathen or no, that he was able to enjoy the rest of this evening and, God willing, many more like it.

"Cousins!" bellowed his savior. "Our trial run has been delayed by this unfortunate friar!"

Only now did Friar Lorenzo see five other horsemen coming right out of the sun, and as they came closer, he began to recognize that he was dealing with a handful of young men involved in some manner of sport. None of the others wore armor, but one of them—a mere boy—held a large hourglass. When the child caught sight of the dead body in the ditch, the device slipped from his fingers and fell to the ground, breaking the glass in half.

"Now here is an evil omen for our race, little cousin," said the knight to the boy, "but maybe our holy friend here can undo it with a prayer or two. What do you say, Friar, do you have a benediction for my horse?"

Friar Lorenzo glared at his savior, thinking he was the victim of a jest. But the other seemed perfectly sincere as he sat there on the mount as comfortably as other men would sit on a chair in their own home. Seeing the monk's furrowed brow, however, the young man smiled and said, "Ah, never mind. No benediction will help this jade anyway. But tell me, before we part, whether I have saved a friend or a foe?"

"Noblest master!" Shocked that he had—for a moment—been tempted to think ill of the man whom God had dispatched to save his life, Friar Lorenzo sprang to his feet and clasped his heart in submission. "I owe you my life! How could I be anything but your devoted subject forever?"

"Fine words! But where lies your allegiance?"

"My allegiance?" Friar Lorenzo looked from one to the other, begging for a clue.

"Yes," urged the boy who had dropped the hourglass, "who do you root for in the Palio?"

Six pairs of eyes narrowed as Friar Lorenzo scrambled to compose an answer, his gaze jumping from the golden beak on the knight's plumed helmet to the black wings on the banner tied to his lance and further on to the giant eagle spread over his breastplate.

"But of course," said Friar Lorenzo hastily, "I root for . . . the Eagle? Yes! The great Eagle . . . the king of the sky!"

To his relief, the answer was received with cheers.

"Then you are truly a friend," concluded the knight, "and I am happy that I killed him and not you. Come, we will take you into town. The Camollia Gate does not allow carts after sunset, so we must hurry."

"Your kindness," said Friar Lorenzo, "humbles me. I beg you to tell me your name that I may bless you in all my prayers from now and forever?"

The beaked helmet dipped briefly in a cordial nod.

"I am the Eagle. Men call me Romeo Marescotti."

"Marescotti is your mortal name?"

"What's in a name? The Eagle lives forever."

"Only Heaven," said Friar Lorenzo, his natural stinginess briefly eclipsing his gratitude, "can grant eternal life."

The knight beamed. "Then obviously," he retorted, mostly for the amusement of his companions, "the Eagle must be the Virgin's favorite bird!"

BY THE TIME ROMEO and his cousins finally delivered monk and cart to the stated destination inside the city of Siena, dusk had turned darkness, and a wary silence had come over the world. Doors and shutters were now closed and barred to the demons that come out at night, and had it not been for the moon and the occasional passerby carrying a torch, Friar Lorenzo would have long since lost his bearings in the sloping labyrinth of streets.

When Romeo had asked him whom he had come to visit, the monk had lied. He knew all about the bloody feud between the Tolomeis and the Salimbenis, and that it could, in the wrong company, be fatal to admit that he had come to Siena to see the great Messer Tolomei. For all their willingness to help, you never knew how Romeo and his cousins would react—nor what lewd stories they would tell their friends and family—if they knew the truth. And so instead, Friar Lorenzo had told them that his destination was Maestro Ambrogio Lorenzetti's workshop, since it was the only other name he could think of in the context of Siena.

Ambrogio Lorenzetti was a painter, a true maestro, who was known far and wide for his frescoes and portraits. Friar Lorenzo had never met him in person, but he remembered someone telling him that this great man lived in Siena. It was with some trepidation he had first spoken the name to Romeo, but when the young man did not contradict him, he dared to assume that, in mentioning the artist, he had chosen wisely.

"Well, then," said Romeo, stopping his horse in the middle of a narrow street, "here we are. It is the blue door."

Friar Lorenzo looked around, surprised that the famous painter did not live in a more attractive neighborhood. Garbage and filth littered the street all around them, and scrawny cats were eyeing him from doorways and dark corners. "I thank you," he said, descending from the cart, "for your great help, gentlemen. Heaven will reward you all in due course."

"Stand aside, monk," replied Romeo, dismounting, "and let us carry that coffin inside for you."

"No! Do not touch it!" Friar Lorenzo tried to position himself between Romeo and the coffin. "You have helped me enough already."

"Nonsense!" Romeo all but pushed the monk aside. "How do you intend to get it into the house without our help?"

"I don't—God will procure a way! The Maestro will help me—"

"Painters have brains, not muscles. Here—" This time, Romeo did move the other aside, but he did it gently, aware that he was engaging a weaker opponent.

The only one not aware of his own weakness was Friar Lorenzo. "No!" he exclaimed, struggling to assert himself as the sole protector of the coffin. "I beg you—I command you—!"

"You command me?" Romeo looked amused. "Such words do little but rouse my curiosity. I just saved your life, monk. Why can you not stomach my kindness now?"

On the other side of the blue door, inside Maestro Ambrogio's workshop, the painter was busy doing what he always did this time of day:

mixing and testing colors. The night belonged to the bold, to the crazed and to the artist—often one and the same—and it was a blessed time to work, for all his customers were now at home, eating and sleeping as humans do, and would not come knocking until after sunrise.

Joyfully engrossed in his work, Maestro Ambrogio did not notice the noise in the street until his dog, Dante, started growling. Without putting down his mortar, the painter stepped closer to the door and tried to gauge the severity of the argument that was—by the sound of it—taking place on his very doorstep. It put him in mind of the grand death of Julius Caesar, stabbed by a throng of Roman senators and dying very decoratively, scarlet on marble, harmoniously framed by columns. Would that some great Sienese could bring himself to die in a like manner, allowing the Maestro to indulge in the scene on a local wall.

Just then, someone banged on the door, and Dante began barking.

"Shush!" said Ambrogio to the dog, "I advise you to hide, in case it is the horned one trying to get in. I know him a great deal better than you."

As soon as he opened the door, a whirlwind of agitated voices burst inside and wrapped the Maestro in a heated argument—something to do with a certain object that needed to be carried inside.

"Tell them, my good brother in Christ!" urged a breathless monk. "Tell them we shall deal with this thing alone!"

"What thing?" Maestro Ambrogio wanted to know.

"The coffin," replied someone else, "with the dead bell ringer! Look!"

"I think you have the wrong house," said Maestro Ambrogio. "I did not order that."

"I beg you," pleaded the monk, "to let us inside. I will explain everything."

There was nothing else to do but step aside, and so Maestro Ambrogio opened the door wide to allow the young men to carry the coffin into his workshop and put it down in the middle of the floor. It did not surprise him at all to see that young Romeo Marescotti and his cousins were—once again—up to no good; what puzzled the Maestro was the presence of the hand-wringing monk.

"That is the lightest coffin I have ever carried," observed one of Romeo's companions. "Your ringer must have been a very slender man, Friar Lorenzo. Make sure to choose a fat one next time that he may stand more firmly in that windy bell tower."

"We shall!" exclaimed Friar Lorenzo with rude impatience. "And now I thank you, gentlemen, for all your services. Thank you, Messer Romeo, for saving our lives—my life! Here"—he extracted a small, bent coin from somewhere underneath his cowl—"a centesimo for your trouble!"

The coin hung in the air for a while, unclaimed. Eventually, Friar Lorenzo stuffed it back underneath his cowl, his ears glowing like coals in a sudden draft.

"All I ask," said Romeo, mostly to tease, "is that you show us what is in that coffin. For it is no monk, fat or slender, of that I am sure."

"No!" Friar Lorenzo's anxious aspect lapsed into panic. "I cannot allow that! With the Virgin Mary as my witness, I swear to you, every one of you, the coffin must remain closed, or a great disaster will undo us all!"

It struck Maestro Ambrogio that he had never before indulged in the features of a bird. A small sparrow that had fallen out of the nest, its feathers ruffled and its eyes little frightened beads . . . that was precisely what this young friar looked like as he stood there, cornered by Siena's most notorious cats.

"Come now, monk," said Romeo, "I saved your life tonight. Have I not by now earned your confidence?"

"I fear," said Maestro Ambrogio to Friar Lorenzo, "that you will have to deliver on your threat and let us all be undone by disaster. Honor demands it."

Friar Lorenzo shook his head heavily. "Very well, then! I shall open the coffin. But allow me first to explain"—for a moment, his eyes darted to and fro in search of inspiration, then he nodded and said—"you are right, there is no monk in this coffin. But there is someone just as holy. She is the only daughter of my generous patron, and"—he cleared his throat to speak more forcefully—"she died, very tragically, two days ago. He sent me here with her body, to beg you, Maestro, to capture her features in a painting before they are lost forever."

"Two days?" Maestro Ambrogio was appalled, all business now. "She has been dead two days? My dear friend—" Without waiting for the monk's approval, he opened the lid of the coffin to assess the damage. But fortunately, the girl inside had not yet been ravished by death. "It seems," he said, happily surprised, "we still have time. Even so, I must begin right away. Did your patron specify a motif? Usually I do a standard Virgin

Mary from the waist up, and in this case I will throw in Babe Jesus for free, since you have come all this way."

"I . . . believe I will go with the standard Virgin Mary, then," said Friar Lorenzo, looking nervously at Romeo, who had knelt down next to the coffin to admire the dead girl, "and our Heavenly Savior, since it is free."

"Ahimè!" exclaimed Romeo, ignoring the monk's warning stance. "How can God be so cruel?"

"Stop!" cried Friar Lorenzo, but it was too late; the young man had already touched a hand to the girl's cheek.

"Such beauty," he said, his voice tender, "should never die. Even death hates his trade tonight. Look, he has not yet brushed her lips with his purple stain."

"Careful!" warned Friar Lorenzo, trying to close the lid. "You know not what infection those lips carry!"

"If she were mine," Romeo went on, blocking the monk's efforts and paying no heed to security, "I should follow her to Paradise and bring her back. Or stay there forever with her."

"Yes-yes-yes," said Friar Lorenzo, forcing the lid down and very nearly slamming it over the other's wrist, "death turns all men into great lovers. Would that they were equally ardent while the lady was still alive!"

"Very true, Friar," nodded Romeo, getting up at last. "Well, I have seen and heard enough misery for one night. The tavern calls. I shall leave you to your sad business and go drink a toast to this poor girl's soul. In fact, I shall drink several, and perchance the wine will send me straight to Paradise that I may meet her in person and . . ."

Friar Lorenzo sprung forward and hissed, for no apparent reason, "Before it throws you from grace, Messer Romeo, bridle your tongue!"

The young man grinned, ". . . pay my respects."

Not until the rogues had left the workshop for good and the sound of hoofbeats had waned, did Friar Lorenzo again lift the lid of the coffin. "It is safe now," he said, "you can come out."

Now at last, the girl opened her eyes and sat up, her cheeks hollow with exhaustion.

"Almighty God!" gasped Maestro Ambrogio, crossing himself with the mortar. "What manner of witchcraft is this?"

"I beg you, Maestro," said Friar Lorenzo, gently helping the girl to stand up, "to escort us to Palazzo Tolomei. This young lady is Messer Tolomei's niece, Giulietta. She has been the victim of much evil, and I must get her to safety as soon as may be. Can you help us?"

Maestro Ambrogio looked at the monk and the girl, still struggling to catch up with reality. Despite her fatigue, the girl stood straight, her tousled hair alive in the candlelight, and her eyes as blue as the sky on a cloudless day. She was, without a doubt, the most perfect creation he had ever beheld. "May I ask," he said to the monk, "what compelled you to trust me?"

Friar Lorenzo made a sweeping gesture at the paintings surrounding them. "A man who can see the divine in earthly things, surely, is a brother in Christ."

The Maestro looked around, too, but all he saw was empty wine bottles, half-finished work, and portraits of people who had changed their mind when they saw his bill. "You are too generous," he said, shaking his head, "but I shall not hold that against you. Have no fear, I will take you to Palazzo Tolomei, but first, do satisfy my rude curiosity and tell me what happened to this young lady, and why she was laid out for dead in that coffin."

Now for the first time, Giulietta spoke. Her voice was as soft and steady as her face was tense with grief. "Three days ago," she said, "the Salimbenis raided my home. They killed everyone by the name of Tolomei—my father, my mother, my brothers—and everyone else who stood in their way, except this man, my dear confessor, Friar Lorenzo. I was in confession in the chapel when the raid took place or I, too, would have been—" She looked away, struggling against despair.

"We have come here for protection," Friar Lorenzo said, taking over, "and to tell Messer Tolomei what happened."

"We have come here for revenge," Giulietta corrected him, her eyes wide with hatred and her fists pressed hard against her chest as if to prevent herself from an act of violence, "and to gut that monster, Salimbeni, and string him up by his own entrails . . ."

"Ahem," said Friar Lorenzo, "we will, of course, exercise Christian forgiveness—"

Giulietta nodded eagerly, hearing nothing. ". . . While we feed him to his dogs, piece by piece!"

"I grieve for you," said Maestro Ambrogio, wishing he could take this beautiful child in his arms and comfort her. "You have borne too much—"

"I have borne nothing!" Her blue eyes pierced the painter's heart. "Do not grieve for me, just be so kind as to take us to my uncle's house without any further questioning." She caught herself, and added quietly, "please."

WHEN HE HAD SAFELY delivered monk and girl to Palazzo Tolomei, Maestro Ambrogio returned to his workshop in something resembling a gallop. He had never felt quite this way before. He was in love, he was in Hell . . . in fact, he was everything all at once as Inspiration flapped its colossal wings inside his skull and clawed painfully at his rib cage, looking for a way out of the prison that is a talented man's mortal frame.

Sprawled on the floor, eternally puzzled by mankind, Dante looked on with half a bloodshot eye as Maestro Ambrogio composed his colors and began the application of Giulietta Tolomei's features onto a painting of a hitherto headless Virgin Mary. He could not help but begin with her eyes. Nowhere else in his workshop was such an intriguing color to be seen; indeed, not in the entire city was the same shade to be found, for he had only invented it on this very night, almost in a fever frenzy, while the image of the young girl was still moist on the wall of his mind.

Encouraged by the immediate result, he did not hesitate to trace the outline of that remarkable face underneath the flaming rivulets of hair. His movements were still magically swift and assured; had the young woman at this very moment sat before him, poised for eternity, the painter could not have worked with more giddy certainty than he presently did.

"Yes!" was the only word escaping him as he eagerly, almost hungrily brought those breathtaking features back to life. Once the picture was complete, he took several steps backwards and finally reached out for the glass of wine he had poured for himself in a previous life, five hours earlier.

Just then, there was another knock on the door.

"Shh!" hushed Maestro Ambrogio, wagging a warning finger at the barking dog. "You always assume the worst. Maybe it is another angel." But as soon as he opened the door to see what demon had been dispatched by fate at this ungodly hour, he saw that Dante had been more right than he.

Outside, in the flickering light of a wall torch, stood Romeo Marescotti, a drunken grin splitting his deceivingly charming face in half. Apart from their encounter only a few hours earlier, Maestro Ambrogio knew the young man only too well from the week before, when the males of the Marescotti family had sat before him, one by one, in order to have their features incorporated into a formidable new mural in Palazzo Marescotti. The paterfamilias, Comandante Marescotti, had insisted on a representation of his clan from past to present, with all credible male ancestors—plus a few incredible ones—in the center, all employed, some-how, in the famous Battle of Montaperti, while the living hovered in the sky above, poised and guised as the Seven Virtues. Much to every-one's amusement, Romeo had drawn the lot least suitable for his charac-ter, and consequently Maestro Ambrogio had found himself forging the present as well as the past as he expertly applied the features of Siena's most infamous playboy to the princely form perched on the throne of Chastity.

Now Chastity reborn pushed his kind creator aside and stepped into the workshop to find the coffin still sitting—closed—in the middle of the floor. The young man was clearly itching to open it and peer once more at the body inside, but that would have meant rudely removing the Mae-stro's palette and several wet paintbrushes that were now resting on top of the lid. "Have you finished the picture yet?" he asked instead. "I want to see it."

Maestro Ambrogio closed the door quietly behind them, only too conscious that his visitor had been drinking too much for perfect balance. "Why would you wish to see the likeness of a dead girl? There are plenty of live ones out there, I am sure."

"True," agreed Romeo, looking around the room and finally spotting the new addition, "but that would be too easy, wouldn't it?" He walked right up to the portrait and looked at it with the gaze of an expert; an ex-pert not of art, but of women. After a while he nodded. "Not bad. Quite the eyes you gave her. How did you—"

"I thank you," said the Maestro hastily, "but the true artistry is God's. More wine?"

"Sure." The young man took the cup and sat down on top of the coffin, carefully avoiding the dripping brushes. "How about a toast to your friend, God, and all the games he plays with us?"

"It is very late," said Maestro Ambrogio, moving the palette and sitting down on the coffin next to Romeo. "You must be tired, my friend."

As if transfixed by the portrait before him, Romeo could not tear away his gaze long enough to look at the painter. And when he finally spoke, there was a sincerity to his voice that was new, even to himself. "I am not as much tired," he said, "as I am awake. I wonder if I was ever this awake before."

"That often happens when one is half-asleep. Only then does the inner eye truly open."

"But I am not asleep, nor do I wish to be. I am never going to sleep again. I think I shall come every night and sit here instead of sleeping."

Smiling at the ardent exclamation, a most enviable privilege of youth, Maestro Ambrogio looked up at his masterpiece. "You approve of her, then?"

"Approve?" Romeo nearly choked on the word. "I adore her!"

"Could you worship at such a shrine?"

"Am I not a man? Yet as a man, I must also feel great sorrow at the sight of such wasted beauty. If only death could be persuaded to give her back."

"Then what?" The Maestro managed to frown appropriately. "What would you do if this angel was a living, breathing woman?"

Romeo took in air, but the words fled from him. "I . . . don't know. Love her, obviously. I do know how to love a woman. I have loved many."

"Perhaps it is just as well she is not real, then. For I believe this one would require extra effort. In fact, I imagine that to court a lady like her, one would have to enter through the front door and not skulk beneath her balcony like a thief in the night." Seeing that the other had fallen strangely silent, a brushstroke of ochre trailing across his noble face, the Maestro proceeded with greater confidence. "There is lust, you know, and then there is love. They are related, but still very different things. To indulge in one requires little but honeyed speech and a change of clothes; to obtain the other, by contrast, a man must give up his rib. In return, his woman will undo the sin of Eve, and bring him back into Paradise."

"But how does a man know when to trade in his rib? I have many friends without a single rib left, and I promise you, they were never once in Paradise."

The earnest concern on the young man's face made Maestro Ambrogio nod. "You said it," he acknowledged. "A man knows. A boy does not."

Romeo laughed out loud. "I admire you!" He put a hand on the Maestro's shoulder. "You have courage!"

"What is so very wonderful about courage?" retorted the painter, bolder now that his role as mentor had been approved. "I suspect this one virtue has killed more good men than all the vices put together."

Again Romeo laughed out loud, as if he did not often have the pleasure of such saucy opposition, and the Maestro found himself suddenly and unexpectedly liking the young man.

"I often hear men say," Romeo went on, unwilling to quit the topic, "that they will do anything for a woman. But then, upon her very first request, they whine and slink away like dogs."

"And you? Do you also slink away?"

Romeo flashed a whole row of healthy teeth, surprising for someone who was rumored to occasion fisticuffs wherever he went. "No," he answered, still smiling, "I have a fine nose for women who ask nothing more than what I want to give. But if such a woman existed"—he nodded towards the painting—"I would happily break all my ribs in pursuit of her. Better still, I would enter through the front door, as you say, and apply for her hand before I had ever even touched it. And not only that, but I would make her my one and only wife and never look at another woman. I swear it! She would be worth it, I am sure."

Pleased with what he heard, and wanting very much to believe that his artwork had had such a profound effect as to turn the young man away from his wanton ways, the Maestro nodded, rather satisfied with the night's work. "She is indeed."

Romeo turned his head, eyes narrow. "You speak as if she were still alive?"

Maestro Ambrogio sat silently for a moment, studying the young man's face and probing the depth of his resolve. "Giulietta," he said at last, "is her name. I believe that you, my friend, with your touch stirred her from death tonight. After you left us for the tavern, I saw her lovely form rise by itself from this coffin—"

Romeo sprang from his seat as if it had burst into flames beneath him. "This is ghostly speech! I know not whether this chill on my arm is from dread or delight!"

"Do you dread the schemes of men?"

"Of men, no. Of God, greatly."

"Then take comfort in what I tell you now. It was not God who laid her out for dead in this coffin, but the monk, Friar Lorenzo, fearing for her safety."

Romeo's jaw dropped. "You mean, she was never dead?"

Maestro Ambrogio smiled at the young man's expression. "She was ever as alive as you."

Romeo clasped his head. "You are sporting with me! I cannot believe you!"

"Believe what you want," said the Maestro, getting up and removing the paintbrushes, "or open the coffin."

After a moment of great distress, pacing back and forth, Romeo finally braced himself and flung open the coffin.

Rather than rejoicing in its emptiness, however, the young man glared at the Maestro with renewed suspicion. "Where is she?"

"That I cannot tell you. It would be a breach of confidence."

"But she lives?"

The Maestro shrugged. "She did when I saw her last, on the threshold of her uncle's house, waving goodbye to me."

"And who is her uncle?"

"As I said: I cannot tell you."

Romeo took a step towards the Maestro, fingers twitching. "Are you saying that I will have to sing serenades beneath every balcony in Siena until the right woman comes out?"

Dante had jumped up as soon as the young man appeared to threaten his master, but instead of growling a warning, the dog merely put its head back and let out a long, expressive howl.

"She will not come out just yet," replied Maestro Ambrogio, bending over to pat the dog. "She is in no mood for serenades. Perhaps she never will be."

"Then why," exclaimed Romeo, all but knocking over the easel and portrait in his frustration, "are you telling me this?"

"Because," said Maestro Ambrogio, amused by the other's exasperation, "it pains an artist's eyes to see a snowy dove dally with crows."

What's in a name? That which we call a rose
By any other word would smell as sweet

...

THE VIEW FROM THE OLD MEDICI FORTRESS, the Fortezza, was spectacular. Not only could I see the terra-cotta roofs of Siena broiling in the afternoon sun, but at least twenty miles of rolling hills were heaving around me like an ocean in shades of green and distant blues. Again and again I looked up from my reading, taking in the sweeping landscape in the hope that it would force all stale air from my lungs and fill my soul with summer. And yet every time I looked down and resumed Maestro Ambrogio's journal, I plunged right back into the dark events of 1340.

I had spent the morning at Malèna's espresso bar in Piazza Postierla, leafing through the official early versions of *Romeo and Juliet* written by Masuccio Salernitano and Luigi da Porto in 1476 and 1530 respectively. It was interesting to see how the plot had developed, and how da Porto had put a literary spin to a story that—Salernitano claimed—was based on real events.

In Salernitano's version, Romeo and Juliet—or rather, Mariotto and Giannozza—lived in Siena, but their parents were not at war. They did get married in secret, after bribing a friar, but the drama only really began when Mariotto killed a prominent citizen and had to go into exile. Meanwhile, Giannozza's parents—unaware that their daughter was already married—demanded that she marry someone else. In desperation, Giannozza had the friar cook up a powerful sleeping potion, and the effect was so great that her imbecilic parents believed she was dead and went ahead and buried her right away. Fortunately, the good old friar was able to deliver her from the sepulchre, whereupon Giannozza traveled secretly by boat to Alexandria, where Mariotto was living the sweet life. However, the messenger who was supposed to inform Mariotto of the sleeping-potion scheme had been captured by pirates, and upon receiving the news of Giannozza's death, Mariotto came blasting back into Siena to die by her side. Here, he was captured by soldiers, and beheaded. Chop. And Giannozza had spent the rest of her life pulling Kleenex in a convent.

As far as I could see, the key elements in this original version were: the secret marriage, Romeo's banishment, the harebrained scheme of the sleeping potion, the messenger gone astray, and Romeo's deliberate suicide mission based on his erroneous belief in Juliet's death.

The big curveball, of course, was that the whole thing supposedly happened in Siena, and if Malèna had been around, I would have asked her if this was common knowledge. I highly suspected it was not.

Interestingly enough, when da Porto took over the story half a century later, he, too, was eager to anchor it in reality, going so far as to call Romeo and Giulietta by their real first names. He chickened out on the location, however, and moved the whole thing to Verona, changing all family names—very possibly to avoid retribution from the powerful clans involved in the scandal.

But never mind the logistics; in my interpretation—aided by several cups of cappuccino—da Porto wrote a far more entertaining story. He was the one who introduced the masked ball and the balcony scene, and his was the genius that first devised the double suicide. The only thing that did not immediately fly with me was that he had Juliet die by holding her breath. But perhaps da Porto had felt that his audience would not appreciate a bloody scene . . . scruples that Shakespeare, fortunately, did not have.

After da Porto, someone called Bandello had felt compelled to write a third version and add a lot of melodramatic dialogue without—as far as I could see—altering the essentials of the plot. But from then on the Italians were done with the story, and it traveled first to France, then England, to eventually end up on Shakespeare's desk, ready for immortalization.

The biggest difference, as far as I could see, between all these poetic versions and Maestro Ambrogio's journal, was that in reality there had been *three* families involved, not just two. The Tolomeis and the Salimbenis had been the feuding households—the Capulets and the Montagues, so to speak—while Romeo, in fact, had been a Marescotti and thus an outsider. In that respect, Salernitano's very early rendition of the story was the one that came closest to the truth; it was set in Siena, and there had been no mention of a family feud.

Later, walking back from the Fortezza with Maestro Ambrogio's journal clutched to my chest, I looked at all the happy people around me and once again felt the presence of an invisible wall between me and them. There they were, walking, jogging, and eating ice cream, not pausing to question the past, nor burdened—as I was—with a feeling that they did not fully belong in this world.

That same morning, I had stood in front of the bathroom mirror trying on the necklace with the silver crucifix that had been in my mother's box, and decided I would start wearing it. After all, it was something she had owned, and by leaving it in the box she had clearly intended it for me. Perhaps, I thought, it would somehow protect me against the curse that had marked her for an early death.

Was I insane? Maybe. But then, there are many different kinds of insanity. Aunt Rose had always taken for granted that the whole world was in a state of constantly fluctuating madness, and that a neurosis was not an illness, but a fact of life, like pimples. Some have more, some have less, but only truly abnormal people have none at all. This commonsense philosophy had consoled me many times before, and it did now, too.

When I returned to the hotel, Direttor Rossini came towards me like the messenger from Marathon, dying to tell me the news. "Miss Tolomei! Where have you been? You must go! Right away! Contessa Salimbeni is waiting for you in Palazzo Pubblico! Go, go"—he shooed me the way one shoos a dog hanging around for scraps—"you must not leave her waiting!"

"Wait!" I pointed at two objects that sat conspicuously in the middle of the floor. "Those are my suitcases!"

"Yes-yes-yes, they were delivered a moment ago."

"Well, I'd like to go to my room and—"

"No!" Direttor Rossini ripped open the front door and waved at me to run through it. "You must go right away!"

"I don't even know where I'm going!"

"Santa Caterina!" Though I knew he was secretly delighted with yet another opportunity to educate me about Siena, Direttor Rossini rolled his eyes and let go of the door. "Come, I will draw directions!"

ENTERING THE CAMPO was like stepping into a gigantic seashell. All around the edge were restaurants and cafés, and right where the pearl would have been, at the bottom of the sloping piazza, sat Palazzo Pubblico, the building that had served as Siena's city hall since the Middle Ages.

I paused for a moment, taking in the hum of many voices under the dome of a blue sky, the pigeons flapping around, and the white marble fountain with the turquoise water—until a wave of tourists came up behind me and swept me along with them, rushing forward in excited wonder at the magnificence of the giant square.

While drawing his directions, Direttor Rossini had assured me that the Campo was considered the most beautiful piazza in all of Italy, and not only by the Sienese themselves. In fact, he could hardly recount the numerous occasions on which hotel guests from all corners of the world—even from Florence—had come to him and extolled the graces of the Campo. He, of course, had protested and pointed out the many splendors of other places—surely, they were out there somewhere—but people had been unwilling to listen. They had stubbornly maintained that Siena was the loveliest, most unspoiled city on the globe, and in the face of such conviction, what could Direttor Rossini do but allow that, indeed, it might be so?

I stuffed the directions into my handbag and began walking down towards Palazzo Pubblico. The building was hard to miss with the tall bell tower, Torre del Mangia, the construction of which Direttor Rossini had described in such detail that it had taken me several minutes to realize that it had not, in fact, been erected before his very eyes, but sometime in the late Middle Ages. A lily, he had called it, a proud monument to female purity with its white stone flower held aloft by a tall red stem. And curiously, it had been built with no foundation. The Mangia Tower, he claimed, had stood for over six centuries, held up by the grace of God and faith alone.

I blocked the sun with my hand and looked at the tower as it stretched against the infinite blue. In no other place had I ever seen female purity celebrated by a 355-foot phallic object. But maybe that was me.

There was a quite literal gravity to the whole building—Palazzo Pubblico and its tower—as if the Campo itself was caving in under its weight. Direttor Rossini had told me that if I was in doubt, I was to imagine that I had a ball and put it on the ground. No matter where I stood on the Campo, the ball would roll right down to Palazzo Pubblico. There was something about the image that appealed to me. Maybe it was the thought of a ball bouncing over the ancient brick pavement. Or maybe it was simply the way he had pronounced the words, with whispering drama, like a magician talking to four-year-olds.

PALAZZO PUBBLICO HAD, like all government, grown with age. From its origins as little more than a meeting room for nine administrators, it was now a formidable structure, and I entered the inner courtyard with a feeling of being watched. Not so much by people, I suppose, as by the lingering shadows of generations past, generations devoted to the life of this city, this small plot of land as cities go, this universe unto itself.

Eva Maria Salimbeni was waiting for me in the Hall of Peace. She sat on a bench in the middle of the room, looking up into the air, as if she was having a silent conversation with God. But as soon as I walked through the door, she snapped to, and a smile of delight spread over her face.

"So, you came after all!" she exclaimed, rising from the bench to kiss me on both cheeks. "I was beginning to worry."

"Sorry to keep you waiting. I didn't even realize—"

Her smile dismissed everything I could possibly say. "You are here now. That is all that matters. Look"—she made a sweeping gesture at the giant frescoes covering the walls of the room—"have you ever seen anything so magnificent? Our great Maestro, Ambrogio Lorenzetti, made them in the late 1330s. He probably finished this one, over the doors, in 1340. It is called *Good Government*."

I turned to look at the fresco in question. It covered the entire length of the wall, and to make it would have required a complex machinery of ladders and scaffolding, perhaps even platforms suspended from the ceiling. The left half depicted a peaceful city scene with ordinary citizens going about their business; the right half was a wide view of the countryside beyond the city wall. Then something occurred to me, and I said, baffled, "You mean . . . *Maestro Ambrogio?*"

"Oh, yes," nodded Eva Maria, not the least bit surprised that I was familiar with the name. "One of the greatest masters. He painted these scenes to celebrate the end of a long feud between our two families, the Tolomeis and the Salimbenis. Finally, in 1339, there was peace."

"Really?" I thought of Giulietta and Friar Lorenzo escaping from the Salimbeni bandits on the high road outside Siena. "I get the impression that in 1340 our ancestors were still very much at war. Certainly out in the countryside."

Eva Maria smiled cryptically; either she was delighted that I had bothered to read up on family lore, or she was miffed that I dared to contradict her. If the latter, she was graceful enough to acknowledge my point, and said, "You are right. The peace had unintended consequences. It happens whenever the bureaucrats try to help us." She threw up her arms. "If people want to fight, you can't stop them. If you prevent them inside the city, they will fight in the country, and out there, they will get away with it. At least inside Siena, the riots were always stopped before things got completely out of hand. Why?"

She looked at me to see if I could guess, but of course, I couldn't.

"Because," she went on, wagging a didactic finger in front of my nose, "in Siena we have always had a militia. And in order to keep the Salimbenis and the Tolomeis in check, the citizens of Siena had to be able to mobilize and have all their companies out in the city streets within minutes." She nodded firmly, agreeing with herself. "I believe this is why the contrada tradition is so strong here even today; the devotion of the old neighborhood militia was essentially what made the Sienese republic possible. If you want to keep the bad guys in check, make sure the good guys are armed."

I smiled at her conclusion, doing my best to look as if I had no horse in the race. Now was not the time to tell Eva Maria that I did not believe in weapons, and that, in my experience, the so-called good guys were no better than the bad ones.

"Pretty, is it not?" Eva Maria continued, nodding at the fresco. "A city at peace with itself?"

"I suppose," I said, "although I have to say people don't look particularly happy. Look"—I pointed at a young woman who appeared to be trapped in a cluster of dancing girls—"this one seems—I don't know. Lost in thought."

"Perhaps she saw the wedding procession passing by?" suggested Eva Maria, nodding at a train of people following what looked like a bride on a horse. "And perhaps it made her think of a lost love?"

"She is looking at the drum," I said, pointing again, "or, the tambourine. And the other dancers look . . . evil. Look at the way they have her trapped in the dance. And one of them is staring at her stomach." I cast a glance at Eva Maria, but it was hard to interpret her expression. "Or maybe I'm just imagining things."

"No," she said, quietly, "Maestro Ambrogio clearly wants us to notice her. He made this group of dancing women bigger than anybody else in the picture. And if you take another look, she is the only one with a tiara in her hair."

I squinted and saw that she was right. "So, who was she? Do we know?"

Eva Maria shrugged. "Officially, we don't know. But between you and me"—she leaned towards me and lowered her voice—"I think she is your ancestor. Her name was Giulietta Tolomei."

I was so shocked to hear her speak the name—*my* name—and articulate the exact same thought I had aired to Umberto over the telephone that it took me a moment to come up with the only natural question: "How on earth do you know? . . . That she is my ancestor, I mean?"

Eva Maria almost laughed. "Isn't it obvious? Why else would your mother name you after her? In fact, she told me so herself—your bloodline comes straight from Giulietta and Giannozza Tolomei."

Although I was thrilled to hear this—spoken with such certainty—it was almost more information than I could handle at once. "I didn't realize you knew my mother," I said, wondering why she had not told me this before.

"She came to visit once. With your father. It was before they were married." Eva Maria paused. "She was very young. Younger than you. It was a party with a hundred guests, but we spent the whole evening talking about Maestro Ambrogio. They were the ones who told me everything I am telling you now. They were very knowledgeable, very interested in our families. It was sad the way things went."

We stood for a moment in silence. Eva Maria was looking at me with a wry smile, as if she knew there was a question that was burning a hole in my tongue, but which I could not bring myself to ask, namely: What was her relationship—if any—with the evil Luciano Salimbeni, and how much did she know about my parents' deaths?

"Your father believed," Eva Maria went on, not leaving me room for inquiry, "that Maestro Ambrogio was hiding a story in this picture. A tragedy that happened in his own time, and which could not be discussed openly. Look"—she pointed at the fresco—"do you see that little birdcage in the window up there? What if I told you that the building is Palazzo Salimbeni, and that the man you see inside is Salimbeni himself, enthroned like a king, while people crouch at his feet to borrow money?"

Sensing that the story somehow gave her pain, I smiled at Eva Maria, determined not to let the past come between us. "You don't sound very proud of him."

She grimaced. "Oh, he was a great man. But Maestro Ambrogio didn't like him. Don't you see? Look . . . there was a marriage . . . a sad girl dancing . . . and now, a bird in a cage. What do you make of that?" When I did not reply right away, Eva Maria looked out the window. "I was twenty-two, you know. When I married him. Salimbeni. He was sixty-four. Do you think that is old?" She looked straight at me, trying to read my thoughts.

"Not necessarily," I said. "As you know, my mother—"

"Well, I did," Eva Maria cut me off. "I thought he was very old and that he would die soon. But he was rich. I have a beautiful house. You must come and visit me."

I was so baffled by her straightforward confession—and subsequent invitation—that I just said, "Sure, I would love to."

"Good!" She put a possessive hand on my shoulder. "And now you must find the hero in the fresco!"

I nearly laughed. Eva Maria Salimbeni was a true virtuoso in the art of changing subjects.

"Come now," she said, like a teacher to a class full of lazy kids, "where is the hero? There is always a hero. Look at the fresco."

I looked up dutifully. "That could be anyone."

"The heroine is inside the city," she said, pointing, "looking very sad. So, the hero must be—? Look! On the left you have life within the city walls. Then you have Porta Romana, the city gate to the south, which cuts the fresco in half. And on the right-hand side—"

"Okay, I see him now," I said, being a good sport. "It's the guy on the horse, leaving town."

Eva Maria smiled, not at me, but at the fresco. "He is handsome, is he not?"

"Drop-dead. What's with the elf hat?"

"He is a hunter. Look at him. He has a hunting bird and is just about to release it, but something holds him back. That other man, the darker man walking on foot, carrying the painter's box, is trying to tell him something, and our young hero is leaning back in the saddle to hear it."

"Perhaps the walking man wants him to stay in town?" I suggested.

"Perhaps. But what might happen to him if he does? Look at what Maestro Ambrogio has put above his head. The gallows. Not a pleasant alternative, is it?" Eva Maria smiled. "Who do you think he is?"

I did not answer right away. If the Maestro Ambrogio who had painted this fresco was, in fact, the same Maestro Ambrogio whose journal I was in the process of reading, and if the unhappily dancing woman with the tiara was indeed my ancestor, Giulietta Tolomei, then the man on the horse could only be Romeo Marescotti. But I was not comfortable with Eva Maria knowing the extent of my recent discoveries, nor the source of my knowledge. She was, after all, a Salimbeni. So, I merely shrugged and said, "I have no idea."

"Suppose I told you," said Eva Maria, "that it is Romeo from *Romeo and Juliet*? ... And that your ancestor, Giulietta, is Shakespeare's Juliet?"

I managed to laugh. "Wasn't that set in Verona? And didn't Shakespeare invent them? In *Shakespeare in Love*—"

"*Shakespeare in Love!*" Eva Maria looked at me as if she had rarely heard anything so revolting. "Giulietta"—she put a hand on my cheek—"trust me when I say that it happened right here in Siena. Long, long before Shakespeare. And here they are, up there, on this wall. Romeo going into exile and Juliet preparing for marriage to a man she cannot love." She smiled at my expression and finally let go of me. "Don't worry. When you visit me, we will have more talk of these sad things. What are you doing tonight?"

I took a step back, hoping to conceal my shock at her intimacy with my family history. "Cleaning my balcony."

Eva Maria didn't miss a beat. "When you are finished with that, I want you to come with me to a very nice concert. Here—" She dug into her handbag and took out an admission ticket. "It is a wonderful program. I chose it myself. You will like it. Seven o'clock. Afterwards we will have dinner, and I will tell you more about our ancestors."

AS I WALKED TO the concert hall later that day, I could feel something nagging me. It was a beautiful evening, and the town was buzzing with happy people, but I was still unable to share in the fun. Striding down the street with eyes for nothing but the pavement ahead, I gradually caught up with myself and was able to identify the cause of my grumpiness.

I was being manipulated.

Ever since my arrival in Siena, people had been on tiptoes to tell me what to do and what to think. Eva Maria most of all. She seemed to find it only natural that her own bizarre wishes and plans should dictate my movements—dress code included—and now she was trying to draw my line of thought as well. Suppose I did not want to discuss the events of 1340 with her? Well, too bad, because I didn't have a choice. And yet, in some strange way I still liked her. Why was that? Was it because she was the very antithesis of Aunt Rose, who had always been so afraid of doing something wrong that she never did anything right either? Or did I like Eva Maria because I was not supposed to? That would have been Umberto's take on it; the surest way of making me hang with the Salimbenis would be to tell me to stay the hell away from them. I guess it was a Juliet thing.

Well, maybe it was time for Juliet to put on her rational hat. According to Presidente Maconi, the Salimbenis would always be the Salimbenis, and according to my cousin Peppo that meant woe unto any Tolomei standing in their way. This had not only held true for the stormy Middle Ages; even now, in present-day Siena, the ghost of maybe-murderer Luciano Salimbeni had not yet left the stage.

On the other hand, maybe it was this kind of prejudice that had kept the old family feud alive for generations. What if the elusive Luciano Salimbeni had never laid a hand on my parents, but had been a suspect solely because of his name? No wonder he had made himself scarce. In a place where you are found guilty by association, your executioner is not likely to sit patiently through a trial.

In fact, the more I thought about it, the more the scales tipped in Eva

Maria's favor; after all, she was the one who seemed most determined to prove that despite our ancestral rivalry, we could still be friends. And if that was really so, I did not want to be the party pooper.

THE EVENING CONCERT was hosted by the Chigiana Musical Academy in Palazzo Chigi-Saracini, right across the street from my friend Luigi's hair salon. I entered the building through a covered gateway to emerge in an enclosed courtyard with a loggia and an old well in the middle. Knights in shining armor, I thought to myself, would have pulled water from that well for their battle horses, and beneath my high-heeled sandals the stone tiles in the floor were worn smooth from centuries of horses' hooves and cartwheels. The place was neither too big nor too imposing, and it had a quiet dignity of its own that made me wonder whether the things going on outside the walls of this timeless quadrangle were truly that important.

As I stood there, gawking at the frescoed ceiling underneath the loggia, an usher handed me a brochure and pointed out the door going up to the concert hall. I glanced at the brochure as I climbed the stairs, expecting it to list the musical program. But instead, it was a brief history of the building written in several different languages. The English version began:

> *Palazzo Chigi-Saracini, one of the most beautiful palazzos in Siena, originally belonged to the Marescotti family. The core of the building is very old, but during the Middle Ages the Marescotti family began to incorporate the neighboring buildings, and, like many other powerful families in Siena, they began the erection of a great tower. It was from this tower that the victory at Montaperti in 1260 was announced, by the sound of a drum, or tambourine.*

I stopped in the middle of the staircase to reread the passage. If this was true, and if I had not completely mixed up the names in Maestro Ambrogio's journal, then the building in which I was currently standing had originally been Palazzo Marescotti, that is, Romeo's home in 1340.

Only when people started squeezing past me in irritation did I shake my surprise and move on. So what if it had been Romeo's home? He and

I were separated by nearly seven hundred years, and besides, back then, he had had a Juliet of his own. Despite my new clothes and hair, I was still nothing but a gangly offshoot of the perfect creature that once was.

Janice would have laughed at me if she had known my romantic thoughts. "Here we go again," she would have jeered, "Jules dreaming about a man she can't have." And she was right. But sometimes, those are the best ones.

My strange obsession with historical figures had been kicked off at age nine with President Jefferson. While everyone else—including Janice—had posters of pop tarts with exposed midriffs plastered all over their walls, my room was a shrine to my favorite Founding Father. I had gone to great lengths to learn how to write out *Thomas* in calligraphy, and had even embroidered a cushion with a giant T, which I hugged every night as I fell asleep. Unfortunately, Janice had found my secret notebook and passed it around in class, making everyone howl with laughter at my fanciful drawings of myself standing in front of Monticello wearing a veil and a wedding gown, hand in hand with a very muscular President Jefferson.

After that, everyone had called me Jeff, even the teachers, who had no idea why they did it, and who—amazingly—never saw me wincing when they called on me in class. In the end I stopped putting up my hand entirely, and just sat there, hiding behind my hair in the back row, hoping no one would notice me.

In high school—thanks to Umberto—I had started looking towards the ancient world instead, and my fancy had jumped from Leonidas the Spartan to Scipio the Roman and even to Emperor Augustus for a while, until I discovered his dark side. By the time I entered college I had finally strayed so far back in time that my hero was an unnamed caveman living on the Russian steppes, killing woolly mammoths and playing haunting tunes on his bone flute under the full moon, all by himself.

The only one to point out that all my boyfriends had one thing in common was, of course, Janice. "Too bad," she had said one night, when we were trying to fall asleep in a tent in the garden and she had managed to extract all my secrets one by one, in exchange for caramels that were originally mine, "that they are all deader than doornails."

"They are not!" I had protested, already regretting telling her my secrets. "Famous people live forever!"

To this, Janice had merely snorted, "Maybe, but who wants to kiss a mummy?"

Despite my sister's best efforts, however, it was no flight of fancy but simple habit for me to now feel a little frisson at the discovery that I was stalking the ghost of Romeo in his own house; the only requirement for us to continue this beautiful relationship was that he stayed just the way he was: dead.

EVA MARIA WAS holding court in the concert hall, surrounded by men in dark suits and women in glittering dresses. It was a tall room decorated in the colors of milk and honey and finished off with touches of gold. About two hundred chairs were set up for the audience, and judging by the number of people already gathered there, it would be no problem filling them. At the far end, members of an orchestra were fine-tuning their instruments, and a large woman in a red dress looked as if she was threatening to sing. As with most spaces in Siena there was nothing modern here to disturb the eye, save the odd rebellious teenager wearing sneakers underneath his pleated pants.

As soon as she saw me entering, Eva Maria summoned me to her entourage with a regal wave. As I approached the group, I could hear her introducing me with superlatives I did not deserve, and within minutes I was best friends with some of the hot dogs of Siena culture, one of whom was the President of the Monte dei Paschi Bank in Palazzo Salimbeni.

"Monte dei Paschi," explained Eva Maria, "is the greatest protector of the arts in Siena. None of what you see around you would have been possible without the financial support of the Foundation."

The President looked at me with a slight smile, and so did his wife, who stood right next to him, draped around his elbow. Like Eva Maria, she was a woman whose elegance belied her years, and although I had dressed up for the occasion, her eyes told me I still had a lot to learn. She even whispered as much to her husband—or so it seemed.

"My wife thinks you don't believe it," said the President teasingly, his accent and dramatic intonation suggesting he was reciting the lyrics of a song. "Perhaps you think we are too"—he had to search for the word—"*proud* of ourselves?"

"Not necessarily," I said, my cheeks heating up under their continuing scrutiny, "I just find it . . . paradoxical that the house of the Marescottis depends on the goodwill of the Salimbenis to survive, that's all."

The President acknowledged my logic with a slight nod, as if to confirm that Eva Maria's superlatives had been appropriate. "A paradox, yes."

"But the world," said a voice behind me, "is full of paradoxes."

"Alessandro!" exclaimed the President, suddenly all jollity and game, "you must come and meet Signorina Tolomei. She is being very . . . *severe* on all of us. Especially on you."

"Of course she is." Alessandro took my hand and kissed it with facetious chivalry. "If she was not, we would never believe she was a Tolomei." He looked me straight in the eye before releasing my hand. "Would we, Miss Jacobs?"

It was an odd moment. He had clearly not expected to encounter me at the concert, and his reaction did not reflect well on either of us. But I could hardly blame him for grilling me; after all, I had never called him back after he stopped by my hotel three days ago. All this time, his business card had been sitting on my desk like a bad omen from a fortune cookie; only this morning I had finally torn it in half and thrown it in the trash, figuring that if he had really wanted to arrest me, he would have done so already.

"Don't you think," said Eva Maria, misinterpreting our intensity, "Giulietta looks lovely tonight, Sandro?"

Alessandro managed to smile. "Bewitching."

"Sì-sì," intervened the President, "but who is guarding our money, when you are here?"

"The ghosts of the Salimbenis," replied Alessandro, still looking straight at me. "A very formidable power."

"Basta!" Secretly pleased by his words, Eva Maria pretended to frown and tapped him on the shoulder with a rolled-up program. "We will all be ghosts soon enough. Tonight we celebrate life."

AFTER THE CONCERT Eva Maria insisted on going out to dinner, just the three of us. When I began protesting, she played the birthday card and said that on this particular night—"as I turn another page in the most excellent and lamentable comedy of life"—her only wish was to go to her favorite restaurant with two of her favorite people. Strangely, Alessandro did not object at all. In Siena, one clearly did not contradict one's godmother on her day of days.

Eva Maria's favorite restaurant was in Via delle Campane, just outside the border of Contrada dell'Aquila, that is, the Eagle neighborhood. Her favorite table, apparently, was on the elevated deck outside, facing a florist shop that was closing down for the night.

"So," she said to me, after ordering a bottle of Prosecco and a plate of antipasto, "you don't like opera!"

"But I do!" I protested, sitting awkwardly, my crossed legs barely fitting beneath the table. "I love opera. My aunt's housekeeper used to play it all the time. Especially *Aida*. It's just that . . . Aida is supposed to be an Ethiopian princess, not a triple-wide wonder in her fifties. I'm sorry."

Eva Maria laughed delightedly. "Do what Sandro does. Close your eyes."

I glanced at Alessandro. He had sat behind me at the concert, and I had felt his eyes on me the whole time. "Why? It's still the same woman singing."

"But the voice comes from the soul!" argued Eva Maria on his behalf, leaning towards me. "All you have to do is listen, and you will see Aida the way she really is."

"That is very generous." I looked at Alessandro. "Are you always that generous?"

He did not reply. He didn't have to.

"Magnanimity," said Eva Maria, testing the Prosecco and deeming it worthy of consumption, "is the greatest of all the virtues. Stay away from stingy people. They are trapped in small souls."

"According to my aunt's housekeeper," I said, "beauty is the greatest virtue. But he would say that generosity is a kind of beauty."

"Truth is beauty," said Alessandro, speaking at last, "beauty truth. According to Keats. Life is very easy if you live like that."

"You don't?"

"I'm not an urn."

I started laughing, but he never even smiled.

Although she clearly wanted us to become friends, Eva Maria was incapable of letting us continue on our own. "Tell us more about your aunt!" she urged me. "Why do you think she never told you who you were?"

I looked from one to the other, sensing that they had been discussing my case, and that they had disagreed. "I have no idea. I think she was afraid that—or maybe she—" I looked down. "I don't know."

"In Siena," said Alessandro, preoccupied with his water glass, "your name makes all the difference."

"Names, names, names!" sighed Eva Maria. "What I don't understand is why this aunt—Rosa?—never took you to Siena before."

"Maybe she was afraid," I said, more sharply this time, "that the person who killed my parents would kill me, too."

Eva Maria sat back, appalled. "What a terrible thought!"

"Well, happy birthday!" I took a sip of my Prosecco. "And thanks for everything." I glared at Alessandro, forcing him to meet my eyes. "Don't worry, I won't stay long."

"No," he said, nodding once, "I imagine it is too peaceful here for your taste."

"I like peace."

Within the coniferous greens of his eyes, I now got a warning glimpse of his soul. It was a disturbing sight. "Obviously."

Rather than replying, I clenched my teeth and turned my attention to the antipasto. Unfortunately, Eva Maria did not pick up on the finer nuances of my emotions; all she saw was my flushed face. "Sandro," she said, riding what she thought was a wave of flirtation, "why have you not taken Giulietta around town and shown her some nice things? She would love to go."

"I'm sure she would." Alessandro stabbed an olive with his fork, but didn't eat it. "Unfortunately, we don't have any statues of little mermaids."

That was when I knew for sure he had checked my file, and that he must have found out everything there was to know about Julie Jacobs—Julie Jacobs the antiwar demonstrator, who had barely returned from Rome before heading off to Copenhagen to protest the Danish involvement in Iraq by vandalizing the Little Mermaid. Sadly, the file would not have told him that it was all a big mistake, and that Julie Jacobs had only gone to Denmark to show her sister that, yes, she dared.

Tasting the dizzying cocktail of fury and fear in my throat, I reached out blindly for the bread basket, hoping very much my panic didn't show.

"No, but we have other nice statues!" Eva Maria looked at me, then at him, trying to grasp what was going on. "And fountains. You must take her to Fontebranda—"

"Maybe Miss Jacobs would like to see Via dei Malcontenti," proposed Alessandro, cutting off Eva Maria. "That was where we used to take the criminals, so their victims could throw things at them on their way to the gallows."

I returned his unforgiving stare, feeling no further need for conceal-ment. "Was anyone ever pardoned?"

"Yes. It was called banishment. They were told to leave Siena and never come back. In return, their lives would be spared."

"Oh, I see," I snapped back, "just like your family, the Salimbenis." I stole a glance at Eva Maria, who was, for a change, dumbstruck. "Am I wrong?"

Alessandro did not answer right away. Judging from the play of the muscles in his jaw, he would have liked very much to respond in kind, but knew that he could not do so in front of his godmother. "The Salimbeni family," he finally said, his voice strained, "was expropriated by the gov-ernment in 1419 and forced to leave the Republic of Siena."

"For good?"

"Obviously not. But they were banished for a long time." The way he looked at me suggested that we were now talking about me again. "And they probably deserved it."

"What if they . . . came back anyway?"

"Then"—he paused for effect, and it struck me that the green in his eyes was not like organic foliage at all, but cold and crystallized, like the slice of malachite I had presented as a special treasure in fourth grade, be-fore the teacher had explained that it was a mineral mined to extract cop-per, with evident harm to the environment—"they must have had a very good reason."

"Enough!" Eva Maria raised her glass. "No more banishment. No more fighting. Now we are all friends."

For about ten minutes we managed to have a civil conversation. After that, Eva Maria excused herself to go to the restroom, and Alessandro and I were left to each other's devices. Glancing at him, I caught him running his eyes over me, and for the briefest of moments I was able to convince myself that it was all just a cat-and-mouse game to see whether I was sufficiently feisty to become his playmate for the week. Well, I thought to myself, whatever the cat was plotting, it was in for a nasty surprise.

I reached out for a slice of sausage. "Do you believe in redemption?"

"I don't care," said Alessandro, pushing the platter towards me, "what you did in Rome. Or anywhere else. But I do care about Siena. So tell me, why are you here?"

"Is this an interrogation?" I spoke with my mouth full. "Should I call my lawyer?"

He leaned towards me, his voice low. "I could have you in jail like this—" He snapped his fingers right in front of my nose. "Is that really what you want?"

"You know," I said, shoveling more food onto my plate and hoping very much he did not notice my hands shaking, "power games have never worked on me. They may have worked wonders for your ancestors, but if you recall, *my* ancestors were never really that impressed."

"Okay—" He leaned back in his chair, changing tactics. "How about this: I'm going to leave you alone on one condition. That you stay away from Eva Maria."

"Why don't you tell that to her?"

"She is a very special woman, and I don't want her to suffer."

I put down my fork. "But *I* do? Is that what you think of me?"

"You really want to know?" Alessandro gave me the once-over as if I were an overpriced artifact put up for sale. "All right. I think you are beautiful, intelligent . . . a great actor—" Seeing my confusion, he frowned and went on, more sternly, "I think someone paid you a lot of money to come here and pretend to be Giulietta Tolomei . . ."

"What?"

". . . and I think part of your job is to get close to Eva Maria. But guess what . . . I'm not going to let that happen."

I barely knew where to start. Fortunately, his accusations were so surreal that I was too flabbergasted to feel truly wounded. "Why," I finally said, "do you not believe I am Giulietta Tolomei? Is it because I don't have baby blue eyes?"

"You want to know why? I'll tell you why." He leaned forward, elbows on the table. "Giulietta Tolomei is dead."

"Then how," I retorted, leaning forward, too, "do you explain that I am sitting right here?"

He looked at me for the longest time, searching for something in my face that somehow wasn't there. In the end he looked away, his lips tight, and I knew that for some reason I had not convinced him, and probably never would.

"You know what—" I pushed back my chair and got up. "I'm going to take your advice and remove myself from Eva Maria's company. Tell her thank you for the concert and the food, and tell her that she can have her clothes back whenever she wants them. I am done with them."

I did not wait for his response, but stalked off the deck and away from the restaurant without looking back. As soon as I had turned the first corner and was out of sight, I could feel tears of anger rising, and despite my shoes I started running. The last thing I wanted was for Alessandro to catch up with me and apologize for his rudeness, should he be so human as to try.

GOING HOME THAT NIGHT, I stuck to the shadows and the streets less traveled. As I walked through the darkness, hoping rather than knowing I was going the right way, I was so preoccupied with my discussion with Alessandro—and, more specifically, with all the brilliant things I could have said, but didn't—that it took me a while to realize I was being followed.

In the beginning it was little more than an eerie feeling of being watched. But soon I began to notice the faint sounds of someone sneaking along behind me. Whenever I forged ahead I could discern a shuffle of clothes and soft soles, but if I slowed down the shuffle disappeared, and I heard nothing but an ominous silence that was almost worse.

Turning abruptly down a random street, I was able to pick up movement and the shape of a man out of the corner of my eye. Unless I was very much mistaken, it was the same thug who had followed me a few days earlier, when I had left the bank in Palazzo Tolomei carrying my mother's box. My brain had obviously filed our previous encounter under danger, and now that it recognized his shape and gait, it set off a deafening evacuation alarm that forced all rational thoughts from my head and made me pull off my shoes and—for the second time that night—start running.

Did my heart love till now? Forswear it, sight.
For I ne'er saw true beauty till this night

...

Siena, A.D. 1340

THE NIGHT WAS RIPE WITH MISCHIEF.

As soon as Romeo and his cousins were out of sight of the Marescotti tower, they threw themselves around a street corner, gasping with laughter. It had been far too easy for them to escape the house this evening, for Palazzo Marescotti was bustling with family visitors from Bologna, and Romeo's father, Comandante Marescotti, had grudgingly put on a banquet with musicians to entertain the lot. After all, what did Bologna have to offer that Siena could not deliver tenfold?

Knowing very well that they were, once again, violating the Comandante's curfew, Romeo and his cousins paused to strap on the gaudy carnival masks they always wore on their nightly escapades. As they stood there, struggling with knots and bows, the family butcher walked by with a rack of ham for the party and an assistant carrying a torch, but he was too wise to recognize the youngsters. One day, Romeo would be the master of Palazzo Marescotti and the one who paid for its deliveries.

When the masks were finally in place, the young men put their velvet hats back on, adjusting both pieces for greatest possible concealment. Grinning at the sight of his friends, one of them picked up the lute he had been carrying and struck a few merry chords. *"Giu-hu-hu-lietta!"* he sang in a teasing falsetto. *"I would I were thy bi-hi-hird, thy little wanton bi-hi-*

hi-hi-hird—" He made a few birdlike hops, causing everyone but Romeo to gag with laughter.

"Very funny!" scowled Romeo. "Keep jesting at my scars and I'll give you a few of your own!"

"Come on," said someone else, champing at the bit, "if we don't hurry, she will be in bed, and your serenade will be nothing but a lullaby."

Measured in footsteps alone, their journey this evening was not long, barely five hundred strides. But in terms of everything else, it was an odyssey. Despite the late hour, the streets were crawling with people—locals mingling with foreigners, buyers with sellers, pilgrims with thieves—and on every corner stood a prophet with a wax candle, condemning the material world while eyeing every passing prostitute with the same stern prohibition one finds in dogs watching the movements of a long string of sausage.

Elbowing their way up the street, jumping over a gutter here, a beggar there, and ducking under deliveries and sedan chairs, the young men at length found themselves stalled on the edge of Piazza Tolomei. Stretching to see why the crowd stood still, Romeo caught a glimpse of a colorful figure bobbing to and fro in the black night air on the front steps of the church of San Cristoforo.

"Look!" said one of his cousins. "Tolomei has invited San Cristoforo to dinner. But he is not dressed up. Shame on him!"

They all watched in awe as the torch-lit procession from the church made its way across the piazza towards Palazzo Tolomei, and Romeo suddenly knew that here was his chance to enter the forbidding house through the front door rather than standing around stupidly beneath Giulietta's presumed window. A long line of self-important people trailed behind the priests carrying the saint, and they were all wearing carnival masks. It was commonly known that Messer Tolomei held masked balls every few months in order to sneak banished allies and lawless family members into his house. Had he not, he would scarcely have been able to fill the dancing floor.

"We are clearly," said Romeo, rallying his cousins, "suspended by the talons of Fortuna. Either that, or she is helping us along only to squash us utterly in a moment and have a good laugh. Come!"

"Wait!" said one of his cousins. "I fear—"

"You fear too early!" Romeo cut him off. "On, lusty gentlemen!"

The confusion on the front steps of the church of San Cristoforo was exactly what Romeo needed in order to steal a torch from a cresset and fall on his unsuspecting prey: an older widow with no companion in sight. "Please," he said, offering his arm. "Messer Tolomei is anxious to ensure your comfort."

The woman seemed not at all displeased with the promising muscularity of his arm and the bold smiles from his companions. "That would be the first time," she said, with some dignity. "But I may say, he is certainly making amends."

It would seem impossible to those who had not seen it with their own eyes, but upon entering their palazzo Romeo had to conclude that the Tolomeis had actually managed to out-fresco the Marescottis. Not only did every single wall tell yet another story about Tolomei triumphs in the past and Tolomei piety in the present, but even the ceilings were vessels of god-fearing self-promotion. Had Romeo been alone, he would have put his head back and gawked at the myriads of exotic creatures traversing this private Heaven. As it were, he was not alone; fully armed, liveried guards stood at attention along every wall, and the fear of detection was enough to check his audacity and ensure that he paid the widow the necessary compliments as they lined up for the opening dance.

If the widow had wondered about Romeo's exact status before—the reassuring quality of his clothes had been somewhat compromised by the suspect manner in which he had obtained her company—at least now, poised for dancing, his bearing assured her of his noble birth.

"What luck I have tonight," she muttered, careful that no one overheard her but he. "But tell me, did you come hither with some particular venture in mind, or are you merely here to . . . dance?"

"I confess," said Romeo smoothly, promising neither too much nor too little, "I am sinfully fond of dancing. I swear, I could go on for hours without a rest."

The woman laughed discreetly, satisfied for now. As the dance went on, she took more liberties with him than he would have liked, occasionally running her hand over his velvet exterior searching for something more solid underneath, but Romeo was too distracted to fend her off.

His one and only interest this evening was to find the young woman whose life he had saved, and whose lovely features Maestro Ambrogio had all but captured in a marvelous portrait. The Maestro had refused to tell him her surname, but it had not taken Romeo long to sniff it out on his own. No more than a week had gone by since the girl's arrival before the rumor was all over town that Messer Tolomei had brought a foreign beauty to mass on Sunday morning—a foreign beauty with eyes as blue as the ocean, and whose name was Giulietta.

Looking around the room once more—a cornucopia of beautiful, swirling women in garish dresses and men poised to catch them—Romeo was at a loss to understand why the girl was nowhere to be seen. Surely, a flower such as she would be going from arm to arm, never free to sit down; the only challenge would be to liberate her from all the other young men craving her attention. It was a challenge Romeo had met many times before, and a game he relished.

Patience was always his initial move, like a Greek prince before the walls of Troy, patience and endurance while all the other contenders in turn made themselves ridiculous. Then would come first contact, a teasing touch of a knowing smile, conspiring with her against them. Later, a long gaze from across the room, a dark, unsmiling stare, and, by God, the next time their hands met in the chain of the dance, her heart would be pounding so wildly in her chest that he could trace its flight up her naked neck. And there, just there, was where he would place his first kiss . . .

But even Romeo's Homeric patience was taxed to oblivion as dance after dance came around, rotating everybody like celestial bodies and creating every possible constellation amongst the dancers, except the very one he was hoping for. Since all were masked he could not be completely sure, but from what was visible of their hair and smiles, the girl he had come to woo was not among them. To miss her this evening would be a disaster, for nothing other than a masked ball would offer him this clandestine admittance to Palazzo Tolomei, and he would be back to singing serenades beneath her balcony—wherever it might be—with a voice the Creator had never intended for song.

There was, of course, the danger that the rumor had misled him, and that the blue-eyed girl at mass had been someone else. If that were the case, his roostering around on Messer Tolomei's dancing floor this evening was no more than a waste of time; the girl he had come to meet was most likely sweetly asleep in some other house in town. Romeo had almost begun to fear as much when suddenly—in the middle of a gallant bow in the ductia—he was overtaken by a strong sensation of being watched.

Introducing a pivot where no pivot was required, Romeo let his eyes sweep the entire room. And now he finally saw it: A visage, half veiled in hair, was looking straight at him from the shades of the upstairs loggia. But no sooner had he recognized the oval form as the head of a woman than it withdrew into the shadows, as if fearing discovery.

He spun back to face his partner, flushed with excitement. Even though chance had afforded him but the faintest glimpse of the lady aloft, there was no doubt in his heart that the figure he had seen was that of the lovely Giulietta. And she had been looking at him, too, as if she somehow knew who he was and why he had come.

Another ductia took him around the room in cosmic majesty, and after that the estampia, before Romeo finally spotted a cousin in the crowd and managed to summon him with a piercing glare. "Where have you been?" he hissed. "Do you not see I am dying here?"

"You owe me thanks, not curses," whispered the other, taking over the dance, "for this is a measly party with measly wine and measly women, and—wait!"

But Romeo was already on his way, deaf to discouraging words and blind to the widow's reproachful gaze as he took flight. On a night like this, he knew, no doors were barred to a bold man. With all servants and guards employed on the ground floor, anything above it was to the lover what a forest pond is to the hunter: a sweet promise for the patient.

Up here, on the first floor, the dizzying fumes from the party below made the old young, the wise foolish, and the stingy generous, and as he walked through the upstairs gallery, Romeo passed by many a dark niche full of rustling silk and hushed giggles. Here and there a flash of white betrayed the strategic removal of garments, and, walking by a particularly salacious corner, he nearly stopped to stare, intrigued by the infinite flexibility of the human body.

The farther from the stairs he went, however, the more silent the corners, and when at last he entered the loggia overlooking the dancing floor, not a single person was left to be seen. Where Giulietta had stood, half concealed by a marble column, there was now only emptiness, and at the end of the loggia was a closed door that even he dared not open.

His disappointment was great. Why had he not extracted himself from the dance earlier, like a shooting star escaping the immortal boredom of the firmament? Why had he been so sure that she would still be here, waiting for him? Folly. He had told himself a story, and now was the time for its tragic end.

Just then, as he was turning to leave, the door at the end of the loggia opened, and a slender figure, hair ablaze, slipped through the doorway— like an ancient dryad through a crack in time—before it closed again with a hollow thud. For a moment there was no movement and no sound save the music downstairs, yet Romeo thought he could sense someone breathing, someone who had been startled to see him standing there, looming in the shadows, and who was now struggling to catch her breath.

Perhaps he should have spoken a word of comfort, but his excitement was too great to be harnessed with good manners. Rather than offering an apology for his intrusion, or even better, the name of the intruder himself, he merely tore off his carnival mask and stepped forward, eagerly, to draw her from the shade and finally unveil her living face.

She neither engaged him nor shrank away; instead she walked over to the edge of the balcony and looked down at the dancers. Encouraged, Romeo followed her, and when she leaned over the balustrade, he had the satisfaction of seeing her profile glowing with the lights from below. While Maestro Ambrogio might have exaggerated the lofty lines of her beauty, he had not done justice to the luminosity of her eyes, or the mystery of her smile. And the ripe softness of her breathing lips, certainly, he had left for Romeo to discover for himself.

"Surely this must be the famous court," the girl now began, "of the king of cowards."

Surprised by the bitterness of her voice, Romeo did not know what to answer.

"Who else," she went on, still not turning, "would spend the night feeding grapes to an effigy while murderers parade around town, bragging about their exploits? And what decent man could contemplate a party such as this, when his own brother has been—" She could not continue.

"Most people," said Romeo, his voice a stranger even to himself, "call Messer Tolomei a brave man."

"Then most people," replied she, "are wrong. And you, Signore, are wasting your time. I will not dance tonight; my heart is too heavy. So, go back to my aunt and feast on her caresses; you will receive none from me."

"I am not here," said Romeo, stepping boldly closer, "as a dancer. I am here . . . because I cannot stay away. Will you not look at me?"

She paused, forcing herself not to move. "Why should I look at you? Is your soul that inferior to your body?"

"I did not know my soul," said Romeo, lowering his voice, "until I saw its reflection in your eyes."

She did not reply right away, but when she did, her voice was sharp enough to graze his courage. "And when did you thus deflower my eyes with your own image? You, to me, are merely the distant form of an excellent dancer. What demon stole my eyes and gave them to you?"

"Sleep," Romeo said, gazing at her profile and hoping for a return of her smile, "was the culprit. He took them from your bed pillow and brought them to me. O, the sweet torment of that dream!"

"Sleep," the girl retorted, her head still stubbornly turned, "is the father of lies!"

"But the mother of hope."

"Perhaps. But the firstborn of hope is tragedy."

"You speak with such familiar fondness as one does only of relatives."

"Oh no!" she exclaimed, her voice shrill with bitterness. "I dare not brag of such high connections. When I am dead, were I to die in a grand, religious manner, let the scholars argue over my bloodline."

"I care not for your bloodline," Romeo said, boldly touching a finger to her neck, "save to trace its secret writing on your skin."

For a moment, his touch made her silent. And when she next spoke, her breathless words rendered void the intended dismissal. "Then I fear," she said, over her shoulder, "that you will be disappointed. For my skin spells no pretty narrative, but a tale of slaughter and revenge."

Braver now that she had allowed his first venture, Romeo cupped his hands over her shoulders and leaned forward to speak through the silken screen of her hair. "I heard of your loss. There is not a heart in Siena that does not feel your pain."

"Yes, there is! It resides in Palazzo Salimbeni, and it is incapable of human feelings!" She shook off his hands. "How often I have wished I was born a man!"

"Being born a man is no safeguard against sorrow."

"Indeed?" She finally turned to face him, taunting his gravity. "And what, pray, are your sorrows, Signore?" Her eyes, vibrant even in the darkness, looked him over with amusement, then settled on his face. "Nay, as I suspected, you are too handsome to have sorrows. Rather, you have the voice and the face of a thief."

Seeing his indignation, she laughed sharply and went on, "Yes, a thief. But a thief that is given more than he takes, and therefore considers himself generous rather than greedy, and a favorite rather than a fiend. Contradict me if you can. You are a man from whom no gift has ever been withheld. How could such a man ever have sorrows?"

Romeo met her teasing stare with confidence. "No man was ever on a quest, who did not seek its end. Yet on his way, what pilgrim says no to a meal and a bed? Do not begrudge me the length of my journey. Were I not a traveler, I never would have landed on your shore."

"But what exotic savage can keep a sailor ashore forever? What pilgrim does not in time weary of his homely chair and set out for still more distant, undiscovered shrines?"

"Your words do justice to neither of us. Pray, do not call me inconstant before you even know my name."

"It is my savage nature."

"I see naught but beauty."

"Then you do not see me at all."

Romeo took her hand and forced it open against his cheek. "I saw you, dear savage, before you saw me. Yet you heard me, before I heard you. And as such we might have lived, our love separated by our senses, had not Fortuna, tonight, granted you eyes, and I ears."

The girl frowned. "Your poetry is mysterious. Do you intend me to comprehend you, or are you hoping that I mistake my own dullness for your wisdom?"

"By God!" exclaimed Romeo, "Fortuna is a tease! She gave you eyes, but took your ears in return. Giulietta, do you not recognize the voice of your knight?" He reached out to touch her cheek the way he had done when she was lying for dead in the coffin. "Do you not," he added, his voice little more than a whisper, "recognize his touch?"

For the briefest of moments, Giulietta softened and leaned against his hand, seeking comfort from his closeness. But just as Romeo thought she was surrendering to him, he was surprised to see her eyes narrow. Rather than opening the door of her heart to him—hitherto suspiciously ajar—she now stepped abruptly backwards, away from his hand. "Liar! Who sent you here to play with me?"

He gasped in surprise. "Sweet Giulietta—"

But she would not listen, and merely pushed at him to leave her. "Go! Go away and laugh at me with all your friends!"

"I swear to you!" Romeo stayed his ground and reached for her hands, but she did not surrender them. For lack of better he took her by the shoulders and held her still, desperate for her to hear him out. "I am the man who saved you and Friar Lorenzo on the high road," he insisted, "and you entered this city under my protection. I saw you in the Maestro's workshop, lying in the coffin—"

As he spoke, he saw her eyes widen in the realization that he was telling the truth, but instead of gratitude, her face filled with anxiety.

"I see," she said, her voice unsteady. "And now, I suppose, you have come to collect your dues?"

Only then, seeing her fear, did it occur to Romeo that he had taken a great liberty in seizing her shoulders like this, and that his grip must have made her wonder about his intentions. Cursing himself for being so impulsive, he gently let go of her and took a step back, hoping very much she would not run away. This encounter was not going the way he had planned it, not at all. For many nights now, he had been dreaming of the moment when Giulietta would come out on her balcony, summoned by his serenade, and clasp her heart in admiration for his person, if not his song.

"I have come," he said, his eyes begging her pardon, "to hear your sweet voice speak my name. That is all."

Seeing his sincerity, she dared to smile. "Romeo. Romeo Marescotti," she whispered, "blessed by Heaven. There, what more do I owe you?"

He nearly stepped forward again, but managed to discipline himself and keep his distance. "You owe me nothing, but I want everything. I have been looking for you all over town since I realized you were alive. I knew I had to see you and . . . speak with you. I even prayed to God—" He broke off, sheepishly.

Giulietta looked at him for the longest time, her blue eyes full of astonishment. "And what did God tell you?"

Romeo could control himself no longer, but grasped her hand and brought it to his lips. "He told me that you were here tonight, waiting for me."

"Then you must be the answer to my prayers." She looked at him in wonder as he kissed her hand again and again. "Only this morning, in church, I prayed for a man—a hero—who could avenge the gruesome death of my family. Now I see that I was wrong in asking for someone new. For you were the one who killed that bandit on the high road, and who protected me from the very moment I arrived. Yes"—she touched her other hand to his face—"I believe you are that hero."

"You honor me," said Romeo, straightening. "I should like nothing better than to be your knight."

"Good," said Giulietta, "then do me no small favor. Seek out that bastard, Salimbeni, and make him suffer as he made my family suffer. And when you are done, bring me his head in a box that he may wander headless through the halls of Purgatory."

Romeo swallowed hard, but managed to nod. "Your wish is my law, dearest angel. Will you allow me a few days for this task, or must he suffer tonight?"

"I will leave that to you," said Giulietta with graceful modesty. "You are the expert on killing Salimbenis."

"And when I am done," said Romeo, holding both her hands, "will you grant me a kiss for my trouble?"

"When you are done," replied Giulietta, watching him as he pressed his lips to her wrists, first one, then the other, "I will grant you anything you desire."

[III.III]

It seems she hangs upon the cheek of night
As a rich jewel in an Ethiop's ear

. . .

THE CITY OF SIENA WAS ASLEEP and beyond compassion. The alleys through which I ran that night were nothing but dark streams of silence, and every object I passed—scooters, trash cans, cars—was veiled in misty moonlight, as if spellbound in the exact same posture for a hundred years. The façades of the houses around me were just as dismissive; the doors seemed to have no handles on the outside, and every single window was closed and covered by shutters. Whatever was going on in the night streets of this ancient town, its dwellers did not want to know.

Pausing briefly, I could hear that—somewhere in the shadows behind me—the thug had started running, too. He was not doing anything to conceal the fact that he was pursuing me; his steps were heavy and irregular, the soles of his shoes scratching against the bumpy paving stones, and even when he paused to catch my scent, he was panting heavily, like someone not used to physical exertion. Even so, I was unable to outrun him, for no matter how silently or swiftly I moved, he managed to stay on track and follow me around every single corner, almost as if he could read my mind.

My naked feet throbbing with pain from slamming against the cold stone, I stumbled through a narrow passageway at the end of an alley, hoping very much there was a way out on the other side, preferably several. But there was not. I had ended up in a cul-de-sac, trapped by tall houses on all sides. In fact, there was not even a wall or fence I could climb, nor a single garbage can to hide behind, and my only means of self-defense were the pointy heels of my shoes.

Turning towards my fate, I braced myself for the encounter. What did this lowlife want from me? My purse? The crucifix around my neck? . . . Me? Or perhaps he wanted to know where the family treasure was, but then, so did I, and there was nothing I could tell him at this juncture that could possibly satisfy him. Unfortunately, most robbers—according to Umberto—did not deal very well with disappointment, and so I quickly dug into my handbag and took out my wallet; hopefully my credit cards looked convincingly flashy. No one but I knew that they represented about twenty thousand dollars' worth of debt.

As I stood there, waiting for the inevitable, the sound of my pounding heart was drowned out by the roar of an approaching motorcycle. And instead of seeing the thug appear, triumphant, at the entrance to the cul-de-sac, there was a flash of black metal as the motorcycle shot past me and continued down the road the other way. But rather than disappearing, it suddenly stopped, tires squealing, and turned around to drive by a couple more times, still not stopping anywhere near me. Only now did I pick up the sounds of someone in sneakers hightailing it down the street, gasping with panic, to disappear around some far corner with the motorcycle hot on his trail, like prey running from a predator.

And then, suddenly, there was silence.

Several seconds passed—perhaps as much as half a minute—but neither the thug nor the motorcycle came back. When I finally dared to emerge from the alley, I could not even see as far as the next street corner in either direction. Being lost in the dark, however, was definitely the lesser of the evils that had befallen me this night, and as soon as I found a public phone, I could call Direttor Rossini back at the hotel and ask for directions. Notwithstanding my being lost and miserable, my request would, undoubtedly, delight him.

Starting up the street, I walked a few yards or so before something suddenly caught my eye in the darkness ahead.

It was a motorcycle and rider, sitting completely still in the middle of the street, looking straight at me. The moonlight was caught in the rider's helmet and the metal of the bike, and it projected an image of a man in black leather, visor closed, who had sat there, very patiently, waiting for me to emerge.

Fear would have been a natural reaction, but as I stood there, awkwardly, shoes in my hand, all I felt was confusion. Who was this guy? And why was he just sitting there, staring at me? Had he actually saved me from the thug? If so, was he waiting for me to come up and thank him?

But my budding gratitude was cut short when he suddenly turned on the headlight of the bike, blinding me with the sharp beam. And as I threw up my hands to shield my eyes, he started the bike and revved the engine a couple of times, just to set me straight.

Spinning around, I started down the street the other way, still partly blinded and cursing myself for being an idiot. Whoever this guy was, he was clearly no friend; in all likelihood he was some local misfit who spent his nights in this sad manner, driving around and terrorizing peaceful people. It just so happened that his latest victim had been my stalker, but that did not make us friends, not at all.

He let me run for a bit, and even waited until I had turned the first corner, before he came after me. Not at high speed, as if he wanted to run me down, just fast enough to let me know that I was not going to get away.

That was when I saw the blue door.

I had just turned another corner, and knew that I only had a small window of opportunity before the headlight would find me again, and there it was, right in front of me: the blue door to the painter's workshop, magically ajar. I did not even pause to consider whether there might be more than just one blue door in Siena, or whether it was really such a good idea to barge into people's homes in the middle of the night. I just did it. And as soon as I was inside, I closed the door and leaned against it, listening nervously to the sounds of the motorcycle passing outside and eventually disappearing.

Admittedly, when we had met in the cloister garden the day before, the long-haired painter had struck me as a bit of an oddball, but when you are being chased through medieval alleys by nefarious characters you can't be picky.

MAESTRO LIPPI'S WORKSHOP was an acquired taste. It looked as if a bomb of divine inspiration had gone off, not just once, but on a regular basis, scattering paintings, sculptures, and bizarre installations everywhere. The Maestro was apparently not someone whose talents could be channeled through a single medium or expression; like a linguistic genius, he spoke in the tongue that fitted his mood, choosing his tools and materials with the commitment of the virtuoso. And in the middle of it all stood a barking dog that looked like the unlikely mix of a fluffy bichon frise and an all-business Doberman.

"Ah!" said Maestro Lippi, emerging from behind an easel as soon as he heard the door closing, "there you are. I was wondering when you would come." Then, without a word, he disappeared. When he returned a moment later, he was carrying a bottle of wine, two glasses, and a loaf of bread. Seeing that I had not yet moved, he chuckled. "You must excuse Dante. He is always suspicious of women."

"His name is *Dante*?" I looked down at the dog, who now came to give me a slimy old slipper, apologizing in his own way for barking at me. "That is so odd—that was the name of Maestro Ambrogio Lorenzetti's dog!"

"Well, this is his workshop." Maestro Lippi poured me a glass of red wine. "Do you know him?"

"You mean, *the* Ambrogio Lorenzetti? From 1340?"

"Of course!" Maestro Lippi smiled and raised his own glass in a toast. "Welcome back. Let us drink to many happy returns. Let us drink to Diana!"

I nearly choked on my wine. He knew my mother?

Before I could sputter out anything, the Maestro leaned closer, conspiratorially. "There is a legend about a river, Diana, deep, deep underground. We have never found her, but people say, sometimes late in the night, they wake up from dreams, and they can feel her. And you know, in the ancient times, there was a Diana temple on the Campo. The Romans had their games there, the bull hunt and the duels. Now we have the Palio in honor of the Virgin Mary. She is the mother who gives us water so we can grow again, like grapevines, out of the darkness."

For a moment we just stood there, looking at each other, and I had a strange feeling that if he had wanted to, Maestro Lippi could have told me many secrets about myself, about my destiny, and about the future of all things; secrets it would take me many lives to discover on my own. But no sooner had the thought been born than it fluttered off, chased away by the Maestro's giddy smile as he suddenly pulled the wineglass from my hand

and put it down on the table. "Come! I have something I want to show you. Remember, I told you?"

He walked ahead of me into another room that was, if possible, even more packed with artwork than the workshop itself. It was an interior room with no windows, clearly used as storage. "Just a minute—" Maestro Lippi went right through the mess to carefully remove a piece of fabric covering a small painting hanging on the far wall. "Look!"

I stepped closer in order to see better, but when I came too near, the Maestro stopped me. "Careful. She is very old. Don't breathe on her."

It was the portrait of a girl, a beautiful girl, with big blue eyes looking dreamily at something behind me. She seemed sad, but at the same time hopeful, and in her hand she held a five-petal rose.

"I think she looks like you," said Maestro Lippi, looking from her to me, and back, "or maybe you look like her. Not the eyes, not the hair, but . . . something else. I don't know. What do you think?"

"I think that's a compliment I don't deserve. Who painted this?"

"Aha!" The Maestro leaned towards me with a furtive smile. "I found it when I took over the workshop. It was hidden inside the wall in a metal box. There was a book, too. A journal. I think—" Even before Maestro Lippi had finished, all the little hairs on my arms were standing up, and I knew exactly what he would say. ". . . No, in fact, I am sure it was Ambrogio Lorenzetti who hid the box. It was his journal. And I think he painted this picture, too. Her name is the same as yours, *Giulietta Tolomei*. He wrote it on the back."

I stared at the painting, scarcely able to believe this was really the portrait I had been reading about. It was every bit as mesmerizing as I had imagined. "Do you still have the journal?"

"No. I sold it. I talked about it to a friend, who talked about it to a friend, and suddenly, there is a man here, who wants to buy it. His name is Professor . . . Professor Tolomei." Maestro Lippi looked at me, eyebrows raised. "You're a Tolomei, too. Do you know him? He is very old."

I sat down on the nearest chair. It had no seat, but I didn't care. "That was my father. He translated the journal into English. I am reading it right now. It's all about her"—I nodded towards the painting—"Giulietta Tolomei. Apparently, she is my ancestor. He describes her eyes in his journal . . . and there they are."

"I knew it!" Maestro Lippi spun around to face the painting with pleased agitation. "She is your ancestor!" He laughed and turned again, grabbing me by the shoulders. "I am so glad you came to see me."

"I just don't understand," I said, "why Maestro Ambrogio felt he had to hide these things in the wall. Or maybe it was not him, but someone else—"

"Don't think so much!" warned Maestro Lippi. "It puts wrinkles on your face." He paused, struck by unexpected inspiration. "Next time you come, I will paint you. When will you be back? Tomorrow?"

"Maestro—" I knew I had to grab hold of his consciousness while its orbit still touched on reality. "I was wondering if I could stay here a bit longer. Tonight."

He looked at me curiously, as if it was me and not him who was showing signs of insanity.

I felt compelled to explain. "There is someone out there—I don't know what's going on. There's this guy—" I shook my head. "I know it sounds crazy, but I am being followed, and I don't know why."

"Ah," said Maestro Lippi. Very carefully, he draped the fabric over the portrait of Giulietta Tolomei and escorted me back into the workshop. Here, he sat me down on a chair and handed me my wineglass before he, too, sat down, facing me like a child expecting a story. "I think you do. Tell me why he is following you."

Over the next half hour I told him everything. I didn't mean to at first, but once I started talking, I couldn't stop. There was something about the Maestro and the way he looked at me—eyes sparkling with excitement, nodding now and then—that made me feel he might be able to help me find the hidden truth behind it all. If indeed there was one.

And so I told him about my parents and the accidents that had killed them, and I hinted that a man named Luciano Salimbeni might have had a hand in them both. After that I went on to describe my mother's box of papers and Maestro Ambrogio's journal, as well as my cousin Peppo's allusion to an unknown treasure called Juliet's Eyes. "Have you ever heard of such a thing?" I asked, when I saw Maestro Lippi frowning.

Instead of answering, he got up and stood for a moment, head in the air, as if listening for a distant call. When he started walking, I knew I had to follow, and so I trailed behind him into another room, up a flight of stairs, and through a long, narrow library with sagging bookcases from floor to ceiling. Once here, all I could do was observe as the Maestro walked back and forth many, many times, trying to locate—I assumed—a particular book that did not wish to be found. When he finally succeeded, he tore it from the shelf and held it up triumphantly. "I knew I had seen it somewhere!"

The book turned out to be an old encyclopedia of legendary monsters and treasures—for apparently, the two go together and cannot be separated—and as the Maestro began leafing through it, I caught sight of several illustrations that had more to do with fairy tales than with my life until now.

"There!" He tapped a finger on an entry. "What do you say to that?" Unable to wait until we were back downstairs, he switched on a wobbly floor lamp and read the text out loud in an animated mix of Italian and English.

The essence of the story was that Juliet's Eyes were a pair of abnormally large sapphires from Ethiopia, originally called The Ethiopian Twins, which were—allegedly—purchased by Messer Salimbeni of Siena in the year 1340 as an engagement present for his bride-to-be, Giulietta Tolomei. Later, after Giulietta's tragic death, the sapphires were set as eyes in a golden statue by her grave.

"Listen to this!" Maestro Lippi ran an eager finger down the page. "Shakespeare knew about the statue, too!" And he went on to read the following lines from the very end of *Romeo and Juliet,* quoted in the encyclopedia in both Italian and English:

> *For I will raise her statue in pure gold,*
> *That whiles Verona by that name is known,*
> *There shall be no figure at such rate be set*
> *As that of true and faithful Juliet.*

When he finally stopped reading, Maestro Lippi showed me the illustration on the page, and I recognized it right away. It was a statue of a man and a woman; the man was kneeling, holding a woman in his arms. Except for a few details, it was the very same statue my mother had tried to capture at least twenty times in the notebook I had found in her box.

"Holy cow!" I leaned closer to the illustration. "Does it say anything about the actual location of her grave?"

"Whose grave?"

"Juliet's, or, I should say, Giulietta's." I pointed at the text he had just read to me. "The book says that a golden statue was put up by her grave . . . but it didn't say where the grave actually *was.*"

Maestro Lippi closed the book and shoved it back in the bookcase on a random shelf. "Why do you want to find her grave?" he asked, his tone suddenly belligerent. "So you can take her eyes? If she doesn't have eyes, how can she recognize her Romeo when he comes to wake her up?"

"I wouldn't take her eyes!" I protested. "I just want to . . . see them."

"Well," said the Maestro, switching off the wobbly lamp, "then I think you have to talk to Romeo. I don't know who else would be able to find it. But be careful. There are many ghosts here, and they are not all as friendly as me." He leaned closer in the darkness, taking some kind of silly pleasure in spooking me, and hissed, "A plague! A plague on both your houses!"

"That's really great," I said. "Thanks."

He laughed heartily and slapped his knees. "Come on! Don't be such a little pollo! I am just teasing you!"

Back downstairs, several glasses of wine later, I finally managed to steer the conversation back to Juliet's Eyes. "What exactly did you mean," I asked, "when you said that *Romeo* knows where the grave is?"

"Does he?" Maestro Lippi now looked perplexed. "I am not sure. But I think you should ask him. He knows more about all this than I do. He is young. I forget things now."

I tried to smile. "You speak as if he is still alive."

The Maestro shrugged. "He comes and goes. It is always late at night . . . he comes here and sits down to look at her." He nodded in the direction of the storage room with the painting of Giulietta. "I think he is still in love with her. That is why I leave the door open."

"Seriously," I said, taking his hand, "Romeo doesn't exist. Not anymore. Right?"

The Maestro glared at me, almost offended. "*You* exist! Why wouldn't *he* exist?" He frowned. "What? You think he is a ghost, too? Huh. Of course, you never know, but I don't think so. I think he is real." He paused briefly to weigh the pros and cons, then said, firmly, "He drinks wine. Ghosts don't drink wine. It takes practice, and they don't like to practice.

They are very boring company. I prefer people like you. You are funny. Here"—he filled up my glass once again—"drink some more."

"So," I said, obediently taking another swig, "if I were going to ask this Romeo some questions . . . how would I do that? Where can I find him?"

"Well," said the Maestro, pondering the question, "I am afraid you will have to wait until he finds you." Seeing my disappointment, he leaned across the table to study my face very intently. "But then," he added, "I think maybe he has already found you. Yes. I think he has. I can see it in your eyes."

With love's light wings did I o'erperch these walls,
For stony limits cannot hold love out

...

Siena, A.D. 1340

ROMEO RAN THE WHETSTONE over the blade with long, careful movements. It had been a while since he had had occasion to use his sword, and there were specks of rust that needed to be ground off before he oiled it. Normally, he preferred to use his dagger for these kinds of jobs, but the dagger was lost in the back of a highway bandit, and in a moment of uncharacteristic distraction he had forgotten to recover it after its use. Besides, Salimbeni was hardly someone you stabbed in the back like a common criminal; no, there would have to be a duel.

It was a new thing for Romeo to question his own involvement with a woman. But then, no woman had ever asked him to commit murder before. He was reminded of his conversation with Maestro Ambrogio on that fateful night two weeks ago, when he had told the painter that he had a fine nose for women who asked nothing more than he was prepared to give, and that he—unlike his friends—was not someone to whine and slink away like a dog at a woman's first request. Did that still hold true? Was he really prepared to approach Salimbeni sword in hand, and very possibly meet his death before he ever collected his reward, or even just looked into Giulietta's heavenly eyes again?

Sighing deeply, he turned over the sword and commenced his work on the other side. His cousins were undoubtedly wondering where he was, and why he did not come out to play, and his father, Comandante Marescotti, had checked on him at least twice, not with questions, but with invitations for target practice. By now, another sleepless night had come and gone, and the sympathetic moon had once more been chased away by a merciless sun. And Romeo, sitting at the table still, wondered yet again if this was to be the day.

Just then, he heard noise on the staircase outside his room, followed by a nervous knock on the door.

"No, thank you!" he growled, as he had done many times already. "I am not hungry!"

"Messer Romeo? You have visitors!"

Now at last, Romeo stood up, his muscles aching from hours without movement or sleep. "Who is it?"

There was a brief mumble on the other side of the door. "A Friar Lorenzo and a Friar Bernardo. They say they have important news, and request a private audience."

The mention of Friar Lorenzo—Giulietta's travel companion, unless he was much mistaken—prompted Romeo to unlock his door. Outside in the gallery stood a servant and two monks in hooded cowls, and behind them, in the courtyard below, several other servants were stretching to see who it might be that had at last prevailed upon the young master to open his door.

"Come quickly!" He ushered both monks inside. "And Stefano"—he fixed an unforgiving stare on the servant—"do not speak of this to my father."

The two monks entered the room with some reserve. Rays of morning sun came in through the open balcony door to fall upon Romeo's untouched bed, and a plate of fried fish sat uneaten on the table, next to the sword.

"Pardon us," said Friar Lorenzo, glancing at the door to make sure it was closed, "for intruding at this hour. But we could not wait—"

He got no further before his companion stepped forward, pulling back the hood of the cowl and revealing a most intricate hairdo. It was no fellow monk who had accompanied Friar Lorenzo to Palazzo Marescotti this morning, but Giulietta herself, despite the disguise lovelier than ever, her cheeks glowing with excitement.

"Please tell me," she said, "that you have not yet . . . done the deed?"

Although thrilled and amazed to see her, Romeo now looked away, embarrassed. "I have not."

"Oh, praised be Heaven!" She folded her hands in relief. "For I have come to apologize, and to beg you forget I ever asked you to do such a horrendous thing."

Romeo started, feeling a twitch of hope. "You no longer want him dead?"

Giulietta frowned. "I want him dead with every beat of my heart. But not at your expense. I was very wrong and very selfish when I took you hostage in my own grief. Can you forgive me?" She looked deeply into his eyes, and when he did not reply right away, her lip trembled slightly. "Forgive me. I beg you."

Now, for the first time in days, Romeo smiled. "No."

"No?" Her blue eyes darkened, threatening a storm, and she took a step backwards. "That is most unkind!"

"No," Romeo went on, teasingly, "I will not forgive you, because you promised me a great reward, and now you are breaking your word."

Giulietta gasped. "I am not! I am saving your life!"

"Oh! And you insult me, too!" Romeo pressed a fist against his heart. "To suggest that I would not survive this duel—woman! You toy with my honor like a cat with a mouse! Bite again and see it limping for cover!"

"Oh, you!" Giulietta's eyes narrowed with suspicion. "You are the one playing with *me*! I did not say you would die by Salimbeni's hand, as you well know, but I do believe they would never let you get away with the murder. And that"—she looked away, still upset with him—"I suppose, would be a shame."

Romeo watched her dismissive profile with great interest. When he saw that she was determined to be stubborn, he turned to Friar Lorenzo. "May I ask that you leave us alone for a moment?"

Friar Lorenzo clearly did not approve of the request, but since Giulietta did not protest, he could hardly refuse. And so he nodded and withdrew to the balcony, his back dutifully turned.

"Now why," said Romeo in a voice so low that only Giulietta could make out the words, "would it be such a shame if I died?"

She took a deep but angry breath. "You saved my life."

"And all I asked in return was to be your knight."

"What good is a knight without a head?"

Romeo smiled and stepped closer. "I assure you, as long you are near me there is no ground for such fears."

"And do I have your word?" Giulietta looked straight into his eyes. "Promise that you will not attempt to engage Salimbeni?"

"It seems," observed Romeo, very much enjoying the exchange, "you are now asking me a second favor . . . and this one far more demanding than the first. But I shall be generous and tell you that my price is still the same."

Her jaw dropped. "Your price?"

"Or my reward, or whatever you choose to call it. It is unchanged."

"You scoundrel!" hissed Giulietta, struggling to quell a smile. "I come here to free you from a lethal vow, and yet you are determined to steal my virtue?"

Romeo grinned. "Surely, a kiss would not tax your virtue."

She squared her shoulders against his charms. "It depends on who kisses me. I highly suspect a kiss from you would instantly void sixteen years of savings."

"What good are savings if you never spend them?"

Just as Romeo was sure he had her ensnared, a loud cough from the balcony made Giulietta jump away. "Patience, Lorenzo!" she said, sternly. "We will be on our way soon enough."

"Your aunt will surely begin to wonder," observed the monk, "what manner of confession is taking so long."

"Just one moment!" Giulietta turned again to Romeo, her eyes full of disappointment. "I have to go."

"Confess to me," whispered Romeo, taking her hands, "and I will give you a blessing that will never wear off."

"The rim of your cup," replied Giulietta, allowing him to draw her back in, "is smeared with honey. I wonder what dreadful poison it contains?"

"If it is poison, it will kill us both."

"Oh dear . . . you must truly like me if you would rather be dead with me than alive with any other woman."

"I believe I do." He closed his arms around her. "Kiss me or I will most certainly die."

"Die yet again? For a man twice doomed you are very much alive!"

There was another noise from the balcony, but this time Giulietta stayed where she was. "Patience, Lorenzo! I beg you!"

"Perhaps my poison," said Romeo, turning her head towards him and not letting go, "has lost its power."

"I really must—"

As a bird swoops down on its prey and assumes this land-bound wretch into heaven, so did Romeo steal her lips before they fled him again. Suspended somewhere between cherubs and devils his quarry ceased to buck, and he spread his wings wide and let the rising wind carry them off across the sky, until even the predator himself had lost every hope of returning home.

Within that one embrace, Romeo became aware of a feeling of certainty he had not thought possible for anyone, even the virtuous. Whatever his erstwhile intentions after learning that the girl in the coffin was alive—obscure even then to himself—he now knew that the words he had spoken to Maestro Ambrogio had been prophetic; with Giulietta in his arms, all other women—past, present, and future—simply ceased to exist.

WHEN GIULIETTA RETURNED to Palazzo Tolomei later that morning, she was received with a very unpleasant barrage of questions and accusations, peppered with comments about her country manners. "Perhaps it is custom among peasants," her aunt had sneered, pulling her niece along by the arm, "but here in town, unmarried women of good breeding do not flit off to confession and return several hours later, their eyes glowing and"—Monna Antonia had glared at Giulietta to detect other signs of mischief—"their hair in disarray! From now on there will be no more such outings, and if you really must converse with your precious Friar Lorenzo, you will please do so under this roof. Hanging about outside, at the mercy of every gossip and rapist in town," she had concluded, pulling her niece up the stairs and shoving her back into her bedchamber, "is no longer permissible!"

"Oh, Lorenzo!" cried Giulietta, when the monk finally came to visit her in her gilded prison, "I am not allowed to go out! I believe I am going distracted! Oh!" She walked up and down the floor of her chamber, pulling her hair. "What must he think of me? I said we would meet—I promised!"

"Hush, my dear," said Friar Lorenzo, trying to sit her down on a chair, "and calm yourself. The gentleman of whom you speak is aware of your distress, and if anything, it has only deepened his affection. He bade me tell you—"

"You spoke with him?" Giulietta grabbed the monk by the shoulders. "Oh, blessed, blessed Lorenzo! What did he say? Tell me, quickly!"

"He said"—the monk reached underneath his cowl and withdrew a roll of parchment sealed with wax—"to give you this letter. Here, take it. It is for you."

Giulietta took the letter reverently, and held it for a moment before breaking the eagle seal. Her eyes wide, she unrolled the missive and looked at the dense pattern of brown ink. "It is beautiful! I never saw anything this elegant in my life." Turning her back to Friar Lorenzo, she stood for a moment, engrossed in her treasure. "He is a poet! How beautifully he writes! Such art, such . . . perfection. He must have labored all night."

"I believe he labored for several nights," said Friar Lorenzo, a drop of cynicism in his voice. "This letter, I assure you, is the work of much parchment and many quills."

"But I do not understand this part—" Giulietta spun around to show him a passage in the letter. "Why would he say that my eyes do not belong in my head, but in the night sky? I suppose it could be construed as a compliment, but surely it would suffice to say that my eyes have a celestial hue. I cannot follow this argument."

"It is not an argument," Friar Lorenzo pointed out, taking the letter, "it is poetry and thus irrational. Its purpose is not to persuade, but to please. I assume you are pleased?"

She gasped. "But of course!"

"Then the letter," said the monk primly, "has served its purpose. And now I propose we forget all about it."

"Wait!" Giulietta snapped the document out of his hands before he could do violence to it. "I must write a reply."

"That," the monk pointed out, "is somewhat complicated by the fact that you have neither quill nor ink nor parchment. Is it not?"

"Yes," said Giulietta, not the least bit discouraged, "but you will get all that for me. Secretly. I meant to ask you anyway, so I may at last write to my poor sister—" She looked eagerly at Friar Lorenzo, expecting him to be standing at attention, eager to fulfill her order. When instead she saw his frown of dissent, she threw up her hands. "What is wrong now?"

"I do not support this endeavor," he grumbled, shaking his head. "An unmarried lady ought not reply to a clandestine letter. Especially . . ."

"But a married one may?"

". . . *especially* considering the sender. As an old and trusted friend I must warn you against the likes of Romeo Marescotti, and—wait!" Friar Lorenzo held up a hand to prevent Giulietta from interrupting him. "Yes, I agree. He has a certain charming way about him, but in God's eyes, I am sure, he is hideous."

Giulietta sighed. "He is not hideous. You are just jealous."

"Jealous?" The monk snorted. "I care nothing for looks, for they are merely of the flesh and live only between the womb and the tomb. What I meant was, his *soul* is hideous."

"How can you speak so," retorted Giulietta, "about the man who saved our lives! A man you had never met before that very moment. A man about whom you know nothing."

Friar Lorenzo held up a warning finger. "I know enough to prophesy his doom. There are some plants and creatures in this world that serve no purpose but to inflict pain and misery on everything with which they come into contact. Look at you! Already you are suffering from this connection."

"Surely"—Giulietta paused to steady her voice—"surely his kind actions towards us have erased whatever vice he may previously have possessed?" Seeing that the monk was still hostile, she very calmly added, "Surely, Heaven would not have chosen Romeo as the instrument of our deliverance had not God himself desired his redemption."

Friar Lorenzo held up a warning finger. "God is a divine being, and as such does not have desires."

"No, but I do. I desire to be happy." Giulietta pressed the letter against her heart. "I know what you are thinking. You wish to protect me, as an old and trusted friend. And you think Romeo will cause me pain. Great love, you believe, carries the seeds of great sorrow. Well, perhaps you are right. Perhaps the wise spurn one to remain safe from the other, but I should rather choose to have my eyes burnt in their sockets than to have been born without."

...

MANY WEEKS AND many letters were to pass before Giulietta and Romeo met again. In the meantime, the tone of their correspondence rose in a fervent crescendo, culminating—despite Friar Lorenzo's best efforts at calming the sentiments—in a mutual declaration of eternal love.

The only other person who was privy to Giulietta's emotions was her twin sister Giannozza—the only sibling Giulietta had left in the world after the Salimbeni raid on her home. Giannozza had been married the year before, and had moved away to her husband's estate in the south, but the two girls had always been close and had remained in frequent contact through letters. Reading and writing were unusual skills for young women to have, but their father had been an unusual man, who hated bookkeeping, and who was happy to leave such indoor tasks to his wife and daughters, seeing that they had little else to do.

However constant their writing to each other, the delivery of Giannozza's letters was infrequent at best, and Giulietta suspected that her own letters going the other way were just as late in arriving—if they ever made it at all. In fact, after her arrival in Siena she had not received a single missive from Giannozza, even though she had sent several reports about the horrendous raid on their home and her own unhappy refuge—and lately imprisonment—in their uncle's house, Palazzo Tolomei.

Although she trusted Friar Lorenzo to get her letters safely and secretly out of the house, Giulietta knew that the monk had no control over their destiny in the hands of strangers. She had no money to pay for a proper delivery, but was dependent on the kindness and diligence of travelers going down her sister's way. And now that she was under house arrest there was always a danger that someone would stop Friar Lorenzo on his way in or out and demand that he empty his pockets.

Aware of the danger, she began to hide her letters to Giannozza under a floorboard rather than sending them right away. It was enough that she was asking Friar Lorenzo to deliver her love letters to Romeo; for him to carry many more reports of her shameless activities would be cruel. And so they all ended up under the floor—the fanciful tales of her amorous encounters with Romeo—awaiting the day when she could pay a messenger to deliver them all at once. Or the day when she would throw them all on the fire.

As for her letters to Romeo, she received smoldering responses to every single one. When she spoke in hundreds, he replied in thousands, and when she said that she liked, he said that he loved. She was bold and called him fire, but he was bolder and called her sun; she dared to think of them together on a dancing floor, but he could think of nothing but to be with her alone ...

Once declared, this ardent love knew only two paths; one led towards fulfillment, the other towards disappointment. Stasis was impossible. And so one Sunday morning, when Giulietta and her cousins were allowed to go to confession in San Cristoforo before mass, she entered the confessional only to discover that there was no priest on the other side of the partition.

"Forgive me, Father, for I have sinned," she began, dutifully, expecting the priest to encourage elaboration.

Instead, a strange voice whispered, "How can love be a sin? If God did not want us to love, then why did he create such beauty as yours?"

Giulietta gasped in surprise and fear. "Romeo?" She knelt down in an attempt at verifying her suspicion through the metal filigree and, indeed, on the other side of the grate she saw the outline of a smile that was anything but priestly. "How dare you come here? My aunt is but ten feet away!"

"There lies more peril in your sweet voice," complained Romeo, "than in twenty such aunts. I beg you, speak again and make my ruin complete." He pressed his hand against the grate, willing Giulietta to do the same. She did, and although their hands did not touch, she could feel his heat against her palm.

"How I wish we were lowly peasants," she whispered, "free to meet whenever we chose."

"And what would we do, we lowly peasants," inquired Romeo, "when we met?"

Giulietta was thankful that he could not see her blushing. "There would be no grate between us."

"That, I suppose," said Romeo, "would be some small improvement."

"You," Giulietta went on, sneaking a fingertip through the filigree, "would undoubtedly speak in rhyming couplets as men do when they seduce reluctant maids. The more reluctant the maid, the finer the poetry."

Romeo swallowed his laughter as best he could. "Firstly, I never heard a lowly peasant utter anything in verse. Secondly, I wonder exactly how fine my poetry would have to be. Not so very much, I think, considering the maid."

She gasped. "You rascal! I shall have to prove you wrong by being very prudish and refusing your kisses."

"Easily said with a wall between us," he smirked.

They stood in silence for a moment, trying to feel each other through the wooden boards.

"Oh, Romeo," sighed Giulietta, suddenly sad, "is this what our love must be? A secret in a dark room, while the world bustles on outside?"

"Not for long, if I can help it." Romeo closed his eyes, pretending the wall was Giulietta's forehead against his own. "I wanted to see you today to tell you that I am going to ask my father to approve of our marriage and approach your uncle as soon as possible with a proposal."

"You wish to . . . marry me?" She was not sure she had understood him properly. He had not posed it as a question, rather as a fact. But perhaps that was the Siena way.

"Nothing else will do," he groaned. "I must have you, completely, at my table and in my bed, or I shall waste away like a starving prisoner. There you have it; forgive the lack of poesy."

When, for a moment, there was nothing but silence on the other side of the wall, Romeo began to fear that he had offended her. He was already cursing his own frankness when Giulietta spoke again, chasing away those small, fluttering fears with the scent of a greater beast. "If it is a wife you seek, it is Tolomei you need to woo."

"As much as I respect your uncle," observed Romeo, "I had hoped to carry you, not him, to my chamber."

Now finally, she giggled, but it was not a lasting pleasure. "He is a man of great ambition. Make sure your father brings a long pedigree when he comes."

Romeo gasped at the perceived insult. "My family wore plumed helmets and served the Caesars, when your uncle Tolomei wore bearskin and served barley mash to his pigs!" Realizing that he was being childish, Romeo went on, more calmly, "Tolomei will not refuse my father. Between our households there has always been peace."

"Would that it was a steady stream of blood!" sighed Giulietta. "Do you not see? If our houses are already at peace, then what is to be gained by our union?"

He refused to understand her. "All fathers wish their children well."

"And so they feed us bitter medicine and make us cry."

"I am eighteen. My father treats me like an equal."

"An old man, then. Why not married? Or have you already buried your childhood bride?"

"My father does not believe in unweaned mothers."

Her shy smile, barely visible through the filigree, was gratifying after so much torment. "But does he believe in old maids?"

"You cannot be sixteen."

"Just. But who counts the petals of a wilting rose?"

"When we are married," whispered Romeo, kissing her fingertips as best he could, "I shall water you and lay you on my bed and count them all."

She attempted a frown. "What of the thorns? Perhaps I shall prick you and ruin your bliss."

"Trust me, the pleasure will far outstrip the pain."

And so they went on, worrying and teasing, until someone tapped impatiently on the wall of the confessional. "Giulietta!" hissed Monna Antonia, making her niece jump in fear. "You cannot have much left to confess. Hurry up, for we are leaving!"

As they made their brief but poetic farewells, Romeo repeated his plan to marry her, but Giulietta dared not believe him. Having seen her sister Giannozza married off to a man who should have been acquiring a coffin for himself rather than a wife, Giulietta knew very well that marriage was not something for young lovers to plan on their own; marriage was first and foremost a matter of politics and inheritance, and had nothing to do with the wishes of the bride and groom, but everything to do with the ambitions of their parents. Love—according to Giannozza, whose first few letters as a married woman had made Giulietta cry—always came later, and with someone else.

IT WAS RARE FOR Comandante Marescotti to be pleased with his first-born. Most of the time, he had to remind himself that—as was the case with most fevers—there existed no remedy for youth but time. Either the subject died, or its affliction eventually wore itself out, leaving no virtue for the wise to cling to but patience. Alas, Comandante Marescotti was not affluent in that particular currency, and his paternal heart, as a result, had grown into a many-headed beast guarding a cavernous store of furies and fears, always alert, but mostly unsuccessful.

Now was no exception.

"Romeo!" he said, lowering his crossbow after the most atrocious marksmanship yet that morning, "I will lay ear to no more. I am Marescotti. For many years, Siena was run from this very house. Wars were planned in this very atrium. The victory at Montaperti was pronounced from this very tower! These walls speak for themselves!"

Comandante Marescotti, standing as tall in his own courtyard as he would in front of his army, glared at the new fresco and its busy, humming creator, Maestro Ambrogio, still unable to fully appreciate the genius of either. Certainly, the colorful battle scene added a little warmth to the monastic space, and the Marescotti family was handsomely poised and appeared convincingly virtuous. But why did it have to take so bloody long to finish it?

"But Father!"

"No more!" This time, Comandante Marescotti raised his voice. "I will not be associated with that kind of people! Can you not appreciate the fact that we have lived in peace these many years, while all those greedy newcomers, the Tolomeis, the Salimbenis, and the Malavoltis have been slaughtering each other in the streets? Do you want their evil blood to spread to our house? Do you want your brothers and cousins murdered in their cribs?"

From across the courtyard, Maestro Ambrogio could not help but look at the Comandante, who so rarely expressed any emotion. Still taller than his son—but mainly because of his posture—Romeo's father was one of the most admirable men the Maestro had ever portrayed. Neither his face nor his figure showed any signs of excess; here was a man who only ate as much as his body needed for healthy upkeep, and who only slept for as long as it needed rest. In contrast, his son Romeo ate and drank whatever he felt like, and happily turned night into day with his escapades and day into night with untimely sleep.

Even so, they were so very like each other to look at—both strong and unbending—and despite Romeo's habit of breaking the house rules, it was a rare sight to have the two of them locked in a verbal duel like this, on tiptoes to make their points.

"But Father!" said Romeo again, and once more, he was ignored.

"And for what? For some woman!" Comandante Marescotti would have rolled his eyes, but he needed them to take aim. This time, the arrow went straight to the heart of the straw puppet. "Some woman, some random woman, when there is a whole city of women out there. As if you did not know!"

"She is no random woman," said Romeo, calmly contradicting his sire. "She is mine."

There was a moment's silence, during which another two arrows hit the target in rapid succession, making the straw puppet dance merrily on its rope like a man at his own hanging. Eventually, Comandante Marescotti drew a deep breath and spoke again, his voice calmer now, the unswerving vessel of reason. "Perhaps, but your lady is the niece of a fool."

"A powerful fool."

"If men are not born fools, politics and flattery certainly help them along."

"I hear he is very generous to family."

"Is there any left?"

Romeo laughed, well aware that his father had never sought to amuse. "Some, surely," he said, "now that the peace has been kept for two years."

"Peace, you call it?" Comandante Marescotti had seen it all before, and vain promises fatigued him even more than blatant falsehoods. "When the ilk of Salimbeni goes back to raiding Tolomei castles and robbing clergy on the high road, mark my words, even this peace is drawing to an end."

"Then why not secure an alliance now," insisted Romeo, "with Tolomei?"

"And make an enemy of Salimbeni?" Comandante Marescotti looked at his son with narrowed eyes. "If you had taken in as much intelligence around town as you have wine and women, my son, you would know that Salimbeni has been mobilizing. His aim is not only to step on the neck of Tolomei and rule all banking out of town, but to lay siege to this very city from his strongholds in the country and, if I am not mistaken, seize the reins of our republic." The Comandante frowned and began pacing up and down. "I know this man, Romeo, I have looked into his eyes, and I have chosen to bar my ears and my door to his ambition. I know not who is worse off, his friends or his foes, and so Marescotti has sworn to be neither. One day, maybe soon, Salimbeni will make a mad push to overthrow the law, and our gutters will run with blood. Foreign soldiers will be brought in, and men will sit in their towers waiting for that knock on the door, regretting the alliances they have made. I will not be one of them."

"Who says all this misery cannot be prevented?" urged Romeo. "If we were to join forces with Tolomei, other noble houses would follow the Eagle banner, and Salimbeni would soon lose ground. We could hunt down the brigands together and make the roads safe again, and with his money and your dignity, great projects could be undertaken. The new tower in the Campo could be finished within months. The new cathedral could be built within years. And the providence of Marescotti would be in everyone's prayers."

"A man should stay out of prayers," said Comandante Marescotti, and stopped to cock his crossbow, "until he is dead." The shot went right through the head of the puppet and landed in a pot of rosemary. "Then he may do whatever he wants. The living, my son, should make sure to pursue true glory, not flattery. True glory is between you and God. Flattery is the food of the soulless. Privately, you may rejoice in the fact that you saved that girl's life, but do not seek acknowledgment or rewards from other men. Vainglory is unbecoming to a nobleman."

"I do not want a reward," Romeo said, his manly face giving in to the stubborn squint of boyhood, "I just want *her*. It moves me little what people know or think. If you do not bless my intention to marry her—"

Comandante Marescotti held up a gloved hand to prevent his son from speaking words that, once heard, could never be unsaid. "Do not threaten me with measures that would hurt you more than me. And let me not see you like this, acting beneath your age, or I shall withdraw my permission for you to ride in the Palio. Even the games of men—nay, especially the games—require the decorum of men. So, too, with marriage. I have never betrothed you to anyone . . ."

"And for that alone I love my father!"

". . . because I traced the outline of your character from the earliest age. Had I been an evil man, with some enemy due for punishment, I might have considered stealing away his only daughter and letting you make worms' meat out of her heart. But I am not such a man. I have waited with great perseverance for you to shed your inconstant self and be satisfied with one pursuit at a time."

Romeo looked crestfallen. But the potion of love was still tingling sweet upon his tongue, and a smile could not be restrained long. His joy broke away like a colt from its handlers, and galloped across his face on unfamiliar legs. "But Father, I have!" was his giddy reply. "Constancy is my true nature! I shall never look at another woman for the rest of my days, or rather, I shall look, but they shall be to me like chairs, or tables. Not that I intend to sit, of course, or eat off them, but in the sense that they are but furniture. Or perhaps I should say that they are to her what the moon is to the sun—"

"Do not compare her with the sun," warned Comandante Marescotti, and walked over to the straw puppet to retrieve his arrows. "You always preferred the company of the moon."

"Because I was living in eternal night! Surely, the moon must be the sovereign of a wretch who has never beheld the sun. But morning has broken, Father, draped in the golds and reds of marriage, and it is the dawn of my soul!"

"But the sun retires," reasoned Comandante Marescotti, "every night."

"And I shall retire, too!" Romeo clenched a fistful of arrows against his heart. "And leave the dark to owls and nightingales. I shall embrace the bright hours with industry, and prey no more on wholesome sleep."

"Make no promises about the dark hours," said Comandante Marescotti, placing a hand on his son's shoulder at last. "If your wife is but half the creature you have laid her out to be, there will be much preying, and little sleep."

And if we meet we shall not 'scape a brawl,
For now these hot days is the mad blood stirring

. . .

I WAS BACK IN MY CASTLE of whispering ghosts. As always, the dream had me walking through room after room, looking everywhere for the people I knew were there, trapped just like me. What was new was that this time, the gilded doors opened before me, even before I had touched them. It was as if the air was full of invisible hands, showing me the way and pulling me along. And so I walked on and on, through vast galleries and deserted ballrooms, forging into hitherto undiscovered parts of the castle, until at last I came to a large, fortified door. Could this be the way out?

I looked at the heavy iron mounting on the door and reached out to try the bolt. But before I had touched it, the door unlocked by itself and swung open, revealing an enormous, black void.

Stopping on the threshold, I squinted and tried to see something—anything—that might indicate whether I had, in fact, reached the world outside, or merely another room.

As I stood there, blind and blinking, an icy wind came at me from the darkness ahead, coiling around me and tugging at my arms and legs, upsetting my balance. When I grabbed the door frame for support, the wind grew in strength and started tearing at my hair and clothes, howling furiously as it worked to pull me over the edge. Its powers were so great that the door frame began to come apart, and the floor crumbled beneath me. Scrambling for safety I let go of the door frame and tried to run back to where I had come from, back into the interior of the castle, but an endless stream of invisible demons—hissing and sneering the Shakespeare quotations I knew so well—were swarming around me on all sides, eager to escape the castle at last and pull me along in their wake.

And so I fell down on the floor and started sliding backwards, desperately scratching for something solid to hold. Just as I was going over the edge, someone dressed in a black motorcycle suit came hurtling towards me to grab my arms and pull me up. "Romeo!" I yelled, reaching out for him, but when I looked up I saw that there was no face behind the visor of the helmet, just emptiness.

After that, I fell down, down, down . . . until I plunged into water. And I was once again back at the marina in Alexandria, Virginia, ten years old, drowning in a soup of seaweed and trash while Janice and her friends were standing on the pier, eating ice cream and crying with laughter.

Just as I came up for air, trying furiously to reach a mooring line, I woke up with a gasp to find myself lying on Maestro Lippi's couch, a prickly blanket kicked into a knot around my legs, and Dante licking my hand.

"Good morning," said the Maestro, placing a mug of coffee in front of me. "Dante doesn't like Shakespeare. He is a very clever dog."

WHEN I WALKED BACK to the hotel later that morning, a bright sun leading my way, the events of the night before seemed oddly unreal, as if it had all been a gigantic theater performance staged for someone else's pleasure. My dinner with the Salimbenis, my flight through the dark streets, and my bizarre refuge in Maestro Lippi's workshop . . . it was all the stuff that nightmares are made of, and the only proof that it had really happened seemed to be the dirt and scrapes on the soles of my feet.

But the bottom line was that it *had* happened, and the sooner I stopped lulling myself into a false sense of safety, the better. It was the second time I had been followed, and this time it was not just by some random thug in a tracksuit, but by a man on a motorcycle as well, whatever his motive. On top of that, there was the growing problem of Alessandro, who clearly knew all about my criminal record, and who would not hesitate to use it against me if I came anywhere near his precious godmother again.

These were all excellent reasons for getting the hell out of Dodge, but

Julie Jacobs was not a quitter, nor—I could feel—was Giulietta Tolomei. There was, after all, a pretty substantial treasure at stake, assuming Maestro Lippi's stories were true and I was ever able to find Juliet's grave and get my hands on the statue with the sapphire eyes.

Or perhaps the statue was simply a legend. Perhaps in reality, it was the discovery that some wackos believed I was related to a Shakespearean heroine that was supposed to be the great reward awaiting me at the end of all my hardship. Aunt Rose had always complained that, even if I could memorize a play backwards and forwards, I did not truly *care* about literature, or about love, and she had maintained that one day I would see the big fat spotlight of truth shine upon the error of my ways.

One of my first memories of Aunt Rose had her seated at the big mahogany desk late at night, a single lamp burning, studying something through a magnifying glass. I still remember the feeling of the teddy-bear paw clutched in my hand, and the fear of being sent back to bed. She did not see me at first, but when she did, she started, as if I were some small ghost come to haunt her. The next thing I remember is being in her lap, looking out over a vast spread of paper.

"Look in here," she had said, holding the magnifying glass for me. "This is our family tree, and here is your mother."

I remember a rush of excitement followed by sour disappointment. It was not a picture of my mother at all, but a line of letters I had not yet learned to read. "What does it say?" I must have asked, for I remembered Aunt Rose's answer only too well.

"It says," she had said with an uncommon degree of theatrics, "dear Aunt Rose, please take good care of my little girl. She is very special. I miss her very much." That was when, to my horror, I realized that she was crying. It was the first time I had seen an adult cry. Until then, it had never occurred to me that they could.

As Janice and I grew older, Aunt Rose would tell us the odd little thing about our mother, but never the grand picture. Once, after starting college and growing a bit of backbone, we had taken her out of the house on a particularly lovely day, and had sat her down on a chair in the garden— coffee and muffins within reach—before deliberately asking her to tell us the whole story. It was a rare moment of synergy between my sister and me. Together, we flooded her with questions: Apart from the fact that they had died in a car accident, what had our parents been like? And why didn't we have any contact with people in Italy, when our passports said we were born there?

Aunt Rose had sat very quietly, listening to our rant without even touching the muffins, and when it was over, she had nodded. "You have a right to ask these questions, and one day, you will get your answers. But for now, you must be patient. It is for your own good that I have told you very little about your family."

I never understood why it could be bad to know everything about one's own family. Or at least just something. But I had respected Aunt Rose's discomfort with the issue and postponed the inevitable conflict until later. One day I would sit her down and demand an explanation. One day she would tell me everything. Even when she turned eighty I kept assuming there would still come a day where she would answer all our questions. But now, of course, she never could.

DIRETTOR ROSSINI WAS on the phone in the back room when I entered the hotel, and I stopped for a moment, waiting for him to come out. Walking back from Maestro Lippi's workshop, I had been mulling over the artist's comments about his late-night visitor called Romeo, and had concluded it was high time I started looking into the Marescotti family and their possible, present-day descendants.

The first logical step, I figured, would be to ask Direttor Rossini for a local phone book, and I intended to do so right away. But after waiting for at least ten minutes, I eventually gave up and stretched across the counter to grab my room key from the wall.

Frustrated with myself for not having interrogated Maestro Lippi about the Marescottis while I had the chance, I walked slowly up the stairs, the cuts on the soles of my feet stinging with every step I took. It didn't help that I wasn't in the habit of wearing high-heeled shoes, especially considering the miles I had been logging over the last two days. As soon as I opened the door to my room, however, all my little aches were forgotten. For the place had been turned upside down, possibly even inside out.

Some very determined invader—if not a whole group—had literally pulled the doors off the wardrobe and the stuffing out of the pillows to find whatever they were looking for, and clothes, trinkets, and bathroom items were scattered everywhere; some of my new underwear was even hanging limply from the chandelier.

I had never actually seen a suitcase bomb go off, but this, I was sure, was what the site would look like afterwards.

"Miss Tolomei!" Panting heavily, Direttor Rossini finally caught up with me. "Contessa Salimbeni called to ask if you were feeling better, but—Santa Caterina!" As soon as he saw the devastation in my room, he forgot everything he had been meaning to say, and for a moment we both stood there, staring at it all in silent horror.

"Well," I said, aware that I had an audience, "at least now I don't have to unpack my suitcases."

"This is terrible!" cried Direttor Rossini, less prepared to look at the upside. "Look at this! Now people will say the hotel is not safe! Oh, careful, don't step in the glass."

The floor was covered in glass from the balcony door. The intruder had clearly come for my mother's box, which was—of course—gone, but the question was why he had proceeded to trash my room. Was there something other than the box that he had been after?

"Cavolo!" sighed Direttor Rossini. "Now I have to call the police, and they will come and take pictures, and the newspapers will write that Hotel Chiusarelli is not safe!"

"Wait!" I said. "Don't call the police. There's no need. We know what they came for." I walked over to the desk where the box had stood. "They won't be back. Bastards."

"Oh!" Direttor Rossini suddenly lit up. "I forgot to tell you! Yesterday, I personally brought up your suitcases . . ."

"Yes, I see that."

". . . and I noticed that you had a very expensive antiquity on that table. So, I made myself the liberty of removing it from this room and putting it in the hotel safe. I hope you do not mind? Normally, I do not interfere—"

I was so relieved, I didn't even think to bristle at his interference, or to marvel at his foresight. Instead, I grabbed his shoulders. "The box is still here?"

Sure enough, when I followed Direttor Rossini downstairs to his office, I found my mother's box sitting very snugly in the hotel safe amongst accounting books and silver candelabra. "Bless you!" I said, meaning it, "this box is very special."

"I know." He nodded gravely. "My grandmother had one just like it. They don't make them anymore. It is an old Sienese tradition. We call it the box of secrets, because they have hidden rooms. You can hide things from your parents. Or from your children. Or from anybody."

"You mean . . . it has a secret compartment?"

"Yes!" Direttor Rossini took the box and began inspecting it. "I will show you. You have to be a Sienese to know how to find them; it is very sneaky. They are never in the same place. My grandmother's was on the side, right here . . . but this is different. This is tricky. Let me see . . . not here . . . not here—" He inspected the box from all angles, enjoying the challenge. "She had a lock of hair, nothing else. I found it one day when she was sleeping. I never asked—*aha!*"

Somehow, Direttor Rossini had managed to locate and trigger the release mechanism to the secret compartment. He smiled in triumph as a quarter of the bottom fell out on the table, followed by a small, rectangular piece of card stock. Turning the box over, we both examined the secret compartment, but it had contained nothing except the card.

"Do you understand this?" I showed Direttor Rossini the letters and numbers that were typed on the card with an old-fashioned typewriter. "It looks like some kind of code."

"This," he said, taking it from me, "is an old—how do you say it?— index card. We used these before we had computers. It was before your time. Ah, the world has changed! I remember when—"

"Do you have any idea where it came from?"

"This? Maybe a library? I don't know. I am not an expert. But"—he glanced at me to gauge whether I was worthy of this level of clearance— "I know someone who is."

IT TOOK ME A while to find the tiny secondhand bookstore that Direttor Rossini had described, and once I did, it was—of course—closed for lunch. I tried to look through the windows to see if there was anyone inside, but saw nothing but books and more books.

Walking around the corner to Piazza del Duomo, I sat down to pass the time on the front steps of the Siena Cathedral. Despite the tourists milling in and out of the church doors, there was something tranquil about the whole place, something very grounded and eternal that made me feel that had I not been on a mission, I could have sat there forever, just like the building itself, and watched with a mix of nostalgia and compassion the perennial rebirth of mankind.

The most striking feature of the cathedral was the bell tower. It was not as tall as the Mangia Tower, Direttor Rossini's virile lily in the Campo, but what made it the more remarkable of the two was the fact that it was zebra-striped. Slim, alternating layers of white and black stone continued all the way to the very top, like a biscuit staircase to Heaven, and I could not help but wonder about the symbolism of the pattern. Perhaps there was none. Perhaps the purpose had simply been to make it striking. Or perhaps it was a reflection of the Siena coat of arms, the Balzana—part black, part white, like a stemless wineglass half filled with the most stygian red wine—which I found equally perplexing.

Direttor Rossini had told me some story about Roman twins escaping their evil uncle on a black and a white horse, but I was not convinced this was the underlying narrative of the colors of the Balzana. It had to be something about contrasts. Something about the perilous art of uniting extremes and forcing compromises, or perhaps about acknowledging that life is a delicate balance of great forces, and that good would lose its potency if there was no evil left to fight in the world.

But I was no philosopher, and the sun was beginning to let me know that it was the hour when only mad dogs and Englishmen exposed themselves to its rays. Walking back around the corner I saw that the bookstore was still closed, and I sighed and looked at my watch, wondering where I should seek refuge until it suited Direttor Rossini's mother's childhood friend to return from lunch.

THE AIR IN THE SIENA CATHEDRAL was full of gold and shadows. Around me on all sides, massive black-and-white pillars held up a vast heaven sprinkled with little stars, and the mosaic floor was a giant jigsaw puzzle of symbols and legends that I somehow knew—as one knows the sounds of a foreign language—but did not understand.

The place was as different from the modern churches of my childhood as one religion from another, and yet I felt my heart responding to it with mystified recognition, as if I had been there before, looking for the same God, a long, long time ago. And it suddenly occurred to me that here, for the first time, I was standing in a building that resembled my dream castle of whispering ghosts. Perhaps, I thought, gaping up at the star-spangled dome in this silent forest of silver-birch columns, someone had brought me to this very cathedral when I was a baby, and I had somehow stored it in my memory without knowing what it was.

The only other time I had been in a church of this size was when Umberto had taken me to the Basilica of the National Shrine in Washington, playing hooky after a dentist appointment. I could not have been more than six or seven years old, but I vividly remembered him kneeling down next to me in the middle of the enormous floor and asking me, "Do you hear it?"

"Hear what?" I had asked, the little plastic bag with a new pink toothbrush clutched in my hand.

He had cocked his head playfully. "The angels. If you are very quiet, you can hear them giggle."

"What are they laughing at?" I had wanted to know. "Us?"

"They take flying lessons here. There is no wind, only the breath of God."

"Is that what makes them fly? The breath of God?"

"There is a trick to flying. The angels told me." He had smiled at my wide-eyed awe. "You need to forget everything you know as a human being. When you are human, you discover that there is great power in hating the earth. And it can almost make you fly. But it never will."

I had frowned, not quite understanding him. "So, what's the trick?"

"Love the sky."

While I was standing there, lost in the memory of Umberto's rare, emotional gush, a group of British tourists came up behind me, their guide talking animatedly about the many failed attempts at finding and excavating the old cathedral crypt—allegedly in existence in the Middle Ages, but now apparently lost forever.

I listened for a while, amused by the sensationalist bent of the guide, before leaving the cathedral to the tourists and strolling down Via del Capitano to end up—much to my surprise—back in Piazza Postierla, right across from Malèna's espresso bar.

The little square had been quite busy the other times I had been there, but today it was pleasantly calm, perhaps because it was siesta time and sizzling hot. A pedestal with a wolf and two suckling babes stood opposite a small water fountain with a fierce-looking metal bird hovering above it. Two children, a boy and a girl, were splashing water on each other and running to and fro, shrieking with laughter, while a row of old men sat in the shade not far away, hats on, jackets off, looking with mild eyes on their own immortality.

"Hello again!" said Malèna when she saw me entering the bar. "Luigi did a good job, no?"

"He's a genius." I walked up to her and leaned on the cool countertop, feeling strangely at home. "I'm never going to leave Siena for as long as he is here."

She laughed out loud, a warm, knowing laughter that made me once again wonder about the secret ingredient in these women's lives. Whatever it was, I was clearly missing it. It was so much more than just self-confidence; it seemed to be the ability to love oneself, enthusiastically and unsparingly, body and soul, naturally followed by the assumption that every man on the planet is dying to get in on the act.

"Here"—Malèna placed an espresso in front of me and added a biscotto with a little wink—"eat more. It gives you . . . you know, *character.*"

"Fierce-looking creature," I said, referring to the fountain outside. "What kind of bird is it?"

"It is our eagle, aquila in Italian. The fountain is our . . . oh, what is it?" She bit her lip, searching for the word. "Fonte battesimale . . . our font for baptism? Yes! This is where we bring our babies so they become aquilini, little eagles."

"This is the Eagle contrada?" I glanced around at the other customers, suddenly all goose-bumpy. "Is it true that the eagle symbol originally came from the Marescotti family?"

"Yes," she said, nodding, "but we didn't invent it, of course. The eagle came originally from the Romans, and then Carlomagno took it over, and since the Marescottis were in his army, we had the right to use this imperial symbol. But nobody knows that anymore."

I stared at her, almost certain she had referred to the Marescottis as if she was, in fact, one of them. But just as I opened my mouth to ask the question, the grinning face of a waiter came between us. "Only the people who are lucky enough to work here. We know everything about her big bird."

"Just ignore him," said Malèna, pretending to hit him over the head with a tray. "He is from Contrada della Torre—the Tower, you know." She grimaced. "Always being funny."

Just then, in the middle of the general amusement, something outside caught my eye. It was a black motorcycle and rider, visor closed, pausing briefly to look through the glass door before speeding up with a roar and disappearing.

"Ducati Monster S4," the waiter recited, as if he had memorized the ad from a magazine, "a real street fighter. Liquid-cooled motor. She makes men dream of blood, and they wake up in a sweat and try to catch her. But she has no grab rails. So"—he patted his belly suggestively—"don't invite a girl on board if you don't have a six-pack antilock braking system."

"Basta, basta, Dario!" scolded Malèna. "Tu parli di niente!"

"Do you know that guy?" I asked, trying to sound casual while feeling everything but.

"That guy?" She rolled her eyes, not impressed. "You know what they say . . . those who make a lot of noise, they are missing something down there."

"I don't make a lot of noise!" protested Dario.

"I was not talking about you, stupido! I was talking about the moscerino on the motorcycle."

"Do you know who he is?" I asked again.

She shrugged. "I like men with cars. Men on motorcycles . . . they are playboys. You can put a girlfriend on a motorcycle, yes, but what about your children and your bridesmaids, and your mother-in-law?"

"Exactly my point," said Dario, wiggling his eyebrows. "I am saving up for one."

By now, several other customers were getting audibly impatient in the queue behind me, and although Malèna seemed quite comfortable ignoring them all for as long as she damn well wanted, I decided to postpone my questions about the Marescottis and their possible present-day descendants to some other time.

As I walked away from the bar, I kept looking around for the motorcycle, but it was nowhere to be seen. Of course, I could not be sure, but my intuition told me this was the same guy who had bullied me the night before, and, honestly, if he really was a playboy looking for someone to hug his abs, I could think of better ways to start that conversation.

WHEN THE OWNER of the bookstore finally came back from lunch, I was sitting on her front step, leaning against the door, very close to giving up on the whole thing. But my patience was rewarded, for the woman—a sweet old lady whose spindly frame seemed to be propelled into motion by little more than an enormous curiosity—took one look at the index card and nodded right away.

"Ah, yes," she said in fluent English, not the least bit surprised, "this is from the university archive. The history collection. I think they still use the old catalogue. Let me see now—yes, see, this stands for *Late Middle Ages*. And this means *local*. And look"—she showed me the codes on the card—"this is the letter of the shelf, K, and this is the number of the drawer, 3-17b. But it doesn't say what is in it. Anyway, that is what the code means." Having solved the mystery so quickly, she looked up at me, hoping for another. "How did you get this card?"

"My mother—or rather, my father—I think he was a professor at the university. Professor Tolomei?"

The old woman lit up like a Christmas tree. "I remember him! I was his student! You know, he was the one who organized that whole collection. It was a mess. I spent two summers gluing numbers on drawers. But . . . I wonder why he took out this card. He was always so upset when people left the index cards lying around."

THE UNIVERSITY OF SIENA was scattered all over town, but the history archive was no more than a brisk walk away, out towards the city gate called Porta Tufi. It took me a while to find the right building among the inconspicuous façades lining the road; in the end what gave it away as a place for education was the patchwork of socialist posters on the fence outside.

Hoping very much to blend in with the general student population, I entered through the door that the bookseller had described to me, and headed straight for the basement. Perhaps because it was still siesta—or perhaps because no one was around during the summer—I was able to get downstairs without meeting a single person; the whole place was blissfully cool and quiet. It was almost too easy.

With nothing but the index card to guide me, I walked through the archive several times, trying in vain to find the appropriate shelves. It was a separate collection, the bookseller had explained, and even back then, people had rarely used it. I had to find the remotest part of the archive, but this instruction was complicated by the fact that every part of the archive seemed remote to me. Furthermore, the shelves I was looking at did not have drawers; they were regular shelves with books, not artifacts. And there was no book labeled K 3-17b.

After walking around for at least twenty minutes, it finally occurred to me to try a door at the far end of the room. It was a sealed metal door, almost like the door to a bank vault, but it opened without a problem, revealing yet another—smaller—room with some sort of climate control that made the air smell very different, like chocolate chip mothballs.

Now, finally, my index card made sense. These shelves were indeed full of drawers, exactly the way the bookseller had described. And the collection was organized chronologically, starting in Etruscan times and ending—I guessed—at the year my father died. It was quite obvious that nobody ever used it, for there was a thick layer of dust everywhere, and when I tried to move the rolling ladder it resisted at first, because the metal wheels had rusted to the floor. When it finally moved, squealing in protest, it left behind little brown imprints on the gray linoleum.

I positioned the ladder by the shelf labeled K, and climbed up to take a closer look at row number 3, which consisted of a couple dozen medium-size drawers, all perfectly out of reach and out of mind, unless you had a ladder and knew precisely what you were looking for. At first, it felt as if drawer number 17b was locked, and only after I knocked on it with my fist several times did it come loose and allow me to pull it open. In all likelihood, no one else had opened that drawer since my father closed it decades ago.

Inside, I found a large package wrapped in airtight, brown plastic. Poking gently at it, I could feel that it contained some kind of spongy fabric, almost like a bag of foam from a textile store. Mystified, I took the package out of the drawer, climbed back down the ladder, and sat down on the bottom step to inspect my findings.

Rather than ripping open the whole thing, I stuck a fingernail into the plastic and made a small hole. As soon as the air seal was broken, the bag seemed to take a deep breath, and a corner of faded blue fabric peeked out. Making the hole a little bigger, I felt the fabric with my fingers. I was no expert, but I suspected it was silk and—despite its fine condition— very, very old.

Knowing full well that I was exposing something delicate to air and light at once, I eased the fabric out of the plastic and began unfolding it in my lap. When I did so, an object fell out and hit the linoleum floor with a metallic clang.

It was a large knife in a golden sheath, which had been hidden within the folds of the silk. As I picked it up, I noticed it had an eagle engraved on the hilt.

Sitting there, weighing this unexpected treasure in my hand, I suddenly heard a noise from the other part of the archive. Only too aware that I was trespassing in a facility that undoubtedly held many irreplaceable treasures, I rose with a guilty gasp and bundled up my loot as best I could. The last thing I wanted was to be discovered in the fancy, climate-controlled vault with canary feathers sticking out of my mouth.

As silently as possible, I slipped back into the main library, pulling the metal door almost shut behind me. Crouching behind the last row of bookcases, I listened intently. But the only sound I could hear was my own unsteady breath. All I had to do was to walk over to those stairs and leave the building as casually as I had entered it.

I was wrong. No sooner had I made the decision to move than I heard the sound of footsteps; not the footsteps of a librarian returning from siesta or a student looking for a book, but the ominous footsteps of some-one who did not want me to hear him coming, someone whose errand in the archive was even more dubious than mine. Peeking out through the shelves I saw him coming my way—and yes, it was the same old scum who had followed me the night before—slithering from bookcase to bookcase, his eyes fixed on the metal door to the vault. But this time, he was carry-ing a gun.

It was only a matter of seconds before he would come to the place where I was hiding. Almost sick with fear, I wormed my way along the bookcase until I reached the far end of it. Here, a narrow aisle went along the wall all the way up to the librarian's desk, and I tiptoed as far as I dared before drawing in my stomach and leaning against the narrow end piece of a bookcase, hoping very much to be exactly out of sight when the thug walked past me in the aisle at the other end.

As I stood there, too afraid to breathe, I had to fight the urge to run like hell. Forcing myself to stay absolutely still, I waited for a few extra seconds before I finally dared to stretch and look, and saw him slipping silently into the vault.

Peeling off my shoes with trembling fingers, I scurried all the way up the aisle, turned the corner by the librarian's desk, and continued up the stairs three steps at a time without even pausing to look behind me.

Not until I was far away from the university premises and safely up some obscure little street did I dare to slow down and feel a kind of relief. But it was not a lasting feeling. In all likelihood, this was the guy who had trashed my hotel room, and the only upside to that was that I had not been asleep in my bed when he came.

PEPPO TOLOMEI WAS almost as surprised to see me as I was to find myself back so soon at the Owl Museum. "Giulietta!" he exclaimed, putting down a trophy and rag, "What is wrong? And what is that?"

We both looked at the messy bundle in my arms. "I have no idea," I confessed. "But I think it belonged to my father."

"Here—" He cleared a space on the table for me, and I put down the blue silk very gently, thus revealing the knife nested within.

"Do you have any idea," I said, picking up the knife, "where this came from?"

But Peppo was not looking at the knife. Instead, he began unfolding the silk with reverent hands. Once it was spread out in its entirety, he took a step backwards, overwhelmed, and crossed himself. "Where on earth," he said, his voice little more than a whisper, "did you find this?"

"Um . . . it was in my father's collection at the university. It was wrapped around the knife. I didn't realize it was something special."

Peppo looked at me in surprise. "You don't know what this is?"

I looked more closely at the blue silk. It was much longer than it was wide, almost like a banner, and a female figure had been painted on it, her hair bound by a halo and her hands raised in a blessing. Time had faded her colors, but the enchantment was still there. Even a philistine like myself could see that it was a picture of the Virgin Mary. "It's a religious flag?"

"This," said Peppo, straightening in respect, "is a cencio, the grand prize of the Palio. But it is very old. See the Roman numbers down in the corner? That is the year." He leaned in once again to verify the numerals. "Yes! Santa Maria!" He turned towards me, eyes glowing. "Not only is this an antique cencio, it is the most legendary cencio there ever was! Everyone thought it was lost forever. But here it is! It is the cencio from the Palio of 1340. A great treasure! It was lined with little tails of . . . I don't know the word in English. Look"—he pointed at the ragged edges of the fabric—"they were here and here. Not squirrels. Special squirrels. But now they are gone."

"So," I said, "what would this kind of thing be worth? In terms of money?"

"Money?" The concept was foreign to Peppo, who looked at me as if I had asked what Jesus charged per hour. "But this is the prize! It is very special . . . a great honor. Ever since the Middle Ages, the winner of the Palio would get a beautiful silk banner lined with expensive fur; the Romans called it a pallium, and this is why our race is called the Palio. Look"—he pointed his cane at some of the banners hanging on the walls around us—"every time our contrada wins the Palio, we get a new cencio for our collection. The oldest ones we have are two hundred years old."

"So, you don't have any other cencios from the fourteenth century?"

"Oh, no!" Peppo shook his head vigorously. "This is very, very special. You see, in the old days, the man who won the Palio would take the cencio and turn it into clothes and wear it on his body in triumph. That is why they are all lost."

"Then it must be worth *something*," I insisted. "If it's so rare, I mean."

"Money-money-money!" he gibed. "Money is not everything. Don't you understand? This is about Siena history!"

My cousin's enthusiasm stood in sharp contrast to my own state of mind. Apparently, this morning, I had risked my life for a rusty old knife and a faded flag. Yes, it was a cencio, and as such it was an invaluable, almost magical artifact to the Sienese, but, unless I was mistaken, a completely worthless old rag if I ever took it beyond the walls of Siena.

"What about the knife?" I said. "Have you ever seen that before?"

Peppo turned back to the table and picked up the knife. "This," he said, pulling the rusty blade out of the sheath and examining it underneath the chandelier, "is a dagger. A very handy weapon." He inspected the engraving very closely, nodding to himself as the whole thing—apparently—began to make sense. "An eagle. Of course. And it was hidden together with the cencio from 1340. To think I should live to see this. Why did he never show me? I suppose he knew what I would say. These are treasures that belong to all of Siena, not just to the Tolomeis."

"Peppo," I said, rubbing my forehead, "what am I supposed to do with this?"

He looked at me, his eyes oddly distant, as if he was partly present, partly in 1340. "Remember I told you that your parents believed Romeo and Juliet lived here, in Siena? Well, in 1340 there was a much-disputed Palio. They say the cencio disappeared—this cencio right here—and that a rider died during the race. They also say that Romeo rode in that Palio, and I think this is his dagger."

Now, finally, my curiosity got the better of my disappointment. "Did he win?"

"I am not sure. Some say he was the one who died. But mark my words"—Peppo looked at me with narrow eyes—"the Marescottis would do anything to get their hands on this."

"You mean, the Marescottis living in Siena now?"

Peppo shrugged. "Whatever you believe about the cencio, the dagger belonged to Romeo. See the engraving of the eagle right here on the hilt? Can you imagine what a treasure this would be to them?"

"I suppose I could return it—"

"No!" The giddy glee in my cousin's eyes now gave way to other emotions, far less charming. "You must leave it here! This is a treasure that now belongs to all of Siena, not just to the aquilini or the Marescottis. You did very well to bring it here. We must discuss it with all the magistrates of all the contrade. They know best. And meanwhile, I will put it in our safe, away from light and air." He began eagerly folding up the cencio. "I promise you, I will take very good care of it. Our safe is very safe."

"But my parents left it for me—" I dared to object.

"Yes-yes-yes, but this is not something that should belong to any one person. Don't worry, the magistrates will know what to do."

"How about—"

Peppo looked at me sternly. "I am your godfather. Do you not trust me?"

What say you, can you love the gentleman?
This night you shall behold him at our feast

...

Siena, A.D. 1340

To MAESTRO AMBROGIO THE NIGHT before Madonna Assunta was as holy as Christmas Eve. Over the course of the evening vigil, the otherwise dark Siena Cathedral would be filled with hundreds of colossal votive candles—some weighing more than fifty pounds—as a long procession of representatives from every contrada made their way up the nave towards the golden altar, to honor Siena's protectress, the Virgin Mary, and celebrate her assumption into Heaven.

Tomorrow, on Madonna Assunta proper, the majestic cathedral would thus be illuminated by a forest of flickering flames when vassals from surrounding towns and villages arrived to pay their tributes. Every year on this day, August 15, they were required by law to donate a carefully calculated quantity of wax candles to the divine queen of Siena, and stern city officials would be posted inside the cathedral to ensure that each subordinate town and village paid their dues. The fact that the cathedral was already illuminated with an abundance of holy lights only confirmed what the foreigners knew well: that Siena was a glorious place, blessed by an all-powerful goddess, and that membership was well worth the price.

Maestro Ambrogio much preferred the nightly vigil to the daylight procession. Something magical happened to people when they carried light into darkness; the fire spread to their souls, and if one looked carefully, the wonder could be observed in their eyes.

But tonight he could not participate in the procession as he usually did. Since he had commenced the large frescoes in Palazzo Pubblico, the Siena magistrates had been treating him like one of their own—undoubtedly because they wanted to ensure that he painted them in a flattering light—and so here he was, stuck on a podium with the Nine, the Biccherna magistrates, the Captain of War, and the Captain of the People. The only consolation was that the perch offered him a full view of the night's spectacle; the musicians in their scarlet uniforms, the drummers and flag throwers with their insignia, the priests in flowing robes, and the candlelit procession that would go on until every contrada had paid its respects to the divine queen who held her protective cape over them all.

There was no mistaking the Tolomei family at the head of the procession from the contrada of San Cristoforo. Dressed in the red and gold of their coat of arms, Messer Tolomei and his wife had the demeanor of royalty approaching their thrones as they walked up the nave towards the main altar. Immediately behind them came a group of Tolomei family members, and it did not take Maestro Ambrogio long to spot Giulietta among them. Even though her hair was covered by blue silk—blue for the innocence and majesty of the Virgin Mary—and even though her face was illuminated solely by the small wax candle in her piously folded hands, her loveliness easily eclipsed everything around her, even the beautiful dowries of her cousins.

But Giulietta did not notice the admiring eyes following her all the way to the altar. Her thoughts were clearly for the Virgin Mary alone, and while everyone around her proceeded towards the high altar with the contentment of the gift giver, the girl had her eyes fixed on the floor until she was able to kneel with her cousins and hand her candle to the priests.

Getting up, she curtsied twice and turned to face the world. Only now did she seem to notice the grandeur surrounding her, and she swayed briefly underneath the vastness of the dome, regarding everything human with nervous curiosity. Maestro Ambrogio would have liked nothing more than to rush to her side to offer his humble assistance, but decency demanded that he stay where he was, and merely appreciate her beauty from a distance.

He was not the only one to notice her. The magistrates, who were busy making deals and shaking hands, fell silent when they saw Giulietta's radiant face. And below the podium, standing close enough to look as if he belonged there, even the grand Messer Salimbeni eventually turned to see what had made everyone so silent. When he caught sight of the young woman, an expression of pleasant surprise spread over his face, and at that exact moment he reminded the Maestro of a fresco that had once caught his attention—when he was young and foolish—in a house of ill repute. The scene had depicted the ancient god Dionysus descending on the island of Naxos to find the princess Ariadne there, abandoned by her perfidious lover Theseus. The myth was vague about the outcome of the encounter between woman and god; some liked to think they flew away together in loving harmony, but others knew that encounters between humans and amorous gods can never have a happy end.

To compare Salimbeni to a divinity might be considered too kind, given his reputation. But then, those ancient pagan gods had been anything but benign and aloof; even though Dionysus had been the god of wine and celebration, he was only too ready to transform himself into the god of raving madness—a terrible force of nature that could seduce women into running wild in the forest and tearing apart animals with their bare hands.

Now, as he stood there looking at Giulietta across the floor of the cathedral, to the untrained eye Salimbeni looked all benevolence and abundance, but the Maestro could see that, beneath the man's plush brocade, the transformation was already taking place.

"I say," mumbled one of the Nine, loud enough for Maestro Ambrogio to hear, "Tolomei is full of surprises. Where did he keep *her* locked up all this time?"

"Do not jest," replied the most senior of the magistrates, Niccolino Patrizi. "I hear that she was orphaned by one of Salimbeni's gangs. They raided her home while she was in confession. I remember her father well. He was a rare man. I never could shake his integrity."

The other man snorted. "Are you sure she was there? It would be unlike Salimbeni to let such a pearl slip between his fingers."

"She was saved by a priest, I believe. Tolomei has taken them both under his protection." Niccolino Patrizi sighed and took a drink of wine from his silver goblet. "I only hope this does not make the feud flare up again, now that we finally have it under control."

...

MESSER TOLOMEI HAD been dreading the moment for weeks. He had known all along that on the vigil of Madonna Assunta he would be face-to-face with his enemy, that most odious of men, Salimbeni, and that his dignity demanded revenge for the death of Giulietta's family. And so after bowing before the altar, he made his way towards the podium, seeking out Salimbeni among the nobles gathered below.

"Good evening to you, my dear friend!" Salimbeni opened his arms in a gesture of affection when he saw his old enemy approaching. "Your family, I hope, are in good health?"

"More or less," replied Tolomei, his jaw tightening. "Some were recently lost to violence, as I am sure you have heard?"

"I heard a rumor," said Salimbeni, his gesture of friendship turning into a dismissive shrug, "but I never trust rumors."

"Then I am more fortunate," replied Tolomei, towering over the other both in stature and manner, yet unable to dominate him, "for I have eyewitnesses who are ready to swear with their hand on the Bible."

"Indeed?" Salimbeni looked away, as if he was already bored with the subject. "What court would be foolish enough to hear them?"

A pregnant silence followed the question. Tolomei, and everyone around him, knew he was challenging a power that could squash him and destroy everything he had—life, liberty, and property—in a matter of hours. And the magistrates would do nothing to protect him. There was too much Salimbeni gold in their private coffers, and too much more to come, for any of them to desire the tyrant's downfall.

"My dear friend," Salimbeni went on, his benevolent smirk returning, "I hope you do not let these faraway events ruin your evening. You should rather congratulate yourself that our fighting days are over, and that we can enter the future in peace and understanding."

"And this is what you call peace and understanding?"

"Perhaps we might consider"—Salimbeni looked across the room, and everyone but Tolomei could see what he was looking at—"sealing our peace with a marriage?"

"But certainly!" Tolomei had proposed the same measure several times before, but had always been refused. If the Salimbenis were to join in the Tolomei blood, he figured, surely they would be inclined to spill less of it.

Anxious to strike while the iron was hot, he summoned his wife impatiently from across the floor. It took a few waves before Monna Antonia finally dared to believe that the men desired her presence, and she joined them with uncharacteristic humility, sidling up nervously to Salimbeni like a slave before an unpredictable master.

"My dear friend Messer Salimbeni," Tolomei explained to her, "has proposed a marriage between our families. What do you say, my dear? Would not that be a marvelous thing?"

Monna Antonia wrung her hands in flattered excitement. "Indeed it would. A marvelous thing." She nearly curtsied to Salimbeni before addressing him directly. "Since you are kind enough to propose it, Messere, I have a daughter, recently thirteen, who would not be entirely inappropriate for your own very handsome son, Nino. She is a silent little thing, but healthy. She stands over there"—Monna Antonia pointed across the floor—"next to my firstborn, Tebaldo, who will ride in the Palio tomorrow, as perhaps you know. And if you lose her, there is always her younger sister, who is now eleven."

"I thank you for the generous offer, dear lady," said Salimbeni, indicating a bow of perfect courtesy, "but I was not thinking of my son. I was thinking of myself."

Tolomei and Monna Antonia both gaped in speechless amazement. All around them, there was a spontaneous outburst of disbelief, soon curbed into a nervous murmur, and even on the podium everyone followed the developments below with intense apprehension.

"Who," Salimbeni went on, oblivious to the commotion, "is that?" He nodded in the direction of Giulietta. "Was she married before?"

Some of Tolomei's former anger returned to his voice as he said, "That is my niece. She alone survived the tragic events I just mentioned. I believe she lives only to seek vengeance on those responsible for the slaughter of her family."

"I see." Salimbeni looked anything but discouraged. In fact, he seemed to relish the challenge. "A spirited one, is she?"

Monna Antonia could remain silent no longer, and stepped eagerly forward. "Very much so, Messere. A thoroughly unpleasant girl. I am confident that you would be much better off taking one of my daughters. They will not object."

Salimbeni smiled, mostly to himself. "As it is, I rather like a little objection."

EVEN FROM A DISTANCE, Giulietta could feel the many eyes on her, and she hardly knew where to go to avoid the scrutiny. Her uncle and aunt had abandoned their kin to mingle with the other nobles, and she could see them talking to a man who exuded the comfort and magnanimity of an emperor, but who had the eyes of a lean and hungry animal. The unsettling thing was that those eyes were—with few interruptions—fixed on her.

Seeking refuge behind a column, she took a few deep breaths and told herself that all would be well. This morning, Friar Lorenzo had brought her a letter from Romeo saying that his father, Comandante Marescotti, would approach her uncle Tolomei with a proposal as soon as possible. Since receiving that letter, she had done little but pray to God that the proposal would be accepted, and that soon her dependency on the Tolomei family would be a thing of the past.

Peeking out from behind the column, Giulietta was able to make out her handsome Romeo in the crowd of nobles—unless she was mistaken, he was stretching and looking around for her, too, getting more and more frustrated that he could not see her anywhere—and next to him stood a man who could only be his father. She felt a surge of joy when she saw them, knowing that they were both determined to claim her as a member of their family, and when she saw them approaching her uncle Tolomei, she could barely contain herself. Moving discreetly closer, from column to column, she tried to bring herself within hearing range of the men without their discovering her presence. Fortunately for her, they were all too absorbed in their heated conversation to pay attention to anything else.

"Comandante!" exclaimed her uncle Tolomei, when he saw the Marescottis advancing. "Tell us, is the enemy at the gates?"

"The enemy," replied Comandante Marescotti, nodding curtly at the man with the animal eyes standing next to her uncle, "is already here. His name is corruption, and he does not stop at the gate." He paused briefly to allow for laughter. "Messer Tolomei, there is a matter of some delicacy that I would like to discuss with you. Privately. When may I pay you a visit?"

Tolomei looked at Comandante Marescotti, clearly mystified. The Marescottis might not have the riches of the Tolomeis, but the torch of history shone upon their name, and the Marescotti family tree had surely sprouted in the camp of Charlemagne, five centuries ago, if not in Eden itself. Nothing, Giulietta suspected, would please her uncle Tolomei more than to enter into a business venture with someone of that name. And so he turned his back to the man with the animal eyes and opened his arms. "Tell me what you have in mind."

Comandante Marescotti hesitated, unhappy about the public setting and the ears surrounding them on all sides. "I cannot imagine," he said, diplomatically, "that Messer Salimbeni would find our business very entertaining."

Hearing the name *Salimbeni,* Giulietta felt her whole body stiffen with fear. Only now did she realize that this man with the animal eyes—the one who had elicited motions of humility from Monna Antonia just a moment ago—was the man responsible for the murder of her family. She had spent many hours imagining what this monster might look like in person, and now that he finally stood before her, she was shocked to see that, apart from his eyes, he did not look the part.

She had imagined someone square and unforgiving, whose whole body was built for war and molestation; instead she saw a man who had surely never wielded a weapon of his own, and who looked as if his arts were those of rhetoric and the dining room. There could be no greater contrast between two men than there was between Comandante Marescotti and Messer Salimbeni; one was an expert at war, yet desired nothing but peace, the other had civility draped around him as a robe, but, underneath his fine fabrics, lusted for conflict.

"You are mistaken, Comandante," said Salimbeni, enjoying his own power over the conversation, "I am always intrigued by any business that cannot wait until morning. And as you know, Messer Tolomei and I are the best of friends; surely he would not scorn my"—Salimbeni was honest enough to chuckle at his own choice of words—"*humble* advice on his very *important* business affairs."

"I beg your pardon," said the Comandante, wisely bowing out, "but you are right. This *can* wait until the morning."

"No!" Romeo was incapable of walking away without having stated their business, and he stepped abruptly forward before his father could hold him back. "It cannot wait! Messer Tolomei, I wish to marry your niece, Giulietta."

Tolomei was so utterly surprised at the straightforward proposition that an immediate response was impossible. He was not the only one silenced by Romeo's impulsive interference in the men's discussion; everywhere around them, people were stretching to see who would have the nerve to speak next. Behind the column, Giulietta held a hand to her mouth; she was thoroughly moved by Romeo's determination, but horrified that he had spoken so impulsively, against his father's wishes.

"As you can hear," said Comandante Marescotti, with remarkable calm, to the gaping Tolomei, "I would like to propose a marriage between my oldest son, Romeo, and your niece, Giulietta. I am sure you know that we are a family of means as well as reputation, and, with all due respect, I believe I can promise that your niece would experience no decrease in comfort or status. After my death and upon the succession of my son, Romeo, as patron of the family, she will become mistress of a large consortium comprising many households and extensive territory, the details of which I have outlined in a document. When would be a good time for us to visit, that I may give you the document in person?"

Tolomei did not reply. Odd shadows traversed his face, like sharks circling their victims beneath the water's surface, and he was clearly in a state of anguish, searching for a way out.

"If you are concerned," Comandante Marescotti went on, not entirely pleased with the hesitation of the other, "for her happiness, it is my good fortune to be able to assure you that my son has no objections to the marriage."

When Tolomei finally spoke, his voice held little encouragement. "Most generous Comandante," he said, grimly, "you do me a great honor by making such a proposal. I shall peruse your document and consider your offer—"

"You shall do no such thing!" Salimbeni stepped in between the two men, furious to have been ignored. "I consider this matter settled."

Comandante Marescotti took a step back. He might be an army commander and always prepared for foul sneak attacks, but Salimbeni was more dangerous than any foreign enemy. "Excuse us!" he said. "I believe Messer Tolomei and I were having a conversation."

"You may have all the conversations you like," Salimbeni shot back, "but that girl is mine. It is my one condition to maintain this ridiculous peace."

Due to the general uproar following Salimbeni's outrageous demand, no one heard Giulietta's cry of horror. Crouched behind the column, she pressed both hands against her mouth and sent up an urgent prayer that she had somehow misunderstood the men's conversation, and that the girl in question was not her, but someone else.

When she finally dared look again, she saw her uncle Tolomei stepping around Salimbeni to address Comandante Marescotti, his face contorted in embarrassment. "Dear Comandante," he said, his voice unsteady, "this is, as you say, a delicate matter. But surely, we can come to some agreement—"

"Indeed!" His wife, Monna Antonia, finally dared speak again, this time to throw herself obsequiously at the frowning Comandante. "I have a daughter, fully thirteen, who would be an excellent wife for your son. She stands over there—see?"

The Comandante did not even turn his head to look. "Messer Tolomei," he said, with as much patience as he could still muster, "our proposal is for your niece Giulietta alone. And you would do well in consulting her on the matter. These are not the barbarous ages, where a woman's wishes can just be ignored—"

"The girl belongs to me!" snapped Tolomei, angry that his wife had intervened, and unhappy to be the victim of a lecture, "and I can do with her as I choose. I thank you for your interest, Comandante, but I have other plans for her."

"I advise you to consider this more carefully," said Comandante Marescotti, taking a warning step forward. "The girl is attached to my son, whom she considers her savior, and she will most certainly give you grief if you ask her to marry someone else. Especially someone"—he cast a disgusted glance at Salimbeni—"who does not seem to appreciate the tragedy that befell her family."

Faced with such unswerving logic, Tolomei was at a loss to come up with a word of objection. Giulietta even felt a brief stab of sympathy for him; standing between these two men, her uncle looked much like a drowning man grasping for the dispersed boards of a boat, and the result was anything but graceful.

"Am I to understand that you are opposing my claim, Comandante?" asked Salimbeni, once again stepping in between the two. "Surely, you do not mean to question Messer Tolomei's rights as head of his own family? And surely"—there was no mistaking the threat in his eyes—"the house of Marescotti does not desire a quarrel with Tolomei *and* Salimbeni?"

Behind the column, Giulietta could no longer fight back her tears. She wanted to run over to the men and stop them, but knew that her presence would only make things worse. When Romeo had first mentioned his intention to marry her—that day in the confessional—he had said that, between their families, there had always been peace. It would seem that now, because of her, those words were no longer true.

NICCOLINO PATRIZI, ONE OF the nine head administrators of Siena, had overheard the escalating conflict beneath the podium with growing apprehension. He was not the only one.

"When they were mortal enemies," mused his neighbor, eyes fixed on Tolomei and Salimbeni, "I feared them greatly. Now that they are friends, I fear them even more."

"We are the government! We must be above such human emotion!" exclaimed Niccolino Patrizi, rising from his chair. "Messer Tolomei! Messer Salimbeni! Why such clandestine airs on the vigil of Madonna Assunta? I hope you are not conducting business in the house of God?"

A pregnant silence fell over the noble assembly at these words spoken from the podium, and beneath the high altar, the bishop momentarily forgot to bless.

"Most honorable Messer Patrizi!" replied Salimbeni with sarcastic civility. "You pay no compliment to either us or yourself by speaking such words. Rather, you should congratulate us, for my very good friend Messer Tolomei and I have decided to celebrate our lasting peace with a marriage."

"My condolences on the death of your wife!" spat Niccolino Patrizi. "I had not heard of her demise!"

"Monna Agnese," said Salimbeni, unstirred, "will not live beyond this month. She lies abed at Rocca di Tentennano and takes no nourishment."

"It is hard," mumbled one of the Biccherna magistrates, "to eat, when you are not fed!"

"You will need to seek the Pope's approval for a wedding between former foes," insisted Niccolino Patrizi, "and I doubt you will get it. Such a torrent of blood has washed away the path between your houses that no decent man can send his daughter across. There is an evil spirit—"

"Only marriage can chase away evil spirits!"

"The Pope believes otherwise!"

"Possibly," said Salimbeni, allowing an unbecoming smile to bend his lips, "but the Pope owes me money. And so do you. All of you."

The grotesque claim had the desired effect; Niccolino Patrizi sat down, flushed and furious, and Salimbeni looked boldly upon the rest of the government as if to challenge anyone else to speak against his enterprise. But the podium was silent.

"Messer Salimbeni!" A voice cut through the murmur of subdued indignation, and everybody stretched to see the challenger.

"Who speaks?" Salimbeni was always delighted to get a chance at putting lesser men in their place. "Do not be shy!"

"Shyness is to me," replied Romeo, stepping forward, "what virtue is to you, Messer Salimbeni."

"And what, pray," said Messer Salimbeni, holding his head high in an attempt at looking down at the contender, "can you possibly have to say to me?"

"Just this," said Romeo, "that the lady you covet already belongs to another man."

"Indeed?" Salimbeni cast a glance at Tolomei. "How so?"

Romeo straightened. "The Virgin Mary delivered her into my hands that I may guard her forever. And what Heaven has entwined, let no man tear apart!"

Salimbeni first looked incredulous, then broke into laughter. "Well spoken, lad, I recognize you now. Your dagger killed a good friend of mine lately, but I shall be generous and bear no grudge, seeing that you took such fine care of my bride-to-be."

Turning away, Salimbeni made it evident that he considered the conversation over. All eyes now fell on Romeo, whose face was aflame with revulsion, and more than one felt sorry for the young man who was so obviously a victim of the wicked little archer.

"Come, my son," said Comandante Marescotti, backing away. "Let us not linger where the game is lost."

"Lost?" cried Romeo. "There never was a game!"

"Whatever the dealings of those two men," said his father, "they have shaken hands beneath the altar of the Virgin. Quarrel with them, and you will be quarreling with God."

"And so I shall!" exclaimed Romeo. "For Heaven has turned against itself in allowing this to happen!"

When the youth stepped forward again, no gesture was needed to bring about silence; everyone's eyes were already fixed on his lips in uneasy expectation.

"Holy Mother of God!" yelled Romeo, surprising the whole assembly by addressing the empty air of the dome above rather than Salimbeni. "A great crime is being committed in this very house, under your very cape, on this very night! I pray that you set the scoundrels straight and show yourself to them, that no one may doubt your divine will! Let the man who wins the Palio be your chosen one! Bestow on me your holy banner that I may drape it over my wedding bed and rest upon it with my rightful bride! Thus satisfied, I shall give it back to you, O merciful Mother, for it was won according to your will, and given to me by your hand alone, to show all mankind your sympathies in this matter!"

When Romeo finally fell silent, there was not a man around him who would meet his eyes. Some were petrified by the blasphemy, others were ashamed to see a Marescotti strike such a selfish and unconventional bargain with the Virgin Mary, but most were merely sorry for his father, Comandante Marescotti, who was a man universally admired. Whether by divine intervention following such a blatant profanation, or by the simple necessity of human politics, young Romeo Marescotti, in most people's minds, would not be allowed to survive the Palio.

Ay, ay, a scratch, a scratch. Marry, 'tis enough.
Where is my page? Go, villain, fetch a surgeon

...

Walking away from the owl museum, I was torn. On the one hand it was a relief that the cencio and Romeo's dagger were now in Peppo's safe; on the other hand I regretted giving them away so quickly. Suppose my mother had wanted me to use them for a specific purpose? Suppose they somehow held a clue to the location of Juliet's grave?

All the way back to the hotel I was resisting the urge to return to the museum and reclaim my treasures. I was successful mainly because I knew that the satisfaction of getting them back would soon be overshadowed by fear of what would happen to them next. Who was to say they were more secure in Direttor Rossini's safe than in Peppo's? After all, the thug knew where I lived—how else could he have broken into my room?—and sooner or later, he would figure out where I kept my things.

I believe I stopped in the middle of the street. Until this moment it had not even occurred to me that going back to the hotel was the least intelligent thing I could possibly do, never mind that I no longer carried the artifacts. Without a doubt, the thug would be waiting for me to do just that. And after our little hide-and-seek in the university archive, he was probably not in a particularly generous mood.

Clearly, I would have to change hotels, and it would have to be done in such a way that my trail went cold. Or maybe this was, in fact, my cue to hop on the next plane back to Virginia?

No. I could not give up. Not now, when I was finally getting somewhere. I would change hotels, maybe tonight, when it was dark. I would become invisible, cunning, mean. This time, Juliet was going to the mattresses.

There was a police station on the same street as Hotel Chiusarelli. I lingered outside for a bit, watching the officers come and go, wondering whether this would be such a smart move—making myself known to the local law and risking their discovering my double identity. In the end I decided it was not. Based on my experiences in Rome and in Copenhagen I knew that police officers are just like journalists; sure, they'll hear your story, but they much prefer to make up their own.

And so I walked back downtown, turning every ten steps to see if I was being followed, and wondering what precisely my strategy should be from now on. I even went into the bank in Palazzo Tolomei to see if Presidente Maconi had time to see me and give me advice; unfortunately, he did not, but the teller with the slim glasses—now my best friend—assured me that he would be more than happy to meet with me when he returned from his vacation at Lake Como in ten days.

I HAD WALKED PAST the forbidding main door of Monte dei Paschi several times since my arrival in Siena. My steps had always quickened to bring me past this Salimbeni fortress without detection, and I would even duck my head, wondering if the office of the Head of Security was facing the Corso or some other way.

But today was different. Today was the day I took the bull by the horns and gave it a good shake. And so I walked up to the Gothic front door and went inside, making sure the surveillance cameras got a good shot of my new attitude.

For a building that had been burnt down by rival families—my own being one—torn apart by an angry populace, rebuilt several times by its owners, confiscated by the government, and finally reborn as a financial institution in the year 1472, making it the oldest surviving bank in the world, Palazzo Salimbeni was a remarkably peaceful place. The interior design blended medieval and modern in a way that made sense of both, and as I walked up to the reception area, the gap of time between now and then closed seamlessly around me.

The receptionist was on the phone, but held a hand over the receiver to ask me—first in Italian, then in English—whom I had come to see.

When I told him I was a personal friend of the Head of Security, and that I had urgent business to discuss with him, the man smiled and said I could find what I was looking for in the basement.

Pleasantly surprised that he let me enter just like that, unescorted and unannounced, I started down the stairs with deliberate detachment, while a chorus line of little mice were riverdancing on the inside of my rib cage. They had been oddly silent while I was running from the tracksuit thug earlier on, but here they were full force, just because I was going to see Alessandro.

When I had left him at the restaurant the night before, I had, quite frankly, harbored no desire ever to see him again. The feeling, I am sure, was mutual. Yet here I was, walking straight into his lair for no other reason than instinct. Janice used to say that instinct was reason in a hurry; I was not so sure about the reason part. My reason told me it was highly likely that Alessandro and the Salimbenis were involved in all the nastiness currently coming my way; however, my gut told me I could count on him, even if it was only to let me know how much he disliked me.

As I descended into the basement the air got considerably cooler, and traces of the original building structure began to emerge as the walls became rough and worn around me. Back in the Middle Ages this foundation had carried a tall tower, perhaps as tall as the Mangia Tower in the Campo. The whole city had been full of these tower-houses; they had served as fortifications in times of unrest.

At the bottom of the stairs, a narrow corridor went off into the darkness, and ironclad doors on either side made the place feel like a dungeon. I was beginning to fear that I had taken a wrong turn somewhere along the way, when there was a sudden outburst of voices, followed by cheers, coming from behind a half-open door.

I approached the door with some apprehension. Whether or not Alessandro was actually down here, there would be a lot of explaining to do, and logic had never been my strong suit. Peeking inside, I could see a table full of metal parts and half-eaten sandwiches, a wall of rifles, and three men in T-shirts and uniform pants—one of them Alessandro—standing around a small television screen. At first I thought they were watching the input from a surveillance camera somewhere in the building, but when they all suddenly moaned and clutched their heads, I realized they were watching a soccer game.

When no one reacted to my initial knocking, I pushed through the door—just a little bit—and cleared my throat. Now finally, Alessandro turned his head to see who had the gall to interrupt the game, and when he saw me standing there, attempting a smile, he looked as if someone had knocked him over the head with a frying pan.

"Sorry to disturb," I said, trying hard not to look like Bambi-on-stilts, although that was precisely how I felt. "Do you have a moment?"

Seconds later, the two other men had left the room, grabbing guns and uniform jackets as they went, half-eaten sandwiches wedged in their mouths.

"So," said Alessandro, killing the soccer game and tossing aside the remote, "satisfy my curiosity." He clearly did not think I needed the rest of the sentence, although the way he looked at me suggested that—notwithstanding the fact that I was a barnacle on the criminal underbelly of society—he was secretly pleased to see me.

I sat down on a vacant chair, looking around at the hardware on the walls. "Is this your office?"

"Yeah—" He pulled the dangling suspenders up on his shoulders and sat down on the other side of the table. "This is where we interrogate people. Americans mostly. It used to be a torture chamber."

The dare in his eyes almost made me forget my general unease and the reason why I had come. "It suits you."

"I thought so." He put a heavy boot against the side of the table and tipped back to lean against the wall. "Okay, I am listening. You must have a very good reason for being here."

"I wouldn't exactly call it reason." I looked away, trying in vain to remember the official story I had rehearsed coming down the stairs. "Obviously, you think I'm a conniving bitch . . ."

"I've seen worse."

". . . and I haven't exactly signed up for your fan club either."

He smiled wryly. "Yet here you are."

I folded my arms across my chest, choking back a nervous laugh. "I know you don't believe I am Giulietta Tolomei, and you know what? I don't care. But here is the bottom line"—I swallowed hard to steady my voice—"someone is trying to kill me."

"You mean, apart from yourself?"

His sarcasm helped me regain my cool. "There's some guy following me," I said, gruffly. "Nasty type. Tracksuit. Bona fide scum. I figured he was a friend of yours."

Alessandro didn't even flinch. "So, what do you want me to do?"

"I don't know—" I searched for a spark of sympathy in his eyes. "Help me?"

There was a spark all right, but it was mostly one of triumph. "And remind me why I would do that?"

"Hey!" I exclaimed, genuinely upset with his attitude. "I'm . . . a maiden in distress!"

"And who am I, Zorro?"

I swallowed a groan, furious with myself for thinking he would care. "I thought Italian men were susceptible to female charms."

He considered the idea. "We are. When we encounter them."

"Okay," I said, sucking in my fury, "fair enough. You want me to go to hell, and I will. I'll go back to the States and never bother you or your fairy godmother again. But first, I want to find out who this guy is, and have someone bust his ass."

"And that someone is me?"

I glared at him. "Maybe not. I just assumed someone like you wouldn't want someone like him running loose in your precious Siena. But"—I made a move to get up—"I see that I got you all wrong."

Now, finally, Alessandro leaned forward with mock concern and put his elbows on the table. "All right, Miss Tolomei, tell me why you think someone is trying to kill you."

Never mind that I had nowhere else to go; I would have walked right out of there, had it not been for the fact that he had finally called me *Miss Tolomei.* "Well—" I moved uncomfortably on the edge of the seat. "How about this: He followed me through the streets, broke into my hotel room, and then, this morning, he came after me with a gun—"

"That," said Alessandro, deploying a great deal of patience, "doesn't mean he intends to kill you." He paused to study my face, then frowned. "How do you expect me to help you, if you are not telling me the truth?"

"But I am! I swear!" I tried to think of some other way of convincing him, but my eyes were drawn to the tattoos on his right forearm, and my brain was busy processing the impulse. This was not the Alessandro I had expected to find coming into Palazzo Salimbeni. The Alessandro

I knew was polished and subtle, if not downright square-toed, and he certainly did not have a dragonfly—or whatever the heck it was—etched into his wrist.

If he could read my thoughts, he didn't show it. "Not the whole truth. There are a lot of pieces missing in the puzzle."

I snapped upright. "What makes you think there is a big picture?"

"There is always a big picture. So, tell me what he is after."

I took a deep breath, only too aware that I had chosen to put myself in this situation, and that a more substantial explanation was due. "Okay," I finally said, "I think he is after something that my mother left for me. Some family heirloom that my parents found years ago, and which she wanted me to have. So, she hid it in a place where only I could find it. Why? Because—whether you like it or not—I am Giulietta Tolomei."

I looked at him defiantly and found him studying my face with something akin to a smile. "And have you found it?"

"I don't think so. Not yet. All I've found is a rusty box full of paper, an old . . . banner, and some kind of dagger, and quite frankly, I don't see—"

"Aspetta!" Alessandro held up a hand to make me slow down. "What kind of paper, what kind of banner?"

"Stories, letters. Silly stuff. Don't get me started. And the banner, apparently, is a cencio from 1340. I found it wrapped around a dagger, like this, in a drawer—"

"Wait! Are you saying you found the cencio from 1340?"

I was surprised to see him reacting even more strongly to this news than my cousin Peppo had. "Yes, I think so. Apparently it is very special. And the dagger—"

"Where is it?"

"In a secure place. I left it at the Owl Museum." Seeing that he did not follow, I added, "My cousin, Peppo Tolomei, is the curator. He told me he would take care of it for me."

Alessandro groaned and ran both hands through his hair.

"What?" I said. "Was that not a good idea?"

"Merda!" He got up, reached into a drawer to pull out a handgun, and slipped it into the holster in his belt. "Come on, let's go!"

"Wait! What's going on?" I got up reluctantly. "You're not suggesting we go see my cousin with that . . . gun?"

"No, it's not a suggestion. Come on!"

As we hurried down the corridor, he glanced at my feet. "Can you run in those things?"

"Look," I said, struggling to keep up, "I just wanna make one thing absolutely clear. I don't believe in guns. I just want peace. Okay?"

Alessandro stopped in the middle of the corridor, took out the gun, and wrapped my hand around it before I realized what he was doing. "Can you feel that? That's a gun. It exists. And there are a lot of people out there who *do* believe in it. So, excuse me for taking care of them so you can have your peace."

WE LEFT THE BANK through a back entrance and ran all the way down a street that was open to motorized traffic. This was not the way I knew, but sure enough, it brought us right to Piazzetta del Castellare. Alessandro took out the gun as we approached the door of the Owl Museum, but I pretended not to notice.

"Stay behind me," he said, "and if things go bad, lie down on the floor and cover your head." Not waiting for me to respond, he put a finger on his lips and slowly opened the door.

I dutifully entered the museum a few steps behind him. There was no question in my mind that he was overreacting, but I was going to let him reach that conclusion on his own. As it was, the whole building was completely silent, and there was no evidence of criminal activity. We walked through several rooms, gun first, but in the end I stopped. "Okay, listen—" But Alessandro immediately put a hand to my mouth to silence me, and as we stood there, both tense, I heard it, too: the sound of someone moaning.

Moving faster through the remaining rooms, we soon circled in on the sound, and once Alessandro had made sure it was not an ambush, we rushed inside to find Peppo lying on the floor of his own office, bruised but alive.

"Oh, Peppo!" I cried, trying to help him. "Are you okay?"

"No!" he shot back. "Of course I am not okay! I think I fell. I can't use my leg."

"Hold on—" I looked around to see where he had put his crutch, and my eyes fell on a safe in the corner, open and empty. "Did you see the man who did this?"

"What man?" Peppo tried to sit up, but winced in pain. "Oh, my head! I need my pills. *Salvatore!* Oh no, wait. It is Salvatore's day off— what day is it?"

"Non ti muovere!" Alessandro knelt down and spent a moment examining Peppo's legs. "I think his tibia is broken. I will call an ambulance."

"Wait! No!" Peppo evidently did not want an ambulance. "I was just going to close the safe. Do you hear me? I must close the safe."

"Let's worry about the safe later," I said.

"The dagger . . . it is in the boardroom. I was looking it up in a book. It must go in the safe, too. It is evil!"

Alessandro and I exchanged glances. Now was not the time to tell Peppo that it was far too late to close the safe. Clearly, the cencio was gone, as was every other treasure that my cousin had been safeguarding. But maybe the thief had not noticed the dagger. And so I got up and walked into the boardroom, and sure enough, Romeo's dagger was lying right there on the table, next to a collector's guide to medieval weaponry.

The dagger clutched in my hand, I returned to Peppo's office just as Alessandro was calling an ambulance.

"Ah yes," said my cousin, seeing the dagger, "there it is. Put it in the safe, quickly. It brings bad luck. See what happened to me. The book says it has the spirit of the devil in it."

PEPPO HAD SUFFERED a minor concussion and a broken bone, but the doctor insisted on keeping him at the hospital overnight, hooked up to various machines, just in case. Unfortunately, she also insisted on telling him precisely what had happened to him.

"She says someone hit him over the head and stole everything in the safe," Alessandro whispered to me, translating the spirited conversation between the doctor and her cranky patient, "and *he* says that he wants to speak to the real doctor, and that no one would hit him over the head in his own museum."

"Giulietta!" exclaimed Peppo, when he had finally succeeded in driving out the doctor, "What do you make of this? The nurse says someone broke into the museum!"

"I'm afraid it's true," I said, taking his hand. "I'm so sorry. This is all my fault. If I hadn't—"

"And who is that?" Peppo eyed Alessandro suspiciously. "Is he here to write a report? Tell him I didn't see anything."

"This is Captain Santini," I explained. "He was the one who saved you, remember? If it wasn't for him, you'd still be . . . in a lot of pain."

"Huh." Peppo was not ready to quit his belligerent mood just yet. "I've seen him before. He's a Salimbeni. Didn't I tell you to stay away from those people?"

"Shh! Please!" I tried to hush him up as best I could, but I knew Alessandro had heard every word. "You need to rest."

"No, I don't! I need to speak with Salvatore. We must find out who did this. There were many treasures in that safe."

"I fear the thief was after the cencio and the dagger," I said. "If I hadn't brought those to you, none of this would have happened."

Peppo looked perplexed. "But who would—oh!" His eyes became oddly distant as he stared into some nebulous past. "Of course! Why didn't I think of this? But would he really do that?"

"Who are you talking about?" I squeezed his hand, trying to make him stay focused. "Do you know who did this to you?"

Peppo grabbed my wrist and looked at me with feverish intensity. "He always said that he would come back. Patrizio, your father. He always said that one day, Romeo would return and take it all back . . . his life . . . his love . . . everything we took from him."

"Peppo," I said, stroking his arm, "I think you should try to sleep." Out of the corner of my eye I could see Alessandro weighing Romeo's dagger in his hand, frowning as if he could sense its hidden powers.

"Romeo," Peppo went on, more drowsily now as the sedative finally began to take effect, "Romeo Marescotti. Well, you can't be a ghost forever. Maybe this is his revenge. On all of us. For how we treated his mother. He was—how do you say—un figlio illegittimo? . . . Capitano?"

"Born outside of marriage," said Alessandro, joining us at last.

"Sì, sì!" nodded Peppo. "Born outside of marriage! It was a big scandal. Oh, she was such a beautiful girl—so, he threw them out—"

"Who?" I asked.

"Marescotti. The grandfather. He was a very old-fashioned man. But very handsome. I still remember the comparsa of '65—it was Aceto's first victory you know—ah, Topolone, a fine horse. They don't make them like that anymore—back then, they didn't twist their ankles and get disqualified, and we didn't need all sorts of veterinarians and mayors to tell us we couldn't run . . . oof!" He shook his head in disgust.

"Peppo?" I patted his hand. "You were talking about the Marescottis. Romeo, remember?"

"Oh, yes! They said the boy had evil hands. Everything he touched . . . it broke. The horses lost. People died. That's what they say. Because he was named after Romeo, you see. He came from that line. It's in the blood . . . *trouble.* Everything had to be fast and noisy—he couldn't sit still. Always scooters, always motorcycles—"

"You knew him?"

"No, I just know what people say. They never came back. Him and his mother. Nobody ever saw them again. They say he grew up wild, in Rome, and that he became a criminal and killed people. They say—they say he died. In Nassiriyah. With a different name."

I turned to glance at Alessandro, and he met my stare, his eyes unusually dark. "Where is Nassiriyah?" I whispered. "Do you know?" For some reason, the question made him glower, but he did not have time to reply before Peppo sighed deeply and went on, "In my opinion, it's just a legend. People like legends. And tragedies. And conspiracies. It's very quiet here in the winter."

"So, you don't believe it?"

Peppo sighed again, his eyelids getting heavy. "How do I know what I believe anymore? Oh, why do they not send a doctor?"

Just then, the door burst open, and the entire Tolomei family came pouring into the room to surround their fallen hero with wails and lamentations. They had obviously been given an overview of the situation by the doctor, for Peppo's wife, Pia, gave me the hairy eyeball as she pushed me aside and took my place next to her husband, and no one expressed anything that could possibly be construed as gratitude. To complete my humiliation, old Nonna Tolomei doddered through the door just as I was eyeing my escape, and there was no doubt in her mind that the perpetrator in this whole business was not the thief, but me.

"Tu!" she growled, aiming an accusatory finger at my heart, "Bastarda!"

She said plenty more, but I did not understand it. Transfixed by her fury like a deer before an oncoming train, I just stood there, unable to move, until Alessandro—fed up with the family fun—grabbed me by the elbow and pulled me through the door to safety.

"Phew!" I gasped. "That's one angry lady. Can you believe she's my aunt? What did she say?"

"Never mind," said Alessandro, walking down the hospital hallway with the expression of someone who wished he had a spare hand grenade.

"She called you a Salimbeni!" I said, proud to have understood that much.

"She did. And it was not a compliment."

"What did she call me? I didn't catch that one."

"It doesn't matter."

"Yes, it does." I stopped in the middle of the hallway. "What did she call me?"

Alessandro looked at me, his eyes suddenly tender. "She said, 'Bastard child. You're not one of us.' "

"Oh." I paused to swallow the words. "I guess nobody believes I am really Giulietta Tolomei. Maybe I deserve this. Maybe this is some special kind of hell reserved for people like me."

"I believe you."

I looked at him, surprised. "Really? That's new. When did that happen?"

He shrugged and started walking. "When I saw you standing in my door."

I did not know how to respond to his sudden kindness, and so we walked the rest of the way in silence, down the stairs and out the front door of the hospital, to emerge in that smooth, golden light that marks the end of day and the beginning of something far less predictable.

"So, Giulietta," said Alessandro, turning towards me, hands on his hips, "anything else I should know?"

"Well," I said, squinting against the light, "there's also a guy on a motorcycle—"

"Santa Maria!"

"But he's different. He just . . . follows me around. I don't know what he wants—"

Alessandro rolled his eyes. "You don't know what he wants! Do you want me to tell you what he wants?"

"No, it's okay." I adjusted my dress. "It's not really an issue. But this other guy—tracksuit guy—he broke into my hotel room. And so . . . I think maybe I should change hotels."

"You *think* so?" Alessandro was not impressed. "I'll tell you what, the first thing we're going to do is go to the police—"

"No, not the police!"

"They're the only ones who can tell you who did that to Peppo. I don't have access to the crime register from Monte dei Paschi. Don't worry, I'll come with you. I know these guys."

"Yeah, right!" I all but poked him in the chest. "This is just a cunning way of having me end up in jail."

He held out his hands. "If I wanted you in jail, I wouldn't really have to be cunning about it, would I?"

"Hey, listen!" I stood as tall as I could. "I still don't appreciate your power games!"

My posture made him smile. "Then why do you keep playing?"

THE SIENA POLICE headquarters was a very quiet place. At ten to seven at some point in the past, the clock on the wall had run down its battery, and as I sat there that evening, dutifully scrolling through page after page of digitized bad guys, I began to feel the same way myself. The more I looked at the faces on the computer screen, the more I realized that, to be honest, I had no idea what my stalker looked like up close. The first time I had seen the creep, he had been wearing sunglasses. The second time it had been too bloody dark to see much, and the third time—this very afternoon—I had been too focused on the gun in his hand to dwell on the finer details of his mug.

"I'm sorry"—I turned to Alessandro, who had sat very patiently next to me, elbows on his knees, waiting for my eureka moment—"but I don't recognize anyone." I smiled apologetically at the female officer in charge of the computer, knowing full well that I was wasting everyone's time. "Mi dispiace."

"It's okay," she said, smiling at me because I was a Tolomei, "it won't take long before we have matched the prints."

The first thing Alessandro had done when we arrived at the police station was to report the break-in at the Owl Museum. Two patrol cars had been dispatched immediately, and the four officers had been only too thrilled that a case of actual crime had come their way. If the thug had been dumb enough to leave any traces of himself at the museum—fingerprints especially—it was only a matter of time before we would know who he was, provided, of course, that he had been arrested before.

"While we wait," I said, "do you think we should look up Romeo Marescotti?"

Alessandro frowned. "You really believe what Peppo said?"

"Why not? Maybe it's him. Maybe it was him all along."

"In a tracksuit? I don't think so."

"Why not? Do you know him?"

Alessandro took in air. "Yes, and he's not in that computer. I already looked."

I stared at him, too amazed to speak. Before I could question him further, two police officers entered the room, one of them carrying a laptop, which he placed in front of me. Neither of them spoke English, so Alessandro had to translate what they were saying to me. "They found a fingerprint at the museum," he explained, "and they want you to take a look at some pictures to see if anyone looks familiar."

I turned to look at the screen. It had a lineup of five male faces, each of which looked out at me with a mix of apathy and disgust. After a moment, I said, "I can't be a hundred percent, but if you want to know which one looks most like the guy who followed me, I'd have to say number four."

After a brief conversation with the officers, Alessandro nodded. "That's the man who broke into the museum. Now they want to know *why* he broke into the museum, and why he has been following you around."

"How about telling me who he is?" I looked around at the grave faces. "Is he some kind of . . . murderer?"

"His name is Bruno Carrera. He's been involved in organized crime in the past, and he's been linked to some very bad people. He disappeared for a while, but now—" Alessandro nodded at the screen. "He is back."

I looked at the photo again. Bruno Carrera was definitely past his prime. Strange that he would come out of retirement in order to steal a piece of old silk with no commercial value whatsoever. "Just out of curiosity," I said without thinking, "was he ever connected to a man called Luciano Salimbeni?"

The officers exchanged glances.

"Very smooth," whispered Alessandro, meaning the exact opposite. "I thought you didn't want to answer any questions."

I looked up and saw the officers studying me with renewed interest. They were clearly wondering what exactly I was doing in Siena, and how much crucial information I had yet to disclose about the museum break-in.

"La signorina conosce Luciano Salimbeni?" one of them asked Alessandro.

"Tell them that my cousin Peppo told me about Luciano Salimbeni," I said. "Apparently he was after some of our family heirlooms twenty years ago. It has the benefit of being true."

Alessandro made my case as best he could, but the police officers were not satisfied and kept asking for more details. It was an odd power struggle, for they obviously respected him very much, and yet there was something about me and my story that just didn't fit. At one point they both left the room, and I turned to Alessandro, mystified. "Is that it? Can we go now?"

"You really think," he said, wearily, "they'll let you go before you explain to them why your family is involved with one of Italy's most wanted criminals?"

"*Involved?* All I said was that Peppo had a suspicion—"

"Giulietta"—Alessandro leaned towards me, not wanting anyone else to overhear us—"why didn't you tell me about all this?"

Before I could reply, the officers returned with a printout of Bruno Carrera's file, asking Alessandro to question me about a specific passage.

"It seems you're right," he said, skimming through the text. "Bruno used to do odd jobs for Luciano Salimbeni. He was arrested once, and told them some story about a statue with golden eyes—" He looked at me, trying to gauge my honesty. "Do you know anything about that?"

A little shocked by the fact that the police knew about the golden statue—even if what they knew was not accurate—I nevertheless managed to shake my head vigorously. "No idea."

For a few seconds, our eyes were locked in a silent battle, but I did not budge. Eventually, he returned to the printout. "It looks like Luciano might have been involved in your parents' deaths as well, just before he went missing."

"Missing? I thought he was dead."

Alessandro did not even look at me. "Careful. I am not going to ask you who told you that. Am I correct in assuming that you do not intend to tell these officers any more than you already have?" He glanced at me for confirmation, then continued, "In that case I suggest you start looking traumatized, so we can get out of here. They've already asked for your Social Security number twice."

"Lest we forget," I said under my breath, "you were the one who dragged me in here!"

"And now I am dragging you out again." He put an arm around me and stroked my hair as if I needed comforting. "Don't be upset about Peppo. He will be fine."

Playing along, I leaned against his shoulder and drew a deep, tearful sigh that felt almost genuine. Seeing my emotional upset the officers finally backed off and left us alone, and five minutes later we walked out of the police station together.

"Nice work," said Alessandro, as soon as we were out of hearing range.

"Likewise. Although . . . this has definitely not been my kind of day, so don't expect pinwheels."

He stopped and looked at me, a small frown on his forehead. "At least now you know the name of the man who followed you. Wasn't that what you wanted when you came to see me this afternoon?"

The world had turned black while we were inside the police station, but the air was still warm, and the streetlamps cast a soft yellow light on everything. Had it not been for the Vespas shooting past us in all directions, the whole piazza would have looked like a stage setting in an opera.

"What does *ragazza* mean?" I asked. "Something nasty?"

Alessandro stuck his hands in his pockets and started walking. "I figured that if I told them you were my girlfriend, they would stop asking for your Social Security number. *And* your phone number."

I laughed. "And they didn't wonder what the heck Juliet is doing dating a Salimbeni?"

Alessandro smiled, but I could see that my question bothered him. "I'm afraid they don't teach Shakespeare at the Police Academy here."

We walked for a while in silence, heading for nowhere in particular. It would have been a natural time for us to part, but then, I did not feel like parting. Never mind the fact that Bruno Carrera might very well be wait-ing for me when I returned to my hotel room; staying close to Alessandro felt like the most natural thing to do.

"Would now," I said, "be a good time to thank you?"

"Now?" He checked his wristwatch. "Assolutamente sì. Now is the time."

"How about dinner? On me?"

My proposal amused him. "Sure. Unless you'd rather hang around on your balcony, waiting for Romeo?"

"Someone broke in through my balcony, remember?"

"I see." His eyes narrowed slightly. "You want me to protect you."

I opened my mouth to fire back something cheeky, but realized I didn't want to. The truth was, after everything that had happened, and everything that might happen still, I would like nothing more than to have Alessandro—gun attached—within arm's length for the remainder of my stay in Siena. "Well," I said, swallowing my pride, "I suppose I would not object if you did."

You are a lover, borrow Cupid's wings
And soar with them above a common bound

. . .

Siena, A.D. 1340

IT WAS THE DAY OF THE PALIO, and the people of Siena were merrily afloat on a sea of song. Every street had become a river, every piazza a whirlpool of religious ecstasy, and those awash in the current kept flapping their flags and banners that they might rise out of the shallows and straddle the slippery swells of fortune, reaching up for their mother in Heaven to feel her tender touch.

The tide of devout mankind had long since broken through the floodgates of the city, spurting out into the countryside all the way to Fontebecci, a few miles north of Porta Camollia. Here, a heaving ocean of heads watched intently as the fifteen horsemen of the Palio emerged from their tents in full battle dress, prepared to honor the newly crowned Virgin by a dashing show of manhood.

It had taken Maestro Ambrogio the better part of the morning to leave town, elbowing his way through the masses, and had he been able to feel less guilt in the matter, he would have given up and turned around a thousand times before he was even halfway to Fontebecci. But he could not. How very wretched the old artist felt this morning! How dreadfully misguided had been his intervention in the affairs of these young people! Had he not been in such a hurry to join beauty with beauty for beauty's sake, Romeo would never have known that Giulietta was alive, and she on her side would never have become infected with his passion.

How very odd, the idea that an artist's love of beauty could so easily turn him into a delinquent. How very cruel it was of Fortuna to teach an old man a lesson at the cost of a young couple's bliss. Or was he mistaken when he tried to explain his own crime through lofty ideas? Was it in fact his base humanity, and nothing else, that had doomed the young lovers from the very outset? Was it possible that he had transferred his own infirm desire to the admirable body of Romeo, and that all his hopes for the happy union of the youngsters had merely been a way of gaining vicarious admittance into Giulietta Tolomei's bridal chamber?

The Maestro was not one to wallow in religious riddles unless they were part of a painting and payment was forthcoming, but it suddenly struck him that the slight nausea he was feeling at the thought of himself as a lascivious old puppeteer must be somewhat near what God was feeling every minute of every day. If indeed He felt anything. He was, after all, a divine Being, and it was entirely conceivable that divinity was incompatible with emotion. If not, then the Maestro sincerely pitied God, for the history of mankind was nothing more than a long tale of tears.

With the Virgin Mary it was different. She had been a human being, and she understood what it meant to suffer. She was the one who would always listen to your woes and make sure God sent his thunderbolts in the right direction. Like the lovely wife of a mighty man, she was the one to befriend and beseech, the one who knew how to reach his divine heart. She was the one to whom Siena had given its front-door keys, the one who had a special fondness for the Sienese, and who would protect them against their enemies, the way a mother protects the little son who seeks her embraces against the harassment of his brothers.

The Maestro's air of imminent apocalypse was not reflected in the faces of the people he pushed aside in his quest to reach Fontebecci before the race began. Everyone was feasting, and no one was in a particular hurry to move forward; as long as one secured a spot along the open road, there was no real need to walk all the way to Fontebecci. Certainly, there would be sights to see at the starting area with all the tents, the many false starts, and the noble families whose sons were participating, but after all, what spectacle could be more worthwhile than the oncoming roar of fifteen galloping warhorses?

When he finally arrived, Maestro Ambrogio headed straight for the colors of the Marescotti eagle. Romeo had already emerged from the yellow tent, surrounded by the men of his family, and there was a remarkable scarcity of smiles among them. Even Comandante Marescotti, who was known to always have an encouraging word for everyone, be it in the most desperate of situations, looked like a soldier who knew he had fallen into an ambush. He was the one who personally held the horse steady while Romeo got into the saddle, and he was the only one who addressed his son directly.

"Fear not," the Maestro heard him say, adjusting the plate armor covering the animal's face, "he stands like an angel, but he will run like the devil."

Romeo merely nodded, too excited to speak, and took the lance with the eagle flag that was handed to him. He would have to ride with it all the way, and if the Virgin Mary was kind, it would be the very one that was exchanged for the cencio at the finish line. If, on the other hand, the Virgin was in a jealous mood, he would be the last rider to plant his flag in front of the cathedral, and in return he would have to pick up a pig as a symbol of his shame.

Just as the helmet was brought out, Romeo caught sight of Maestro Ambrogio, and his surprise was so great that the horse became nervous beneath him. "Maestro!" he exclaimed, and there was understandable bitterness in his voice, "have you come to draw a picture of my downfall? I assure you, it will be quite the spectacle for an artist's eye."

"You are right," replied Maestro Ambrogio, "to taunt me. I gave you a map leading straight to disaster; now I am eager to undo the damage."

"Undo away, old man!" said Romeo. "You had better hurry, though, for I see the rope is ready."

"Indeed I shall," replied the Maestro, "if you will allow me to speak bluntly."

"Blunt speech is all we have time for," said Comandante Marescotti. "So let us hear it!"

Maestro Ambrogio cleared his throat. The carefully rehearsed monologue he had worked on all morning now quite escaped him, and he barely knew his first line. But necessity soon overruled eloquence, and he blurted out his information in the order it occurred to him. "You are in great danger!" he began. "And if you do not believe me—"

"We believe you!" barked Comandante Marescotti. "Tell us the details!"

"One of my students, Hassan," the Maestro went on, "overheard a conversation in Palazzo Salimbeni last night. He was working on an angel in the ceiling, a cherub, I believe—"

"To Hell with the cherub!" roared Comandante Marescotti. "Tell us what Salimbeni is planning to do to my son!"

Maestro Ambrogio drew in air. "I believe their plan is as follows: Nothing will be attempted here at Fontebecci, as so many eyes are watching. But halfway to Porta Camollia, where the road widens, the son of Tolomei and someone else will attempt to block your way or push you into the ditch. If Salimbeni's son is far ahead of you, they will be content with just slowing you down. But that is only the beginning. Once you enter town, be careful when you go through the contrade controlled by Salimbeni. When you pass the houses in the neighborhoods of Magione and Santo Stefano, there will be people in the towers, and they will throw things at you, if you are among the three front riders. Once you get into San Donato and Sant'Egidio, they will not be as bold, but if you are ahead of the field and look like a winner, they will risk it."

Romeo looked at his father. "What do you make of that?"

"The same as you do," said Comandante Marescotti. "This is no surprise, I was expecting it. But thanks to the Maestro, we now have certainty. Romeo, you must start ahead of the field and stay in front. Do not spare the horse, just go. Once you reach Porta Camollia, you must let them pass you, one by one, until you are in the fourth position."

"But—"

"Do not interrupt me! I want you to stay in the fourth position until you are clear of Santo Stefano. Then you may climb up to the third or second position. But not the first. Not until you have passed Palazzo Salimbeni, do you understand?"

"It is too close to the finishing line! I can't pass!"

"But you will."

"It is too close! Nobody has ever done that before!"

"Since when," said Comandante Marescotti, more softly, "did that ever stop my son?"

A clarion signal from the starting line ended all conversation, and the eagle helmet was placed over Romeo's head, its visor closed. The family priest quickly executed the—very likely last—blessing of the young man, and the Maestro found himself extending the wishes to the nervous horse; after that it was up to the Virgin alone to protect her champion.

As the fifteen horses lined up at the rope, the crowd began chanting the names of favorites as well as foes. Every noble family had its supporters and its antagonists; no one household was universally loved, or despised. Even the Salimbenis had their throng of devoted clients, and it was on occasions such as these that great, ambitious men expected to see their year-round generosity rewarded with a lavish show of public support.

Among the horsemen themselves, few had thoughts for much except the road ahead. Eye contact was sought and avoided, patron saints were mobilized like locusts onto Egypt, and last-minute insults were hurled like missiles at a closing city gate. The time for prayers had passed, advice was no longer heard, and no deals could now be undone. Whatever demons, evil or good, had been conjured from the collective soul of the people of Siena, they had been given life, and only the battle itself, the race, could execute justice. There was no law but fate, no rights but the favors of chance; victory was the only truth worth knowing.

"So, let this be the day," thought Maestro Ambrogio, "where you, divine Virgin, celebrate your coronation in Heaven by leniency towards us poor sinners, old as young. I beg you to take pity on Romeo Marescotti and protect him against the forces of evil that are about to eat up this city from within its own bowels. And I promise you, if you let him live, I shall devote the rest of my life to your beauty. But if he dies today, he has perished by my hand, and for sorrow and shame, that hand shall never paint again."

AS ROMEO RODE UP to the starting area with the eagle banner, he felt the sticky web of a conspiracy closing around him. Everyone had heard of his brash challenge to Salimbeni, and knew that a family battle must ensue. Knowing the contestants, the question in most people's minds was not so much who would win the race, but who would be alive at the end of it.

Romeo looked around at the other riders, trying to guess his odds. The Crescent Moon—Tolomei's son, Tebaldo—was clearly in alliance with the Diamond—Salimbeni's son, Nino—and even the Rooster and the Bull looked at him with eyes full of treason. Only the Owl nodded at him with the stern sympathy of a friend, but then, the Owl had many friends.

When the rope dropped, Romeo was not even fully inside the official starting area. He had been too busy looking at the other riders and judging their game to keep an eye on the magistrate in charge. Besides, the Palio always began with many false starts, and the starter had no qualms about bringing everyone back and starting over a dozen or so times—in fact, it was all part of the game.

But not today. For the first time in Palio history, the clarions did not sound a cancellation after the first start: Despite the confusion and the one horse left behind, the fourteen other riders were allowed to continue, and the race was on. Too shocked to feel more than a flash of fury at the foul play, Romeo tilted the lance forward until it sat tightly under his arm, dug his heels into the horse, and took up the pursuit.

The field was so far ahead that it was impossible to say who was in the lead; all he could see through the eye slit of the helmet was dust and incredulous faces turning towards him, faces of bystanders who had expected to see the young lover already far ahead of his rivals. Ignoring their cries and gestures—some encouraging, others anything but—Romeo rode right through the fray, giving the horse full rein and praying that it would return the favor.

Comandante Marescotti had run a calculated risk by giving his son a stallion; with a mare or a gelding Romeo had a fair chance, but a fair chance is not enough when your life is at stake. At least with a stallion it was all or nothing. Yes, it was possible that Cesare would get into a fight, pursue a mare, or even throw his rider to show the boy who was in charge, but on the other hand, he had the extra power needed to pull away from a dangerous situation, and, most important, he had the winning spirit.

Cesare also had another quality, something that was, under normal circumstances, entirely irrelevant to the Palio, but which now occurred to Romeo as being the only possible way in which he could ever hope to catch up with the field: The horse was an uncommonly powerful jumper.

The rules of the Palio said nothing about staying on the road. As long as a rider started at Fontebecci and ended up at the Siena Cathedral he was eligible to win the prize. It had never been necessary to stipulate the exact route, for no one had ever been foolish enough not to follow the road. The fields on either side of it were bumpy, filled with livestock or heaps of drying hay, as well as being crisscrossed by numerous fences and gates. To attempt a shortcut through the fields, in other words, meant facing an army of obstacles, obstacles that might be fun for a rider wearing a tunic, but which were murder for a horse carrying a knight with plate armor and a lance.

Romeo did not hesitate for long. The fourteen other riders were heading southwest, following a two-mile-long curve in the road that would eventually bring them to Porta Camollia. This was his chance.

Spotting an opening in the screaming crowd, he steered Cesare right off the road, into a recently harvested grain field, and beelined for the city gate.

The horse relished the challenge and tore through the field with more energy than it had displayed on the road, and when Romeo saw the first wooden fence coming up ahead, he pulled off the eagle helmet and tossed it into a passing haystack. There were no rules outlining a rider's wear apart from the lance with the family colors; riders wore their battle dress and helmets exclusively in the interest of self-protection. In throwing away his helmet, Romeo knew he would be vulnerable to punches from the other riders as well as to objects deliberately dropped from the tower-houses of the city, but he also knew that if he did not lighten its load, the horse—strong as it was—would never make it into town.

Flying over the first fence, Cesare came down heavily on the other side, and Romeo wasted no time in stripping the breastplate from his shoulders and tossing it into the middle of the pigsty he was riding through. The next two fences were lower than the first, and the horse jumped them with ease as Romeo held the lance high above his head to avoid getting it caught on the rails. Losing the lance with the Marescotti colors meant losing the race, even if he came in as number one.

Everyone who saw him that day would have sworn that Romeo was attempting the impossible. The distance saved by the shortcut was easily nullified by the many jumps, and once back on the road, he would—at best—be as far behind the other riders as he had been before. To say nothing of the harm done to the horse from galloping across heaps and holes and jumping like a mad dog under the August sun.

Luckily, Romeo did not know his odds. He also did not know that he emerged on the road ahead of the field due to very unusual circumstances. Somewhere along the way, an anonymous bystander had let loose a hamper of geese right in front of the Palio riders, and in the confusion, rotten eggs had been very accurately launched at a particular horseman—belonging to a particular tower-house—in retaliation for a similar incident the year before. Such pranks were part of the Palio, but only rarely did they have any profound influence on the race.

There were those who saw the Virgin Mary's hand in it all: the geese, the delay, and Romeo's magical flight over seven fences. But to the fourteen riders, who had dutifully followed the road, Romeo's sudden appearance ahead of them could be nothing but the work of the devil. And so they pursued him with hateful vehemence as the road gradually narrowed to funnel them all through the arch of Porta Camollia.

Only the boys who had climbed up onto the brickwork of the city gate had been able to see the latter part of Romeo's daring ride with their own eyes, and whatever their previous allegiances, whatever the loves and hates of their kin crowding below, those boys could not help but cheer on the reckless challenger as he shot through the gate beneath them, eminently vulnerable without his body armor and helmet, and immediately followed by a band of frenzied foes.

MANY A PALIO HAD been decided at Porta Camollia; the rider who had the good fortune to be first through the city gate stood a decent chance of maintaining the lead through the narrow city streets and ending up the winner in Piazza del Duomo. The greatest challenge from now on was the tower-houses lining the road on both sides; despite the law stipulating that if objects had been deliberately thrown from a tower, then that tower must be torn down, flowerpots and bricks kept falling—miraculously or devilishly, depending on your allegiance—onto rivals passing in the street below. Despite the law, such acts were rarely punished, for to gather a sober and unanimous account of events leading to accidents along the Palio racetrack was something very few city officials had ever bothered to attempt.

As he rode under the fateful gate and entered Siena in the lead position, Romeo was only too aware of disobeying his father. Comandante Marescotti had instructed him to avoid being in the lead, precisely because of the danger of projectiles thrown from the towers. Even with a helmet on his head, a man could easily be knocked from his horse by a well-aimed terra-cotta pot; with no helmet on, he was sure to be dead before he even hit the ground.

But Romeo could not let the others pass him. He had struggled so hard to catch up and pass the field that the idea of falling back to the fourth position—even in the interest of strategy and self-preservation— was as repulsive as giving in completely and letting the others finish the race without him.

And so he spurred on the horse and thundered into town, trusting in the Virgin to carve his way with her heavenly staff and deliver him from any evil falling from aloft.

He saw no faces, no limbs, no bodies; Romeo's path was lined with walls studded with screaming mouths and wide-open eyes, mouths that made no sound, and eyes that saw nothing but black and white, rival and ally, and which would never be able to recount the facts of the race, for in a maddened crowd there are none. All is emotion, all is hope, and the wishes of the crowd will always trump the truth of one.

The first projectile hit him just as he entered the neighborhood of Magione. He never saw what it was, just felt a sudden, burning pain in his shoulder as the object merely grazed him and fell to the ground somewhere in his wake.

The next one—a terra-cotta pot—hit his thigh with a numbing thud, and for a brief instant he thought the impact might have crushed the bone. But when he touched a hand to his leg, he felt nothing, not even pain. Not that it mattered whether the bone was broken or not, as long as he was still in the saddle and his foot still firmly in the stirrup.

The third object to hit him was smaller, and that was fortunate, for it hit him right on the forehead and nearly knocked him out. It took Romeo a few gasps to shake the darkness and regain control of the horse, and meanwhile, all around him, the wall of screaming mouths was laughing at his confusion. Only now did he fully understand what his father had known all along: If he stayed in the lead through the neighborhoods controlled by the Salimbenis, he would never finish the race.

Once the decision was made, it was not hard to fall back from the lead position; the challenge was to avoid being passed by more than three other riders. They all glared at him as they passed him—the son of

Tolomei, the son of Salimbeni, and someone else who did not matter—and Romeo glared right back at them, hating them for thinking he was giving up, and hating himself for resorting to tricks.

Taking up the pursuit, he stayed as close to the three as he could, keeping his head down and trusting that no tower-dwelling Salimbeni supporter would risk hurting the son of their patron. His calculation proved right. The sight of the Salimbeni banner with the three diamonds made everyone hesitate one moment too long in throwing their bricks and pots, and as the four riders galloped through the neighborhood of San Donato, Romeo was not struck by a single object.

Riding by Palazzo Salimbeni at last, he knew the time had come for him to do the impossible: pass his three rivals, one by one, before the track turned sharply up Via del Capitano and into Piazza del Duomo. This was truly the moment when divine intervention would show itself; were he to succeed and win the race from his current position, it could only be a result of heavenly favor.

Spurring on the horse, Romeo managed to catch up with the son of Tolomei and the son of Salimbeni—side by side as if they had been allies forever—but just as he was about to pass them, Nino Salimbeni drew back his arm like a scorpion its tail, and sunk a shiny dagger into the flesh of Tebaldo Tolomei, right above the harness where the tender neck was visible between the body armor and the helmet.

It happened so quickly that no one else could possibly have seen exactly who attacked and how. There was a flash of gold, a brief struggle. Then seventeen-year-old Tebaldo Tolomei tumbled from the horse, limply, in the middle of Piazza Tolomei, to be pulled aside by his father's screaming clients, while the assassin continued at full speed without even looking back.

The only one to react to the atrocity was the third rider, who—fearing for his own life now that he seemed the only serious contender left—began swinging his banner at the murderer, trying to knock him out of the saddle.

Giving Cesare full rein, Romeo tried to pass the two wrestling riders, but was thwarted when Nino Salimbeni broadsided him in an attempt at avoiding the third rider's banner. Hanging by little more than a stirrup, Romeo saw Palazzo Marescotti fly by and knew that the most lethal corner of the Palio was coming up ahead. If he was not back in the saddle when the road turned, his Palio—and maybe his life—would come to a very ignoble end.

IN PIAZZA DEL DUOMO, Friar Lorenzo regretted—for the twentieth time that morning—not staying in his lonely cell with his prayer book. Rather, he had allowed himself to be swept outside and away by the madness of the Palio. Here he was, trapped in the crowd and barely able to see the finish line, never mind that demonic cloth flying from a tall pole, that silken noose around the neck of innocence: the cencio.

Next to him was the podium holding the heads of the noble families, not to be confused with the podium of the government, which held fewer luxuries, and fewer ancestors, but—for all the self-effacing rhetoric—an equal amount of ambition. Both Tolomei and Salimbeni were visible on the former, opting to watch their sons triumph from the comfort of cushioned seats rather than suffering the dust of the starting line at Fontebecci only to toss their paternal advice at an ungrateful youngster who would never heed it anyway.

As they sat there, waving at their cheering supporters with measured condescension, they were not deaf to the fact that, this year, the tone of the masses had changed. The Palio had always been a cacophony of voices with everyone singing the songs of their own contrada and their own heroes—including the houses of Tolomei and Salimbeni, if they had a rider in the race—but this year it seemed many more people were joining in the songs of Aquila, the Marescotti eagle.

Sitting there, listening to it all, Tolomei looked worried. Only now, Friar Lorenzo ventured to guess, did the great man wonder whether it had been such a good idea to bring along with him the true prize of the Palio: his niece Giulietta.

The young woman was hardly recognizable as she sat there between father and husband-to-be, her regal attire at odds with her wan cheeks. She had turned her head once, to look right at Friar Lorenzo, as if she had known all along that he was standing there, observing her. The look on her face sent a stab of compassion through his heart, immediately followed by a stab of fury that he was unable to save her.

Was this why God had delivered her from the slaughter that befell her family—only to thrust her into the arms of the very villain who had shed their blood? It was a cruel, cruel fate, and Friar Lorenzo found himself suddenly wishing that neither she, nor he, had survived that evil day.

IF GIULIETTA HAD KNOWN her friend's thoughts as she sat there on the podium, displayed for everyone to pity, she would have agreed that marriage to Salimbeni was a fate worse than death. But it was too early to give in to despair; the Palio was not yet over, Romeo was—as far as she knew—still alive, and Heaven might still be on their side.

If the Virgin Mary had truly been offended by Romeo's behavior in the cathedral the night before, she would surely have struck him dead on the spot; the fact that he had been allowed to live, and return home unharmed, must mean that Heaven wanted him to ride in the Palio. But then . . . the design of Heaven was one thing, and quite another was the will of the man sitting next to her, Salimbeni.

A distant rumble of oncoming horses made the crowd around the podium contract in expectation and erupt in frenzied cheers, calling out the names of their favorites and rivals as if shouting could somehow direct fate. Everywhere around her, people stretched to see which of the fifteen Palio riders would be first into the piazza, but Giulietta could not look. Closing her eyes to the turmoil, she pressed her folded hands to her lips and dared to speak the one word that would make everything right, "Aquila!"

One breathless moment later, that word was repeated everywhere around her by thousands of voices: *Aquila! Aquila! Aquila!* It was cried, it was chuckled, it was sneered . . . and Giulietta opened her eyes excitedly to see Romeo sweeping through the piazza—his horse skidding on the uneven track and foaming with exhaustion—heading straight for the angel wagon with the cencio. His face was torn with rage, and she was shocked to see him smeared in blood, but he still had the eagle banner in his hand, and he was first. First.

Not pausing to cheer, Romeo rode right up to the angel wagon, pushed aside the chubby choirboys dressed with wings and suspended with ropes, grabbed the pole with the cencio, and planted his own banner instead. Holding his prize high in unrestrained triumph, he turned to face his closest rival, Nino Salimbeni, and to relish the other's rage.

Nobody cared about the riders coming in third, fourth, and fifth; almost as one, the crowd's heads were turning to see what Salimbeni was going to do about Romeo and this unexpected turn of events. By now, there was not a man or woman in Siena who was ignorant of Romeo's defying Salimbeni, and his pledge to the Virgin Mary—that if he won the Palio, he would not turn the cencio into clothes, but drape it over his wedding bed—and there were few hearts,that did not harbor some sympathy for the young lover.

Seeing that Romeo had secured the cencio, Tolomei got up abruptly, swaying in the crosswinds of fortune. All around him, the people of Siena were wailing and pleading, begging him to change his heart. Yet next to him sat a man who would surely squash that heart if he did.

"Messer Tolomei!" bellowed Romeo, holding the cencio high as the horse reared up beneath him, "Heaven has spoken in my favor! Do you dare ignore the wishes of the Virgin Mary? Will you sacrifice this city to her wrath? Does the pleasure of that man"—he pointed boldly at Salimbeni—"mean more to you than the safety of us all?"

A roar of outrage went through the crowd at the idea, and the guards surrounding the podium positioned themselves to draw and defend. There were those among the townspeople who defied the guards and boldly reached for Giulietta, urging her to jump from the podium and let them deliver her to Romeo. But Salimbeni put a stop to their attempts by standing up and placing a firm hand on her shoulder.

"Very well, boy!" he yelled to Romeo, counting on his many friends and supporters to cheer him on and turn the tide. "You won the race! Now go home and turn that cencio into a nice dress for yourself, and maybe I'll let you be my bridesmaid when—"

But the crowd had heard enough and would not let him finish. "Shame on the Salimbenis," cried someone, "for violating the will of Heaven!" And the rest responded immediately, screaming out their indignation against the noble gentlemen and preparing to turn rage into riot. Old Palio rivalries were now quite forgotten, and the few imbeciles still singing were quickly shut up by their peers.

The people of Siena knew that if they all united against the few, they might be able to storm the podium and steal away the lady who so obviously belonged to another. It would not be the first time they had rebelled against Salimbeni, and they knew that if only they kept pushing, they would soon have the mighty men hiding within their tall towers, all stairs and ladders pulled up and out of reach.

To Giulietta, who sat on the podium like an inexperienced sailor on a stormy sea, it was frightening and intoxicating to feel the power of the elements raging about her. There they were, thousands of strangers, whose names she did not know, but who were ready to brave the halberds of the guards to bring her justice. If only they kept pushing, the podium would soon keel over, and all the noble gentlemen would be busy saving themselves and their fine robes from the rabble.

In such a pandemonium, Giulietta figured, she and Romeo might be able to disappear, and the Virgin Mary would surely keep the riot going long enough for them to escape the city together.

But it was not to be. Before the mob had gathered momentum, a new group of people came bursting into the piazza, to scream terrible news at Messer Tolomei. "Tebaldo!" they cried, pulling at their hair in despair, "it is Tebaldo! Oh, the poor boy!" And when they finally reached the podium and found Tolomei on his knees, begging them to tell him what had happened to his son, they replied in tears, waving a bloody dagger in the air, "He is dead! Murdered! Stabbed to death during the Palio!"

As soon as he understood the message, Tolomei fell over in convulsions, and the whole podium erupted in fear. Shocked by the sight of her uncle like this, looking as if he was possessed by a demon, Giulietta at first recoiled, then forced herself to kneel down and attend to him as best she could, shielding him from the scuffle of feet and legs until Monna Antonia and the servants were able to get through. "Uncle Tolomei," she urged him, not knowing what else to say, "calm yourself!"

The only man to stand straight through it all was Salimbeni, who demanded to see the murder weapon and instantly held it up for everyone to behold. "Look!" he roared. "There you have your hero! This is the dagger that killed Tebaldo Tolomei during our holy race! See?" He pointed at its shaft. "It has the Marescotti eagle engraved! What do you make of that?"

Giulietta looked out in horror to see the crowd staring at Salimbeni and the dagger in disbelief. Here was the man they had wanted to punish just a moment ago, but the shocking news of the misdeed and the sight of

Messer Tolomei's grieving figure had distracted them. Now they did not know what to think, and they just stood there, gaping, waiting for a cue.

Seeing the changing expression on their faces, Giulietta understood right away that Salimbeni had planned this moment in advance, in order to turn the mob against Romeo in case he won the Palio. Now they were quite forgetting their reasons for attacking the podium in the first place, yet their emotions were still running wild, ravenous for some other object to tear apart.

They did not have to wait long. Salimbeni had enough loyal clients in the crowd that, as soon as he waved the dagger in the air, someone yelled out, "Romeo is the murderer!"

Within a moment, the people of Siena were once again united, this time in disgusted hatred against the young man they had just hailed as their hero.

Afloat on such a full sea of commotion, Salimbeni now dared to order Romeo's immediate arrest, and to call everyone who disagreed a traitor. But to Giulietta's immense relief, when the guards returned to the podium a quarter of an hour later, they brought only a foaming horse, the eagle banner, and the cencio. Of Romeo Marescotti there had been no trace. No matter how many people they had asked, they had received the same reply: Not a single person had seen Romeo leaving the piazza.

Only when they started making house calls later that night did one man—in the interest of saving his wife and daughters from the uniformed villains—confess that he had heard a rumor saying Romeo Marescotti had escaped through the underground Bottini aqueduct in the company of a young Franciscan friar.

When Giulietta heard this rumor whispered by the servants later that evening, she sent up a grateful prayer to the Virgin Mary. There was no doubt in her mind that the Franciscan friar had been Friar Lorenzo, and she knew him well enough to be sure that he would do everything in his power to save the man he knew she loved.

O, he's a lovely gentleman.
Romeo's a dishclout to him. An eagle, madam,
Hath not so green, so quick, so fair an eye
As Paris hath

...

THE MONTE DEI PASCHI BANK was dark and empty after hours, greeting us with soothing silence as we walked up the central staircase together. Alessandro had asked if I minded a quick stop on the way to dinner, and I had, of course, said no. Now, following him to the very top of the stairs, I began to wonder where exactly he was taking me, and why.

"After you—" He opened a heavy mahogany door and waited for me to enter what turned out to be a large corner office. "Just give me a minute." Switching on a lamp, he disappeared into a back room, leaving the door ajar. "Don't touch anything!"

I glanced around at the plush couches and stately desk and chair. The office bore few signs of actual work. A lonely file folder sitting on the desk looked as if it had been placed there mostly for show. The only wall decorations were the windows overlooking Piazza Salimbeni; there were no personal effects such as diplomas or photographs anywhere in the room, nor anything else to identify its owner. I had just touched a finger to the edge of the desk to feel the dust when Alessandro reemerged, buttoning a shirt. "Careful!" he said. "Desks like that kill many more people than guns do."

"This is your office?" I asked, stupidly.

"Sorry," he said, grabbing a jacket from a chair. "I know you prefer the basement. To me"—he cast an unenthusiastic look around the opulent décor—"this is the real torture chamber."

Back outside, he stopped in the middle of Piazza Salimbeni and looked at me with a teasing smile. "So, where are you taking me?"

I shrugged. "I'd like to see where the Salimbenis go for dinner."

His smile faded. "I don't think so. Unless you want to spend the rest of the evening with Eva Maria." Seeing that I did not, he went on, "Why don't we go somewhere else? Somewhere in your neighborhood."

"But I don't know anybody in the Owl contrada," I protested, "except cousin Peppo. And I wouldn't have a clue where to eat."

"Good." He started walking. "Then nobody will bother us."

WE ENDED UP AT Taverna di Cecco, just around the corner from the Owl Museum. It was a small place, off the beaten track and bustling with contrada locals. All the dishes—some served in clay bowls—looked like Mamma's best home cooking. Looking around, I saw no artsy experiments with herbs sprinkled on the edge of half-empty plates; here, the plates were full, and the spices were where they belonged: in the food.

Most tables had five or six people at them, all laughing or arguing animatedly, not the least bit worried about being too loud or staining the tablecloths. I now understood why Alessandro had wanted to go to a place where no one knew him; judging by the way people hung out with their friends here—inviting everyone and their dog to join in and making a big fuss if they refused—it was hard to have a quiet dinner for two in Siena. As we made our way past them all and into an undisturbed corner, I could see that Alessandro was visibly relieved to recognize no one.

As soon as we sat down, he reached into his jacket, took out Romeo's dagger, and put it on the table between us. "It seems," he said, speaking the unfamiliar words very slowly, if not reluctantly, "I owe you an apology."

"Oh well"—I stuck my nose in a menu to hide my smirk—"don't get too carried away. You read my file. I'm still a threat to society."

But he was not ready to laugh it off just yet, and for a while we sat in awkward silence, pretending to study the menu and taking turns poking at the dagger.

Not until we had a bottle of Prosecco and a plate of antipasto in front of us did Alessandro smile—albeit apologetically—and raise his glass. "I hope you'll enjoy it better this time. Same wine, new bottle."

"Getting to the main course would definitely be an improvement," I said, touching my glass to his. "And if I can avoid being chased barefoot through the streets afterwards, I'd say this evening is bound to trump last night."

He winced. "Why didn't you come back to the restaurant?"

"I'm sorry," I laughed, "but my scummy friend Bruno was far better company than you. At least he believed I was Giulietta all along."

Alessandro looked away, and it occurred to me that I was the only one who appreciated the comedy of the situation. I knew he had humor—and certainly sarcasm enough to go around—but right now it clearly did not amuse him to be reminded of his own ungentlemanly behavior.

"When I was thirteen years old," he finally said, leaning back in his chair, "I spent a summer with my grandparents here in Siena. They had a beautiful farm. Vineyards. Horses. Plumbing. One day, they had a visitor. It was an American woman, Diane Tolomei, and her two little girls, Giulietta and Giannozza—"

"Wait!" I interrupted him. "You mean, *me*?"

He looked at me with a strange, lopsided smile. "Yes. You were wearing a—what is the word?—diaper." Ignoring my protests, he went on, "My grandmother told me to play with you and your sister while they talked, and so I took you out to the barn to show you the horses. Unfortunately, you got scared and fell down on a hayfork"—he shook his head, reliving the moment—"it was terrible. You were screaming, and there was blood everywhere. I carried you into the kitchen, but you were kicking and crying, and your mother looked at me as if I had tortured you on purpose. Fortunately, my grandmother knew what to do, and she gave you a big ice cream and stitched up the cut the way she had done with all her children and grandchildren many times." Alessandro took a sip of Prosecco before he went on, "Two weeks later my parents read in the newspaper that Diane Tolomei had died in a car accident, together with her little girls. They were devastated." He looked up and met my eyes at last. "That is why I didn't believe you were Giulietta Tolomei."

For a moment we just sat there, looking at each other. It was a sad story for both of us, but at the same time there was something bittersweet and irresistible about the idea that we had met before, as children.

"It is true," I said quietly, "that my mother died in a car crash, but she didn't have us with her that day. The newspaper got it wrong. Now, as for the hayfork," I went on, more cheerfully, "I appreciate knowing what happened. Do you have any idea how unsettling it is to have a scar and not know where it came from?"

Alessandro looked incredulous. "You still have a scar?"

"Absolutely!" I pulled up my skirt and let him see the white mark on my thigh. "Pretty nasty, huh? But now I finally know who to blame."

Checking to see if he looked remorseful, I found him staring at my thigh with an expression of shock that was so very unlike him, it made me burst out laughing. "Sorry!" I pushed down my skirt again. "I got carried away by your story."

Alessandro cleared his throat and reached for the Prosecco bottle. "Let me know when you want another one."

HALFWAY THROUGH DINNER, he got a call from the police station. When he returned to the table, I could see that he had good news.

"Well," he said, sitting down, "it looks like you don't have to change hotels tonight. They found Bruno at his sister's, his trunk full of stolen goods from your cousin's museum. When his sister discovered that he was back in his old business, she beat him up so bad he begged them to arrest him right away." He grinned and shook his head, but when he noticed my raised eyebrows, he quickly sobered. "Unfortunately, they did not find the cencio. He must have hidden it somewhere else. Don't worry, it will turn up. There's no way he can sell that old rag—" Seeing my dismay with his choice of words, he shrugged. "I didn't grow up here."

"A private collector," I said, sharply, "would pay a lot of money for that old rag. These things have great emotional value to people around here . . . as I'm sure you are well aware. Who knows, maybe it's Romeo's family, the Marescottis, who are behind all this. Remember, my cousin Peppo said that Romeo's descendants think the cencio and this dagger belong to them."

"If it is," said Alessandro, leaning back as the waiter took away our plates, "we'll know tomorrow, when the boys have a little talk with Bruno. He is not the silent type."

"What about you? Do you believe it? . . . That the Marescottis hired him to steal the cencio?"

I could see that Alessandro was not at all comfortable with the subject. "If they were really behind this," he eventually said, "they would not have used Bruno. They have their own people. And they would not have left the dagger on the table."

"Sounds like you know them?"

He shrugged. "Siena is a small place."

"I thought you said you didn't grow up here."

"True." He tapped his fingers on the table a few times, clearly annoyed at my perseverance. "But I spent my summers here, with my grandparents. I told you. Me and my cousins played in the Marescotti vineyard every day. We were always afraid of being discovered. It was part of the fun. Everyone was afraid of old man Marescotti. Except Romeo, of course."

I nearly knocked over my wineglass. "You mean, *the* Romeo? The one that my cousin Peppo talked about, who might have stolen the cencio?" When Alessandro did not reply, I went on, more quietly, "I see. So, that's how it hangs together. You were childhood friends."

He grimaced. "Not exactly friends." Seeing that I was bursting to ask more questions, he handed me the menu. "Here. Time to think of sweet things."

Over dessert, dipping almond cookies—cantucci—in vin santo, I tried to circle back to the issue of Romeo, but Alessandro did not want to go there. Instead, he asked about my own childhood, and what had triggered my involvement with the antiwar movement. "Come on," he said, clearly amused by my scowl, "it can't all be your sister's fault."

"I never said it was. We just have very different priorities."

"Let me guess . . ." He pushed the cookies towards me. "Your sister is in the military? She went to Iraq?"

"Ha!" I helped myself to more cantucci. "Janice couldn't find Iraq on a foam puzzle. She thinks life is all about . . . having fun."

"Shame on her." Alessandro shook his head. "Enjoying life."

I exhaled sharply. "I knew you wouldn't understand! When we—"

"I do understand," he cut me off. "She is having fun, so you can't have fun. She is enjoying life, so you can't enjoy life. It's too bad someone carved that in stone."

"Look"—I swirled my empty wineglass, not willing to give him the point—"the most important person in the world to Janice Jacobs is Janice Jacobs. She will skewer anybody to score a point. She's the kind of person who—" I stopped myself, realizing that I, too, didn't want to conjure the ugly past on this pleasant evening.

"And what about Julie Jacobs?" Alessandro filled up my glass. "Who is the most important person to her?"

I looked at his smile, not sure if he was still making fun of me.

"Let me guess." He gave me a playful once-over. "Julie Jacobs wants to save the world and make everybody happy—"

"But in the process, she makes everybody miserable," I went on, hijacking his morality tale, "including herself. I know what you're thinking. You're thinking that the ends don't justify the means, and that sawing the heads off little mermaids is not how you make wars go away. I know that. I know it all."

"Then why did you do it?"

"I didn't! It wasn't supposed to be that way." I looked at him to see if we could possibly forget that I had mentioned the Little Mermaid and move on to a happier subject. But we couldn't. Even though he was half smiling, his eyes told me this was an issue that could be postponed no longer.

"Okay," I sighed, "this is what happened. I thought we were going to dress her up in army fatigues, and the Danish press would come and take pictures—"

"Which they did."

"I know! But I never wanted to cut her head off—"

"You were holding the saw."

"That was an accident!" I buried my face in my hands. "We didn't realize she was so small. It's a tiny little statue. The clothes didn't fit. And then someone—some moron—pulled out a saw—" I couldn't go on.

We sat for a moment in silence, until I peeked out through my fingers to see if he still looked disgusted. He didn't. In fact, he looked mildly amused. Although he wasn't actually smiling, there was that little sparkle in his eye.

"What's so funny?" I grumbled.

"You," said Alessandro. "You really are a Tolomei. Remember? . . . 'I will show myself a tyrant; when I have fought with the men I will be civil with the maids, I will cut off their heads.' " When he saw that I recognized the quotation, he finally smiled. " 'Ay, the heads of the maids, or their maidenheads; take it in what sense thou wilt.' "

I let my hands drop to my lap, partly relieved and partly embarrassed by the shift in our conversation. "You surprise me. I didn't realize you knew *Romeo and Juliet* by heart."

He shook his head. "Only the fighting parts. I hope that's not a disappointment."

Not entirely sure whether he was flirting with me or just making fun, I started fiddling with the dagger again. "It's strange," I said, "but I know the whole play. I always did. Even before I understood what it was. It was like a voice in my head—" I started laughing. "I don't know why I'm telling you this."

"Because," said Alessandro plainly, "you've only just discovered who you are. And it's all finally beginning to make sense. Everything you've done, everything you've chosen not to do . . . now you understand. This is what people call destiny."

I looked up to find him staring not at me, but at the dagger. "And you?" I asked. "Have you discovered your destiny?"

He took in air. "I've known it all along. And if I forget, Eva Maria will quickly remind me. But I never liked the idea that your future is already made. All my life, I tried to run away from my destiny."

"Did you succeed?"

He thought about it. "For a while. But, you know, it always catches up with you. No matter how far away you go."

"And did you go far?"

He nodded, but just once. "Very far. To the edge."

"You're making me curious," I said lightly, hoping he would elaborate. But he didn't. Judging from the frown on his forehead, it was no happy subject. Dying to know more about him, but without wanting to spoil the evening, I merely asked, "And are you planning to go back there?"

He almost smiled. "Why? Do you want to come?"

I shrugged, absentmindedly spinning the dagger on the tablecloth between us. "I'm not trying to run away from my destiny."

When I didn't meet his eyes, he put a hand gently on top of the weapon to stop it from spinning. "Maybe you should."

"I think," I countered, teasingly inching out my treasure from beneath his palm, "I prefer to stay and fight."

...

AFTER DINNER, ALESSANDRO insisted on walking me back to the hotel. Seeing that he had already won the battle over the restaurant bill, I didn't resist. Besides, even if Bruno Carrera was now behind bars, there was still a misfit on a motorcycle at large in town, preying on scaredy-mice like me.

"You know," he said, while we walked though the darkness together, "I used to be just like you. I used to think you had to fight for peace, and that, between you and a perfect world, there would always be sacrifice. Now I know better." He glanced at me. "Leave the world alone."

"Don't try to make it better?"

"Don't force people to be perfect. You'll die trying."

I couldn't help smiling at his mundane conclusion. "Notwithstanding the fact that my cousin is in the hospital, being slapped around by female doctors, I'm having such a good time. It's too bad we can't be friends."

This was news to Alessandro. "We can't?"

"Obviously not," I said. "What would all your other friends say? You're a Salimbeni, I'm a Tolomei. We're destined to be enemies."

His smile returned. "Or lovers."

I started laughing, mostly with surprise. "Oh, no! You are a Salimbeni, and as it turns out, Salimbeni was Shakespeare's Paris, the rich guy who wanted to marry Juliet *after* she had secretly married Romeo!"

Alessandro took the news in stride. "Ah yes, now I remember: the rich, handsome Paris. That's me?"

"Looks like it." I let out a theatrical sigh. "Lest we forget, my ancestor, Giulietta Tolomei, was in love with Romeo Marescotti, but was forced into an engagement with the evil Salimbeni, *your* ancestor! She was trapped in a lovers' triangle, just like Shakespeare's Juliet."

"I am evil, too?" Alessandro liked the story better and better. "Rich, handsome, and evil. Not a bad role." He thought about it for a moment, then added, more quietly, "You know, between you and me, I always thought Paris was a much better man than Romeo. In my opinion, Juliet was an idiot."

I stopped in the middle of the street. "Excuse me?"

Alessandro stopped, too. "Think about it. If Juliet had met Paris first, she would have fallen in love with him instead. And they would have lived happily ever after. She was ready to fall in love."

"Not so!" I countered. "Romeo was cute . . ."

"Cute?" Alessandro rolled his eyes. "What kind of man is *cute*?"

". . . and an excellent dancer . . ."

"Romeo had feet of lead! He said so himself!"

". . . but most importantly," I concluded, "he had nice hands!"

Now, at last, Alessandro looked defeated. "I see. He had nice hands. You got me there. So, that is what great lovers are made of?"

"According to Shakespeare it is." I glanced at his hands, but he foiled me by sticking them in his pockets.

"And do you really," he asked, walking again, "want to live your life according to Shakespeare?"

I looked down at the dagger. It was awkward to walk around with it like this, but it was too big to fit in my handbag, and I did not want to ask Alessandro to carry it for me again. "Not necessarily."

He glanced at the dagger, too, and I knew that we were thinking the same thing. If Shakespeare was right, this was the weapon with which Giulietta Tolomei had killed herself. "Then why don't you rewrite it?" he proposed. "And change your destiny."

I glared at him. "You mean, rewrite *Romeo and Juliet*?"

He did not meet my eyes, but kept looking straight ahead. "And be my friend."

I studied his profile in the darkness. We had spent the whole night talking, but I still knew almost nothing about him. "On one condition," I said. "That you tell me more about Romeo." But I regretted the words as soon as I had said them, seeing the frustration on his face.

"Romeo, Romeo," he gibed, "always Romeo. Is that why you came to Siena? To find the cute guy with the dancing feet and the nice hands? Well, I'm afraid you'll be disappointed. He's nothing like the Romeo you think you know. He won't make love in rhyming couplets. Take it from me: He's a real bastard. If I were you"—he looked at me at last—"I'd share my balcony with Paris this time around."

"I have no intention," I said, tartly, "of sharing my balcony with anyone. All I want is to get the cencio back, and the way I see it, Romeo is the only one with a motive for taking it. If you don't think he did it, then say so, and I'll drop the subject."

"Okay," said Alessandro. "I don't think he did it. But that doesn't mean he is clean. You heard your cousin: Romeo has evil hands. Everyone would like to think he is dead."

"What makes you so sure he is not?"

He squinted. "I can feel it."

"A nose for scumbags?"

He didn't reply right away. When he finally spoke, it was to himself as much as to me. "A nose for rivals."

DIRETTOR ROSSINI KISSED the feet of an imaginary crucifix when he saw me walking through the front door of his hotel that night. "Miss Tolomei! Grazie a Dio! You are safe! Your cousin called from the hospital many times—" Only now did he notice Alessandro behind me, and nodded a brief greeting. "He said that you were in bad company. Where have you been?"

I cringed. "As you can see, I'm in the best of hands."

"The second best," Alessandro corrected me, taking an absurd amount of pleasure in the situation. "For now."

"And he also," Direttor Rossini continued, "told *me* to tell *you* to put the dagger in a safe place."

I looked down at the dagger in my hand.

"Give it to me," said Alessandro. "I'll take care of it for you."

"Yes," urged Direttor Rossini. "Give it to Captain Santini. I don't want any more break-ins."

And so I gave Romeo's dagger to Alessandro, and saw it disappearing once more into his inner pocket. "I'll be back tomorrow," he said, "at nine o'clock. Don't open your door to anyone else."

"Not even my balcony door?"

"*Especially* not your balcony door."

CRAWLING INTO BED that night, I curled up with the document from my mother's box called *Giulietta and Giannozza Family Tree*. I had looked at it before, but had not found it very illuminating. Now, after Eva Maria had more or less confirmed that I was descended from Giulietta Tolomei, it suddenly made much more sense that my mother should have cared about tracing our bloodline.

My room was still a mess, but I did not feel like addressing my baggage just yet. At least the broken glass was gone, and a new pane had been installed while I was out; if someone else wanted to get into my room tonight, he would have to wake me first.

Unrolling the lengthy document on top of the bed, I spent a long time trying to orient myself in its forest of names. It was no ordinary family tree, for it traced our roots exclusively through the female line, and it was only concerned with logging the direct connection between the Giulietta Tolomei of 1340 and me.

I eventually found myself and Janice at the very bottom of the document, right below the names of our parents:

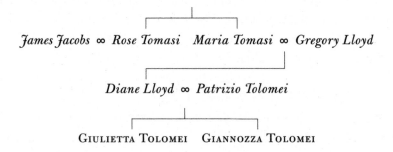

After my initial guffaw at the fact that Janice's given name really was Giannozza—she had always hated being Janice, and had maintained, to the point of tears, that it was not her name—I went all the way to the top of the document to find the exact same names right there:

And so forth. The list in between was so long that I could have used it as a rope ladder from my balcony. It was impressive that someone—or rather, dozens of people over the centuries—had so diligently kept track of our bloodline, starting all the way back in 1340, with Giulietta and her sister, Giannozza.

Every now and then those two names—Giulietta and Giannozza—popped up side by side on the family tree, but always with a different last name; they were never called Tolomei. What was particularly interesting was that, as far as I could see, Eva Maria had not been entirely right in saying that Giulietta Tolomei was my ancestor. For according to this document, we were all—Mom, Janice, and me—descended from Giulietta's sister, Giannozza, and her husband, Mariotto da Gambacorta. As for Giulietta, there was no record of her having married anyone, and certainly not of her having children.

Full of foreboding, I eventually put the document aside and dove back into the other texts. The knowledge that it was, in fact, Giannozza Tolomei who was my real ancestor made me much more appreciative of Giulietta's fragmented letters to her and occasional comments on Giannozza's quiet country life far away from Siena.

"You are lucky, my dearest," she had written at one point, "that your house is so large and your husband so hard of walking—" and later on she had mused, "Oh, to be you, sneaking outside and lying in the wild thyme for a stolen hour of peace—"

I eventually nodded off and slept soundly for a couple of hours, until a loud noise woke me up while it was still dark.

SOMEWHAT BLURRY ON the sounds of the waking world, it took me a moment to recognize the bedlam as a motorcycle revving its engine in the street beneath my balcony.

For a while I just lay there, annoyed at the inconsiderate nature of Siena youth in general, and it took me longer than it should have to realize that this was no ordinary gang rally, but a single biker trying to catch someone's attention. And that someone, I began to fear, was me.

Peeking out through the cracks in the shutters, I could not see much of the street below, but as I stood there, stretching this way and that, I started hearing noise all around me in the building. The other hotel guests, it seemed, were also getting out of bed and banging open the shutters to see what on earth was going on.

Emboldened by the collective uproar, I opened my French doors to peek out, and now I finally saw him; it was indeed my motorcycle stalker, making textbook figure-eights beneath a streetlamp. There was no doubt in my mind that it was the same guy who had followed me twice before—once to save me from Bruno Carrera, and once to look at me through the glass door of Malèna's espresso bar—for he was still black on black, visor closed, and I had never seen another bike just like his.

At one point he turned his head and spotted me in the balcony door. As the engine noise suddenly waned to a purr, it was nearly drowned out by angry shouts from the other windows and balconies of Hotel Chiusarelli, but he could not care less; reaching into his pocket, he took out a round object, pulled back his arm, and pitched whatever it was at my balcony with perfect aim.

It landed before my feet with an odd, squishy sound, and even bounced a bit before it finally rolled to a halt. With no other attempt at communication, my leather-clad friend jerked the Ducati into a frenzied acceleration that very nearly made it rear up and throw him off. Seconds later he disappeared around a corner and was gone, and had it not been for the other hotel guests—some grumbling, some laughing—the night would once again have been quiet.

I stood for a moment, staring at the missile, before I finally dared pick it up and bring it back into my room, closing the balcony door tightly behind me. Turning on the lights, I found that it was a tennis ball wrapped in heavy bond paper and secured with rubber bands. The paper, it turned out, was a message drafted by a strong, confident hand in the dark red ink of love letters and suicide notes. This was what it said:

Giulietta ~

Forgive me that I am carefulle, I have very good reason. Soon you will understand. I must talk with you and explain to you every thing. Meet me in the top of the Torre del Mangia tomorrow morning on 9, and do not tell it to any body.

~ Romeo

[V.I]

Why I descend into this bed of death
Is partly to behold my lady's face
But chiefly to take thence from her dead finger
A precious ring

...

Siena, A.D. 1340

On the night of the fatal palio, the body of young
Tebaldo Tolomei was laid out in the church of San Cristoforo, across the
piazza from Palazzo Tolomei. In a gesture of friendship, Messer Salimbeni had stopped by to drape the cencio over the dead hero and to promise the grieving father that the murderer would soon be found. After that,
he had excused himself and left the Tolomei family to their grief, pausing
only briefly on his way out to bow to the Lord and appreciate Giulietta's
slender form kneeling rather invitingly in prayer before the bier of her
cousin.

All the women of the Tolomei family were gathered in the church of
San Cristoforo that night, wailing and praying with Tebaldo's mother,
while the men ran back and forth between church and palazzo, wine on
their breath, athirst to execute justice on Romeo Marescotti. Whenever
Giulietta heard snippets of their hushed conversations, her throat tightened in fear, and her eyes welled up at the imagined sight of the man she
loved, caught by his enemies and punished for a crime she was certain he
had not committed.

It spoke in her favor that she was seen to grieve so profoundly over a
cousin with whom she had never exchanged a single word; the tears

Giulietta cried that night mingled with those of her cousins and aunts like rivers running into one and the same lake; they were so plentiful that no one cared to explore their true source.

"I suppose you *are* truly sorry," her aunt had said, looking up briefly from her own grief to see Giulietta crying into the cencio that was draped over Tebaldo. "And you should be! Had it not been for you, that bastard Romeo would never have dared—" Before she could finish the sentence, Monna Antonia had once again collapsed in tears, and Giulietta had discreetly removed herself from the center of attention to sit down in a pew in one of the darker corners of the church.

As she sat there, lonely and miserable, she was sorely tempted to try her luck and escape from San Cristoforo on foot. She had no money, and no one to protect her, but, God willing, she might be able to find her way back to Maestro Ambrogio's workshop. The city streets, however, were awash with soldiers searching for Romeo, and the entrance to the church was lined with guards. Only an angel—or a ghost—would be able to get past them unnoticed.

Sometime past midnight she looked up from her folded hands to see Friar Lorenzo making the rounds of the mourning party. The sight surprised her; she had heard the Tolomei guards talking about a Franciscan friar who had—allegedly—helped Romeo escape through the Bottini right after the Palio, and she had naturally assumed the man was Friar Lorenzo. Now, seeing him walking around the church so calmly, comforting the mourning women, her chest became heavy with disappointment. Whoever it was that had helped Romeo to escape, it was no one she knew or was ever likely to know.

When he eventually caught sight of her sitting alone in the corner, he joined her right away. Squeezing into the pew, Friar Lorenzo took the liberty of sharing her kneeler, and mumbled, "Forgive me for intruding on your grief."

Giulietta replied softly, making sure no one overheard them. "You are my grief's oldest friend."

"Would it console you to know that the man for whom you are *truly* crying is on his way to foreign lands where his foes will never find him?"

Giulietta pressed a hand to her mouth to strangle her emotion. "If he is indeed safe, then I am the happiest creature on earth. But I am also"—

her voice trembled—"the most pitiful. Oh, Lorenzo, how can we live like this . . . he there, I here? Would that I had gone with him! Would that I were a falcon on his arm and not a wanton bird in this putrid cage!"

Aware that she had spoken too loudly, and far too frankly, Giulietta looked around nervously to see if anyone had heard her. But fortunately, Monna Antonia was too absorbed in her own misery to notice much around her, and the other women were still flocking around the bier, busying themselves with flower arrangements.

Friar Lorenzo looked at her intently from behind his folded hands. "If you could follow him, would you go?"

"Of course!" Giulietta straightened up in spite of herself. "I would follow him throughout the world!" Realizing that, once again, she was being carried away, she sank lower on the kneeler, and added, in a solemn whisper, "I would follow him through the valley of the shadow of Death."

"Then compose yourself," whispered Friar Lorenzo, putting a warning hand on her arm, "for he is here, and—calm yourself! He would not leave Siena without you. Do not turn your head, for he is right—"

Giulietta could not help but twist around to catch a glimpse of the hooded monk crouched on the kneeler behind her, head bent in perfect concealment; if she was not mistaken, he was wearing the very same cowl Friar Lorenzo had made her wear when they once went together to Palazzo Marescotti.

Light-headed with excitement, Giulietta eyed her aunts and cousins with nervous calculation. If anyone discovered that Romeo was here, in this very church on this very night, surely neither he, nor she, nor even Friar Lorenzo would live to see the sun rise. It was too bold, too devilish for a presumed murderer to defile poor Tebaldo's vigil in order to woo the dead hero's cousin, and no Tolomei would ever tolerate the insult.

"Are you moonstruck?" she hissed over her shoulder. "If they discover you, they will kill you!"

"Your voice is sharper than their swords!" complained Romeo. "I beg you, be sweet; these may be the last words you ever speak to me." Giulietta more felt than saw the sincerity in his eyes, gleaming at her from within the shade of the hood as he went on, "If you meant what you said just now, take this"—he pulled a ring off his finger and held it out for her to take—"here, I give you this ring—"

Giulietta gasped, but took the ring nonetheless. It was a golden signet ring with the Marescotti eagle, but through Romeo's words, *I give you this ring*, it had become her wedding band.

"May God bless you both forever after!" whispered Friar Lorenzo, knowing full well that forever after might not extend beyond this night. "And may the holy saints in Heaven be the witnesses of your happy union. Now listen carefully. Tomorrow, the funeral will be held at the Tolomei sepulchre, outside the city walls—"

"Wait!" exclaimed Giulietta. "Surely, I am coming with you now?"

"*Shh!* It is impossible!" Friar Lorenzo laid another hand on her to calm her. "The guards at the door would stop you. And it is too danger-ous inside the city tonight—"

The sound of someone hushing them across the room made the three of them jolt with fear. Glancing nervously at her aunts, Giulietta saw them grimacing at her to be quiet and not upset Monna Antonia any further. And so she ducked her head dutifully and held her tongue until they were no longer looking at her. Then, turning around once more, she looked pleadingly at Romeo.

"Do not marry me and leave me!" she begged. "Tonight is our wed-ding night!"

"Tomorrow," he whispered, all but reaching out to touch her cheek, "we will look back on all this and laugh."

"Tomorrow," sobbed Giulietta, into the palm of her hand, "may never come!"

"Whatever happens," Romeo assured her, "we will be together. As man and wife. I swear it to you. In this world . . . or the next."

THE TOLOMEI SEPULCHRE was part of a vast cemetery outside Porta Tufi. Ever since antiquity, the people of Siena had buried their dead be-yond the city walls, and every noble family had kept up—or usurped—an ancient vault containing a suitable quantity of deceased ancestors. The Tolomei sanctuary sat among them all like a marble castle in this city of death; most of the structure was subterranean, but it had a grandiose en-trance above ground, much like the tombs of those august Roman states-men with whom Messer Tolomei so liked to compare himself.

Scores of family members and close friends had come along to the cemetery on this sad day, to comfort Tolomei and his wife as their first-born was laid to rest in the granite sarcophagus Tolomei had originally commissioned for himself. It was a sin and a shame to see such a healthy young man surrendered to the netherworld; no words could console the wailing mother or the young girl to whom Tebaldo had been betrothed since the day she was born, twelve years ago. Where was she to find another suitable husband now, so close to womanhood, and so used to thinking of herself as mistress of Palazzo Tolomei?

But Giulietta was too anxious about her own immediate future to wallow long in sympathy for her grieving family. She was also exhausted from lack of rest. The vigil had lasted all night, and now, far into the afternoon of the following day—with all hopes of resurrection proving idle—Monna Antonia looked as if she herself was likely to join her son in his untimely grave. Pale and drawn, she supported herself heavily on the arms of her brothers; only once did she turn towards Giulietta, her ghoulish face contorted in hatred.

"And there she is, the snake at my bosom!" she snarled, wanting everyone to hear her. "Had it not been for her shameless encouragement, Romeo Marescotti would never have dared lift a hand against this house! Look at her conniving face! Look at those traitorous tears! I wager they are not for my Tebaldo, but for his murderer, Romeo!" She spat on the ground twice to rid herself of the taste of the name. "It is time for you to act, brothers! Stand no more like frightened sheep! A foul crime has been committed against the house of Tolomei, and the murderer is prancing around town thinking himself above the law—" She withdrew a shiny stiletto from her shawl and waved it in the air. "If you are men, gut this town and find him, wherever he may be hiding, and let a grieving mother bury this blade in his black heart!"

After this outburst of emotion, Monna Antonia fell back into the arms of her brothers, and there she hung, limp and miserable, while the procession continued down the stone stairs into the underground sepulchre. Once everyone was gathered below, Tebaldo's shrouded body was placed in the sarcophagus, and the last rites performed.

Throughout the funeral, Giulietta looked stealthily around at every nook and cranny of the tenebrous receptacle, trying to decide on a convenient hiding place. For Friar Lorenzo's plan demanded that she stay behind in the burial chamber after the ceremony, undetected by all the people leaving, and that she wait there in solitude until nightfall, when it would be safe for Romeo to come and retrieve her. It was, the monk had explained, the only place where the Tolomei guards would not be vigilant in herding the family members, and because the cemetery was outside the city walls, Romeo's movements would not be constrained by constant fear of discovery and arrest.

Once delivered from the sepulchre, Giulietta would accompany Romeo into banishment, and as soon as they were safely settled in foreign lands, they would write a secret letter to Friar Lorenzo, telling him a long tale of health and happiness and encouraging him to join them at his earliest convenience.

Such was the plan on which they had all hastily agreed in San Cristoforo the night before, and it did not occur to Giulietta to question its particulars until the very moment when she herself had to act. Sickness rising in her throat, she eyed the sealed sarcophagi surrounding her to all sides—giant vessels of death that they were—wondering how she could possibly steal away and hide among them unseen and unheard.

Not until the very end of the ceremony, when the priest gathered everyone in head-bent prayer, did Giulietta see her chance to silently back away from her oblivious family and crouch down behind the nearest sarcophagus. And when the priest engaged them in a long-drawn, melodious *amen* to end the ceremony, she seized the opportunity to crawl farther into the shadows on her hands and knees, her arms already trembling from the contact with the cool, damp earth.

As she sat there, leaning against the rough stone of a coffin and trying not to breathe, the members of the funeral party left the burial chamber one by one, placed their candles on the small altar beneath the feet of Christ Crucified, and embarked upon the long, tearful walk home. Few had slept since the Palio on the previous day, and—as Friar Lorenzo had anticipated—no one had the presence of mind to ascertain that the number of people leaving the sepulchre was equal to the number originally entering. After all, what living person would choose to stay behind in a vault of terror and loathsome smells, trapped behind a heavy door that could not be opened from the inside?

When they had all left, the door to the sepulchre fell shut with a hollow thud. Although the candles were still flickering on the altar by the en-

trance, the darkness that now enfolded Giulietta as she sat panting between the tombs of her ancestors seemed, in every way, complete.

SITTING THERE, WITH NO sense of time, Giulietta slowly began to
comprehend that death was, more than anything, a matter of waiting.
Here they lay, all her illustrious forebears, patiently anticipating that divine tap on the lid of their coffins that would rouse their spirits once again
to an existence they could never have imagined when they were still alive.

Some would come out wearing a knight's armor, perhaps missing an
eye or a limb, and others would appear in their nightclothes, looking
sickly and full of boils; some would be mere wailing infants, and others
would be their young mothers, drenched in blood and gore . . .

While Giulietta did not doubt that, one day, there would be such a tap
on the lid for everyone deserving, the sight of all these ancient sarcophagi
and the thought of all those dormant centuries filled her with horror. But
shame on her, she thought, for being afraid and restless while waiting for
Romeo amongst the immovable stone coffins; what were a few anxious
hours in the face of such eternity?

When the door to the sepulchre finally opened, most of the candles on
the altar had burned out, and the few that were still going cast frightful,
contorted shadows that were almost worse than darkness. Not even pausing to see if it might be someone other than Romeo who had arrived,
Giulietta ran eagerly towards her savior, hungry for his living touch and
thirsty for a breath of wholesome air.

"Romeo!" she cried, only now giving in to weakness. "Thank
Heaven—!"

But it was not Romeo who stood in the door, torch in hand, regarding
her with a cryptic smile; it was Messer Salimbeni.

"It would seem," he said, his strained voice at odds with his mirthful
air, "you weep immoderately for your cousin's death, staying behind at
his grave like this. But then, I see no sign of tears on those rosy cheeks.
Could it be"—he took a few steps down the stairs, but stopped in disgust
at the smell of rot—"that my honey bride has gone distracted? I fear it is
the case. I fear I shall have to look for you in graveyards, my dear, and find
you playing madly with bones and hollow skulls. But"—he made a lewd

grimace—"I am no stranger to such games. In truth, I believe we shall fit well together, you and I."

Standing frozen at the sight of him, Giulietta did not know how to reply; she had barely understood his meaning. The only thing on her mind was Romeo, and why it was not he, but the odious Salimbeni, who had come to deliver her from the grave. But that was, of course, a question she did not dare to ask.

"Come here!" Salimbeni gestured for her to leave the burial chamber, and Giulietta had no choice but to obey. And so she emerged from the sepulchre by his side to find herself in black night, encircled by a ring of torches held by liveried Salimbeni guards.

Looking around at the faces of the men, Giulietta thought she saw pity and indifference in equal measures, but what was most unsettling was the impression that they knew something she did not.

"Are you not desirous," asked Salimbeni, relishing her confusion, "to know how I was able to rescue you from death's festering embrace?"

Giulietta could barely bring herself to nod, but then, she did not really have to, for Salimbeni was quite happy to continue his monologue without her consent.

"Fortunately for you," he went on, "I had an excellent guide. My men saw him wandering about, and instead of skewering him right away—as their orders would have them do—they wisely asked themselves what manner of treasure could tempt a banished man to return to his forbidden city and risk detection and violent death? His path, as you have already guessed, led us straight to this monument, and since it is well known that you cannot murder the same man twice, I easily divined that his motive for descending into your cousin's tomb must be something other than blood-thirst."

Seeing that Giulietta had turned sufficiently pale during his speech, Salimbeni now finally gestured for his men to produce the person in question, and they did so by tossing the body into their circle the way butchers toss aside a sickly carcass for the grinder.

Giulietta screamed when she saw him lying there, her own Romeo, bloody and broken, and if Salimbeni had not restrained her, she would have thrown herself at him to stroke his grimy hair and kiss the blood from his lips while there was still breath left in his body.

"You devil incarnate!" she roared at Salimbeni, struggling like an animal to rid herself of his grip, "God will punish you for this! Let me to his side, you fiend, that I may die with my husband! For I carry his ring on my finger, and I swear by all the angels in Heaven that I shall never, ever be yours!"

Now at last, Salimbeni frowned. Grabbing Giulietta's wrist, he nearly broke the bone to inspect the ring on her finger. When he had seen enough, he shoved her into the arms of a guard and stepped forward to kick Romeo hard in the stomach. "You slithering thief!" he sneered, spitting in disgust. "You couldn't help yourself, could you? Well, know this: It was your embrace that killed your lady! I was going to kill you alone, but now I see she is as worthless as you!"

"I beg you," coughed Romeo, struggling to lift his head off the ground and see Giulietta one last time, "let her live! It was only a vow! I never lay with her! Please! I swear it by my soul!"

"How touching," observed Salimbeni, looking from one to the other, not convinced. "What say you, girl"—he took Giulietta by the chin—"is he telling the truth?"

"Damn you!" she spat, trying to shake off his fist. "We are man and wife, and you had better kill me, for just as I lay with him on our wedding bed, so will I lie with him in our grave!"

Salimbeni's grip tightened. "Is that so? And will you, too, swear on his soul? Mind you, if you lie, he will go straight to Hell on this very night."

Giulietta looked down at Romeo, so miserable on the ground before her, and the desperation of it all strangled the words in her throat and made her unable to speak—and lie—any further.

"Ha!" Salimbeni towered over them both triumphantly. "So, here is one flower you did not pick, you dog." He kicked Romeo once more, indulging in the moans of his victim and the sobs of the woman begging him to stop. "Let us make sure"—reaching into his cotehardie, he pulled out Romeo's dagger and unsheathed it—"you pick no more."

With one slow, indulgent motion, Salimbeni sank the eagle dagger into its owner's abdomen and pulled it back out, leaving the youth in breathless agony, his whole body contorted around the gruesome wound.

"No!" screamed Giulietta and sprang forward, her panic so strong that the men could not hold her. Throwing herself down by Romeo's side, she wrapped her arms around him, desperate to go where he was going, and not be left behind.

But Salimbeni had had enough of her theatrics, and pulled her back up by the hair. "Quiet!" he barked, slapping her across the face until she obeyed. "This howling will not help anyone. Compose yourself, and re-member that you are a Tolomei." Then, before she understood what he was doing, he pulled the signet ring from her finger and tossed it on the ground, where Romeo lay. "There go your vows with him. Be glad they are so easily undone!"

Through the veil of her bloody hair, Giulietta saw the guards pick up Romeo's body and fling it down the stairs to the Tolomei sepulchre as if it was no more than a sack of grain thrown into storage. But she did not see them slamming the door after him, nor making sure the handle was se-curely locked. In her horror she had forgotten how to breathe, and now, at last, a merciful angel closed her eyes and let her fall into the embrace of soothing oblivion.

Virtue itself turns vice being misapplied,
And vice sometime's by action dignified

. . .

SEEN FROM THE TOP OF THE Mangia Tower, the half-moon-shaped Campo looked like a hand of cards with the picture side down. How suitable, I thought, for a city that held so many secrets. Who would have thought that men like the evil Messer Salimbeni could thrive in such a beautiful place—or rather, that he had been allowed to.

There was nothing in Maestro Ambrogio's journal to suggest that this medieval Salimbeni had had redeeming qualities—such as the generosity of Eva Maria or the charms of Alessandro—and even if he did, it didn't change the fact that he had brutally murdered everyone Giulietta had ever loved, with the exception of Friar Lorenzo and her sister, Giannozza.

I had spent most of the night in anguish over the brutal events described in the journal, and the dwindling number of pages left told me that a bitter end loomed. There was, I feared, not going to be a happily-ever-after for Romeo and Juliet; it was not merely literary acrobatics but solid facts that had turned their lives into a tragedy. As far as I could tell, Romeo was already dead, stabbed in the stomach with his own dagger—or rather, *my* dagger—and Giulietta was now in the clutches of a loathed enemy. What remained to be seen was whether she, too, would die before the pages ran out.

Perhaps this was why I was not in a merrier mood as I stood at the top of the Mangia Tower that morning, waiting for my motorcycle Romeo to appear. Or perhaps I was apprehensive because I damn well knew I shouldn't have come. What kind of woman agrees to a blind date at the top of a tower? And what kind of man spends his nights with a helmet on his head, visor closed, communicating with people via tennis balls?

But here I was.

For if this mysterious man was truly the descendant of medieval Romeo, I simply had to see what he looked like. It was more than six hundred years since our ancestors had been torn apart under very violent circumstances, and between then and now, their disastrous romance had become one of the greatest love stories the world had ever known.

How could I not be excited? Surely, I ought to be all steamed up at the idea that one of my historical figures—undeniably the most important of them all, at least to me—had finally come alive. Ever since Maestro Lippi had first made me aware that there was a contemporary, art-loving, wine-drinking Romeo Marescotti at large in Siena by night, I had secretly dreamt of a meeting. Yet now that I finally had it before me—fleshed out in red ink and signed with a swirl—it occurred to me that what I really felt was nausea . . . the kind of nausea you feel when you are betraying someone whose good opinion you cannot afford to lose.

That someone, I realized, sitting on the embrasure overlooking a city at once achingly beautiful and irresistibly arrogant, was Alessandro. Yes, he was a Salimbeni, and no, he did not like my Romeo one bit, but his smile—when he allowed it to surface—was so genuine and so contagious that I had already become hooked.

Then again, it was ridiculous. We had known each other for a week, no more, and for most of that time we had been at each other's throats, eagerly spurred on by my own prejudiced family. Even Romeo and Giulietta—the real ones—could not boast that kind of initial enmity. It was ironic that the story of our ancestors should come full circle like this, leaving us looking like Shakespearean wannabes, while at the same time seriously reshuffling our little love triangle.

No sooner had I deigned to acknowledge my infatuation with Alessandro, however, than I started feeling sorry for the Romeo I was about to meet. According to my cousin Peppo, he had fled to foreign lands to escape the viciousness that had driven him and his mother out of town, and whatever his ultimate purpose in returning to Siena, he was very possibly risking it all by offering to meet me in the Mangia Tower today. For that alone, I owed him thanks.

And even if he was not Alessandro's equal, the least I could do was to give him a chance to wow me, if that was what he wanted to do, and not stubbornly close my heart to him the way Juliet had closed her heart to Paris after meeting Romeo. Or ... perhaps I was jumping to conclusions. Perhaps all he wanted was to talk with me. If that were the case, it would— quite frankly—be a relief.

When I finally heard steps on the stairs, I got up from my perch on the stony embrasure and brushed off my dress with stiff hands, steeling myself for the quasi-legendary encounter about to happen. It took a while, though, before my hero made it to the very top of the spiral stairs, and as I stood there, poised to like him, I could not help but notice that— judging from his heavy breathing and the way he dragged his feet the last little bit—between the two of us, I was in far better shape.

Then, finally, my panting stalker appeared, leather suit draped over one arm, helmet dangling from the other, and all of a sudden, everything stopped making sense.

It was Janice.

IT WOULD BE HARD to pinpoint the exact moment when things had started going south in my relationship with Janice. Our childhood had been full of conflicts, but so are most people's childhoods, and the overwhelming majority of mankind seems to be able to reach maturity without having completely lost the love of their siblings.

Not so with us. Now, at twenty-five, I could no longer remember when I had last embraced my sister, or had a conversation with her that did not deteriorate into a juvenile spat. Whenever we met, it was as if we were eight-year-olds again, falling back on the most primitive forms of argument. "Because I say so!" and "I had it first!" tend to be expressions most people leave happily behind as vestiges from a barbarian age the way they do blankies and pacifiers; to Janice and me, they were the philosophical cornerstones of our entire relationship.

Aunt Rose had generally taken the approach that it would all straighten itself out in due course, as long as there was an even distribution of love and candy. Whenever we applied to her for arbitration, she would be tired of the case before she even heard it—it was, after all, only one of many piling up around her—and would always give us a standard reply to do with sharing, or being nice to each other. "Come now!" she would say, reaching for the crystal bowl with chocolate pretzels sitting on a side table, within easy reach of her armchair. "Be good girls! Julie, be fair to Janice now, and let her borrow your"—whatever it was . . . doll, book, belt, bag, hat, boots—"so we can have some peace around here, for heaven's sake!"

And so, inevitably, we would walk away from her with a whole new can of worms, Janice snickering at my losses and her own undeserved gains. The reason she wanted my things in the first place was that her own had broken or gotten "tired," and it was easier for her to take over mine than to make money and go out and buy new ones. And so we would leave the armchair after yet another wealth redistribution that had taken away what was mine and replaced it with nothing but a dry chocolate pretzel from the bowl. For all her litanies about fairness, Aunt Rose was a perpetual generator of nasty unintended consequences; the whole hellish path of my childhood was paved with her good intentions.

By the time I reached high school, I didn't even bother to go to her for help, but ran straight out into the kitchen to complain to Umberto, who was—in my memory—always in the process of sharpening the knives, opera blaring. Whenever I defaulted to the old, "But it isn't fair!" he would counter with, "Who told you life is fair?" and, when I finally calmed down, he would ask me, "So, what do you want me to do about it?"

As I grew older and wiser, I learned that the correct answer to his question was, "Nothing. I have to do it myself." And it was true. I did not run to him because I really wanted him to take Janice to task—although that would have been nice—but because he was not afraid of telling me, in his way, that I was better than her, and that I deserved more from life. But, that said, it was up to me to get it. The only problem was, he never told me how.

All my life, it seemed, I had been running around with my tail between my legs, trying to dig up opportunities that Janice could not somehow steal or spoil, but no matter where I buried my treasures, she was always able to sniff them out and chew them up beyond recognition. If I had saved my new satin ballet shoes for the end-of-season recital, I would open the box only to discover that she had tried them on and left the ribbons in a tangle, and once, when I had spent weeks making a collage of figure skaters in art class, she had inserted a cutout of Big Bird from *Sesame Street* as soon as I brought it home.

It didn't matter how far away I ran, or how much rot I rolled in to camouflage my scent, she would always come running, tongue hanging out, to bounce around me with playful mischief and leave a steaming number two right in the middle of my path.

As I stood there in the Mangia Tower, it all hit me at once—my countless reasons for hating Janice. It was as if someone had started a slide show of bad memories in my head, and I felt a surge of fury that I had never felt in the company of anyone else.

"Surprise!" she now said, dropping the leather suit and helmet and opening her arms for applause.

"What the hell," I finally gasped, my voice shrill with anger, "do you think you are doing here? Was that you, chasing me around on that ridiculous bike? And the letter—" I pulled the handwritten note out of my purse, creased it into a ball and flung it at her. "How stupid do you think I am?"

Janice grinned, enjoying my fury. "Stupid enough to climb up the friggin' tower! . . . Oh!" She made a grimace of faux sympathy that she had patented at the age of five. "Is that it? You weally fought I was Womeo?"

"Okay," I said, trying to cut through her laughter, "so, you had your joke. I hope it was worth the flight. Now excuse me, I'd love to stay, but I'd rather go stick my head in a bidet."

I tried to walk around her to get to the stairs, but she immediately backed up, blocking the door. "Oh, no you don't!" she hissed, her expression shifting from fair to stormy. "Not until you give me my share!"

I started. "Excuse me?"

"No, not this time," she said, her lower lip trembling as she tried on the role of the wounded party for a change. "I'm broke. Bankrupt."

"So, call the millionaire help line!" I retorted, falling right back into our sister act. "I thought you recently inherited a fortune from someone? Someone we both know?"

"Oh, ha ha!" Janice wrung out a smile. "Yeah, that was priceless. Good old Aunt Rose and all her gazillions."

"I have no idea," I said, shaking my head, "what you are whining about. Last time I saw you, you had just won the lottery. If it's more money you want, I'm the last person you should be talking to." I made another push for the door, and this time, I was determined to get through. "Get–out–of–my–way," I said. And amazingly, she did.

"Why look at you!" she jeered as I walked past her. If I hadn't known better, I might have seen jealousy in her eyes. "The little runaway princess. How much of my inheritance have you blown on clothes? Huh?"

When I just kept walking without even pausing to reply, I could hear her scrambling to pick up her gear and follow me. All the way down the spiral staircase she was hot on my trail, yelling after me first in anger, then in frustration, and finally in something as unusual as desperation. "Wait!" she cried, using the crash helmet as a buffer against the brick wall. "We have to talk! Stop! Jules! Seriously!"

But I had no intention of stopping. If Janice really had something important to tell me, why had she not done so right away? Why the shenanigans with the motorcycle and the red ink? And why had she wasted our five minutes in the tower with her usual antics? If, as she had hinted in her little rant, she had already managed to squander Aunt Rose's fortune, then I could certainly understand her frustration. But the way I saw it, that was, for dead sure, her own problem.

As soon as I reached the bottom of the tower I walked away from Palazzo Pubblico and crossed the Campo with firm strides, leaving Janice to her own mess. The Ducati Monster was parked right in front of the building, like a limo pulled up for the Oscars, and as far as I could see, at least three police officers were waiting impatiently—muscular arms akimbo, sunglasses on—for the return of its owner.

MALÈNA'S ESPRESSO BAR was the only place I could think of going where Janice wouldn't immediately find me. If I went back to the hotel, I figured, she would show up within minutes to resume her figure eights beneath my balcony.

And so I practically ran all the way up to Piazza Postierla, turning every ten steps to make sure she wasn't following, my throat still tight with anger. When I finally came shooting through the door of the bar, slamming it shut behind me, Malèna greeted me with a burst of laughter. "Dio mio! What are you doing here? You look like you are already drinking too much coffee."

Seeing that I didn't even have air to reply, she spun around to pour a tall glass of water from the tap. While I was drinking, she leaned on the counter with a look of barefaced curiosity. "Someone . . . giving you some trouble?" she suggested, her expression hinting that if that were the case, she had a few cousins—apart from Luigi the hairdresser—who would be more than happy to help me out.

"Well—" I said. But where to start? Looking around I was relieved to see that we were almost alone in the bar, and that the other customers were absorbed in conversations of their own. It occurred to me that here was the opportunity I had been hoping for ever since Malèna's mention of the Marescotti family the day before.

"Did I hear you correctly—" I began, taking the plunge before I could change my mind. "Did you say your name was *Marescotti*?"

The question had Malèna break into an ebullient smile. "Certamente! I was born a Marescotti. Now I am married, but"—she pressed a hand to her heart—"I will always be a Marescotti in here. Did you see the palazzo?"

I nodded with polite vigor, thinking of the rather painful concert I had attended with Eva Maria and Alessandro two days earlier. "It's beautiful. I was wondering—someone told me—" Grinding to a halt, I could feel embarrassment rising in my cheeks as I realized that, no matter how I phrased my follow-up question, I would be making an ass of myself.

Seeing my fluster, Malèna fished out a bottle of something homemade from beneath the counter—she didn't even have to look—and poured a hearty slug into my water glass. "Here," she said. "A Marescotti special. It will make you happy. Cin cin."

"It's ten o'clock in the morning," I protested, feeling very little desire to taste the cloudy liquid, never mind its ancestry.

"Bah!" she shrugged. "Maybe in Firenze it is ten o'clock—"

After dutifully gulping down the foulest concoction I had tasted since Janice's attempt at brewing beer in her bedroom closet—and hacking out a compliment, too—I at last felt I had earned the right to ask, "Are you related to a guy called Romeo Marescotti?"

The transformation in Malèna when she registered my question was almost uncanny. From being my best friend, leaning on her elbows to hear my troubles, she snapped upright with a gasp, and brusquely corked the bottle. "Romeo Marescotti," she said, taking away my empty glass and wiping the counter with a whiplash swipe of a tea towel, "is dead." Only then did she meet my eyes, and where there had been kindness a moment ago, I saw only fear and suspicion. "He was my cousin. Why?"

"Oh!" The disappointment fell heavily through my body, leaving me oddly light-headed. Or maybe it was the drink. "I'm so sorry. I shouldn't have—" Now, I thought, was probably not the time to tell her that my cousin Peppo had suspected Romeo of being behind the museum break-in. "It's just that Maestro Lippi, the artist—he says he knows him."

Malèna snorted, but at least she looked relieved. "Maestro Lippi," she whispered, circling a finger around her ear, "talks to ghosts. Don't listen to him. He is . . ." She searched for an appropriate word, but found none.

"There's also someone else," I said, figuring I might as well have it all shot to pieces once and for all. "The Head of Security at Monte dei Paschi. Alessandro Santini. Do you know him?"

Malèna's eyes widened briefly in surprise, then quickly narrowed. "Siena is a small place." From the way she said it I knew there was a smelly rat buried somewhere in all this.

"Why," I went on more quietly, hoping that my questions would not further rip open an old wound, "do you think anyone would go around saying that your cousin Romeo was still alive?"

"He said that?" Malèna studied my face intently, more incredulous than sad.

"It's kind of a long story," I said, "but the bottom line is that *I* was the one asking about Romeo. Because . . . I am Giulietta Tolomei."

I was not expecting her to understand the implications of my name in conjunction with Romeo's, but the shock on her face told me that she knew exactly who I was, ancestor and all. Once she had processed this little curveball, her reaction was very sweet; she reached out to pinch my nose.

"Il gran disegno," she muttered. "I knew there was a reason you came to me." Then she paused, as if there was something she wanted to say, but which she knew she shouldn't. "Poor Giulietta," she said instead, with a sympathetic smile, "I wish I could tell you he was alive, but . . . I can't."

...

W H E N I F I N A L L Y L E F T· the espresso bar, I had forgotten all about Janice. It was therefore an unpleasant surprise to find her waiting for me right outside, leaning comfortably against the wall like a cowgirl killing time until the saloon opens.

As soon as I saw her standing there, beaming with triumph because she had tracked me down, it all came back to me—motorcycle, letter, tower, argument—and I sighed loudly and started walking in the other direction, not really caring where I was headed as long as she didn't follow.

"What is it with you and Yummy Mummy in there?" Janice was nearly tripping over her own feet to catch up. "Are you trying to make me jealous?"

I was so sick of her at this point that I stopped in the middle of Piazza Postierla and spun around to yell at her, "Do I really have to spell it out? I'm trying to get rid of you!"

During all our years together, I had said plenty of nasty things to my sister, and this was nowhere near the worst. But perhaps due to the unfamiliar turf it hit her right between the eyes, and for a brief moment she looked stunned, almost as if she was going to cry.

Turning away in disgust I resumed walking, laying some distance between us before—once again—she came stumbling along in my wake, her stiletto boots twisting this way and that on the irregular stone pavement.

"Okay!" she exclaimed, arms flapping for balance, "I'm sorry about the bike, okay? And I'm sorry about the letter. Okay? I didn't know you'd take it that way." Seeing that I neither replied nor slowed down, she moaned and kept going, still not quite able to catch me. "Listen, Jules, I know you're pissed off. But we really have to talk. Remember Aunt Rose's will? It was bo—*ow*!"

She must have twisted something, for when I turned around to look, Janice was sitting in the middle of the street, rubbing her ankle.

"What did you say?" I asked warily, walking back towards her a few steps. "About the will?"

"You heard me," she said glumly, inspecting her broken boot heel, "the whole thing was bogus. I thought you were part of it, and that's why I was lying low, trying to figure out what you were up to, but . . . I'm willing to give you the benefit of the doubt."

...

IT HAD NOT BEEN a good week for my evil twin. For starters, she told me, limping along with an arm around my neck, she had discovered that our family lawyer, Mr. Gallagher, was not, in fact, Mr. Gallagher. How? Well, the *real* Mr. Gallagher had shown up. Secondly, the will he had shown us after the funeral had been nothing but fiction. In reality, Aunt Rose had had nothing left to leave to anybody, and to be her heir would have meant inheriting nothing but debt. Thirdly, two police officers had arrived at the house the day after I left, and they had given Janice hell for removing the yellow tape. What yellow tape? Well, the tape they had wrapped around the building when they had discovered it was a crime scene.

"A crime scene?" Even though the sun was high in the sky, I felt a chill. "You mean, Aunt Rose was *murdered*?"

Janice shrugged as best she could, struggling to keep her balance. "God knows. Apparently, she was covered with bruises, even though supposedly she died in her sleep. Go figure."

"Janice!" I barely knew what to say, except to chastise her for being so flippant. This unexpected news—that Aunt Rose might not have died peacefully, the way Umberto had described—closed around my throat like a noose, almost choking me.

"What?" she snapped, her voice thick with emotion. "Do you think it was fun sitting in that interrogation room all night and . . . answering questions about whether or not"—she could barely get out the words—"I really loved her?"

I looked at her profile, wondering when I had last seen my sister cry. With her mascara smeared and her clothes messed up from the fall, she actually seemed human, and almost likable, maybe because of the throbbing ankle, the grief, and all the disappointment. Suddenly realizing that, for a change, *I* would have to be the strong one, I took a better grip on her and tried to suppress all thoughts of poor old Aunt Rose for the time being. "I don't get it! Where on earth was Umberto?"

"Ha!" The question gave Janice an opportunity to recover some of her zest. "You mean, *Luciano*?" She glanced at me to see if I was suitably shocked. "That's right. Good old Birdie was a fugitive, a desperado, a gangster . . . take your pick. All these years, he's been hiding out in our rose garden while the cops *and* the Mafia were looking for him. Apparently, they found him—his old Mob buddies—and he just"—with her free hand, she snapped her fingers in the air—"poof, gone!"

I stopped to catch my breath, swallowing hard to keep down Malèna's Marescotti special that was supposed to make me happy but tasted like heartbreak. "His name wouldn't happen to be . . . Luciano Salimbeni, would it?"

Janice was so flabbergasted by my insight that she completely forgot about not being able to put weight on her left foot. "My-my!" she exclaimed, removing her arm from my shoulder. "You *do* have a hand in this shit!"

AUNT ROSE USED TO say that she had hired Umberto for his cherry pie. And while this was true to a certain extent—he always did produce the most outrageous desserts—the fact was that she was helpless without him. He took care of everything, the kitchen, the garden, the general maintenance around the house, but even more admirably, he managed to convey a sense that his contribution was trifling in comparison with the enormous tasks undertaken by Aunt Rose herself. Such as arranging flowers for the dinner table. Or looking up troublesome words in the dictionary.

The true genius of Umberto was his ability to make us believe we were self-sustained. It was almost as if he had somehow failed in his endeavors if we were able to identify his touch in the blessings that came to us; he was like a year-round Santa Claus who only enjoyed giving presents to those soundly asleep.

As with most things in our childhood, the original arrival of Umberto on the doorstep of our American lives was veiled in silence. Neither Janice nor I could remember a time when he had not been there. When we occasionally, under the scrutiny of a full moon, would lie in our beds and outdo each other in remembering our exotic infancies in Tuscany, Umberto was somehow always in the picture.

In a way I loved him more than I ever loved Aunt Rose, for he always took my side and called me his little princess. It was never explicit, but I am sure we all felt his disapproval of Janice's deteriorating manners and his subtle support of me, whenever I chose not to emulate her naughtiness.

When Janice asked him for a good-night story, she would get a brief morality tale ending with someone's head being chopped off; when I curled up on the bench in the kitchen, he would fetch the special cookies in the blue tin and tell me stories that went on forever, stories about knights and fair maidens, and buried treasures. And when I grew old enough to understand, he would assure me that Janice would be punished soon enough. Wherever she went in life, she would bring along with her an inescapable piece of Hell, for she herself was Hell, and in time, she would come to realize that she was her own worst punishment. I, on the other hand, was a princess, and one day—if only I made sure to stay away from corrupting influences and irreversible mistakes—I would meet a handsome prince and find my own magic kingdom.

How could I not love him?

IT WAS WAY PAST NOON when we had finally caught up on each other's news. Janice told me everything the police had said about Umberto—or rather, Luciano Salimbeni—which wasn't much, and in return I told her everything that had happened to me since arriving in Siena, which was a lot.

We ended up having lunch in Piazza del Mercato, with a view of Via dei Malcontenti and a deep, green valley. The waiter informed us that beyond the valley ran the gloomy one-way road Via di Porta Giustizia, at the end of which—in the old days—criminals were executed in public.

"Lovely," said Janice, slurping ribollita soup, elbows on the table, her brief sadness long since evaporated, "no wonder old Birdie didn't feel like coming back here."

"I still don't believe it," I muttered, poking at my food. Watching Janice eat was enough to relieve me of my appetite, to say nothing of the surprises she had brought with her. "If he really killed Mom and Dad, why didn't he kill us, too?"

"You know," said Janice, "sometimes I thought he was going to. Seriously. He had that serial-killer look in his eyes."

"Maybe," I suggested, "he felt guilty about what he had done—"

"Or maybe," Janice cut me off, "he knew that he needed us—or at least *you*—in order to get Mom's box from Mister Macaroni."

"I suppose," I said, trying to apply logic where logic was not enough, "he could have been the one hiring Bruno Carrera to follow me?"

"Well, obviously!"—Janice rolled her eyes—"and you can be damn sure he is puppeteering your little toyboy as well."

I shot her a glare that she didn't even seem to notice. "I hope you're not referring to Alessandro?"

"Mmm, Alessandro . . ." She savored his name as if it was a chocolate caramel. "I gotta give it to you, Jules, he was worth waiting for. Too bad he's already in bed with Birdie."

"You are disgusting," I said, not allowing her to upset me, "and you're wrong."

"Really?" Janice didn't like being wrong. "Then explain to me why he broke into your hotel room?"

"What?"

"Oh, yes—" She took her sweet time dipping the last slice of bread in olive oil. "That night when I saved you from Gumshoe Bruno, and you ended up three sheets to the wind with the artmeister . . . Alessandro was having one helluva party in your room. You don't believe me?" She reached into her pocket, only too happy to oblige my suspicion. "Then check this out."

Pulling out her cell phone, she showed me a series of bleary photos of someone climbing up to my balcony. It was hard to tell whether it was really Alessandro, but Janice insisted that it *was,* and I had known her long enough to identify those rare twitches around her mouth as honesty.

"Sorry," she said, looking almost as if she meant it, "I know this is blowing your little fantasy, but I thought you'd like to know your Pooh is not just in it for the honey."

I flung the phone back at her without knowing what to say. There had been too much to absorb in the last few hours, and I had definitely reached my saturation point. First Romeo . . . dead and buried. Then Umberto . . . reborn as Luciano Salimbeni. And now Alessandro . . .

"Don't look at me like that!" hissed Janice, usurping the moral high ground with habitual dexterity. "I'm doing you a favor! Imagine if you'd gone ahead and fallen for this guy, only to discover that he was after the family jewels all along."

"Why don't you do me another favor," I said, leaning back in my chair to get as far away from her point as possible, "and explain how you found me in the first place? And what's up with that stupid Romeo act?"

"Not a word of thanks! Story of my life!" Janice reached into her pocket once more. "If it hadn't been for me chasing Bruno away, you could have been dead now. But see if you care. Nag, nag, nag!" She tossed a letter across the table, narrowly missing the dipping bowl. "Here. See for yourself. This is the *real* letter from the *real* Aunt Rose, handed to me by the *real* Mr. Gallagher. Make sure you inhale. It's all she left for us."

As she lit up her once-a-week cigarette, hands shaking, I brushed a few crumbs from the letter and took it out of the envelope. It consisted of eight sheets of paper, all of them covered in Aunt Rose's own handwriting, and if the date was correct, she had left it with Mr. Gallagher several years ago.

This is what it read:

My dearest girls,

You have often asked me about your mother, and I have never told you the truth. It was for your own good. I was afraid that if you knew what she was like, you would want to be just like her. But I do not wish to take it with me to the grave, so here they are, all the things I was afraid to tell you.

You know that Diane came to live with me when her parents and little brother died. But I never told you how they died. It was very sad, and a great shock for her, and I think she never got over it. It was a car accident in terrible holiday traffic, and Diane told me that they were having an argument, and that it was her fault for fighting with her brother. It was Christmas Eve. I think she never forgave herself. She would never open her presents. She was a very religious girl, much more than her old aunt, especially at Christmas. I wish I could have helped her, but in those days people did not run to doctors all the time.

Her great interest was genealogy. She believed that our family was descended from Italian nobility through the female line, and she told me that, before she died, my mother had told her a great secret. I thought it was very strange that my mother would tell her granddaughter something she never told me or Maria, her own daughters, and I never believed a word of it, but Diane was so stubborn and kept saying that we were descended from Shakespeare's Juliet, and that there was a curse on our bloodline. She also said that was why poor Jim and I never had children, and why her parents and brother had to die. I never encouraged her when she talked like that, I just let her talk. After she died I kept thinking that I should have done something to help her, but that is too late now.

Poor Jim and I tried to make Diane finish her degree, but she was too restless. Before we knew it, she was off to Europe with her backpack, and the next thing I know she writes that she is getting married to some Italian professor. I did not go to the wedding. Poor Jim was very ill at the time, and after he died I did not feel like traveling. Now I regret that. Diane was all alone, having twins, and then after that, there was a terrible house fire that killed her husband, so I never even met him, poor soul.

I wrote many letters to her telling her to come home, but Diane did not want to, stubborn creature that she was, bless her heart. She had bought a house of her own, and she kept saying that she wanted to continue her husband's research. She told me over the phone that he had spent all his life looking for a family treasure that could stop the curse, but I did not believe a word of it. I told her that it was very foolish to marry back into your own family, even if it was a very distant connection, but she said that she had to, because _she_ had the Tolomei genes from her mother and grandmother, but _he_ had the Tolomei name, and the two must go together. It was all very strange, if you ask me. You two were baptized in Siena with the names Giulietta and Giannozza Tolomei. Your mother said the names were a family tradition.

I tried very hard to make her come home, just for a visit I said, and we had even bought tickets. But she was so busy with her research, and she kept saying that she was very close to finding the treasure, and that she had to see a man about an old ring. One morning I received a call from a police officer in Siena, who told me that there had been a dreadful accident, and that your poor mother was dead. He told me that you two were with your godpar-

ents, but that you were likely in danger, and that I must come and get you right away. When I arrived to pick you up, the police asked me if Diane had ever mentioned a man called Luciano Salimbeni, and this made me very afraid. They wanted me to stay for a hearing, but I was so afraid that I took you to the airport right away and flew home, without even waiting for the adoption papers to go through. I changed your names, too. I called Giulietta Julie, and Giannozza Janice. And instead of Tolomei, I gave you my name, Jacobs. I did not want some crazy Italian to come looking for you, or say that they wanted to adopt you. I even hired Umberto to protect you and keep an eye out for that Luciano Salimbeni. Fortunately, we never heard anything about him again.

I do not know much about what Diane was doing those years alone in Siena. But I think she found something very valuable, and that she left it behind in Siena, for you to find. I hope that if you ever find it, you will share it equally. She also owned a house, and I believe her husband was wealthy. If there is anything of value left for you in Siena, perhaps you will take care of dear Umberto, too?

It is very painful for me to say this, but I am not as rich as you think. I have been living on poor Jim's pension, but when I die, there will be nothing left for you two, just debt. Maybe I should have told you, but I was never good with these things.

I wish I knew more about Diane's treasure. She talked about it sometimes, but I did not listen. I thought it was just one of her crazy stories. But there is a man in the bank in Palazzo Tolomei who may be able to help you. I cannot for the life of me remember his name. He was your mother's financial advisor, and I think he was fairly young, so maybe he is still alive.

If you decide to go, just remember that there are people in Siena who believe in the same stories your mother believed in. I wish I had paid attention when she told me all that. Do not tell anyone your real names, except the man in the bank. Maybe he can help you find the house. I would like you to go together. Diane would have wanted that. We should have gone years ago, but I was afraid something would happen to you.

Now you know that I left nothing for you to live on. But I hope that with this letter, at least you have a chance of finding what your mother left behind. I met with Mr. Gallagher this morning. I really should not have lived this long, there will be nothing left, not even the memories, because I never wanted you to know them. I was always afraid that you would run off like Diane and get yourselves into trouble. Now I know that you will find trouble wherever you are. I know what it means, the look in your eyes. Your mother had it, too. And I want you to know that I pray for you every day.

Umberto knows where the funeral instructions are kept. God bless your innocent hearts!

Much love, Aunt Rose

Is there no pity sitting in the clouds
That sees into the bottom of my grief?

...

Siena, A.D. 1340

TRAPPED IN HER ROOM at the very top of the Tolomei tower, Giulietta knew nothing of what was going on in the city below. She had been kept there ever since the day of Tebaldo's funeral, and no one had been allowed to visit her. The window shutters had been nailed in place by one of the Tolomei guards, and food was delivered through a slit in the door, but that hardly mattered, since—for the longest time—she took none of it.

For the first few hours of her imprisonment, she had implored whoever could hear her through the door to let her out. "Kindest aunt!" she had begged, her teary cheek against the door, "please do not treat me this way! Remember whose daughter I am! . . . Dear cousins? Can you hear me?" But when no one had dared to respond, she had begun yelling at the guards instead, cursing them for obeying the orders of a devil in the guise of man.

When no one responded with a single word, she eventually lost her spirit. Weak with grief, she lay on her bed with a sheet over her head, unable to think of anything but Romeo's molested body and her own inability to prevent his grisly death. Only now did fearful servants come to the door to offer food and drink, but Giulietta refused it all, even water, in the hope of expediting her own demise and following her lover to Paradise before he got too far ahead.

Her only duty left in life, she felt, was to pen a secret letter to her sister Giannozza. It was meant as a goodbye note, but in the end it became just one letter out of many, written by the light of a candle stump and hidden under a loose floorboard with all the others. To think, she wrote, that she had once been so intrigued by this world and everyone in it; now she understood that Friar Lorenzo had been right all along. "The mortal world is a world of dust," he used to say. "Everywhere you step it crumbles away right beneath your foot, and if you do not walk carefully, you will fall over the edge and into limbo." This limbo was where she must surely be right now, thought Giulietta—the abyss from which no prayers could be heard.

GIANNOZZA, SHE KNEW, was no stranger to this sort of misery. For all his novel ideas that his daughters should be able to read and write, their father had been an old-fashioned man when it came to marriage. Daughters, to him, were emissaries that could be sent out to build alliances with important people in foreign places, and so when his wife's cousin—a nobleman with a large estate north of Rome—had expressed an interest in closer ties with the Tolomeis, he had informed Giulietta that she would have to go. She was, after all, four minutes older than her sister, Giannozza, and it is the duty of the eldest to go first.

Hearing this news, the sisters had spent many days in tears at the prospect of being torn apart and settled at such a distance from each other. But their father was unbending, and their mother even more so— after all, the groom was her cousin and no stranger—and in the end the girls had approached their parents with a humble proposal.

"Father," Giannozza had said, as she was the only one bold enough to speak her mind, "Giulietta is honored that you have such plans for her, but she begs you to consider whether it might not be better to send me instead. The truth is, her heart was always bent on the convent, and she fears she would not make a very happy bride to anyone other than Christ. I, on the other hand, have no objection to an earthly marriage; in fact, I believe I should rather like to run a house on my own. And so we were wondering"—now, for the first time, Giannozza had eyed their mother as well, hoping for her aquiescence—"whether you would consider dispatching us both together—me as a bride, and Giulietta as a novice at a nearby convent. That way, we can see each other whenever we wish, and you will not have to worry about our well-being."

Seeing that Giulietta was so against the idea of marriage, their father finally agreed to let Giannozza take her place. But when it came to the other half of the plan, he remained dismissive. "If Giulietta will not marry now," he had said, seated behind his large desk, arms crossed, as his women stood before him in supplication, "she will marry later, when she grows out of this . . . nonsense." He had shaken his head, angry at this interference in his affairs. "I should never have taught you girls to read! I suspect you have been reading the Bible behind my back—that is enough to fill a girl's head with folly!"

"But Father—"

Only now had their mother stepped forward, eyes ablaze. "Shame on you," she had hissed at her daughters, "for putting your father in this situation! We are not poor, and yet you ask him to behave as if we were! You both have dowries large enough to tempt a prince! But we have been selective. Many have come calling for you, Giulietta, but your father has turned them all away, because he knew we could do better. And now you want him to rejoice in seeing you as a *nun*? . . . As if we did not have the means and connections for you to marry? Shame on you for putting your own selfish desires before the dignity of your family!"

And so Giannozza had been married to a man she had never seen before, and had spent her wedding night with a groom thrice her age, who had the eyes of her mother but the hands of a stranger. When she said goodbye to her family the next morning—to leave her home forever with her new husband—she had clung to them all one by one, without a word, her lips pressed tightly together to prevent herself from cursing her parents.

The words came later, in endless letters from her new home, addressed not to Giulietta directly, but to their friend, Friar Lorenzo, that he might deliver her missives in stealth, when he had Giulietta in confession in the chapel. These were letters that could never be forgotten, letters that must haunt the reader forever, and Giulietta would often allude to them in her own writing, such as when she agreed with her sister that "there are, indeed, as you say, men in this world who thrive on evil, men who live only to see others suffer." But she would always encourage Giannozza to look at the positive side of things—her husband was old and sickly, and would surely die while she was still young, and even though she was not allowed out of doors, at least the view from her castle was magnificent—and would even go as far as to point out that "contrary to what you say, my dearest, there is *some* pleasure to be found in the company of men. They are not all rotten through and through."

In her farewell letter to Giannozza, however, composed in her prison cell the day after Tebaldo's funeral, Giulietta could no longer speak so bravely in favor of the future. "You were right," she wrote simply, "and I was wrong. When life hurts more than death, it is not worth living."

AND SO SHE HAD decided to die, and to refuse all nourishment until her body gave in, setting her soul free to reunite with Romeo. But on the third day of her hunger strike—her lips parched and her head throbbing—a new thought began to haunt her, namely, the question of where exactly in Paradise she would have to go in order to find him. It was obviously a vast place—it had to be—and there was no saying whether the two of them would be sent to the same region. In fact, she rather feared they would not.

While she might not be perfectly blameless in the eyes of God, she was still an innocent maid; Romeo, on the other hand, had undoubtedly left behind a long trail of mischief. Furthermore, there had been no funerary rites and no prayers said over his body, and so it was even doubtful whether he would go to Paradise at all. Perhaps he was doomed to wander around as a ghost, wounded and bloody, until—if ever—some kind Samaritan took pity on him and finally put his body to rest.

Giulietta sat up in bed with a gasp. If she died now, who was to make sure Romeo was properly buried? Leave it to the Tolomeis to discover the body next time there was a family funeral—in all likelihood her own—and they would most certainly give it anything but peace. No, she thought, reaching out for the water at last, her weak fingers barely able to grasp the cup, she would have to stay alive until she had spoken with Friar Lorenzo and explained the situation to him.

Where on earth was the monk? In her misery, Giulietta had not wanted to speak to anyone, not even her old friend, and it had been a relief that he had never come to see her. But now—her heart set on a plan she could not possibly execute on her own—she was furious with him for not being at her side. Only later, after wolfing down every scrap of food she could find in the room, did it occur to her that her uncle Tolomei might have prohibited the monk's visits altogether, in an attempt at preventing him from spreading reports of her misery.

Pacing up and down the floor, occasionally pausing to peek out through a crack in the sealed shutters to guess the time of day, Giulietta eventually concluded that death would have to wait. Not because she had a desire to live, but because there were still two tasks left in life that only she could accomplish. One of them was to get hold of Friar Lorenzo—or some other holy man more bent on obeying the law of God than that of her uncle—and to have him ensure that Romeo was properly buried; the other was to make Salimbeni suffer in a way no man had ever suffered before.

MONNA AGNESE DIED on All Saints' Day, after having been confined to her bed for over half a year. There were those who whispered that the poor lady had stayed alive for so long simply to annoy her husband, Messer Salimbeni, whose new wedding clothes had been laid out for wear ever since his August engagement to Giulietta Tolomei.

The funeral was held at Rocca di Tentennano, the impregnable Salimbeni fortress in Val d'Orcia. No sooner had he tossed earth over the coffin than the widower took off for Siena with the fluttering dispatch of a winged cupid. Only one child accompanied him on his return to town: his nineteen-year-old son Nino—already a hardened Palio assassin, according to some—whose own mother had preceded Monna Agnese into the Salimbeni sepulchre several years earlier, following a similar affliction, commonly known as starvation.

Tradition demanded a period of mourning after such a loss, but few were surprised to see the great man so soon back in town. Salimbeni was renowned for his celerity of mind; while other men spent several days mourning the death of a wife or child, he would shrug it off within hours, never missing an important business transaction.

Despite his occasional, suspect dealings and tireless rivalry with the house of Tolomei, Salimbeni was a man most people could not help but admire to the point of toadying. Whenever he was present in a gathering, he was the undisputed center of attention. And whenever he sought to amuse, everyone responded with laughter, even if they had barely heard what he said. His unstinting ways endeared him immediately to strangers, and his clients knew that once you had earned his trust, you would be handsomely rewarded. Understanding the dynamics of the city better than anyone, he knew when to hand out food to the poor, and he knew when to stand firm in the face of the government. It was no coincidence that he liked to dress like a Roman emperor in a fine woolen toga with scarlet edging, for he ran Siena like a small empire of his own, and anyone who opposed his authority was treated as a traitor to the city at large.

In the light of Salimbeni's political and fiscal savvy, it astounded the people of Siena to witness his enduring infatuation with Messer Tolomei's melancholy niece. There he was, bowing politely to her pale figure at mass, when she could barely look at him. Not only did she despise him for what had happened to her family—her tragedy was, by now, widely known—but he was also the man who had driven her lover Romeo out of town after incriminating him in the suspicious murder of Tebaldo Tolomei.

Why, people asked themselves, did a man of Salimbeni's stature put his dignity at stake in order to marry a girl who could never warm to him, were they both to live a thousand years? She was beautiful, certainly, and most young men were able to conjure up Giulietta's perfect lips and dreamy eyes whenever they felt the need. But it was quite another thing for a man as settled as Salimbeni to toss aside all respectability and claim her for his own so soon after her sweetheart's disappearance and his own wife's passing.

"It is all a matter of honor!" said some, approving of the engagement. "Romeo challenged Salimbeni to a fight over Giulietta, and such a fight can only have one logical outcome: The winner must live, the loser die, and the lady fall to the man standing, whether he wants her or not."

Others were more candid and confessed that they saw the touch of the devil in Salimbeni's actions. "Here is a man," they would whisper to Maestro Ambrogio over wine in taverns late at night, "whose power has long been checked by no one. Now at last that power has turned malignant, and as such it is threatening not only us, but him as well. You have said it yourself, Maestro: Salimbeni's virtues have ripened to a point where they are turning into vice, and, now that they are long sated, his immense appetites for glory and influence must naturally seek new sources of nourishment."

To name an example of such nourishment was not mere guesswork; there were certain females about town who would readily testify to Salimbeni's increasingly wicked ways.

From being a man who sought to please and be pleased, Salimbeni had, one lady told the Maestro, gradually come to resent those who too readily bent to his wishes. He had begun to seek out the unwilling, or the downright hostile, in order that he might have reason to fully exercise his faculties of dominance, and nothing pleased him more than an encounter with someone—most often a defiant foreigner newly arrived—who did not yet know that he was a man who must be obeyed.

But even defiant foreigners listen to friendly advice, and before long, Salimbeni was once again, much to his irritation, met by nothing but sickening smiles and charades whenever he ventured out on the town in what he considered disguise. Most business owners would have liked nothing more than to bar their door to the rapacious customer, but in the absence of men willing to enforce the law against the tyrant, how could private industry ever be safe from such infringement? And so the satyr play was allowed to continue, its lead on a perennial quest for ever more worthwhile challenges to his potency, while the chorus of people left in his wake could do little but recount the myriad dangers of hubris and the tragic blindness to reason that will, invariably, ensue.

"So you see, Maestro," concluded the lady—always happy to exchange gossip with those of her neighbors who did not spit in the street when they saw her—"this certain man's obsession with that certain young lady is no mystery at all." She leaned on her broom and waved him closer, anxious that no one overhear her insight. "Here is a girl—a lovely, nubile creature—who is not only the niece of his enemy, but who, herself, has every reason in the world to despise him. There is no risk of her fierce resistance degenerating into sweet submission . . . no risk that she will ever willingly admit him to her chamber. Do you see, Maestro? In marrying *her,* he will secure for himself the very wellspring of his preferred aphrodisiac—hatred—and that is a source that will surely never run dry."

...

THE SALIMBENI WEDDING succeeded the Salimbeni funeral by a week and a day. The graveyard soil still moist underneath his fingernails, the widower wasted no time in dragging his next wife to the altar that she might forthwith infuse his sagging family tree with the luxurious blood of the Tolomeis.

For all his charisma and generosity, this blatant display of egoism was disgusting to the people of Siena. As the wedding procession passed through town, more than one bystander remarked on its semblance to a military triumph in Roman times; here came the booty from foreign lands—men and beasts hitherto unseen, and a chained queen upon a horse, crowned for mockery—all presented to the slack-jawed mob lining the road by an exulting general waving at them all from a passing chariot.

The sight of the tyrant in his glory like this brought back in full force all the suspicious murmurings that had followed Messer Salimbeni wherever he went since the Palio. Here was a man—some said—who had committed murder, not just once, but whenever he damn well pleased, and yet no one dared speak against his actions. Clearly, a man who could get away with such crimes—and force a wedding with an unwilling bride on top of it—was a man who could, and would, do anything to anyone.

As he stood by the wayside in the drizzling November rain, looking at the woman whose path had been crossed by every star in Heaven, Maestro Ambrogio found himself praying that someone would step forward and save Giulietta from her fate. In the eyes of the crowd she was no less beautiful now than she had been before, but it was evident to the painter—who had not seen her since the night before the fatal Palio—that hers had become the stony beauty of Athena, rather than the smiling charms of Aphrodite.

How he wished that Romeo would return to Siena this very instant and come charging into town with a band of foreign soldiers to steal away his lady before it was too late. But Romeo, said people, shaking their heads, was far away in distant lands, seeking comfort in women and drink where Salimbeni would never find him.

All of a sudden, standing there with his hood up against the rain, Maestro Ambrogio knew how he must conclude the large fresco in Palazzo Pubblico. There must be a bride, a sad girl lost in bitter memories, and a man on a horse leaving town, but leaning back in the saddle to hear a painter's plea. Only by confiding in the silent wall, thought the Maestro, would he be able to ease the pain in his heart on this hateful day.

GIULIETTA KNEW IT as soon as she had finished the breakfast that was to be her last meal in Palazzo Tolomei: Monna Antonia had put something in her food to calm her down. Little did her aunt know that Giulietta had no intention of obstructing the wedding by refusing to go. How else would she get close enough to Salimbeni to make him suffer?

She saw it all in a haze—the wedding procession, the gaping street hordes, the stern assembly in the dark cathedral—and only when Salimbeni lifted her veil to reveal her bridal crown to the bishop and the awestruck wedding guests did she snap out of her trance and recoil at their gasps and his closeness.

The crown was a sinful vision of gold and sparkling stones, which rivaled anything that had ever been seen before, in Siena or elsewhere. It was a treasure more suited for royalty than for a sullen country girl, but then, it was not really for her. It was for him.

"How do you like my gift?" he asked, studying her face as he spoke. "It has two Ethiopian sapphires that reminded me of your eyes. Priceless. But then . . . they seemed so forlorn that I gave them the company of two Egyptian emeralds that reminded me of the way that fellow—Romeo—used to look at you." He smiled at the shock in her face. "Tell me, my dear, do you not find me generous?"

Giulietta had to steel herself before addressing him. "You, Messere, are so much more than generous."

He laughed delightedly at her reply. "I am glad to hear it. You and I will get along very well, I think."

But the bishop had heard the evil remark and was not amused. Nor were the priests who attended the wedding feast later, and who entered the bridal chamber to bless it with holy water and incense, only to discover that Romeo's cencio was spread out on top of the bed. "Messer Salimbeni!" they exclaimed, "you cannot make up your bed with this cencio!"

"Why not?" Salimbeni asked, wine goblet in hand, musicians in tow.

"Because," they replied, "it belongs to another man. It was given to

Romeo Marescotti by the Virgin Mary herself, and it was meant for his bed alone. Why would you challenge the will of Heaven?"

But Giulietta knew very well why Salimbeni had put the cencio on the bed, for he had put the green emeralds in her bridal crown for the very same reason: to remind her that Romeo was dead, and that there was nothing she could do to bring him back.

In the end, Salimbeni threw out the priests without getting their blessing for the night, and when he had heard enough sycophantic drivel from the drunken wedding guests, he threw them out as well, together with the musicians. If some people were surprised by their patron's sudden lack of generosity, they all understood his reason for ending the party—she sat in the corner, more asleep than awake, but even in her state of disarray was far too lovely to be left alone much longer.

While Salimbeni was busy taking leave of them all and receiving their good wishes, Giulietta saw her chance to grab a knife from the banquet table and conceal it beneath her clothes. She had been eyeing that particular weapon all night, and had seen it capture the light from the candles as the servants had used it to cut meat for the guests. Even before she held it in her hand, she had already begun to plan how she would use it to carve her loathsome groom. She knew from Giannozza's letters that—this being her wedding night—there would be a point where Salimbeni would come to her, undressed and with thoughts for everything but fighting, and she knew that this would have to be the moment when she struck.

She could hardly wait to do him such mortal harm that the bed would be covered in his blood rather than hers. But most important, she longed to drink in his reaction to his own mutilation before she plunged the blade right into his demonic heart.

After that, her plans were less defined. Because she had had no communication with Friar Lorenzo since the night after the Palio—and had found no other sympathetic ear in his absence—she knew that, in all likelihood, Romeo's body was still lying unburied at the Tolomei sepulchre. It was conceivable that her aunt, Monna Antonia, had returned to Tebaldo's grave the next day to pray and light a candle, but Giulietta rather suspected that, if her aunt had actually stumbled upon Romeo's body, she—and the rest of Siena—would have heard about it, or, even more likely, witnessed the grieving mother dragging the body of her son's presumed murderer through the streets by the heels, strapped to her carriage.

WHEN SALIMBENI JOINED Giulietta in the candlelit wedding chamber, she had barely finished her prayers, and had not yet found a suitable place to hide the knife. Turning to face the intruder, she was shocked to see him wearing little more than a tunic; the sight of him holding a weapon would have been less unsettling than that of his naked arms and legs.

"I believe it is custom," she said, her voice shaking, "to allow your wife time to prepare herself—"

"Oh, I think you are quite ready!" Salimbeni closed the door and walked right up to her, taking her by the chin. He smiled. "No matter how long you make me wait, I will never be the man you want."

Giulietta swallowed hard, nauseated by his touch and smell. "But you are my husband—" she began meekly.

"Am I now?" He looked amused, head to one side. "Then why do you not greet me more heartily, my love? Why these cold eyes?"

"I—" She struggled to get the words out. "I am not yet used to your presence."

"You disappoint me," he said, smiling obscurely. "They told me you would have more spirit than this." He shook his head, feigning exasperation. "I am beginning to think you could grow to like me."

When she did not respond, he ran a hand down to challenge the neckline of her wedding gown, seeking access to her bosom. Giulietta gasped when she felt his greedy fingers, and for a moment quite forgot her cunning plan of letting him believe he had conquered her.

"How dare you touch me, you stinking goat!" she hissed, working to pry his hands off her body. "God will not let you touch me!"

Salimbeni laughed delightedly at her sudden resistance and stuck a claw in her hair to hold her still while he kissed her. Only when she gagged with revulsion did he let go of her mouth and say, his sour breath warm against her face, "I will tell you a secret. Old God likes to watch." With that he picked her up only to throw her down again on top of the bed. "Why else would he create such a body as yours, but leave it for me to enjoy?"

As soon as he let go of her to undo the belt around his tunic, Giulietta tried to crawl away. Unfortunately, when he pulled her back by the ankles, the knife became perfectly visible underneath her skirts, strapped to her thigh. The mere sight of it made its intended victim burst out laughing.

"A concealed weapon!" he exclaimed, pulling it free and admiring its flawless blade. "You already know how to please me."

"You gutter pig!" Giulietta tried to take it from him and nearly cut herself. "It is mine!"

"Indeed?" He looked at her distorted face, his amusement growing. "Then go get it!" One quick throw later, the knife sat quivering in a wooden beam far out of reach, and when Giulietta tried to kick him in frustration, he pushed her right back down and pinned her against the cencio, easily evading her attempts at scratching him and spitting in his face. "Now, then," he said, taunting her with false tenderness, "what other surprises do you have for me tonight, my dearest?"

"A curse!" she sneered, struggling to get her arms free. "A curse on everything you hold dear! You killed my parents, and you killed Romeo. You will burn in Hell all right, and I will shit on your grave!"

As she lay there helplessly, her weapon lost, looking up into the triumphant face of the man who ought, by now, to have been prostrate in a pool of blood, dismembered if not dead, Giulietta should have been despairing. And for a few ghastly moments, she was.

But then something happened. At first it was little more than a sudden warmth, penetrating her whole body from the bed below. It was a curious, prickling heat, as if she were lying on a skillet over a slow fire, and when the sensation deepened, it made her burst out laughing. For she suddenly understood that what she felt was a moment of religious ecstasy, and that the Virgin Mary was working a divine wonder through the cencio on which she was lying.

To Salimbeni, Giulietta's maniacal laughter was far more unsettling than any insult or weapon she could possibly have hurled at him, and he slapped her across the face once, twice, even thrice, without accomplishing anything but to boost her mad amusement. Desperate to shut her up, he started tearing at the silk covering her bosom, but in his agitation was unable to solve the mystery of her apparel. Cursing the Tolomei tailors for the strength of their thread, he turned instead to her skirts, rifling through their intricate layers in search of a less fortified access point.

Giulietta did not even struggle. She just lay there, still chuckling, while Salimbeni made himself ridiculous. For she knew, with a certainty that could only come from Heaven itself, that he could not harm her tonight. No matter how determined he was to put her in her place, the Virgin Mary was by her side, sword drawn, to bar his invasion and protect the holy cencio from an act of barbarous sacrilege.

Chuckling again, she looked at her assailant with eyes full of jubilation. "Did you not hear me?" she asked, simply. "You are cursed. Can you not feel it?"

THE PEOPLE OF SIENA knew very well that gossip is either a plague or an avenger, depending on whether you yourself are the victim. It is cunning, tenacious, and fatal; once you have been marked, it will stop at nothing to bring you down. If it cannot corner you in its present form, it will alter slightly and leap on you from aloft or below; it does not matter how far you run, or how long you crouch in silence: It will find you.

Maestro Ambrogio first heard the rumor at the butcher's. Later that day, he heard it whispered at the baker's. And by the time he returned home with his groceries, he knew enough to feel a need to act.

Putting aside his basket of food—all thoughts of dinner gone—he went straight into the back room of his workshop to retrieve the portrait of Giulietta Tolomei and put it back on the easel. For he had never completely finished it. Now he finally knew what she must hold in her piously folded hands; not a rosary, not a crucifix, but a five-petal rose, the rosa mistica. An ancient symbol for the Virgin Mary, this flower was thought to express the mystery of her virginity as well as her own immaculate conception, and in Maestro Ambrogio's mind there existed no more appropriate emblem of Heaven's patronage of innocence.

The troublesome task for the painter was always to represent this intriguing plant in a way that steered men's thoughts towards religious doctrine, rather than distracting them with the alluring, organic symmetry of its petals. It was a challenge the Maestro embraced wholeheartedly, and as he began mixing his colors to produce the perfect shades of red, he did his best to purge his mind of anything but botany.

But he could not. The rumors he had heard around town were too marvelous—too welcome—for him not to enjoy them a little further. For it was said that on the very eve of Salimbeni's wedding to Giulietta Tolomei, Nemesis had paid a timely visit to the bridal chamber and had stopped, most mercifully, an act of unspeakable cruelty.

Some called it magic, others called it human nature or simple logic; whatever the cause, however, they all agreed on the effect: The groom had been unable to consummate the marriage.

The proofs of this remarkable situation, Maestro Ambrogio had been given to understand, were abundant. One had to do with Salimbeni's movements, and it went like this: A mature man marries a lovely young girl and crowns their nuptials by joining her in the marriage bed. After three days he leaves the house and seeks a lady of the night, yet is unable to benefit from her services. When that lady kindly offers him an assortment of potions and powders, he cries out furiously that he has already tried them all, and that they are nothing but humbug. What could be concluded but that he had spent his nuptial night incapacitated, and that not even a consultation with a specialist had produced a cure?

Another proof of this presumed state of affairs came from a far more trustworthy quarter, for it had originated in Salimbeni's own household. For as long as anyone cared to remember, it had been a tradition in that family to scrutinize the bedsheet after every wedding night to ensure that the bride had been a virgin. If there was no blood on the sheet, the girl would be returned to her parents in disgrace, and the Salimbenis would add yet another name to their long list of enemies.

On the morning after Salimbeni's own wedding, however, no such sheet was displayed, nor was Romeo's cencio waved around in triumph. The only one who knew of its fate was the servant who was ordered to deliver it in a box to Messer Tolomei that same afternoon, apologizing for its unjustified removal from Tebaldo's corpse. And when finally, several days after the wedding, a piece of bloodstained linen was handed over to the chambermaid, who gave it to the housekeeper, who promptly gave it to the oldest grandmother of the house . . . then that old grandmother instantly dismissed it as a falsification.

The purity of a bride was so great a question of honor that it sometimes necessitated great deception, and so, all over town, grandmother was pitted against grandmother in developing and detecting the most convincing concoctions that could quickly be dabbed onto a nuptial sheet for lack of the real thing. Blood itself was not enough; it had to be mixed with other substances, and every grandmother of every family had her own secret recipe as well as a method of detection. Like the alchemists of old, these women spoke not in mundane, but in magical terms; to them the eternal challenge was to forge the perfect combination of pleasure and pain, of male and female.

Such a woman, trained and seasoned in all but witchcraft, could never be fooled by Salimbeni's wedding sheet, which was clearly the work of a man who had never taken a second look at his bride or his bed after their initial skirmish. Even so, nobody dared to bring up the issue with the master himself, for it was already widely known that the problem lay not with his lady, but with him.

COMPLETING THE PORTRAIT of Giulietta Tolomei was not enough. Filled with restless energy, Maestro Ambrogio went to Palazzo Salimbeni a week after the wedding to inform its inhabitants that their frescoes needed inspection and possibly maintenance. No one dared to contradict the famous Maestro, nor did anyone feel a need to consult Salimbeni on the matter, and so, for the next many days, Maestro Ambrogio was free to come and go in the house as he pleased.

His motive, of course, was to catch a glimpse of Giulietta and, if possible, offer her his assistance. With what, exactly, he was not sure, but he knew that he could not be calm until she knew she still had friends left in this world. But no matter how long he waited—climbing around on ladders pretending to find fault with his own work—the young woman never came downstairs. Nor did anyone mention her name. It was almost as if she had ceased to exist.

One evening, when Maestro Ambrogio was stretched at the very top of a tall ladder, inspecting the same coat of arms for the third time and wondering if perhaps he ought to rethink his strategy, he accidentally came to overhear a conversation between Salimbeni and his son, Nino, taking place in the neighboring room. Clearly under the impression that they were alone, the two men had withdrawn into this remote part of the house to discuss an issue that required some discretion; little did they know that, through the gap between a side door and frame, standing very still on his ladder, Maestro Ambrogio could hear every word.

"I want you," said Salimbeni to his son, "to take Monna Giulietta to Rocca di Tentennano and see to it that she is properly . . . installed."

"So soon?" exclaimed the young man. "Do you not think people will talk?"

"People are already talking," observed Salimbeni, apparently used to having such frank exchanges with his son, "and I do not want everything to come to a boil. Tebaldo . . . Romeo . . . all that. It would be good for you to leave town for a while. Until people forget. Too much has happened lately. The mob is stirring. It worries me."

Nino made a sound that could only be an attempt at laughter. "Perhaps you should go instead of me. A change of air—"

"Quiet!" There was a limit to Salimbeni's camaraderie. "You will go, and you will bring her with you. Out with her, disobedient baggage! It sickens me to have her in my house. And once you are there, I want you to stay—"

"Stay *there*?" Nino could think of nothing more odious than a sojourn in the country. "For how long?"

"Until she is pregnant."

There was an understandable silence, during which Maestro Ambrogio had to cling to the ladder with both hands so as to not lose his balance as he coped with the shocking demand.

"Oh no—" Nino backed away from his father, finding the whole thing absurd. "Not me. Someone else. Anyone."

His face flushed with rage, Salimbeni walked right up to his son and took him by the collar. "I do not have to tell you what is going on. Our honor is at stake. I would happily do away with her, but she is a Tolomei. So, I will do the second best, and plant her in the country where no one is looking, busy with her children and out of my way." He finally let go of his son. "People will say I have been merciful."

"Children?" Nino liked the plan less and less. "For how many years do you want me to sleep with my mother?"

"She is sixteen!" retorted Salimbeni, "and you will do as I say. Before this winter is over, I want everyone in Siena to know that she is pregnant with my child. Preferably a boy."

"I shall endeavor to give satisfaction," said Nino, sarcastically.

Seeing that his son was being flippant, Salimbeni held up a warning finger. "But God help you if you let her out of your sight. No one else may touch her but you. I do not want to show off a bastard."

Nino sighed. "Very well. I will play Paris and take your wife, old man. Oh, wait. She is not actually your wife, is she?"

The slap on the face did not come as a surprise to Nino; he was asking for it. "That's right," he said, backing away, "hit me every time I tell the truth, and reward me whenever I do wrong. Just tell me what you want— kill a rival, kill a friend, kill a maidenhead—and I'll do it. But don't ask me to respect you afterwards."

AS MAESTRO AMBROGIO walked back to his workshop later that night, he could not stop thinking of the conversation he had overheard. How could there be such perversity at large in the world, let alone in his own city? And why did no one move to stop it? He suddenly felt old and obsolete, and began to wish he had never gone to Palazzo Salimbeni in the first place and never overheard those wicked plans.

When he arrived at his workshop, he found the blue door unlocked. Hesitating on the threshold, he wondered briefly whether he had forgotten to lock it when he left, but when he could not hear Dante barking, he began to fear a break-in. "Hello?" He pushed open the door and stepped inside fearfully, confused by the burning lamps. "Who is here?"

Almost immediately, someone pulled him away from the door and closed it firmly behind him. When he turned to face his adversary, however, he saw that it was no malevolent stranger, but Romeo Marescotti. And right next to him stood Friar Lorenzo with Dante in his arms, holding the dog's mouth closed.

"Heaven be praised!" exclaimed Maestro Ambrogio, looking at the youngsters and marveling at their full beards. "Back from foreign lands at last?"

"Not so foreign," said Romeo, limping slightly as he walked over to the table to sit down. "We've been in a monastery not far from here."

"Both of you?" asked the painter, dumbfounded.

"Lorenzo," said Romeo, grimacing as he stretched out his leg, "saved my life. They left me for dead—the Salimbenis, in the cemetery—but he found me and brought me back to life. These past months—I should have been dead, but for him."

"God," said Friar Lorenzo, putting down the dog at last, "wanted you to live. And he wanted me to help you."

"God," said Romeo, retrieving a bit of his former mischief, "wants a lot from us, doesn't he?"

"You could not," said Maestro Ambrogio, looking around for wine and cups, "have returned at a better time. For I have just heard—"

"We have heard it, too," Romeo cut him off, "but I don't care. I am not leaving her with him. Lorenzo wanted me to wait until I had recovered fully, but I am not sure I ever will. We have men and horses. Giulietta's sister, Monna Giannozza, wants her out of Salimbeni's clutches as much as we do." The young man leaned back on his chair, slightly out of breath from talking. "Now, you're the master of frescoes, so you know all the houses. I need you to paint me a map of Palazzo Salimbeni—"

"Pardon me," said Maestro Ambrogio, shaking his head in bewilderment, "but what exactly is it that you have heard?"

Romeo and Friar Lorenzo glanced at each other.

"I understood," said the monk, defensively, "that Giulietta was married to Salimbeni some weeks ago. Is this not true?"

"And that is really," asked the painter, "all you have heard?"

Once again, the young men looked at each other.

"What is it, Maestro?" Romeo frowned in anticipation. "Don't tell me she is already carrying his child?"

"Heavens, no!" laughed the painter, suddenly giddy. "Quite the opposite."

Romeo looked at him with narrow eyes. "I am aware that she has known him for three weeks now"—he swallowed with difficulty, as if the words were making him sick—"but I am hoping she has not yet grown too fond of his embraces."

"My dearest friends," said Maestro Ambrogio, locating a bottle at last, "brace yourselves for a most unusual story."

Sin from my lips? O trespass sweetly urg'd.
Give me my sin again

...

IT WAS DAWN BY THE TIME Janice and I finally fell asleep in my
hotel room, both of us collapsing on a bed of documents, our heads spinning with family lore. We had spent all night going back and forth between now and 1340, and by the time our eyes finally fell shut, Janice
knew almost as much about the Tolomeis, the Salimbenis, the Marescottis, and their Shakespearean alter egos as I did. I had shown her every
scrap of paper in our mother's box, including the mangy volume of *Romeo
and Juliet* and the notebook full of sketches. Amazingly, she had not dis-
puted my taking the silver crucifix and wearing it around my neck; she
was more interested in our family tree and in tracing her own ancestry
back to Giulietta's sister, Giannozza.

"Look," she had pointed out, scrolling down the long document,
"there are Giuliettas and Giannozzas all over the place!"

"Originally, they were twins," I had explained, pointing out a passage
in one of Giulietta's last letters to her sister, "see? She writes, 'You have
often said that you are four minutes younger, but four centuries older,
than me. I now understand what you mean.' "

"Creepers!" Janice had stuck her nose in the family tree once more.
"Maybe these are all twins! Maybe it's a gene that runs in our family."

But apart from the fact that our medieval namesakes had been twins,
too, it was hard for us to find many other similarities between their lives
and ours. They had lived in an age where women were the silent victims

of men's mistakes; we, it would seem, were free to make our own and to shout about it as loudly as we pleased.

Only when we had read on—together—in Maestro Ambrogio's journal had the two very different worlds finally fused in a language we could both understand, namely that of money. Salimbeni had given Giulietta a bridal crown with four supersized gemstones—two sapphires and two emeralds—and those were supposedly the stones that would later end up in the statue by her grave. But we had fallen asleep before we got that far.

After only the barest bones of sleep, I was woken up by the telephone.

"Miss Tolomei," chirped Direttor Rossini, enjoying the role of early bird, "are you upright?"

"I am now." I grimaced to see the face of my wristwatch. It was nine o'clock. "What's wrong?"

"Captain Santini is here to see you. What should I tell him?"

"Uh—" I looked around at the mess. Janice was still snoring soundly beside me. "I'll be down in five minutes."

My hair still dripping from a drive-thru shower, I ran downstairs as fast as I could to find Alessandro sitting on a bench in the front garden, playing absentmindedly with a flower from the magnolia tree. The sight of him filled me with warm expectation, but as soon as he looked up to meet my eyes, I was reminded of the photos of him breaking into my hotel room, and the happy tickle immediately turned into stings of doubt.

"Top of the morning," I said, not quite meaning it. "Any news about Bruno?"

"I came by yesterday," he replied, looking at me pensively, "but you weren't here."

"I wasn't?" I did my best to sound surprised. In my frenzy of meeting motorcycle Romeo in the Mangia Tower the day before, I had completely forgotten my appointment with Alessandro. "That's strange. Oh, well—so what did Bruno say?"

"Not much." Alessandro tossed aside the flower and stood up. "He's dead."

I gasped. "That was sudden! What happened?"

As we strolled through town together, Alessandro explained that Bruno Carrera—the man who had broken into my cousin Peppo's museum—had been found dead in his cell the morning after his arrest. It was hard to say whether it was suicide or whether someone on the inside had been paid to silence him, but, Alessandro pointed out, it requires quite a bit of expertise—if not downright magic—to hang yourself from your frayed old shoelaces without breaking them in the fall.

"So, you're saying he was murdered?" Despite his character, behavior, and gun, I felt sorry for the guy. "I guess someone didn't want him to talk."

Alessandro looked at me as if he suspected I knew more than I let on. "That is what it looks like."

FONTEBRANDA WAS AN old public fountain—thanks to plumbing it was no longer used—which sat at the bottom of a sloping maze of city streets in a large open area. It was a detached, loggialike building in ancient, reddish brick, and leading down to it were broad stairs grown over with weeds.

Sitting down on the edge next to Alessandro, I looked around at the crystal-green water in the large stone basin and the kaleidoscope of light reflected onto the walls and vaulted ceiling above.

"You know," I said, having a hard time accepting all this beauty, "your ancestor was a real piece of shit!"

He laughed in surprise, an unhappy laughter. "I hope you are not judging me by my ancestors. And I hope you are not judging yourself by yours either."

How about, I thought to myself as I leaned down to run my fingers through the water, *judging you by a photo on my sister's cell phone*? But instead, I said, "That dagger—you can keep it. I don't think Romeo would ever want it back." I looked up at him, needing very much to hold someone responsible for Messer Salimbeni's crimes. "Peppo was right, it has the spirit of the devil in it. But so do some people."

We sat for a moment in silence, Alessandro smiling at my frown. "Come on," he finally said, "you are alive! Look! The sun is shining. This is the time to be here, when the light comes through the arches and hits the water. Later in the day, Fontebranda becomes dark and cold, like a grotto. You would not recognize it."

"What a strange thing," I muttered, "that a place can change so much in a few hours."

If he suspected I was referring to him, he didn't show it. "Everything has a shadow-side. In my opinion, that is what makes life interesting."

Despite my general gloom, I couldn't help smiling at his logic. "Should I be frightened?"

"Well—" He took off his jacket and leaned back against the wall of the arch, a challenge in his eyes. "The old people will tell you that Fonte-branda holds special powers."

"Go on. I will let you know when I am sufficiently spooked."

"Take off your shoes."

Much against my will, I burst out laughing. "Okay, I'm spooked."

"Come on, you'll like it." I watched him as he took off his own shoes and socks, rolled up his pant legs, and stuck his feet into the water.

"Don't you have to work today?" I asked, staring at his dangling legs.

Alessandro shrugged. "The bank is over five hundred years old. I think it can survive without me for an hour."

"So," I said, folding my arms across my chest, "tell me about those special powers."

He thought for a moment, then said, "I believe there are two kinds of madness in this world. Creative madness and destructive madness. The water from Fontebranda, it is believed, will make you mad, pazzo, but in a good way. It is hard to explain. For almost a thousand years, men and women have been drinking this water and have been filled with pazzia. Some have become poets, and some have become saints; the most famous of them all, of course, is Santa Caterina, who grew up right here, around the corner, in Oca, the contrada of the Goose."

I was not in the mood to agree with anything he said, or allow him to distract me with fairy tales, and so I made a point of shaking my head. "This whole saint thing—women starving themselves and getting burned on the stake—how can you call that creative? It's just plain insanity."

"I think that, to most people," he countered, still smiling, "throwing rocks at the Roman police would be insanity, too." He laughed at my expression. "Especially when you won't even put your feet in this nice fountain."

"All I am saying," I said, taking off my shoes, "is that it depends on your perspective. What seems perfectly creative to you might, in fact, be destructive to me." I stuck my feet tentatively into the water. "I think it all comes down to what you believe in. Or . . . whose side you are on."

I could not interpret his smile. "Are you telling me," he said, looking at my wiggling toes, "that I need to rethink my theory?"

"I think you should always rethink your theories. If you don't, they stop being theories. They become something else"—I waved my hands menacingly in the air—"they become dragons beneath your tower, letting no one in and no one out."

He glanced at me, probably wondering why I continued to be so prickly this morning. "Did you know that here, the dragon is a symbol of virginity and protection?"

I looked away. "How ironic. In China, the dragon represents the bridegroom, the very enemy of virginity."

For a while, neither of us spoke. The water in Fontebranda rippled quietly, projecting its lustrous beams onto the vaulted ceiling with the patient confidence of an immortal spirit, and for an instant, I almost felt I could be a poet. "So," I said, shaking the idea before it took root, "do you believe it? That Fontebranda makes you pazzo?"

He looked down at the water. Our feet seemed submerged in liquid jade. Then he smiled languidly, as if he somehow knew that I did not really need an answer. For it was right there, reflected in his eyes, the glittering green promise of rapture.

I cleared my throat. "I don't believe in miracles."

His eyes dropped to my neck. "Then why do you wear that?"

I touched my hand to the crucifix. "Normally I don't. Unlike you." I nodded at his open shirt.

"You mean this—?" He fished out the object that was hanging around his neck by a leather string. "This is not a crucifix. I don't need a crucifix to believe in miracles."

I stared at the pendant. "You're wearing a *bullet*?"

He smiled wryly. "I call it a love letter. The report called it 'friendly fire.' Very friendly. It stopped two centimeters from my heart."

"Tough rib cage."

"Tough partner. These bullets, they're made to go through many people. This one went through someone else first." He let it slide back down inside his shirt. "And if I hadn't been in the hospital, I would have been blown to pieces. So, it looks like God knows where I am even if I'm not wearing a crucifix."

I barely knew what to say. "When was this? *Where* was this?"

He leaned forward, feeling the water. "I told you. I went to the edge."

I tried to catch his eyes, but couldn't. "That's it?"

"That's it for now."

"Well," I said, "I'll tell you what *I* believe in. I believe in science."

His expression never changed, even as his eyes wandered over my face. "I think," he said, "that you believe in more than that. Against your will. And that is why you are afraid. You are afraid of the pazzia."

"Afraid?" I tried to laugh, "I am not the least bit—"

He interrupted me by scooping up a handful of water and holding it towards me. "If you don't believe, then drink. You have nothing to lose."

"Oh, come on!" I leaned away in disgust. "That stuff is full of bacteria!"

He shook the water from his hands. "People have been drinking it for hundreds of years."

"And gone mad!"

"See?" He smiled. "You do believe."

"Yes! I believe in microbes!"

"Have you ever seen a microbe?"

I glared at his teasing smile, annoyed that he had treed me so easily. "Honestly! Scientists see them all the time."

"Santa Caterina saw Jesus," said Alessandro, his eyes sparkling, "right up there in the sky, over Basilica di San Domenico. Who do you believe? Your scientist, or Santa Caterina, or both?"

When I did not answer, he cupped his hands, scooped up more water from the font, and drank a few mouthfuls. Then he offered the rest to me, but once again, I leaned away.

Alessandro shook his head in fake disappointment. "This is not the Giulietta I remember. What did they do to you in America?"

I snapped upright. "All right, give it here!"

By now, there was not much water left in his hands, but I slurped it up anyway, just to make a point. It did not even occur to me how intimate the gesture was, until I saw the look on his face.

"There is no escaping the pazzia now," he said, his voice hoarse. "You are a true Sienese."

"A week ago," I pointed out, squinting to get my bearings straight, "you told me to go home."

Smiling at my frown, Alessandro reached out to touch my cheek. "And here you are."

It took all my willpower not to lean into his hand. Despite my many excellent reasons for not trusting him—never mind flirting with him—all I could think of saying was, "Shakespeare wouldn't like it."

Not the least bit discouraged by my breathless dismissal, Alessandro ran a finger slowly across my cheek to pause at the corner of my mouth. "Shakespeare wouldn't have to know."

What I saw in his eyes was as strange to me as a foreign coast after end-less nights on the ocean; behind the jungle foliage I could sense the pres-ence of an unknown beast, some primordial creature waiting for me to come ashore. What he saw in mine I don't know, but whatever it was, it made his hand drop.

"Why are you afraid of me?" he whispered. "Fammi capire. Make me understand."

I hesitated. This had to be my chance. "I know nothing about you."

"I'm right here."

"Where"—I pointed at his chest and the bullet I knew was there— "did that happen?"

He closed his eyes briefly, then opened them again and allowed me to see right into his weary soul. "Oh, you'll love this. Iraq."

With that one word, all my anger and suspicion was briefly buried under a mudslide of sympathy. "Do you wanna talk about it?"

"No. Next question."

It took me a moment to process the fact that—with remarkably little ef-fort—I had come to learn Alessandro's big secret, or at least one of them. However, it was highly unlikely that he would allow me to extract the rest as easily as that, especially the one to do with breaking into my room.

"Did you—" I began, but quickly lost my nerve. Then another angle occurred to me, and I started over, saying, "Are you in any way related to Luciano Salimbeni?"

Alessandro did a double take, clearly expecting something completely different. "Why? You think he killed Bruno Carrera?"

"It was my impression," I said, speaking as calmly as I could, "that Lu-ciano Salimbeni was dead. But maybe I was misinformed. Considering everything that has happened, and the possibility that he killed my parents, I believe I have a right to know." I pulled first one foot, then the other out of the fountain. "You are a Salimbeni. Eva Maria is your godmother. Please tell me how it all hangs together."

Seeing that I was serious, Alessandro groaned and ran both hands through his hair. "I don't think—"

"Please."

"All right!" He took a deep breath, possibly more angry with himself than with me. "I will explain." He thought for quite a while, perhaps wondering where to start, then finally said, "Do you know Charlemagne?"

"Charlemagne?" I repeated, not sure I had heard him properly.

"Yes," nodded Alessandro. "He was . . . very tall."

Just then, my stomach growled, and I realized that I hadn't eaten a proper meal since lunch the day before—not unless you consider a bottle of Chianti, a tub of marinated artichokes, and half a chocolate panforte dinner.

"How about," I suggested, putting on my shoes, "you tell me the rest over coffee?"

IN THE CAMPO, preparations for the Palio were under way, and as we passed a heap of sand meant for the racetrack, Alessandro knelt down to pick up a handful as reverently as if it had been the finest saffron. "See?" He showed it to me. "La terra in piazza."

"Let me guess; it means 'this piazza is the center of the universe'?"

"Close. It means earth in the piazza. Soil." He put some in my hand. "Here, feel it. Smell it. It means *Palio*." As we walked towards the nearest café and sat down, he pointed out the workmen putting up padded barriers all around the Campo. "There is no world beyond the Palio barriers."

"How poetic," I said, discreetly brushing the sand from my hands. "Too bad Shakespeare was such a Veronaphiliac."

He shook his head. "Do you never get tired of Shakespeare?"

I very nearly retorted, *hey, you started it,* but was able to stop myself. There was no need to remind him that, the first time we had met, back in his grandparents' garden, I had been wearing diapers.

We sat like that for a moment, our eyes locked in a silent battle over the Bard and so much else, until the waiter came to take our orders. As soon as he had left, I leaned forward and put my elbows on the table. "I'm still waiting," I reminded Alessandro, not open for negotiation, "to hear about you and Luciano Salimbeni. So why don't we skip the Charlemagne part, and go—"

Just then, his cell phone rang, and after checking the display he excused himself and left the table, no doubt relieved to have his story postponed yet again. As I sat there watching him in the distance, however, it suddenly struck me how very unlikely it was that *he* was the person who had broken into my hotel room. Although I had only known him for a week, I was ready to swear that it took a lot more than your average pickle to make this man lose his calm. Even though Iraq had nearly killed him, it had definitely not broken him, quite the opposite. So, if he really *had* been sneaking around in my room for whatever reason, he would surely not have gone through my suitcases like a Tasmanian Devil, leaving my dirty panties dangling from the chandelier. It simply did not make sense.

When Alessandro returned to the table five minutes later, I pushed his espresso towards him with what I hoped was a forgiving smile. But he barely even looked at me as he took the cup and stirred in a pinch of sugar. Something in his behavior had changed, and I could sense that whoever had called him had told him something troubling. Something to do with me.

"Now, where were we?" I asked lightly, sipping my cappuccino through the milk foam. "Oh yes! Charlemagne was very tall—?"

"Why," countered Alessandro, his voice too casual to be sincere, "don't you tell me about your friend on the motorcycle?" When he saw that I was too stunned to reply, he added, more sternly, "I thought you told me you were being followed by a guy on a Ducati."

"Oh!" I managed to laugh, "*that* guy! No idea. Never saw him again. Guess my legs weren't long enough."

Alessandro didn't smile. "Long enough for Romeo."

I nearly spilled my cappuccino. "Wait! Are you suggesting I am being stalked by your old childhood rival?"

He looked away. "I am not suggesting anything. Just curious."

We sat for a moment in painful silence. He was clearly still brooding over something, and I was racking my brain to figure out what it was. Obviously, he knew about the Ducati, but not that it was my sister riding it.

Perhaps he was aware that the police had impounded the bike the day be-fore after waiting in vain at the bottom of the Mangia Tower for the owner to return. According to Janice she had taken one look at the indignant po-lice officers and decided to stick her tail between her legs. A single guy would have been a piece of cake, and two might even have been fun, but three boy scouts in uniform had been too big a mouthful, even for my sis-ter.

"Look," I said, trying to salvage a bit of our former intimacy, "I hope you don't think I'm still . . . dreaming about Romeo."

Alessandro did not respond right away. When he finally did, he spoke reluctantly, well aware that he was revealing part of his hand. "Just tell me," he said, doodling on the tablecloth with a teaspoon, "did you like the view from the Mangia Tower?"

I glared at him. "Wait a minute! Are you . . . *following* me?"

"No," he said, not too proud of himself, "but the police have been keeping an eye on you. For your own sake. Just in case the guy who killed Bruno comes looking for you, too."

"Did you ask them to?" I looked him straight in the eye and saw the confirmation before he even spoke it. "Why, thank you," I went on, drily, "it's too bad they weren't around when that lowlife broke into my room the other night!"

Alessandro didn't flinch. "Well, they were around last night. They said they saw a man in your room."

I actually burst out laughing because the whole thing was so absurd. "That's too ridiculous! A man in my room? *My* room?" Seeing that he was not yet convinced, I stopped laughing. "Look," I said, earnestly, "there was no man in my room last night, and no man in the tower either." I was just about to add, "Not that it's any of your goddamn business if there was," but stopped myself, realizing that I didn't actually mean it. In-stead, I laughed. "My-my! We sound like an old married couple."

"If we were an old married couple," said Alessandro, still not smiling, "I would not have to ask. The man in your room would be me."

"The Salimbeni genes," I observed, rolling my eyes, "are yet again rearing their ugly head. Let me guess, if we were married, you would chain me in the dungeon every time you left the house?"

He considered it, but not for long. "I wouldn't have to. Once you get to know me, you will never want anyone else. And"—he finally put down the teaspoon—"you will forget everyone you knew before."

His words—half teasing, half not—coiled around me like a school of eels around a drowned body, and I felt a thousand little teeth testing my composure.

"I believe," I said firmly, crossing my legs, "you were going to tell me about Luciano Salimbeni?"

Alessandro's smile faded. "Yes. You are right." He sat for a while, frowning, playing once again with the teaspoon, then finally said, "I should have told you this a long time ago—well, I should have told you the other night, but . . . I didn't want to scare you."

Just as I opened my mouth to urge him on and say that I was not so easily scared, another customer squeezed by my chair to sit down with a deep sigh at the table right next to us.

Janice again.

She was wearing Eva Maria's red-and-black outfit and a pair of super-sized sunglasses, but despite the glamour she made no big spectacle of herself, merely picked up the menu and pretended to consider her options. I noticed Alessandro glancing at her, and for a brief moment I feared he might see some similarity between us, or perhaps even recognize his godmother's clothes. But he did not. However, the close presence of someone else discouraged him from commencing the story he had wanted to tell me, and we sat once again in frustrated silence.

"Ein cappuccino, bitte!" said Janice to the waiter, sounding an awful lot like an American pretending to be a German, "und zwei biscotti."

I could have killed her. There was no doubt in my mind that Alessandro had been just about to disclose something of tremendous importance, and now he went on to talk about the Palio again, while the waiter lingered like a begging dog to tease out of my shameless sister where in Germany she was from.

"Prague!" she blurted out, but quickly corrected herself. "Prague . . . heim . . . stadt."

The waiter looked sufficiently convinced and totally smitten, and ran off to fulfill her order with the dispatch of an Arthurian knight.

"Look at the Balzana—" Alessandro was showing me the Siena coat of arms on the side of my cappuccino cup, thinking I was paying attention. "Everything is simple here. Black and white. Curses and blessings."

I looked at the cup. "Is that what it means? Curses and blessings?"

He shrugged. "It can mean anything you want. To me, it is an attitude indicator."

"Attitude? As in . . . the cup is half full?"

"It is an instrument. In a cockpit. It shows you if you are upside down. When I look at the Balzana, I know I am right side up." He put his hand on top of mine, ignoring Janice. "And when I look at you, I know—"

I quickly pulled my hand away, not wanting Janice to see our intimacy and then harass me afterwards. "What kind of pilot," I snapped, "wouldn't know if he was upside down?"

Alessandro stared at me, not understanding the sudden rejection. "Why," he asked, quietly, "do you always want to fight? Why are you so afraid"—he reached out for my hand again—"of being happy?"

That was it. Janice could take no more, and she exploded in laughter behind her German guidebook. Even though she tried to mask it by coughing, it was obvious even to Alessandro that she had been listening to every word we said, and he shot her a glare that endeared him to me even more. "I'm sorry," he sighed, reaching for his wallet, "I have to get back."

"I'll take care of this," I assured him, staying where I was. "I might have another coffee. Are you free later? You still owe me a story."

"Don't worry," he said, touching my cheek before he got up, "you'll get your story."

As soon as he was out of hearing range, I turned to Janice, beyond furious. "Did you really have to come and ruin everything?" I hissed, keeping an eye on Alessandro's disappearing figure. "He was just about to tell me something. Something about Luciano Salimbeni!"

"Oh, I'm sorry," said Janice with saccharine insincerity, "to interrupt your little tête-à-tête with the guy who trashed your room. Honestly, Jules, have you lost your friggin' mind?"

"I'm not so sure—"

"Oh, yes you are! I *saw* him, remember?" Seeing that I was still reluctant to believe her, Janice snorted and threw down the guidebook. "Yes, he is cute as a skunk, and yes, I'd like to lick his stamp collection, but come on! How can you let him play you like this? It would be one thing if he was just after your tail, but you know what it is he really wants."

"Actually," I quipped, "I'm not sure I do. But you clearly have ample experience with shysters, so pray enlighten me."

"Puh-*leez!*" Janice couldn't believe my naïveté. "It's obvious that he's hanging around to see when you go tomb raiding. Let me guess, he's never explicitly asked you about the grave and the statue?"

"Wrong!" I said. "When we were at the police station, he asked me whether I knew anything about a statue with golden eyes. Golden eyes! He obviously had no idea—"

"He obviously had every idea!" snapped Janice. "Oldest trick in the book: Pretend you are clueless. Don't you see he is playing you like a glockenspiel?"

"So, what are you suggesting? That he is going to wait until we've found the stones, and then . . . steal them?" Even as I spoke the words, I could hear they made perfect sense.

Janice threw up her hands. "Welcome to reality, bonehead. I say you dump this guy *pronto,* and move to my hotel. We'll make it look as if you're going to the airport—"

"And then what? Hide in your room? This is a very small place, in case you hadn't noticed."

"Just let me do the legwork." Janice was visualizing the whole thing. "I'll get this spettacolo on the road in no time."

"You are so hilarioso," I said. "We're in this together . . ."

"*Now* we are."

". . . and for your information I'd rather be screwed by him than by you."

"Well," said Janice, miffed, "then why don't you run after him right now? I'm sure he would be more than happy to deliver. Meanwhile, *I* am going to see how cousin Peppo is doing, and no, you're not invited."

I WALKED BACK to the hotel alone, deep in thought. No matter how I twisted and turned it, Janice was right; I should not be trusting Alessandro. The problem was, I was not just trusting him, I was falling for him. And in my infatuation I could almost make myself believe that Janice's blurry photos were of someone else, and that, later on, he had only had me followed out of some mistaken idea of chivalry.

Furthermore, he had promised to tell me how it all hung together, and it was not his fault that we had been interrupted several times. Or was it? If he had really wanted me to know, why had he waited for me to initiate the conversation? And just now, when Janice interrupted us, why had he not simply asked me to walk back to Monte dei Paschi with him, and told me the highlights of the story on the way?

As I approached Hotel Chiusarelli, a black limo with tinted windows rolled up beside me, and a rear window went down halfway to reveal Eva Maria's smiling face. "Giulietta!" she exclaimed. "What a coincidence! Come and have a piece of Turkish Delight!"

Climbing into the creamy leather seat facing Eva Maria, I caught myself wondering if it was some sort of trap. But then, if Eva Maria wanted me kidnapped, why not just have Alessandro do it? Undoubtedly, he had already told her that he had me eating—or at least drinking—out of his hand.

"I am so happy you are still here!" Eva Maria gushed, offering me a piece of candy from a satin box. "I called, you know. Did you not get my messages? I was afraid my godson had scared you away. I must apologize for him. He is not usually like that."

"No worries," I said, licking confectioner's sugar from my fingers and wondering what exactly she knew about my interactions with Alessandro. "He's been very nice lately."

"Has he?" She looked at me with raised eyebrows, at the same time happy to hear the news and annoyed at being kept out of the loop. "That is good."

"Sorry to walk away from your birthday dinner like that—" I went on, feeling a little sheepish for not having called her back once since that awful night. "And about the clothes you lent me—"

"Keep them!" She waved dismissively. "I have too many as it is. Tell me, are you here this weekend? I am having a party, and there will be some people you should meet . . . people who know much more about your Tolomei ancestors than I do. The party is tomorrow night, but I would like you to stay for the whole weekend." She smiled like a fairy godmother conjuring a pumpkin carriage. "You will love Val d'Orcia, I know it! Alessandro will drive you. He is coming, too."

"Uh—" I said. How could I possibly refuse? Then again, if I didn't, Janice would strangle me. "I'd love to come, but—"

"Wonderful!" Eva Maria leaned over to open my door so I could get out. "Until tomorrow, then. Don't bring anything, just yourself!"

How oft when men are at the point of death
Have they been merry! Which their keepers call
A lightning before death. O how may I
Call this a lightning?

...

Siena, A.D. 1340

ROCCA DI TENTENNANO was a formidable structure. It sat like a vulture on a hill in Val d'Orcia, perfectly perched to scavenge far and wide. Its massive walls were built to withstand innumerable hostile sieges and attacks, and considering the manners and morals of its owners, those walls were not an inch too thick.

Throughout her journey there, Giulietta had wondered why Salimbeni had been so kind as to send her to the country, far away from him. When he had seen her off the day before, standing in the courtyard outside Palazzo Salimbeni and looking at her with an air of benevolence, she had wondered whether he now—thanks to the curse on his manliness—felt remorse for what he had done, and whether his sending her away had been a way of compensating her for all the pain he had caused her.

In her hopeful state, she had observed him as he took leave of his son Nino—who was to accompany her to Val d'Orcia—and had thought she saw genuine affection in Salimbeni's eyes as he gave his last instructions for the road. "May God bless you," he had said, as Nino mounted the horse he had ridden in the Palio, "on your journey and beyond."

The young man had not replied; in fact, he had acted as if his father was not even there, and for all his wickedness, Giulietta had—ever so briefly—felt embarrassed for Salimbeni.

But later, seeing the view from her window at Rocca di Tentennano, she began to grasp his true intention in sending her here, and to understand that it was not meant as a gesture of generosity, merely as a new and ingenious form of punishment.

The place was a fortification. Just as no one could get in who did not belong there, so would no one ever be able to leave who was not allowed to. Now she finally understood what people had meant when they gravely referred to Salimbeni's previous wives as having been sent to the island; Rocca di Tentennano was a place from which the only possible escape was death.

Much to Giulietta's surprise, a servant girl came right away to light the fireplace in her room, and to help her out of her travel clothes. It was a cool day in early December, and for the last of the many hours of the journey, her fingertips had been white and numb. Now she stood in a woolen dress and dry slippers, turning herself about in front of the open fire, trying to remember when she had last felt comfortable.

Opening her eyes, she saw Nino standing in the door, regarding her with something as unexpected as kindness. It was too bad, she thought, that he was a scoundrel like his father, for he was a handsome young man, strong and able, to whom smiling seemed to come far more easily than perhaps it ought, considering the weight—surely—of his conscience.

"May I ask," he said, his tone as cordial as if he had addressed her on the dancing floor, "that you join me downstairs for dinner tonight? I understand you have been eating alone these past three weeks, and I apologize on behalf of my ill-mannered family." Seeing her surprise, he smiled charmingly. "Do not be afraid. I assure you, we are completely alone."

AND INDEED THEY WERE. Posed at either end of a dinner table that could comfortably seat twenty, Giulietta and Nino ate most of their meal in silence, their eyes only occasionally meeting through the candelabra. Whenever he saw her looking at him, Nino smiled, and at length Giulietta found the necessary boldness within herself to speak the words that were on her mind. "Did you kill my cousin Tebaldo in the Palio?"

Nino's smile disappeared. "Of course not. How could you think that?"

"Then who did?"

He looked at her curiously, but neither of her questions had visibly upset him. "You know who did. Everyone knows."

"And does everyone know"—Giulietta paused to steady her voice—"what your father did to Romeo?"

Instead of answering, Nino rose from his chair and walked along the table all the way down to where she sat. Here, he knelt down next to her and took her hand the way a knight would take the hand of a maiden in distress. "How can I ever make good the evil my father has done?" He pressed her hand to his cheek. "How can I ever eclipse that mad moon shining upon my kin? Please tell me, dearest lady, how I may please you?"

Giulietta studied his face for the longest time, then simply said, "You can let me go."

He looked at her, puzzled, not sure what she meant.

"I am not your father's wife," she went on. "There is no need to keep me here. Just let me go, and I will never bother you again."

"I am sorry," said Nino, pressing her hand to his lips this time, "but I cannot do that."

"I see," said Giulietta, withdrawing her hand. "In that case you can let me return to my room. That would please me very much."

"And I will," said Nino, getting up, "after another glass of wine." He poured more wine into the glass she had barely touched. "You have not eaten much. You must be hungry?" When she did not reply, he smiled. "Life around here can be very pleasant, you know. Fresh air, good food, wonderful bread—not the stones we are served at home—and"—he opened his arms—"excellent company. Everything is yours to enjoy. All you have to do is take it."

Only when he offered her the glass, still smiling, did Giulietta begin to understand his full meaning. "Are you not afraid," she said, lightly, taking the glass, "of what your father would say?"

Nino laughed. "I think we both would appreciate a night of not thinking about my father." He leaned against the table, waiting for her to drink. "I trust you can see that I am nothing like him."

Putting down her glass, Giulietta stood up. "I thank you," she said, "for this meal and your kind attention. But now it is time for me to retire, and I bid you good night—"

A hand around her wrist prevented her from leaving.

"I am not a man without feeling," said Nino, serious at last. "I know you have suffered, and I wish it were otherwise. But fate has ordained that we be here together—"

"Fate?" Giulietta tried to free herself, but could not. "You mean, your father?"

Only now did Nino give up all pretense and look at her wearily. "Do you not realize that I am being generous? Believe me, I do not have to be. But I like you. You are worth it." He let go of her wrist. "Now go, and do whatever it is that women do, and I will come to you." He had the nerve to smile. "I promise, you will not think me quite so offensive by midnight."

Giulietta looked him in the eye, but saw only determination. "Is there nothing I can say or do to convince you otherwise?"

But all he did was smile and shake his head.

THERE WAS A GUARD posted on every corner as Giulietta walked back to her room. And yet, despite all the protection, there was no lock on her door, no way of keeping Nino out.

Opening her shutters to the frosty night outside, she looked up at the stars and was amazed at their number and brightness. It was a dazzling spectacle, put on by Heaven for her alone, it seemed, to give her one last chance to fill her soul with beauty before it all went away.

She had failed at everything she set out to do. Her plans to bury Romeo and kill Salimbeni had both come to naught, and she must conclude that she had kept herself alive only to be abused. Her sole consolation was that they had not managed to void her vows with Romeo no matter how they had tried; she had never belonged to anyone else. He was her husband, and yet was not. While their souls were entwined, their bodies were separated by death. But not for long. All she had to do now was remain faithful to the end, and then perhaps, if Friar Lorenzo had told her the truth, she would be reunited with Romeo in the afterlife.

Leaving the shutters open, Giulietta walked over to her luggage. So many dresses, so much finery . . . but nested in a brocade slipper lay the only thing she wanted. It was a vial for perfume, which had been on her bedstand at Palazzo Salimbeni, but which she had soon decided to put to other use.

Every night after her wedding, an old nurse had come to serve her a measure of sleeping potion on a spoon, her eyes full of unspoken compassion. "Open up!" she had said, briskly, "and be a good girl. You want happy dreams, do you not?"

The first few times Giulietta had promptly spat out the potion in her chamber pot as soon as the nurse had left the room, determined to be fully awake in case Salimbeni came to her bed again, that she might remind him of his curse.

But after those first few nights, it had occurred to her to empty the vial of rosewater Monna Antonia had given her as they said goodbye, and—instead of the perfume—slowly fill it up with the mouthfuls of sleeping potion she was served every night.

In the beginning, she thought of the concoction as a weapon that might somehow be used against Salimbeni, but as his visits to her room became more and more rare, the vial sat on her bedstand with no dedicated purpose, except to remind Giulietta that, once it was full, it would surely be lethal to anyone who drank it all.

From the earliest age, she remembered hearing fanciful tales of women killing themselves with sleeping potion when abandoned by their lovers. Although her mother had tried to shield her daughters from that kind of gossip, there had been too many servants around the house who enjoyed the wide-eyed attention of the little girls. And so Giulietta and Giannozza had spent many afternoons in their secret ditch of daisies, taking turns being dead, while the other played out the horror of the people discovering the body and the empty bottle. Once, Giulietta had remained still and unresponsive for so long that Giannozza had, in fact, believed she was really dead.

"Giu-giu?" she had said, pulling at her arms. "Please stop! It is not funny anymore. Please!"

In the end, Giannozza had started crying, and although Giulietta had eventually sat up, laughing, Giannozza had been inconsolable. She had cried all afternoon and all evening, and had run away from dinner without eating. They had not played the game since.

During Giulietta's imprisonment at Palazzo Salimbeni, there were days when she sat with the vial in her hands, wishing it was already full, and that she possessed the power to end her own life. But it was only on the last night before her morning departure for Val d'Orcia that the vial had finally run over, and throughout the journey she had consoled herself with thoughts of the treasure nested in a slipper in her luggage.

Now, sitting down on the bed with the vial in her hands, she felt confident that what she held would stop her heart. This, then, she thought, must have been the Virgin Mary's plan all along; that her marriage with Romeo was to be consummated in Heaven, and not on earth. The vision was sweet enough to make her smile.

Taking out the quill and ink that was also hidden in her luggage, she settled down briefly to write a final letter to Giannozza. The inkwell Friar Lorenzo had given her when she was still at Palazzo Tolomei was by now almost empty, and the quill had been sharpened so many times that only a feeble tuft was left; even so, she took her time composing one last message to her sister before rolling up the parchment and hiding it in a crack in the wall behind the bed. "I will wait for you, my dearest," she wrote, tears smearing the ink, "in our patch of daisies. And when you call my name, I shall wake up right away, I promise."

ROMEO AND FRIAR LORENZO came to Rocca di Tentennano with ten horsemen trained in all manner of combat. Were it not for Maestro Ambrogio, they would never have known where to find Giulietta, and were it not for Giulietta's sister, Giannozza, and the warriors she lent them, they would never have been able to follow words with action.

Their connection with Giannozza had been Friar Lorenzo's doing. When they were in hiding in the monastery—Romeo still immobilized from his stomach wound—the monk had sent a letter to the only person he could think of who might sympathize with their situation. He knew Giannozza's address only too well from having been the sisters' secret courier for more than a year, and not two weeks had passed before he received an answer.

"Your most painful letter reached me on a good day," she wrote to him, "for I have just buried the man who ran this house, and am now finally in charge of my own destiny. Yet I cannot express the grief I felt, dear

Lorenzo, when I read about your tribulations, and about my poor sister's fate. Please let me know what I may do to help. I have men, I have horses. They are yours."

But even Giannozza's capable warriors stood helpless against the massive gate of Rocca di Tentennano, and as they observed the place from afar in the twilight hour, Romeo knew he would have to resort to trickery to get inside and save his lady.

"It reminds me," he said to the others, who had all fallen silent at the sight of the fortress, "of a giant wasp's nest. To attack it in broad daylight would mean death to us all, but perhaps we stand a chance come nightfall, when they are all asleep but for a few sentinels."

And so he waited until dark to pick out eight men—one of them Friar Lorenzo, who could not be left behind—and to make sure they were equipped with ropes and daggers, before taking them stealthily to the foot of the cliff on which the Salimbeni stronghold was built.

With no audience but the twinkling stars in a moonless sky, the intruders climbed the hill as quietly as possible, to eventually arrive at the very base of the great building. Once here, they crept along the bottom of the slanting wall until someone spotted a promising opening some twenty feet up and poked Romeo on the shoulder, indicating the opportunity without a word.

Allowing no one else the honor of going first, Romeo secured a rope around his waist and proceeded to take a firm, stabbing grip of two daggers before commencing his ascent by hacking the blades into the mortar between the boulders and pulling himself up, laboriously, by the arms. The wall was slanted just enough to make such a venture possible, but not enough to make it easy, and Friar Lorenzo gasped more than once as Romeo's foot slipped from its hold and left him hanging by the arms. He would not have been so concerned if Romeo had been in perfect health, but he knew that every motion his friend made as he climbed the wall must cause him almost unbearable pain, since his abdominal wound had never properly healed.

But Romeo barely felt his old injury as he climbed up the wall, for it was drowned out by the ache in his heart at the thought of Giulietta being forced into submission by Salimbeni's ruthless son. He remembered Nino only too well from the Palio, where he had seen him expertly stabbing Tebaldo Tolomei, and he knew that no woman would be able to bar her door to his will. Nor was Nino likely to fall prey to threats of a curse; surely the young man knew that, as far as Heaven was concerned, he was already cursed for all eternity.

The opening aloft turned out to be an arrow slit, just wide enough to let him through. As Romeo came down heavily on the floor tiles, he saw that he was in an armory, and he almost smiled at the irony. Untying the rope around his waist and securing it to a cresset on the wall, he jiggled it twice to let the men at the other end know they could safely follow.

ROCCA DI TENTENNANO was as joyless on the inside as it was on the outside. There were no frescoes to brighten the walls, no tapestries to keep out the drafts; unlike Palazzo Salimbeni, which was a display of refinement and abundance, this place was built for no other purpose than dominance, and any attempt at adornment would have been but an obstacle to the swift movements of men and arms.

As Romeo traversed the endless, winding corridors—Friar Lorenzo and the others trailing closely behind—he began to fear that finding Giulietta in this living mausoleum and escaping with her unnoticed would be a matter of luck rather than courage.

"Careful!" he hissed at one point, holding up a hand to stop the others as he caught sight of a guard. "Back up!"

To avoid the guard they had to embark upon a labyrinthine detour, and in the end they found themselves back exactly where they had been before, crouching silently in the shadows, where the wall torches did not reach.

"There are guards posted on every corner," whispered one of Giannozza's men, "but mostly in that direction—" He pointed ahead.

Romeo nodded gravely. "We may have to take them one at a time, but I would rather wait as long as possible."

He did not have to explain why he wanted to postpone the clamor of weapons. They were all keenly aware of being vastly outnumbered by the guards currently asleep in the bowels of the castle, and they knew that once the fighting began, their only hope would be to run. For that purpose, Romeo had left three men outside to keep the horses ready, but he was beginning to suspect their job would merely be to return to Giannozza and tell the sorry tale of failure.

Just then, as he was despairing over their lack of progress, Friar Lorenzo poked him on the shoulder and pointed out a familiar figure carrying a torch at the other end of a hallway. The person—Nino—was walking slowly, even reluctantly, as if his was an errand that could happily be postponed. Despite the cold night he was dressed in a tunic, and yet he had a sword strapped to his belt; Romeo knew right away where he was headed.

Waving Friar Lorenzo and Giannozza's men along, he crept down the corridor in silent pursuit of the malefactor, stopping only when the other paused to address two guards flanking a closed door.

"You may leave now," Nino told them, "and rest until tomorrow. I will personally ensure that Monna Giulietta is safe. In fact"—he turned to address all the guards at once—"everyone may leave! And tell the kitchen that, tonight, there is no limit to the wine."

Only when the guards had disappeared down the corridor—already grinning at the prospect of a carousal—did Nino take a deep breath and reach for the door handle. But as he did so, a noise right behind him made him start. It was the unmistakable sound of a sword being drawn from a sheath.

Nino turned around slowly to face his assailant with incredulity. When he recognized the person who had come this far to challenge him, his eyes all but sprang from their sockets. "Impossible! You are dead!"

Romeo stepped into the torchlight with a baleful smile. "If I were dead, I would be a ghost, and you would not need to fear my blade."

Nino gazed at his rival in silent wonder. Here was a man he had never expected to see again; a man who had defied the grave to save the woman he loved. It was possible that—for the first time in his life—it now occurred to Salimbeni's son that here was a true hero, and that he, Nino, was the villain. "I believe you," he said, calmly, and placed the torch in a cresset on the wall, "and I respect your blade, but I do not fear it."   .

"That," observed Romeo, waiting for the other to prepare himself, "is a big mistake."

Just around the corner, Friar Lorenzo listened to the exchange with futile agitation. It was beyond his comprehension that Nino did not call back the guards in order to overpower Romeo without a fight. This was an ignominious break-in, not a public spectacle; Nino did not have to risk this duel. Nor, however, did Romeo.

Right beside him, crouched in the darkness, Friar Lorenzo could see Monna Giannozza's men exchanging glances, asking themselves why Romeo did not call them out to cut Nino's throat before the cocky offender could even cry for help. After all, this was no tournament to win a lady's heart; this was a case of downright theft. Romeo, surely, did not owe an honorable joust to the man who had stolen his wife.

But the two rivals thought otherwise.

"The mistake is yours," countered Nino, unsheathing his sword with gleeful anticipation. "Now I shall have to say you were cut down by a Salimbeni twice. People will think you grew to like the feeling of our iron."

Romeo threw his opponent a derisive smile. "Might I remind you," he said, positioning himself for combat, "that your family is short on iron these days. Indeed, I believe people are too busy talking about your father's . . . empty crucible to care about much else."

The insolent remark would have made a less experienced fighter lunge at the speaker in fury, forgetting that anger destroys your focus and makes you an easy victim, but Nino was not so easily fooled. He restrained himself and merely touched the tip of his blade to Romeo's in acknowledgment of the point. "True," he said, moving in a circle around his opponent, searching for an opening, "my father is wise enough to know his limitations. That is why he sent me to deal with the girl. How very rude of you to delay her pleasure like this. She is behind that very door, waiting for me with moist lips and rosy cheeks."

This time it was Romeo who had to restrain himself, testing Nino's blade with but the slightest touch and absorbing the vibration in his hand. "The lady of whom you speak," he pointed out, "is my wife. And she will cheer me on with cries of pleasure as I chop you into pieces."

"Will she now?" Nino lunged forward, hoping to surprise, but missed. "As far as I know, she is no more your wife than she is my father's. And soon"—he grinned—"she will be no one's wife, but my little whore, pining all day for me to come and entertain her at night—"

Romeo lunged at Nino, and missed the other only by a hair as Nino had the presence of mind to parry and deflect the blade. It was enough, however, to put a halt to their conversation, and for a while there was no sound other than that of their blades crossing with hateful clangs as they entered into a circular dance of death.

While Romeo was no longer the nimble-footed fighter he had been before his injury, his tribulations had taught him resilience, and, most important, they had filled him with a white-hot hatred that—if properly mastered—might trump any fighting skill. And so, even as Nino danced around him in a taunting manner, Romeo did not take the bait, but waited patiently for his moment of revenge . . . a moment he was confident the Virgin Mary would grant him.

"How very fortunate I am!" exclaimed Nino, taking Romeo's inaction for a sign of fatigue. "I get to indulge in my two favorite sports on the same evening. Tell me, how does it feel—"

Romeo needed no more than a brief, careless imbalance in Nino's stance to spring forward with impossible speed and drive his sword in between the other's ribs, to penetrate his heart and pin him, briefly, to the wall.

"How it feels?" he sneered, right into Nino's astounded face. "Did you really want to know?"

With that, he withdrew his blade in disgust and watched the lifeless body slide to the ground, leaving a trail of crimson on the wall.

From around the corner, Friar Lorenzo was shocked to witness the conclusion of the brief duel. Death had come so abruptly to Nino that the young man's face showed nothing but surprise; the monk would have liked for Nino to realize his own defeat—even if it was only within the blink of an eye—before expiring. But Heaven had shown itself more merciful than he, and had ended the scoundrel's sufferings before they had even begun.

Not pausing to wipe down his sword, Romeo stepped right over the dead body to turn the door handle that Nino had guarded with his life. Seeing his friend disappearing through the fateful door, Friar Lorenzo at last got up from his hiding place and hastened across the hallway— Giannozza's men in tow—to follow Romeo into the unknown.

Stepping through the door, Friar Lorenzo paused to let his eyes adjust. There were no lights in the room save the glow from a few embers in the fireplace and the faint shine of the stars through an open window; even so, Romeo had walked straight over to the bed to wake its sleeping tenant.

"Giulietta, my love," he urged, embracing her and showering her pale face with kisses, "wake up! We are here to save you!"

When the girl finally stirred, Friar Lorenzo saw right away that something was wrong. He knew Giulietta well enough to grasp that she was beyond herself, and that some power stronger than Romeo was working at her to put her back to sleep.

"Romeo . . ." she murmured, struggling to smile and touch his face, "you found me!"

"Come," Romeo encouraged her, trying to make her sit up, "we must go before the guards come back!"

"Romeo . . ." Giulietta's eyes were closing again, her head drooping limply like the bud of a flower felled by a scythe. "I wanted to—" She would have said more, but her tongue failed her, and Romeo looked at Friar Lorenzo in desperation.

"Come and help me!" he urged his friend, "she is ill. We'll have to carry her." When he saw the other hesitating, Romeo followed the monk's eyes and saw the vial and cork on the bedstand. "What is that?" he demanded, his voice hoarse with fear. "A poison?"

Friar Lorenzo leapt across the floor to inspect the vial. "It was rosewater," he said, smelling the empty vessel, "but also something else—"

"Giulietta!" Romeo shook the girl violently. "You must wake up! What did you drink? Did they poison you?"

"Sleeping potion . . ." mumbled Giulietta without opening her eyes, "so you could wake me up—"

"Merciful Mother!" Friar Lorenzo helped Romeo sit her up. "Giulietta! Come to! It's your old friend, Lorenzo!"

Giulietta frowned and managed to open her eyes. Only now, seeing the monk and all the strangers surrounding her bed did she seem to understand that she was not yet dead, not yet in Paradise. And when the truth reached her heart, she gasped, her face contorted with panic.

"Oh, no!" she whispered, clinging to Romeo with all her remaining strength. "This is not right! My dear—you are alive! You are—"

As she started coughing, violent spasms ran through her body, and Friar Lorenzo could see the pulse in her neck pounding as if the skin was about to burst. Not knowing what else to do, the two men tried to soothe her pains and calm her down, and they kept holding her, even as sweat ran from her body and she fell back on the bed in convulsions.

"Help us!" cried Romeo to the men standing around the bed. "She is suffocating!"

But Giannozza's warriors were trained to end life, not sustain it, and they stood uselessly around the bed as the husband and the childhood friend struggled to save the woman they loved. Although they were strangers, the men were so engrossed in the tragedy unfolding before their eyes that they did not notice the advent of the Salimbeni guards until these were at the door and escape was impossible.

It was a cry of horror from the hallway that first alerted them to the danger. Someone had clearly caught sight of young master Nino, sprawled in his own blood. Now at last, Giannozza's men had occasion to draw their weapons as the Salimbeni guards began pouring into the room.

In a situation as desperate as theirs, a man's only hope of survival was to have none. Knowing they were already dead, Giannozza's men threw themselves at the Salimbeni guards with fearless frenzy, cutting them down without mercy and not even pausing to ensure that their victims were beyond suffering before moving on to the next. The only armed man who did not turn to fight was Romeo, who could not let go of Giulietta.

For a while, Giannozza's men were able to defend their position and kill anyone who came into the room. The door was too narrow to admit more than one enemy at a time, and as soon as someone burst inside, he would be met by seven blades in the hands of men who had not spent the evening drinking themselves into a stupor. In a space as narrow as this, a few determined men were not as helpless against a hundred opponents as they would have been in an open field; as long as the hundred came to them one by one, there was no strength in numbers.

But not all Salimbeni's guards were imbeciles; just as Giannozza's men began to entertain a hope that they might, in fact, live through the night, they were distracted by a loud clamor from the back of the room, and spun around to see a secret door open and a stream of guards pouring through it. Now, with enemies coming at them from the front and rear at once, the men were quickly overwhelmed. One by one, Giannozza's men fell to their knees in defeat—some dying, some already dead—as the room flooded with guards.

Even now, with all hope lost, Romeo still did not turn to fight. "Look at me!" he urged Giulietta, too focused on reviving her lifeless body to think of defending himself. "Look at—" But a spear thrown from across the room struck him right between the shoulder blades, and he collapsed over the bed without another word, even in death unwilling to let go of Giulietta.

As his body went limp, the eagle signet ring fell from his hand, and Friar Lorenzo understood that Romeo's last wish had been to put the ring back on his wife's finger where it belonged. Without thinking, he grabbed the holy object from the bed—lest it be confiscated by men who would never respect its destiny—but before he could put it on Giulietta's finger, he was pulled away from her by strong hands.

"What happened here, you blithering monk?" demanded the captain of the guards. "Who is that man, and why did he kill Monna Giulietta?"

"That man," replied Friar Lorenzo, too numb from shock and grief to feel any real fear, "was her true husband."

"Husband?" The captain took the monk by the hood of his cowl and shook him. "You're a stinkin' liar! But"—he bared his teeth in a smile—"we have ways to fix that."

MAESTRO AMBROGIO SAW it with his own eyes. The wagon came in from Rocca di Tentennano late at night—just as he was passing by Palazzo Salimbeni—and the Salimbeni guards did not falter in unloading their miserable cargo before the very feet of their master on the front steps of his home.

First came Friar Lorenzo—bound and blindfolded and barely able to climb off the wagon by himself. Judging by the unforgiving way in which the guards hauled him into the building, they were taking him straight to the torture chamber. Next, they proceeded to unload the bodies of Romeo, Giulietta, and Nino . . . all wrapped together in the same bloody sheet.

There were those who would later say that Salimbeni had looked at his son's dead body without emotion, but the Maestro was not fooled by the man's stony features as Salimbeni beheld his own tragedy. Here was the outcome of his wicked dealings; God had punished him by serving up his son to him like a butchered lamb, smeared in the blood of the two people he himself had sought to separate and annihilate against the will of Heaven. Surely, at that moment, Salimbeni understood that he was already in Hell, and that, wherever he went in the world and however long he lived, his demons would always follow him.

When Maestro Ambrogio returned to his workshop later that night, he knew the Salimbeni soldiers might come knocking at any moment. If the rumors about Salimbeni's torture methods were true, poor Friar Lorenzo was likely to blurt out everything he knew—as well as an abundance of falsehoods and exaggerations—before midnight.

But, the Maestro wondered, would they really dare come for him, too? After all, he was a famous artist with many noble patrons. Yet he could not be sure. Only one thing was certain: Running away and hiding would surely fix his guilt, and—once a runaway—there could be no return to the city he loved above any other.

And so the painter looked around his workshop for anything incriminating, such as the portrait of Giulietta and his journal, lying on the table. Pausing only to enter one last paragraph—a few jumbled sentences about what he had seen that night—he took the book and the portrait, wrapped them both in cloth, put them in an airtight box, and hid that box in a secret hollow in the wall where, surely, no one else would ever find it.

Can I go forward when my heart is here?
Turn back, dull earth, and find thy centre out

. . .

*J*ANICE HAD NOT LIED when she said she was a good climber. For some reason, I had never put much faith in her postcards from exotic places, except when they spoke of disappointment and debauchery. I preferred to think of her lying dead drunk in a motel in Mexico rather than snorkeling around coral reefs in water so clean that you—as she had once scribbled, not to me, but to Aunt Rose—jump in like the dirty old sinner you are and come out feeling like Eve on her first morning in Paradise, before Adam shows up with newspaper and cigarettes.

Standing on my balcony, observing her efforts to climb up to me, I was struck by how much I had looked forward to my sister's return. For after pacing up and down the floor of my room for at least an hour, I had come to the frustrating conclusion that I would never be able to make sense of the situation on my own.

It had always been like that. Whenever I would describe my problems to Aunt Rose as a child, she would fuss and fuss, but never solve anything, and in the end I would feel much worse than I had before. If a boy was bugging me at school, she would call the principal and all the teachers and demand that they call his parents. Janice, in contrast—accidentally overhearing our conversation—would merely shrug and say, "He has a crush on her. It'll pass. What's for dinner?" And she was always right, even though I hated to admit it.

In all likelihood, she was right now, too. It was not that I particularly liked her snarky comments about Alessandro and Eva Maria, but then, someone had to make them, and my own mind was clearly embroiled in a conflict of interest.

Panting with the ongoing effort of staying alive, Janice readily grasped the hand I held out for her and eventually managed to swing a leg over the railing. "Climbing . . ." she gasped, coming down like a sack of potatoes on the other side, "is such sweet sorrow!"

"Why," I asked, as she sat gasping on the floor of the balcony, "did you not use the stairs?"

"Very funny!" she shot back. "Considering there's a mass murderer out there who hates my guts!"

"Come on!" I said. "If Umberto had wanted to wring our necks he would have done it a long time ago."

"You never know when these people will suddenly snap!" Janice finally got up, brushing off her clothes. "Especially now that we have Mom's box. I say we get out of here prontissimo, and—" Only now did she actually look at my face and notice my red and puffy eyes. "Jesus, Jules!" she exclaimed. "What's wrong?"

"Nothing," I said, dismissively. "I just finished reading about Romeo and Giulietta. Sorry to spoil the plot, but there's no happy end. Nino tries to seduce her—or, rape her—and she kills herself with sleeping potion, just before Romeo comes blasting in to save her."

"What the hell did you expect?" Janice went inside to wash her hands. "People like the Salimbenis don't change. Not in a million years. It's hardwired into their system. Evil with a smile. Nino . . . Alessandro . . . cut from the same cloth. You either kill them, or you let them kill you."

"Eva Maria is not like that—" I began, but Janice wouldn't let me finish.

"Oh, really?" she sneered from the bathroom. "Allow me to broaden your horizon. Eva Maria has been playing you since day one. Do you seriously think she was on that plane by accident?"

"Don't be ridiculous!" I gasped. "No one else knew I was arriving on that plane except—" I stopped.

"Precisely!" Janice tossed aside the towel and threw herself down on the bed. "They're obviously working together, her and Umberto. I wouldn't be surprised if they're brother and sister. That's how the Mafia works, you know. It's all about family, all about favors and covering each other's ass—mind you, I'd love to cover your boyfriend's ass, except I'm not sure I want to end up sleeping under a floor."

"Oh, would you give it a break!"

"No, I won't!" Janice was on a roll, feet in the air. "Cousin Peppo says that Eva Maria's husband, Salimbeni, was a *bastardo classico*. He was definitely into some über-organized badass behavior with limos and guys in shiny suits and Sicilian ties, the whole scene. Some people think Eva Maria had her little sugar daddy put down so she could take over the biz and get rid of the limit on her credit card. And your Mister Candypants is obviously her favorite muscle, if not downright toy dawg. But now— ta-daa!—she's sicced him on you, and the question is: Will he dig up a bone for her, or for you? Can the virgitarian turn the playboy from his wicked ways, or will the scary godmother prevail and steal back her family jewels as soon as you get your cute little hands on them?"

I just looked at her. "Are you finished?"

Janice blinked a couple of times, recovering from her solo flight of fancy. "Definitely. I'm so outta here. You?"

"Oh, crap!" I sat down next to her, suddenly exhausted. "Mom was trying to leave us a treasure. And we've screwed it up. *I've* screwed it up. Don't I owe it to her to straighten things out?"

"The way I see it, all we owe her is to stay alive." Janice dangled a pair of keys in front of me. "Let's go home."

"What are those for?"

"Mom's old house. Peppo told me all about it. It's southeast of here, in a place called Montepulciano. It's been empty all these years." She looked at me with guarded hopefulness. "Wanna come?"

I stared at her, amazed that she could bring herself to ask. "You really want me to come?"

Janice sat up. "Jules," she said, with unusual sobriety, "I really want us both to get out of here. This is not just about a statue and some gemstones. There is something really spooky going on. Peppo told me about a secret society of people who believe there is a curse running in our family, and that they need to stop it. And guess who runs the whole show? Yes, your little mobster-queen. This is the same kind of sick stuff that Mom was into . . . something about secret blood rituals to conjure the spirits of the dead. Excuse me for not being enthusiastic."

I got up and walked over to the window, frowning at my own reflection. "She has invited me to a party. At her place in Val d'Orcia."

When Janice didn't answer, I turned to see what was wrong. She was lying back on the bed, clutching her face. "God help us!" she moaned. "I don't believe this! Let me guess: El Niño is going, too?"

I threw up my arms. "Come on, Jan! Don't you want to get to the bottom of this? I do!"

"And you will!" Janice sprang from the bed and started stomping back and forth, fists clenched. "You'll end up on the bottom of something, that's for sure, with your heart broken and your feet in cement. I swear to God . . . if you do this, and you end up dead like all our ancestors that are supposedly buried under Eva Maria's front steps, I will never speak to you again!"

She looked at me belligerently, and I stared back in disbelief. This was not the Janice I knew. The Janice I knew could not have cared less about my movements, or my fate, except to hope that I failed miserably in everything I set out to do. And the idea of me with my feet in cement would have made her slap her knees laughing, not bite her lip as if she was just about to cry.

"All right," she said more calmly, when I remained silent, "go ahead, then, and get yourself killed in some . . . satanic ritual. See if I care."

"I didn't say I was going."

She deflated a bit. "Oh! Well, in that case, I think it's high time you and I had a gelato."

WE SPENT A GOOD CHUNK of the afternoon sampling old and new flavors in Bar Nannini, an ice cream parlor conveniently located in Piazza Salimbeni. Not exactly reconciled, we had at least come to agree on two things: We knew far too little about Alessandro to be comfortable with him driving away with me tomorrow, and, secondly, gelato was better than sex.

"Just trust me on that one," said Janice, winking to cheer me up.

For all her faults, my sister had always had tremendous perseverance, and she single-handedly kept watch for over an hour, while I was crouched on a bench in the far corner of the shop, mortified in advance at the idea of being discovered.

Suddenly, Janice pulled at me to get up. She didn't say anything; she didn't have to. Peeking out through the glass door together, we watched Alessandro as he crossed Piazza Salimbeni on foot and continued down the Corso.

"He's going downtown!" observed Janice. "I knew it! Guys like that don't live in the burbs. Or maybe"—she made eyes at me—"he's going to meet his mistress." We both stretched our necks to see better, but Alessandro was no longer visible. "Damn!"

We shot out of Bar Nannini and cantered down the street as best we could without attracting too much attention, which was always a challenge in Janice's company. "Wait!" I grabbed her by the arm to slow her down. "I see him! He's right—*uh-oh!*"

Just then, Alessandro stopped, and we both ducked into a doorway. "What's he doing?" I hissed, too afraid of disclosure to see for myself.

"Talking to some guy," said Janice, stretching. "Some guy with a yellow flag. What's up with the flag thing? Everybody has a flag here—"

Moments later, we were once again on the prowl, slithering along shopwindows and doorways to avoid detection, following our prey all the way down the road, past the Campo, and up towards Piazza Postierla. He had already stopped several times to greet people going the other way, but as the road became steeper, the number of friends increased.

"Honestly!" exclaimed Janice, when Alessandro stopped yet again to goochi-gooch a baby in a stroller. "Is this guy running for friggin' mayor?"

"It's called interhuman relationships," I muttered, "you should try it."

Janice rolled her eyes. "Why, listen to the social butterfly!"

I was brewing a retort when we both realized our target had disappeared.

"Oh no!" gasped Janice. "Where did he go?"

We hurried up to where we had last seen Alessandro before he vanished—practically across the street from Luigi's hair salon—and here we discovered the entrance to the tiniest, darkest alley in all of Siena.

"Can you see him?" I whispered, hiding behind Janice.

"No, but it's the only place he could have gone." She took my hand and pulled me along. "Come!"

As we tiptoed down the covered alley, I could not help giggling. Here we were, sneaking around hand in hand the way we used to when we were children. Janice glanced at me sternly, worried about the noise, but when she saw the laughter in my face, she softened and started giggling, too.

"I can't believe we are doing this!" I whispered. "It's embarrassing!"

"Shh!" she hissed, "I think this is a bad neighborhood." She nodded at the graffiti on one of the walls. "What's a *galleggiante*? Sounds pretty obscene. And what the hell happened in '92?"

At the bottom, the alley turned a sharp right, and we stood for a moment at the corner, listening for disappearing footsteps. Janice even stuck out her head to assess the situation, but she pulled it back again very quickly.

"Did he see you?" I whispered.

Janice drew in air. "Come!" She grabbed me by the arm and pulled me around the corner before I could protest. Fortunately, there was no sign of Alessandro, and we scampered on in nervous silence, until we suddenly caught sight of people guarding a horse at the far end of the narrow alley.

"Stop!" I pushed Janice up against a wall, hoping no one had spotted us. "This is no good. Those guys—"

"What are you dong?" Janice pushed away from the wall and continued down the alley towards the horse and its handlers. Seeing that, thankfully, Alessandro was not among them, I ran after her, pulling at her arm to make her stop.

"Are you crazy!" I hissed. "That's gotta be a horse for the Palio, and those guys don't want tourists running around—"

"Oh, I'm not a tourist," said Janice, shaking off my hands and walking on, "I'm a journalist."

"No! Jan! Wait!"

As she approached the men guarding the horse, I was filled with a strange mix of admiration and the desire to kill her. The last time I had felt quite like this was in ninth grade, when she had spontaneously picked up the phone and dialed the number of a boy in our class, merely because I had said I liked him.

Just then, someone opened a pair of shutters right above us and, as soon as I realized that it was Alessandro, I sprang back against the wall, pulling Janice with me, desperate that he shouldn't see us there, sniffing around in his neighborhood like lovesick teenagers.

"Don't look!" I hissed, still shell-shocked from the near miss. "I think he lives up there, on the third floor. Mission accomplished. Case closed. Time to go."

"What do you mean, *mission accomplished*?" Janice leaned back to look up at Alessandro's window, eyes gleaming. "We came here to find out what he's up to. I say we stick around." She tried the nearest door, and when it opened without a problem, she wiggled her eyebrows and stepped inside. "Come on!"

"Are you out of your mind?" I eyed the men nervously. They were all staring at us, clearly wondering who we were and what we were up to. "I am not setting foot in that building! That's where he lives!"

"Fine by me." Janice shrugged. "Stay here and loiter. I'm sure they won't mind."

AS IT TURNED OUT, we were not in a stairway. Walking along in the semidarkness behind Janice, I had been afraid she would race me all the way to the third floor, determined to kick in Alessandro's door and bombard him with questions. But seeing that there were no stairs, I gradually started relaxing.

At the end of the long corridor a door was ajar, and we both stretched to see what was on the other side.

"Flags!" observed Janice, clearly disappointed. "More flags. Someone has a thing with yellow around here. And birds."

"It's a museum," I said, spotting a few cencios hanging on the walls. "A contrada museum, just like Peppo's. I wonder—"

"Cool!" Janice pushed open the door before I could protest. "Let's see it. You always liked dusty old junk."

"No! Please don't—" I tried to hold her back, but she shook off my hand and walked boldly into the room. "Come back here! Jan!"

"What kind of man," she mused, looking around at the displayed artifacts, "lives in a museum? It's kind of creepy."

"Not in," I corrected her. "On top. And it's not as if they have mummies here."

"How do you know?" She tipped open the visor on a suit of armor, just to check. "Maybe they have horse-mummies. Maybe this is where they have those secret blood rituals and conjure the spirits of the dead."

"Yeah." I threw her a hairy eyeball from behind the door. "Thanks for getting to the bottom of that when you had the chance."

"Hey!" She all but gave me the finger. "Peppo didn't know any more than that, okay!"

I stood and watched her as she tiptoed around for another minute or so, pretending to be interested in the exhibition. We both knew she was only doing it to irritate me. "Okay," I finally said, "have you seen enough flags now?" But instead of answering, Janice simply walked through a door into another room, leaving me to stand there, half hiding, all by myself.

It took me a while to find her; she was walking around in a tiny chapel with candles burning on the altar and magnificent oil paintings on every wall. "Wow!" she said when I joined her. "How would you like this for a living room? What do they do in here? Read entrails?"

"I hope they read yours! Do you *mind* if we leave now?"

But before she could give me a cheeky answer, we both heard footsteps. Nearly tripping over each other's feet in our panic, we scrambled to get out of the chapel and find a place to hide in the next room.

"In here!" I pulled Janice into a corner behind a glass cabinet with beat-up riding helmets, and five seconds later an elderly woman walked right past us with an armful of folded-up yellow clothes. Behind her came a boy of eight or so, hands in his pockets, a scowl on his face. Though the woman walked straight through the room, unfortunately the boy stopped ten feet from the place where we were hiding, to look at antique swords on the wall.

Janice made a face, but neither of us dared to move an inch, let alone whisper, as we crouched in the corner like textbook evildoers. Luckily for us, the boy was too focused on his own mischief to pay much attention to anything else. Making sure his grandmother was good and gone, he stretched to lift a rapier off its hooks on the wall, and to assume a couple of fencing positions that were not half bad. He was so engrossed in his illicit project that he did not even hear someone else entering the room until it was too late.

"No-no-no!" scolded Alessandro, crossing the floor and taking the rapier right out of the boy's hand. But instead of putting the weapon back on the wall, as any responsible adult would do, he merely showed the boy the correct position and gave him the rapier right back. "Tocca a te!"

The weapon went back and forth a few times until finally Alessandro plucked another rapier from the wall and indulged the boy in a play-fight, which only ended when an impatient woman's voice yelled, "Enrico! Dove sei?"

Within seconds, the weapons were back on the wall, and when Grandmother materialized in the doorway, both Alessandro and the boy were standing innocently with their hands behind their backs.

"Ah!" exclaimed the woman, delighted to see Alessandro and kissing him on both cheeks. "Romeo!"

She said a lot more than that, but I didn't hear it. If Janice and I had not been standing so close, I might even have sunk to my knees, seeing that my legs had turned to soft-serve ice cream.

Alessandro was Romeo.

Of course he was. How could I have missed that? Was this not the Eagle Museum? Had I not already seen the truth in Malèna's eyes? . . . And in his?

"Jesus, Jules," grimaced Janice, without a sound, "get a grip!"

But there was nothing left for me to get a grip on. Everything I had thought I knew about Alessandro spun before my eyes like numbers on a roulette wheel, and I realized that—in every single conversation with him—I had put all my money on the wrong color.

He was not Paris, he was not Salimbeni, he was not even Nino. He had always been Romeo. Not Romeo the party-crashing playboy with the elf hat, but Romeo the exile, who had been banished long ago by gossip and superstition, and who had spent his whole life trying to become someone else. Romeo, he had said, was his rival. Romeo had evil hands, and people would like to think he was dead. Romeo was not the man I thought I knew; he would never make love to me in rhyming couplets. But then, Romeo was also the man who came to Maestro Lippi's workshop late at night, to have a glass of wine and contemplate the portrait of Giulietta Tolomei. That, to me, said more than the finest poetry.

Even so, why had he never told me the truth? I had asked him about Romeo again and again, but each and every time he had replied as if we were talking about someone else. Someone it would be very bad for me to know.

I suddenly remembered him showing me the bullet hanging from a leather string around his neck, and Peppo telling me from his hospital bed that everybody thought Romeo had died. And I remembered the expression on Alessandro's face when Peppo had talked about Romeo being born outside of marriage. Only now did I understand his anger towards my Tolomei family members, who—in their ignorance of his true identity—had taken such pleasure in treating him like a Salimbeni and thus an enemy.

Just like I had.

When everyone had finally left the room—Grandmother and Enrico in one direction, Alessandro in another—Janice took me by the shoulders, eyes blazing. "Would you pull yourself together already!"

But that was asking a lot. "Romeo!" I groaned, clutching my head. "How can he be Romeo? I'm such an idiot!"

"Yes you are, but that's hardly news." Janice was not in the mood to be nice. "We don't know if he *is* Romeo. *The* Romeo. Maybe it's just his middle name. Romeo is a completely common Italian name. And if he really is *the* Romeo—that doesn't change anything. He's still in cahoots with the Salimbenis! He still trashed your friggin' hotel room!"

I swallowed a few times. "I don't feel so good."

"Well, let's get the hell out of here." Janice took my hand and pulled me along, thinking she was taking us towards the main entrance of the museum.

Instead, we ended up in a part of the exhibition we had not seen before; it was a dimly lit room with very old and worn cencios on the wall, sealed in glass cabinets. The place had the vibe of an ancestral shrine, and off to one side a curved staircase in darkened stone led steeply into the underground.

"What's down there?" whispered Janice, stretching to see.

"Forget it!" I shot back, recovering some of my spirit. "We're not getting trapped in some dungeon!"

But Fortuna clearly favored Janice's boldness over my jitters, for the next thing I knew we heard voices again—coming at us, it seemed, from all sides—and we nearly fell down the stairs in our hurry to get out of sight. Panting with the fear of discovery we crouched at the bottom of the stairwell as the voices came closer and the footsteps eventually stopped right overhead. "Oh no," I whispered, before Janice could slap a hand over my mouth, "it's *him*!"

We looked at each other, eyes wide. At this point—quite literally squatting, as we were, in Alessandro's basement—even Janice did not seem to embrace the prospect of a meeting.

Just then, the lights came on around us, and we saw Alessandro starting down the stairs, then stopping. "Ciao, Alessio, come stai—?" we heard him say, greeting someone else, and Janice and I glared at each other, acutely aware that our humiliation had been postponed, if only for a few minutes.

Looking around frantically to assess our options, we could see that we were truly trapped in a subterranean dead end, precisely as I had predicted we would be. Apart from three gaping holes in the wall—the black mouths of what could only be Bottini caves—there was no way of leaving the place other than going back upstairs, past Alessandro. And any attempt at entering the caves was made impossible by black iron grates covering the holes.

But you never say never to a Tolomei. Bristling at the idea of being trapped, we both got up and started examining the grates with trembling fingers. I was mostly trying to figure out if we would be able to squeeze through with brute force, while Janice expertly felt her way around every bolt, every hinge, clearly refusing to believe that the structures could not somehow be opened. To her, every wall had a door, every door had a key; in short, every jam had an eject button. All you had to do was dig in and find it.

"Psst!" She waved at me excitedly, demonstrating that, indeed, the third and last grate did swing open, just like a door, and without the slightest squeak at that. "Come on!"

We went as far into the cave as the lights allowed, then scrambled on a few more feet in absolute darkness, until we finally stopped. "If we had a flashlight—" began Janice. "Oh, *shit*!" We nearly banged our heads together when suddenly a beam of light came down the entire length of the cave to where we stood, stopping only inches before it hit us, and then retracting, like a wave rolling ashore and back out to sea.

Smarting from the close call, we stumbled farther into the cave until we found something resembling a niche that was big enough to swallow us both. "Is he coming? Is he coming?" hissed Janice, trapped behind me and unable to see. "Is it him?"

I stuck my head out briefly, then pulled it back in. "Yes, yes, and yes!"

It was hard to see anything other than the sharp flashlight bouncing to and fro, but at some point everything stabilized, and I dared to look out again. It was indeed Alessandro—or, I should say, some version of Romeo—and as far as I could see he had stopped in order to unlock a small door in the cave wall, holding the flashlight tightly under one arm.

"What's he doing?" Janice wanted to know.

"It looks like some kind of safe—he's taking something out. A box."

Janice clawed me excitedly. "Maybe it's the cencio!"

I looked again. "No, it's too small. More like a cigar box."

"I knew it! He's a smoker."

I watched Alessandro intently as he locked the safe and walked back towards the museum with the box. Moments later, the iron grate fell shut behind him with a clang that echoed through the Bottini—and our ears— for far too long.

"Oh no!" said Janice.

"Don't tell me—!" I turned towards her, hoping she would quickly put my worry to rest. But even in the darkness I could see the frightened expression on her face.

"Well, I was wondering why it wasn't locked before—" she said, defensively.

"But that didn't stop you, did it!" I snapped. "And now we're trapped!"

"Where's your sense of adventure?" Janice always tried to make a virtue out of necessity, but this time she failed to convince even herself. "This is great! I always wanted to go spelunking. It's gotta come out somewhere, right?" She looked at me, relieving her nerves by taunting me. "Or would wittle Wulietta wather be wescued by Womeo?"

UMBERTO HAD ONCE described the Roman catacombs to us, after we had spent a whole evening plaguing Aunt Rose with questions about Italy and why we couldn't go. Giving us each a dish towel so we could make ourselves useful while he had his hands in the sink, he had explained how the early Christians had been assembling in secret caves underground in order to hold communion where no one could see them and report their activities to the heathen Emperor. Similarly, these early Christians had defied the Roman tradition of cremation by wrapping their dead in shrouds and bringing them down into the caves, laying the bodies on shelves in the rock wall and performing funerary rites that hinged on the hope of a second coming.

If we were really so keen on going to Italy, Umberto concluded, he would make sure to take us down into those caves first thing and show us all the interesting skeletons.

As Janice and I walked through the Bottini, stumbling in the dark and taking turns at leading the way, Umberto's ghostly stories came back to me with a vengeance. Here we were—just like the people in his story— scrambling around underground to avoid detection, and like those early Christians, we also did not know exactly when and where we would eventually surface, if at all.

It helped a bit that we had the lighter for Janice's once-a-week cigarette; every twenty steps or so we would stop and flick it on for a few seconds, just to make sure we were not about to plunge into a bottomless hole or—as Janice at one point whimpered, when the cave wall suddenly turned slimy—walk right into a massive spiderweb.

"Creepy-crawlies," I said, taking the lighter away from her, "are the least of our concerns. Don't use up the liquid. We could be spending the night down here."

We walked for a while in silence—me in front, Janice right behind, mumbling something about spiders liking it humid—until my foot caught on protruding rock and I fell down on the uneven floor, hurting my knees and wrists so badly I could have cried, had I not been so anxious to check that the lighter was still intact.

"Are you okay?" asked Janice, her voice full of fear. "Can you walk? I don't think I could carry you."

"I'm fine!" I grunted, smelling blood on my fingers. "Your turn to go first. Here . . ." I fumbled the lighter into her hands. "Break a leg."

With Janice in the lead, I was free to fall back and examine my scrapes—both physical and mental—as we inched further into the unknown. My knees were more or less in shreds, but that was nothing compared to the turmoil in my soul.

"Jan?" I touched my fingers to her back as we walked. "Do you think that maybe he didn't tell me he was Romeo because he wanted me to fall in love with him for the right reasons, not just because of his name?"

I suppose I couldn't blame her for moaning.

"Okay—" I went on, "so, he didn't tell me he was Romeo because the last thing he needed was to have some pain-in-the-ass virgitarian cramp his incognito style?"

"Jules!" Janice was so focused on picking her way through the perilous blackness that she had little patience for my speculations. "Would you stop torturing yourself! And me! We don't even know *if* he is Romeo. Mind you, even if he is, I'm still gonna turn his ass inside out for treating you like this."

Despite her angry tone, I was once again astounded to hear her expressing concern for my feelings, and began to wonder if it was something new, or something I just hadn't noticed before.

"The thing is," I went on, "he never actually said he was a Salimbeni. It was always *me*—oops!" I nearly fell again, and clung to Janice until I had regained my balance.

"Let me guess," she said, flicking on the lighter so I could see her raised eyebrows, "he also never said he had anything to do with the museum break-in?"

"That was Bruno Carrera!" I exclaimed. "Working for Umberto!"

"Oh no, Julie-Baby," Janice mimicked, not sounding the least bit like Alessandro, "I didn't steal Romeo's cencio . . . why would I do that? To me, it's just an old rag. But hey, let me take care of that sharp knife for you, so you don't hurt yourself. What did you call it? . . . A *dagger?*"

"It wasn't like that at all," I muttered.

"Honey, he lied to you!" She flicked off the lighter at last and started walking again. "The sooner you can get that into your little Julie box, the better. Trust me, this guy has zero feelings for you whatsoever. It's all just a big charade to get to the—*ow!*" By the sound of it, she hit her head on something, and once again, we stopped. "What the hell was that?" Janice flicked the lighter to check—she had to try three or four times before it finally came on—only to discover that I was crying.

Shocked by the unusual sight, she put her arms around me with clumsy tenderness. "I'm sorry, Jules. I'm just trying to save you from heartache."

"I thought I didn't have a heart?"

"Well"—she gave me a squeeze—"you seem to have grown one lately. Too bad, you were more fun without it." Jiggling my chin with a sticky hand that still smelled like mocha-vanilla, she finally succeeded in making me laugh, and went on, more generously, "It's my fault anyway. I should have seen it coming. He drives a goddamn Alfa Romeo for Christ's sake!"

Had we not stopped right there, in the last, feeble flicker of the dying lighter, we might never have noticed the opening in the cave wall on our left. It was barely a foot and a half wide, but as far as I could see when I knelt down and stuck my head inside, it sloped upwards for at least thirty or forty feet—like an air duct in a pyramid—to end in a tiny seashell pattern of blue sky. I could even convince myself that I heard traffic noise.

"Hail Mary!" exclaimed Janice. "We're back in business! You go first. Age before beauty."

The pain and frustration of walking through the dark tunnel was nothing compared to the claustrophobia I felt crawling up the narrow shaft and the torment of scraping along on my raw knees and elbows. For every time I managed to pull myself up half a foot, painfully, by my toes and fingertips, I kept sliding back down several inches.

"Come on!" urged Janice, right behind me. "Let's get moving!"

"Then why didn't you go first?" I snapped back. "You're the fancy-ass rock climber."

"Here—" She placed a hand underneath my high-heeled sandal. "Push away on this."

Slowly and agonizingly, we made our way up the shaft, and although it widened considerably at the very top, allowing Janice to crawl up beside me, it was still a revolting place to be.

"Eek!" she said, looking around at the junk that people had tossed in there through the grate. "This is disgusting. Is that . . . a cheeseburger?"

"Does it have cheese in it?"

"Hey, look!" She picked something up. "It's a cell phone! Hang on—no, sorry. Out of battery."

"If you are finished rifling through the garbage, can we move on?"

We elbowed our way through a mess too nasty for words before finally coming up to the vertical, artsy sewer cover separating us from the earth's surface. "Where are we?" Janice pressed her nose against the bronze filigree, and we both looked out at the legs and feet walking by. "It's some kind of piazza. But huge."

"Holy cow!" I exclaimed, realizing that I had seen the place before, many times, but from very different angles. "I know exactly where we are. It's the Campo." I knocked on the sewer cover. "Ow! It's pretty solid."

"Hello? *Hello?*" Janice stretched to see better. "Can anyone hear me? Is anyone there?"

A few seconds later, an incredulous teenager with a snow cone and green lips came into view, stooping down to see us. "Ciao?" she said, smiling uncertainly, as if suspecting she was the victim of a prank. "I am Antonella."

"Hi, Antonella," I said, trying to make eye contact with her. "Do you speak English? We're kind of trapped down here. Do you think you could . . . find someone who can help us out?"

Twenty deeply embarrassing minutes later, Antonella returned with a pair of naked feet in sandals.

"Maestro Lippi?" I was so astounded to see my friend, the painter, that my voice almost escaped me. "Hello? Do you remember me? I slept on your couch."

"Of course I remember you!" he beamed. "How are you doing?"

"Uh—" I said, "do you think it would be possible to . . . remove this thing?" I wiggled my fingers through the sewer cover. "We're kind of stuck down here. And—this is my sister, by the way."

Maestro Lippi knelt down to see us better. "Did you two go somewhere you shouldn't go?"

I smiled as timidly as I could. "I'm afraid we did."

The Maestro frowned. "Did you find her grave? Did you steal her eyes? Did I not tell you to leave them where they are?"

"We didn't do anything!" I glanced at Janice to make sure she, too, looked sufficiently innocent. "We got trapped, that's all. Do you think we can somehow"—once again, I knocked on the sewer cover, and once again, it felt pretty rigid—"unscrew this thing?"

"Of course!" he said, without hesitation. "It is very easy."

"Are you sure?"

"Of course I'm sure!" He got back on his feet. "I made it!"

DINNER THAT NIGHT was pasta primavera from a can, spruced up with a twig of rosemary from Maestro Lippi's windowsill and accompanied by a box of Band-Aids for our bruises. There was barely room for the three of us at the table in his workshop, seeing that we were sharing the space with artwork and potted plants in different stages of demise, but even so, he and Janice were having a grand old time.

"You are very quiet," observed the artist at one point, recovering from laughter and pouring more wine.

"Juliet had a little run-in with Romeo," explained Janice, on my behalf. "He swore by the moon. Big mistake."

"Ah!" said Maestro Lippi. "He came here last night. He was not happy. Now I understand why."

"He came here last night?" I echoed.

"Yes," nodded the Maestro. "He said you don't look like the painting. You are much more beautiful. And much more—what was it he said?— oh, yes . . . *lethal*." The Maestro grinned and raised his glass to me in playful communion.

"Did he happen to mention," I said, failing to take the edge off my voice, "why he has been playing schizo games with me instead of telling me that he was Romeo all along? I thought he was someone else."

Maestro Lippi looked surprised. "But didn't you recognize him?"

"No!" I clutched my head in frustration. "I didn't recognize him. And he sure as hell didn't recognize me either!"

"What exactly can you tell us about this guy?" Janice asked the Maestro. "How many people are aware he is Romeo?"

"All I know," said Maestro Lippi, shrugging, "is that he does not want to be called Romeo. Only his family calls him that. It is a big secret. I don't know why. He wants to be called Alessandro Santini—"

I gasped. "You knew his name all along! Why didn't you tell me?"

"I thought you knew!" the Maestro shot back. "You are Juliet! Maybe you need glasses!"

"Excuse me," said Janice, rubbing a scratch on her arm, "but how did *you* know he was Romeo?"

Maestro Lippi looked stunned. "I . . . I—"

She reached out to help herself to another Band-Aid. "Please don't say you recognized him from a previous life."

"No," said the Maestro, frowning, "I recognized him from the fresco. In Palazzo Pubblico. And then I saw the Marescotti eagle on his arm"—he took me by the wrist and pointed at the underside of my forearm—"right here. Did you never notice that?"

For a few seconds I was back in the basement of Palazzo Salimbeni, trying to ignore Alessandro's tattoos while we discussed the fact that I was being followed. Even then I had been aware that his were not—unlike Janice's muffin-top tramp stamps—mere souvenirs from boozy spring breaks in Amsterdam, but it had not occurred to me that they held important clues to his identity. In fact, I had been too busy looking for diplomas and ancestors on his office wall to realize that here was a man who did not display his virtues in a silver frame, but carried them around on his body in whatever form they took.

"It's not glasses she needs," observed Janice, enjoying my cross-eyed introspection, "it's a new brain."

"Not to change the subject," I said, picking up my handbag, "but would you mind translating something for us?" I handed Maestro Lippi the Italian text from our mother's box, which I had been carrying around for days, hoping to stumble upon a willing translator. I had originally toyed with the idea of asking Alessandro, but something had held me back. "We think it might be important."

The Maestro took the text and perused the headline and first few paragraphs. "This," he said, a little surprised, "is a story. It is called *La Maledizione sul Muro . . . The Curse on the Wall.* It is quite long. Are you sure you want to hear it?"

[VI.II]

A plague o' both your houses,
They have made worms' meat of me

...

The Curse on the Wall

Siena, A.D. 1370

THERE IS A STORY THAT NOT MANY people have heard, because it was hushed up by the famous families involved. It starts with Santa Caterina, who had been known for her special powers since she was a little girl. People would come to her from all over Siena with their pains and aches, and would be healed by her touch. Now, as a grown woman, she spent most of her time taking care of the sick at the hospital by the Siena Cathedral, the Santa Maria della Scala, where she had her own room with a bed.

One day Santa Caterina was called to Palazzo Salimbeni, and when she arrived, she saw that everyone in the house was sick with worry. Four nights ago, they told her, there was a great wedding held here, and the bride was a woman of the Tolomeis, the lovely Mina. It had been a magnificent feast, for the groom was a son of Salimbeni, and the two families were there together, eating and singing, celebrating a long peace.

But when the groom went to his wedding chamber in the midnight hour, his bride was not there. He asked the servants, but no one had seen her, and he was filled with fear. What had happened to his Mina? Did she run away? Or was she abducted by enemies? But who would dare do such a thing to the Tolomeis and the Salimbenis? It was impossible. So, the groom ran everywhere, looking for his bride, upstairs, downstairs, asking the servants, asking the guards, but everyone told him that Mina could not have left the house unseen. And his heart as well said no! He was a kind young man, a handsome man. She would never run away from him. But now, this young Salimbeni must tell his father, and her father, and when they heard what was wrong, the whole house began searching for Mina.

For hours they searched—in the bedrooms, the kitchen, even in the servants' quarters—until the lark started singing, and they finally gave up. But now that a new day had begun, the oldest grandmother of the wedding party, Monna Cecilia, came downstairs to find them sitting there, all in tears and talking of war against these, war against those. And old Monna Cecilia listened to them, and then she said to them, "Sad gentlemen, come with me, and I will find your Mina. For there is one place in the house you have not looked, and I feel in my heart that she is there."

Monna Cecilia took them down, down, deep underneath the earth and into the ancient dungeons of Palazzo Salimbeni. And she showed them that the doors had been opened with the household keys that were given to the bride in the wedding ceremony, and she told them what they already knew: that these were caverns where no one had come for many years, for fear of the darkness. The old men in the wedding party were terrified, for they could not believe that the new bride had been given keys to all these secret doors, and they got more and more angry as they went, and more and more afraid. For they knew that there was much darkness down there, and that many things had happened in the past, before the Plague, that were best forgotten. So there they were, all the great men, walking after old Monna Cecilia with their torches, not believing their eyes.

At last they came to a room that was used in the old days for punishment, and now Monna Cecilia stopped, and all the men stopped too, and they heard the sound of someone crying. Without hesitation, the young groom rushed forward with his torch, and when the light reached the far corner of the cell, he saw his bride there, sitting on the floor in her fine blue nightgown. She was shivering with cold, and so afraid that she screamed when she saw the men, for she did not recognize anyone, even her own father.

Of course, they picked her up and brought her upstairs into the light, and they wrapped her in wool and gave her water to drink and nice things

to eat, but Mina kept shaking and pushed them all away. Her father tried
to talk to her, but she turned her head away and would not look at him. At
last the poor man took her by the shoulders and asked his daughter, "Do
you not remember that you are my little Mina?" But Mina pushed him
away with a sneer and said, in a voice that was not hers, a voice as dark as
death, "No," she said, "I am not your Mina. My name is Lorenzo."

You can imagine the horror of both families when they realized that
Mina had lost her mind. The women started praying to the Virgin Mary,
and the men started accusing each other of being bad fathers, and brothers, and of finding poor Mina so late. The only one who was calm was old
Monna Cecilia, who sat down with Mina and stroked her hair and tried to
make her speak again.

But Mina rocked back and forth and would not look at anyone until
Monna Cecilia finally said, "Lorenzo, Lorenzo, my dear, I am Monna Cecilia. I know what they did to you!"

Now at last, Monna Mina looked at the old woman and started crying
again. And Monna Cecilia embraced her and let her cry, for hours, until
they fell asleep together on the wedding bed. For three days Monna Mina
slept, and she had dreams, terrible dreams, and she woke up the whole
house with her screams, until at last the families decided to call for Santa
Caterina.

After she had heard the whole story, Santa Caterina understood that
Monna Mina had become possessed by a spirit. But she was not afraid.
She sat by the young woman's bed all night and prayed without a pause,
and by morning, Monna Mina woke up and remembered who she was.

There was much joy in the house, and everybody praised Santa Caterina, even though she scolded them and said that the praise was due only
to Christ. But even in this hour of great joy, Monna Mina was still trou-
bled, and when they asked her what was troubling her, she told them that
she had a message for them, from Lorenzo. And that she could not rest
until she had delivered it. You can imagine how everyone must have been
terrified to hear her speak of this Lorenzo again, this spirit who had possessed her, but they said to her, "Very well, we are ready to hear the message." But Monna Mina could not remember the message, and she started
crying again, and everyone was horrified. Maybe, they worried to each
other in hushed voices, she would lose her mind once more.

But now, the wise Santa Caterina handed Monna Mina a feather dipped in ink and said, "My dear, let Lorenzo write his message with your hand."

"But I cannot write!" said Mina.

"No," said Santa Caterina, "but if Lorenzo has the skill, his hand will move yours."

So, Monna Mina took the feather and sat for a while, waiting for her hand to move, and Santa Caterina prayed for her. At last, Monna Mina got up without a word and went out onto the stairs like a sleepwalker and down, down, deep into the basement, with everyone following her. And when she came into the room where they found her, she went to the wall and started running her finger over it, as if she was writing, and the men came forward with torches to watch what she was doing. They asked her what she was writing, but Monna Mina said, "Just read!" And when they told her that her writing was invisible, she said, "No, it is right there, do you not see?"

Now Santa Caterina had the good idea to send a boy to fetch clothes dye from her father's workshop, and she made Monna Mina dip her finger in the dye and write once again what she had already written before. And Monna Mina filled the whole wall, this woman who had never learned to read or write, and what she wrote made all the great men cold with fear. This was the message that the spirit Lorenzo made Monna Mina write:

> *A plague on both your houses*
> *You shall all perish in fire and gore*
> *Your children forever wail under a mad moon*
> *Till you undo your sins and kneel before the Virgin*
> *And Giulietta wakes to behold her Romeo*

When Monna Mina had finished writing, she fell into the arms of her groom, calling him by his name, and asked him to take her away from the room, as her task was over. So he did, crying with relief, and brought her upstairs, into the light, and Monna Mina never spoke with the voice of Lorenzo again. But she never forgot what had happened to her, and decided that she wanted to understand who this Lorenzo had been, and why he had spoken through her, even though her father and father-in-law did everything in their power to keep the truth from her.

Monna Mina was a stubborn woman, a true Tolomei. She spent many hours with old Monna Cecilia when her husband was away on business, listening to stories of the past, and asking many questions. And although the old woman was afraid at first, she also knew that it would give her peace to pass on this heavy burden to someone else, so that the truth would not die with her.

Monna Cecilia told Monna Mina that just where she had written that terrible curse on the wall, was where a young monk named Friar Lorenzo had written the same words many, many years earlier, in his own blood. It was the room where they had kept and tortured him until he died.

"But who?" Monna Mina asked, leaning over the table to clasp Monna Cecilia's gnarled hands in her own. "Who did this to him, and why?"

"A man," Monna Cecilia said, her head drooping with sorrow, "whom I have long since stopped thinking of as my father."

THIS MAN, MONNA CECILIA explained, had ruled the Salimbeni household in the era of the great Plague, and he had ruled it like a tyrant. Some people tried to pardon him by saying that, when he was a little boy, Tolomei bandits had killed his mother before his very eyes, but that does not excuse a man for doing the same to others. And that was what Salimbeni did. He was cruel to his enemies, and severe on his family; whenever he was tired of his wives, he locked them away in the countryside and instructed the servants to never feed them quite enough. And as soon as they were dead, he married anew. As he grew older, his wives grew younger, but in the end not even youth could please him anymore, and in his desperation he developed an unnatural desire for a young woman whose parents he himself had ordered killed. Her name was Giulietta.

Despite the fact that Giulietta was already secretly betrothed to another, and that the Virgin Mary was believed to have blessed the young couple, Salimbeni forced his own marriage with the girl, and by doing so provoked the most formidable enemy a man could have. For everyone knew that the Virgin Mary did not like human interference in her plans, and, indeed, the whole thing ended in death and misery. Not only did the young lovers kill themselves, but Salimbeni's oldest son perished, too, in a desperate struggle to defend his father's honor.

For all these insults and griefs, Salimbeni arrested and tortured Friar Lorenzo, holding him responsible for secretly helping the young lovers in their disastrous affair. And he invited Giulietta's uncle, Messer Tolomei, to witness the punishment of the insolent monk who had destroyed their plans of uniting the two feuding families through marriage. These were the men Friar Lorenzo cursed with his writing on the wall: Messer Salimbeni and Messer Tolomei.

After the monk had died, Salimbeni buried the body under the floor of the torture chamber as was his custom. And he had his servants wash off the curse and put new chalk on the wall. But he soon discovered that these measures were not sufficient to undo what had happened.

When Friar Lorenzo appeared to him in a dream a few nights later, warning him that no soap and no chalk could ever erase the curse, Salimbeni became filled with fear and closed off the old torture chamber to contain the evil powers of the wall. And now, suddenly, he began to listen to the voices of people saying he was cursed, and that the Virgin Mary was looking for a way to punish him. The voices were everywhere; in the street, in the market, in church—even when he was all alone he heard them. And when, one night, a great fire broke out in Palazzo Salimbeni, he was sure it was all part of Friar Lorenzo's curse, which called for his family to "perish in fire and gore."

It was about this time that the first rumors of the Black Death came to Siena. Pilgrims came back from the Orient with stories of a terrible plague that had destroyed more villages and towns than a mighty army, but most people thought it was only something that would strike the heathens. They were sure that the Virgin Mary would—as she had done many times before—spread her protective cape over Siena, and that prayers and candles could keep the evil at bay, should it ever cross the ocean.

But Salimbeni had long lived with the illusion that everything good that happened around him was an effect of his brilliance. Now that something bad was coming, it was only natural for him to think that this, too, was his doing. And so he became obsessed with the idea that he and he alone was the cause of every disaster that happened around him, and that it was his fault the Plague was threatening to come to Siena. In his madness he dug up the bodies of Giulietta and Romeo from their unholy ground, and made for them a most holy grave in order to silence the voices of the people or, maybe more accurately, the voices in his own head blaming him for the deaths of a young couple whose love had been blessed by Heaven.

He was so eager to make peace with the ghost of Friar Lorenzo that he spent many nights looking at the curse written out on a piece of parchment, trying to find a way of meeting the demand to "undo your sins and kneel before the Virgin." He even had clever professors from the university come to his house and speculate on how to make Giulietta "wake to behold her Romeo," and they were the ones who finally came up with a plan.

In order to do away with the curse, they said, Salimbeni must begin by understanding that riches are evil, and that a man who possesses gold is no happy man. Once he has admitted that much, he will not be sorry to pay large sums of his fortune to people devoted to ridding him of his guilt, such as clever professors from the university. Also, such a man will be happy to commission an expensive sculpture that will, most certainly, do away with the curse and help its owner at last sleep soundly at night, knowing that he alone, by sacrificing his wicked money, has bought forgiveness for his entire city, and credits against the rumored plague.

The statue, they told him, must be placed on Giulietta and Romeo's grave, and it must be covered in the purest gold. It must depict the young couple and do it in such a way that it would become an antidote to Friar Lorenzo's curse. Salimbeni must take the precious gems from Giulietta's bridal crown and use them as eyes in the sculpture: two green emeralds in the head of Romeo, and two blue sapphires in the head of Giulietta. And underneath the statue, an inscription must read:

> *Here sleeps true and faithful Giulietta*
> *By the love and mercy of God*
> *To be woken by Romeo, her rightful spouse*
> *In an hour of perfect grace*

In that way, Salimbeni could artificially re-create their moment of resurrection, allowing the two young lovers to behold each other again and forever, and allowing every citizen of Siena to see the sculpture and call Salimbeni a generous and religious man.

To aid this impression, however, Salimbeni must make sure to cultivate a story of his own benevolence, and to commission a tale that freed
him from guilt altogether. The tale must be of Romeo and Giulietta, and it
must contain much poetry and much confusion, as good art does, for an
accomplished storyteller brimming with dazzling falsehoods commands
far more attention than an honest bore.

As for those people who would still not be silent on the issue of Salimbeni's guilt, they must be silenced, either by gold in their hands or iron
in their backs. For only by getting rid of such malicious tongues could Salimbeni ever hope to be purified in the eyes of the people and find his way
back into their prayers and thus into the holy ears of Heaven.

Those were the recommendations from the university professors, and
Salimbeni set about meeting their demands with much vigor. Firstly—
following their own advice—he made sure to silence the professors before
they could slander him. Secondly, he employed a local poet to fabricate a
tale about two star-crossed lovers whose tragic deaths were no one's fault
but their own, and to circulate it among the reading classes, not as fiction,
but as a truth shamefully ignored. Finally, Salimbeni employed the great
artist, Maestro Ambrogio, to oversee the work with the golden statue. And
once it was ready—with the precious eyes in place—he posted four armed
guards in the chapel at all times, to protect the immortal couple.

But even the statue and the guards could not hold the Plague at bay.
For over a year the horrible disease ravaged Siena, covering healthy bodies in black boils and killing almost everyone it touched. Half the entire
population perished—for every person that lived, another died. In the
end, there were not enough survivors to bury the dead; the streets ran
with rot and gore, and those who could still eat were starving for lack of
food.

Once it was over, the world had changed. The slate of men's memory
had been wiped clean, for better and for worse. Those who had survived
were too busy with their needs to care much for art and old gossip, and so
the story of Romeo and Giulietta became little more than a faint echo
from another world, occasionally remembered, but only in fragments. As
for the grave, it was gone forever, buried under a mountain of death, and
few people were left who knew the value of the statue. Maestro Ambrogio,
who had personally affixed the gemstones and knew what they were, was
one of the many thousand Sienese who had died during the Plague.

...

WHEN MONNA MINA had heard everything Monna Cecilia knew about Friar Lorenzo, she decided that there was still something that could be done to appease his ghost. And so on a day when her husband had seemed particularly enamored with her before riding off on business, she ordered six capable servants to follow her into the basement and break up the floor of the old torture chamber.

Naturally, the servants were not happy with their morbid task, but seeing their mistress standing so patiently next to them as they worked, urging them on with promises of cakes and sweets, they dared not complain.

Over the course of the morning, they found the bones not just of one, but of several people. At first, the discovery of death and molestation made them all sick to the stomach, but when they saw that Monna Mina— although pale—did not budge, they soon overcame their horror and picked up their tools to continue their work. And as the day went on, they were all filled with ardent admiration for the young woman, who was so determined to rid the house of its evil.

Once all the bones had been recovered, Monna Mina had the servants wrap them in shrouds and take them to the cemetery, except for the most recent remains, which, she was sure, must be Friar Lorenzo's. Not quite sure what to do, she sat for a while with the body, looking at the silver crucifix that had been clutched in its hand, until a plan formed in her head.

Before her marriage, Monna Mina had had a confessor, a holy and wonderful man, who came from the south, from the town of Viterbo, and who had often spoken of the town's cathedral, San Lorenzo. Would not this be the right place to send the monk's remains, she wondered, that his holy brothers might help him find peace at last, far away from the Siena that had caused him such unspeakable woes?

When her husband returned that evening, Monna Mina had everything prepared. Friar Lorenzo's remains were now in a wooden coffin, ready to be loaded onto a cart, and a letter had been written to the priests at San Lorenzo, explaining just enough to make them understand that here was a man who deserved an end to his sufferings. The only thing wanting was her husband's permission and a handful of money for the venture to be launched, but Monna Mina was a woman who had already learned—in just a few months of marriage—how a pleasant evening could extract such things from a man.

Early next morning, before the mists had lifted from Piazza Salimbeni, she stood at her bedroom window, her husband blissfully asleep in the bed behind her, and saw the cart with the coffin leaving for Viterbo. Around her neck hung Friar Lorenzo's crucifix, cleaned and polished. Her first instinct had been to put it in the coffin with the monk's remains, but in the end she had decided to keep it as a token of their mystical connection.

She did not yet understand why he had chosen to speak through her and force her hand to write an old curse that had called down a plague on her own family, but she had a feeling he had done it out of kindness, to tell her that she must somehow find a cure. And until she did, she would keep the crucifix to remind her of the words on the wall, and of the man whose last thoughts had not been for himself, but for Romeo and Giulietta.

By a name
I know not how to tell thee who I am:
My name, dear saint, is hateful to myself

...

AFTER MAESTRO LIPPI STOPPED READING, we sat for a while in silence. I had originally pulled out the Italian text to get us off the topic of Alessandro being Romeo, but had I known it would take us to such dark places, I would have left it in my handbag.

"Poor Friar Lorenzo," said Janice, emptying her wineglass, "no happy end for him."

"I always thought Shakespeare let him off the hook too easily," I said, trying to strike a lighter tone. "There he is, in *Romeo and Juliet,* walking around red-handed in the cemetery—bodies sprawled everywhere—even admitting that he was behind the whole double-crossing screw-up with the sleeping potion . . . and that's it. You'd think the Capulets and the Montagues would at least *try* to hold him responsible."

"Maybe they did," said Janice, "later on. 'Some shall be pardon'd, and some punished' . . . sounds like the story wasn't over just because the curtain dropped."

"Clearly it wasn't." I glanced at the text Maestro Lippi had just read to us. "And according to Mom it still isn't."

"This," said the Maestro, still frowning over the evil deeds of old man Salimbeni, "is very disturbing. If it is true that Friar Lorenzo wrote such a curse, with those exact words, then it would—in theory—go on forever, until"—he checked the text to get the wording straight—" 'you undo your sins and kneel before the Virgin . . . and Giulietta wakes to behold her Romeo.' "

"Okay," said Janice, never a great fan of superstitious mumbo jumbo, "so, I have two questions. One: who is this *you*—?"

"That's obvious," I interjected, "seeing that he is calling down 'a plague on both your houses.' He is obviously talking to Salimbeni and Tolomei, who were right there in the basement, torturing him. And since you and I are of the house of Tolomei, we're cursed, too."

"Listen to you!" snapped Janice. "Of the house of Tolomei! What difference does a name make?"

"Not just a name," I said. "The genes *and* the name. Mom had the genes, and Dad had the name. Not much wiggle room for us."

Janice was not happy with my logic, but what could she do? "Okay, fair enough," she sighed. "Shakespeare was wrong. There never was a Mercutio, dying because of Romeo and calling down a plague on him and Tybalt; the curse came from Friar Lorenzo. Fine. But I have another question, and that is: *If* you actually believe in this curse, then what? How can anybody be stupid enough to think they can stop it? We're not just talking repent here. We're talking *un*-friggin'-*do* your sins! Well . . . *how*? Are we supposed to dig up old Salimbeni and make him change his mind and . . . and . . . and drag him to the cathedral so he can fall to his knees in front of the altar or whatever? Puh-*leez*!" She looked at us both belligerently, as if it was the Maestro and me who had brought this problem upon her. "Why don't we just fly home and leave the stupid curse here in Italy? Why do we have to care?"

"Because Mom cared," I said, simply. "This was what she wanted: to stick it out and end the curse. Now we have to do it for her. We owe her that."

Janice pointed at me with the rosemary twig. "Allow me to quote myself: All we owe her is to stay alive."

I touched the crucifix hanging around my neck. "That's exactly what I mean. If we want to stay alive happily ever after, then—according to Mom—we *have* to end the curse. You and me, Giannozza. There's no one else left to do it."

The way she looked at me, I could see her coming around, realizing I was right, or, at least, telling a convincing story. But she didn't like it. "This," she said, "is so far out. But okay, let's assume for a moment that there really *is* a curse, and that—if we don't stop it—it really *will* kill us, like it killed Mom and Dad. The question is still *how?* How do we stop it?"

I glanced at the Maestro. He had been unusually present-minded all evening—and still was—but even he didn't have the answer to Janice's question. "I don't know," I confessed. "But I suspect the golden statue plays a part. And maybe the dagger and the cencio, too, although I don't see how."

"Oh, well!" Janice threw up her hands. "Then we're cooking! . . . Except that we have absolutely no clue where the statue is. The story just says that Salimbeni 'made for them a most holy grave' and posted guards at 'the chapel,' but that could mean anywhere! So . . . we don't know where the statue is, and you lost the dagger and the cencio! I'm amazed you've managed to hang on to that crucifix, but I suspect that's because it has no significance whatsoever!"

I looked at Maestro Lippi. "The book you had, which talked about Juliet's Eyes and the grave . . . are you sure it didn't say anything about where it is? When we talked about it, you just told me to go ask Romeo."

"And did you?"

"No! Of course not!" I felt a surge of irritation, but knew that I could not reasonably blame the painter for my own blindness. "I didn't even know he was Romeo until this afternoon."

"Then why," said Maestro Lippi, as if nothing could be more straightforward, "do you not ask him next time you see him?"

IT WAS MIDNIGHT BY the time Janice and I returned to Hotel Chiusarelli. As soon as we entered the lobby, Direttor Rossini rose behind the reception counter and handed me a stack of folded-up notes. "Captain Santini called at five o'clock this afternoon," he informed me, clearly blaming me for not being in my room, on tiptoes to take the call. "And many times since. Last time he called was"—he leaned forward to check the clock on the wall—"seventeen minutes ago."

Walking up the stairs in silence, I saw Janice glaring at my handful of messages from Alessandro—evidence of his keen interest in my whereabouts. I began bracing myself for the inevitable next chapter in our ongoing discussion of his character and motives, but as soon as we entered the room we were met by an unexpected breeze from the balcony door, which had sprung open by itself with no immediate signs of a break-in. Instantly apprehensive, however, I quickly checked that no papers were missing from Mom's box; we had left it right there, sitting on the desk, since we were now convinced that it contained nothing like a treasure map.

"Please call me back—" sang Janice, leafing through Alessandro's messages one by one. "Please call me back—Are you free for dinner?—Are you okay?—I'm sorry—Please call—By the way, I'm a cross-dresser—"

I scratched my head. "Did we not lock that balcony door before we left? I specifically remember locking it."

"Is anything missing?" Janice tossed Alessandro's messages on the bed in a way that had them scatter in all directions.

"No," I said, "all the papers are there."

"Plus," she observed, wiggling out of her top in front of the window, "half the law enforcement in Siena is keeping an eye on your room."

"Would you get away from there!" I cried, pulling her away.

Janice laughed delightedly. "Why? At least they'll know it's not a *man* you're sleeping with!"

Just then, the phone rang.

"That guy," sighed Janice, shaking her head, "is a nutcase. Mark my words."

"Why?" I shot back, making a dash for the receiver. "Because he happens to like me?"

"*Like* you?" Janice had clearly never heard anything so naïve in her entire life, and she embarked upon a long-drawn, snorting laugh, which only stopped when I threw a bed pillow at her.

"Hello?" I picked up the phone and carefully shielded the receiver from the noise of my sister stomping defiantly about the room, humming the sinister theme from a horror film.

It was Alessandro all right, concerned that something had happened to me, since I had not returned his calls. Now, of course, he acknowledged, it was too late to think about dinner, but could I at least tell him whether I was, in fact, planning to attend Eva Maria's party tomorrow?

"Yes, Godmother . . ." mimicked Janice in the background, "whatever you say, Godmother—"

"I hadn't actually—" I began, trying to remember all my excellent reasons for saying no to the invitation. But somehow they all seemed utterly groundless now that I knew he was Romeo. He and I were, after all, on the same team. Weren't we? Maestro Ambrogio and Maestro Lippi would have agreed, and so would Shakespeare. Furthermore, I had never been completely convinced that it was really Alessandro who had broken into my hotel room. It certainly would not be the first time my sister had made a mistake. Or told me a lie.

"Come on," he urged, in a voice that could talk a woman into anything, and probably had, many times, "it would mean a lot to her."

Meanwhile, in the bathroom, Janice was wrestling loudly with the shower curtain, pretending—by the sound of it—to be stabbed to death.

"I don't know," I replied, trying to block out her shrieks, "everything is so . . . insane right now."

"Maybe you need a weekend off?" Alessandro pointed out. "Eva Maria is counting on you. She has invited a lot of people. People who knew your parents."

"Really?" I could feel curiosity tearing at my feeble resolve.

"I'll pick you up at one o'clock, okay?" he said, choosing to interpret my hesitation as a yes. "And I promise, I'll answer all your questions on the way."

When Janice came back into the room, I was expecting a scene, but it never came.

"Do as you wish," she merely said, shrugging as if she couldn't care less, "but don't say I didn't warn you."

"It's so easy for you, isn't it?" I sat down on the edge of the bed, suddenly exhausted. "You're not Juliet."

"And you're not either," said Janice, sitting down next to me. "You're just a girl who had a weird mom. Like me. Look"—she put an arm around me—"I know you want to go to this party. So, go. I just wish—I hope you don't take it too literally. The whole Romeo-and-Juliet thing. Shakespeare didn't create you, and he doesn't own you. You do."

Later, we lay in bed together and looked through Mom's notebook one more time. Now that we knew the story behind the statue, her drawings of a man holding a woman in his arms made perfect sense. But there was still nothing in the book that indicated the actual location of the grave.

Most of the pages were crisscrossed with sketches and doodles; only one page was unique in that it had a border of five-petal roses all around, and a very elegantly written quotation from *Romeo and Juliet:*

> *And what obscur'd in your fair volume lies,*
> *Find written in the margent of my eyes.*

As it turned out, it was the only explicit Shakespeare quotation in the entire notebook, and it made us both pause.

"That," I said, "is Juliet's mother talking about Paris. But it's wrong. It's not *your* fair volume or *my* eyes, it's *this* fair volume and *his* eyes."

"Maybe she got it wrong?" proposed Janice.

I glared at her. "Mom get Shakespeare wrong? I don't think so. I think she did this on purpose. To send someone a message."

Janice sat up. She had always loved riddles and secrets, and for the first time since Alessandro's phone call she looked genuinely excited. "So, what's the message? Someone is obviously obscured. But we can find him. Right?"

"She talks about a *volume,*" I said, "and a *margent,* which means *margin.* That sounds like a book to me."

"Not just one book," Janice pointed out, "but two books: *our* book, and *her* book. She calls her own book her *eyes,* which sounds to me a lot like a sketchbook"—she knocked on the page of the notebook—"as in *this* book. Wouldn't you agree?"

"But there's nothing written in the margin—" I started flipping through the notebook, and now, for the first time, we both noticed all the numbers that were jotted down—seemingly randomly—on the edges of the pages. "Oh my—you're right! Why didn't we see this before?"

" 'Cause we weren't looking," said Janice, taking the book from me. "If these numbers do not refer to pages and lines, you can call me Ishmael."

"But the pages and lines of what?" I asked.

The truth hit us both at the same time. If the notebook was *her* volume, then the paperback edition of *Romeo and Juliet*—the only other book in the box—would have to be *our* volume. And the page and line numbers would have to refer to select passages in Shakespeare's play. How very appropriate.

We both scrambled to get to the box first. But neither of us found what we were looking for. Only then did it occur to us what had gone missing since we left the room that afternoon. The mangy old paperback was no longer there.

JANICE HAD ALWAYS been a sound sleeper. It used to annoy me to no end that she could sleep through her alarm without even reaching out for the snooze button. After all, our rooms were right across the corridor from each other, and we always slept with our doors ajar. In her desperation, Aunt Rose went through every alarm clock in town in search of something that was monstrous enough to get my sister out of bed and off to school. She never succeeded. While I had a pink little Sleeping Beauty alarm on my bedstand until I left for college, Janice ended up with some industrial contraption—which Umberto had personally modified with a set of pliers at the kitchen counter—that sounded like an evacuation alarm from a nuclear power plant. And even so, the only one it woke up—usually with a yelp of terror—was me.

On the morning after our dinner with Maestro Lippi, I was amazed to see Janice lying awake, looking at the first golden blades of dawn as they came sliding in through the shutters.

"Bad dreams?" I asked, thinking of the nameless ghosts that had chased me around my dream castle—which looked more and more like the Siena Cathedral—all night.

"I couldn't sleep," she replied, turning to face me. "I'm going to drive down to Mom's house today."

"How? Are you renting a car?"

"I'm gonna get the bike back." She wiggled her eyebrows, but her heart was not in it. "Peppo's nephew runs the car pound. Wanna come?" But I could see that she already knew I wouldn't.

When Alessandro came to pick me up at one o'clock, I was sitting on the front steps of Hotel Chiusarelli with a weekend bag at my feet, flirting with the sun through the branches of the magnolia tree. As soon as I saw his car pull up, my heart started racing; maybe because he was Romeo, maybe because he had broken into my room once or twice, or maybe simply because—as Janice would have it—I needed to get my head checked. It was tempting to blame it all on the water in Fontebranda, but then, you could argue that my madness, my pazzia, had started long, long before that. Six hundred years at least.

"What happened to your knees?" he asked, coming up the walkway and stopping right in front of me, looking anything but medieval in jeans and a shirt with rolled-up sleeves. Even Umberto would have had to agree that Alessandro looked remarkably trustworthy despite his casual attire, but then, Umberto was—at best—a rapscallion, so why should I still live under his morality code?

The thought of Umberto sent a little pang through my heart; why was it that the people I cared about—perhaps with the exception of Aunt Rose, who had been practically non-dimensional—always had a shadow-side?

Shaking my gloomy thoughts, I pulled at my skirt to cover the evidence of my marine crawl through the Bottini the day before. "I tripped over reality."

Alessandro looked at me quizzically, but said nothing. Leaning forward, he picked up my bag, and now, for the first time, did I notice the Marescotti eagle on his forearm. To think that it had been right there all the time, literally staring me in the face when I drank from his hands at Fontebranda . . . but then, the world was full of birds, and I was certainly no connoisseur.

IT WAS ODD TO be back in his car, this time in the passenger seat. So much had happened since my arrival in Siena with Eva Maria—some of it charming, some anything but—thanks in part to him. As we drove out of town, one topic, and one topic only, was scalding my tongue, but I could not bring myself to raise it. Nor could I think of much else to talk about that would not, inevitably, bring us right back to the mother of all questions: Why had he not told me he was Romeo?

In all fairness, I had not told him everything either. In fact, I had told him next to nothing about my—admittedly pathetic—investigations into the golden statue, and absolutely nothing about Umberto and Janice. But at least I had told him who I was from the beginning, and it had been his own decision not to believe me. Of course . . . I had only told him I was Giulietta Tolomei to prevent him from finding out that I was Julie Jacobs, so it probably didn't really count for much in the big blame game.

"You're very quiet today," said Alessandro, glancing at me as he drove. "I have a feeling it's my fault."

"You never got around to telling me about Charlemagne," I countered, putting a lid on my conscience for now.

He laughed. "Is that it? Don't worry, by the time we get to Val d'Orcia, you'll know more about me and my family than you could ever want. But first, tell me what you already know, so I don't repeat it."

"You mean"—I tried to read his profile, but couldn't—"what do I know about the Salimbenis?"

As always when I mentioned the Salimbenis, he smiled wryly. Now, of course, I knew why. "No. Tell me about your own family, the Tolomeis. Tell me everything you know about what happened in 1340."

And so I did. Over the next little while I told him the story I had pieced together from Friar Lorenzo's confession, Giulietta's letters to Giannozza, and Maestro Ambrogio's journal, and he did not interrupt me once. When I had come to the end of the drama at Rocca di Tentennano, I wondered briefly if I should go on to mention the Italian story about the possessed Monna Mina and Friar Lorenzo's curse, but decided not to. It was too strange, too depressing, and besides, I didn't want to get into the issue of the statue with the gemstone eyes again, after having flatly denied knowing anything about it that day at the police station, when he had first asked me.

"And so they died," I concluded, "at Rocca di Tentennano. Not with a dagger and a vial of poison, but with sleeping potion and a spear in the back. Friar Lorenzo saw it all with his own eyes."

"And how much of this," said Alessandro teasingly, "did you make up?"

I shrugged. "A bit here and there. Just to fill in the blanks. Thought it might make the story more entertaining. It doesn't change the essentials, though—" I looked at him only to find him grimacing. "What?"

"The essentials," he said, "are not what most people think. In my opinion, your story—and *Romeo and Juliet* as well—is not about love. It is about politics, and the message is simple: When the old men fight, the young people die."

"That," I chuckled, "is remarkably unromantic of you."

Alessandro shrugged. "Shakespeare didn't see the romance either. Look at how he portrays them. Romeo is a little whiner, and Juliet is the real hero. Think about it. He drinks poison. What kind of man drinks poison? *She* is the one who stabs herself with his dagger. The manly way."

I couldn't help laughing at him. "Maybe that's true for Shakespeare's Romeo. But the *real* Romeo Marescotti was no whiner. He was tough as nails." I glanced at him to see his reaction, and caught him smiling. "It is no mystery why Giulietta loved him."

"How do you know she did?"

"Isn't it obvious?" I shot back, starting to get a little miffed. "She loved him so much that—when Nino tried to seduce her—she committed suicide to remain faithful to Romeo, even though they had never actually . . . you know." I looked at him, upset that he was still smiling. "I suppose you think that's ridiculous?"

"Absolutely!" said Alessandro, as we surged forward to pass another car. "Think about it. Nino was not so bad—"

"Nino was outrageous!"

"Maybe," he countered, "he was outrageously good in bed. Why not find out? She could always kill herself the morning after."

"How can you say that?" I protested, genuinely upset. "I don't believe you actually mean it! If you were Romeo, you would not want Juliet to . . . test-drive Paris!"

He laughed out loud. "Come on! You were the one who told me I was Paris! Rich, handsome, and evil. Of course I want Juliet to test-drive me." He looked over and grinned, enjoying my scowl. "What kind of Paris would I be if I didn't?"

I pulled at my skirt once more. "And when exactly did you plan on that to happen?"

"How about," said Alessandro, gearing down, "right now?"

I had been too absorbed in our conversation to pay attention to the drive, but now I saw that we had long since turned off the highway and were crawling along a deserted gravel road flanked by scruffy cedars. It ended blindly at the foot of a tall hill, but instead of turning around, Alessandro pulled into an empty parking lot and stopped the car.

"Is this where Eva Maria lives?" I croaked, unable to spot a house anywhere near.

"No," he replied, getting out of the car and grabbing a bottle and two glasses from the trunk, "this is Rocca di Tentennano. Or . . . what's left of it."

...

WE WALKED ALL THE way up the hill until we were at the very base of the ruined fortress. I knew from Maestro Ambrogio's description that the building had been colossal in its day; he had called it "a forbidding crag with a giant nest of fearsome predators, those man-eating birds of old." It was not hard to imagine what it had once looked like, for part of the massive tower was still standing, and even in its decay it seemed to loom over us, reminding us of the power that once had been.

"Impressive," I said, touching the wall. The brick felt warm under my hand—much different, I was sure, than it would have felt to Romeo and Friar Lorenzo on that fateful winter evening in 1340. In fact, the contrast between the past and the present was never more striking than here. Back in the Middle Ages, this hilltop had been buzzing with human activity; now it was so quiet you could hear the happy hum of the tiniest insects. Yet around us in the grass lay the odd piece of freshly crumbled brick, as if somehow the ancient building—left for dead many, many years ago—was still quietly heaving, like the chest of a sleeping giant.

"They used to call it 'the island,' " explained Alessandro, strolling on. "L'Isola. It is usually windy here, but not today. We are lucky."

I followed him along a small, rocky path, and only now did I notice the spectacular view of Val d'Orcia dressed in the bold palette of summer. Bright yellow fields and green vineyards stretched all around us, and here and there was a patch of blue or red, where flowers had taken over a verdant meadow. Tall cypresses lined the roads that snaked through the landscape, and at the end of every road sat a farmhouse. It was the kind of view that made me wish I had not dropped out of art class in eleventh grade, just because Janice had threatened to sign up.

"No hiding from the Salimbenis," I observed, holding up a hand against the sun. "They sure knew how to pick their spots."

"It has great strategic importance," nodded Alessandro. "From here, you can rule the world."

"Or at least some of it."

He shrugged. "The part worth ruling."

Walking ahead of me, Alessandro looked surprisingly at home in this semi–state of nature with the glasses and a bottle of Prosecco, apparently in no hurry to pop the cork. When he finally stopped, it was in a little hollow grown over with grass and wild spices, and as he turned to face me—smiling with boyish pride—I felt my throat tighten.

"Let me guess," I said, wrapping my arms around myself although there was barely a breeze, "this is where you bring all your dates? Mind you, it didn't work too well for Nino."

He actually looked hurt. "No! I haven't—my uncle took me up here when I was a boy." He made a sweeping gesture at the shrubs and scattered boulders. "We had a sword fight right here . . . me and my cousin, Malèna. She—" Perhaps realizing that his big secret might begin to unravel from the wrong end if he went on, he stopped abruptly and said instead, "Ever since, I always wanted to come back."

"Took you a long time," I pointed out, only too aware that it was my nerves speaking, not me, and that I was doing neither of us a favor by being so skittish. "But . . . I'm not complaining. It's beautiful here. A perfect place for a celebration." When he still didn't speak, I pulled off my shoes and walked forward a few steps, barefoot. "So, what are we celebrating?"

Frowning, Alessandro turned to look at the view, and I could see him wrestling with the words he knew he had to say. When he finally turned to face me, all the playful mischief I had come to know so well had disappeared from his face and, instead, he looked at me with tortured apprehension. "I thought," he said slowly, "it was time to celebrate a new beginning."

"A new beginning for who?"

Now at last, he put the bottle and glasses down in the tall grass and walked over to where I stood. "Giulietta," he said, his voice low, "I didn't take you up here to play Nino. Or Paris. I took you up here because this is where it ended." He reached out and touched my face with reverence, like an archaeologist who finally finds that precious artifact he has spent his whole life digging for. "And I thought it would be a good place to start over." Not quite able to interpret my expression, he added, anxiously, "I am sorry I didn't tell you the truth before. I was hoping I wouldn't have to. You kept asking about Romeo and what he was really like. I was hoping that"—he smiled wistfully—"you would recognize me."

Although I already knew what he was trying to tell me, his solemnity and the tension of the moment struck me unexpectedly, right in the heart, and I could not have been more shocked had I arrived at Rocca di Tentennano—and heard his confession—knowing absolutely nothing.

"Giulietta—" He tried to catch my eye, but I didn't let him. I had been desperate for this conversation ever since discovering who he really was, and now that it was finally happening, I wanted him to say the words over and over. But at the same time, I had been running an emotional gauntlet for the last couple of days, and although, obviously, he couldn't know the details, I needed him to feel my pain.

"You lied to me."

Instead of backing up, he came closer. "I never lied to you about Romeo. I told you he was not the man you thought."

"And you told me to stay away from him," I went on. "You said I would be better off with Paris."

He smiled at my accusatory frown. "You were the one who told me I was Paris—"

"And you let me believe it!"

"Yes, I did." He touched my chin gently, as if wondering why I would not allow myself to smile. "Because it was what you wanted me to be. You wanted me to be the enemy. That was the only way you could relate to me."

I opened my mouth to protest, but realized he was right.

"All this time," Alessandro went on, aware that he was winning me over, "I was waiting for my moment. And I thought—after yesterday, at Fontebranda, I thought you would be happy." His thumb paused at the corner of my mouth. "I thought you . . . liked me."

In the silence that followed, his eyes confirmed everything he had said and begged me to reply. But rather than speaking right away I reached up to put a hand on his chest, and when I felt his warm heartbeat against my palm, an irrational, ecstatic joy bubbled up inside me from a place I had never known was there, to find its way to the surface at last. "I do."

How long our kiss lasted, I will never know. It was one of those moments that no scientist can ever reduce to numbers, try as she might. But when the world eventually came whirling back, from somewhere pleasantly far away, everything was brighter, more worthwhile, than ever before. It was as if the entire cosmos had undergone some exorbitant renovation since the last time I looked . . . or maybe I had just never looked properly before.

"I am so glad you are Romeo," I whispered, my forehead against his, "but even if you were not, I would still—"

"You would still what?"

I looked down in embarrassment. "I would still be happy."

He chuckled, knowing full well that I had been about to say something far more revealing. "Come . . ." He pulled me down in the grass beside him. "You make me forget my promise. You are very good at that!"

I looked at him as he sat there, so determined to collect his thoughts. "What promise?"

"To tell you about my family," he replied, helplessly. "I want you to know everything—"

"Oh, but I don't want to know everything," I cut him off, straddling his lap. "Not right now."

"Wait!" He tried in vain to stop my misbehaving hands. "First, I have to tell you about . . ."

"Shh!" I put my fingers over his mouth. "First, you want to kiss me again."

". . . Charlemagne—"

". . . can wait." I removed my fingers and touched my lips to his in a lingering kiss that left no room for contradictions. "Wouldn't you say?"

He looked at me with the expression of a lone defender facing a barbarian invasion. "But I want you to know what you're getting yourself into."

"Oh, don't you worry," I whispered, "I think I know what I'm getting myself into—"

After struggling for three noble seconds, his resolve finally caved in, and he pulled me as close as Italian fashion permitted. "Are you sure?" The next thing I knew I was lying on my back in a bed of wild thyme, giggling with surprise. "Well, Giulietta . . ." Alessandro looked at me sternly, "I hope you're not expecting a rhyming couplet."

I laughed. "It's too bad Shakespeare never wrote any stage directions."

"Why?" He kissed me softly on the neck. "Do you really think old William was a better lover than me?"

In the end, it was not my modesty that put an end to the fun, but the unwelcome specter of Sienese chivalry.

"Did you know," Alessandro growled, pinning my arms to the ground

in an attempt at saving his remaining shirt buttons, "that it took Columbus six years to discover the mainland of America?" As he hovered above
me, constraint incarnate, the bullet dangled between us like a pendulum.

"What took him so long?" I asked, savoring the sight of his valiant
struggle against the backdrop of blue sky.

"He was an Italian gentleman," replied Alessandro, speaking to himself as much as to me, "not a conquistador."

"Oh, he was after the gold," I said, trying to kiss his clenched jaw, "just
like them."

"Maybe at first. But then"—he reached down to pull my skirt back
where it belonged—"he discovered how much he loved to explore the
coastline and get to know this strange, new culture."

"Six years is a long time," I protested, not yet ready to get up and on
with reality. "Far too long."

"No." He smiled at my invitation. "Six *hundred* years is a long time. So
I think you can be patient for half an hour while I tell you my story."

THE PROSECCO WAS warm by the time we finally got around to it, but
it was still the best glass of wine I had ever had. It tasted like honey and
wild herbs, of love and giddy plans, and as I sat there, leaning against
Alessandro, who was leaning against a boulder, I could almost believe that
my life would be long and full of joy, and that I had finally found a blessing to put my ghosts to rest.

"I know you are still upset because I didn't tell you who I was," he
said, stroking my hair. "Maybe you think I was afraid you would fall in
love with the name and not the man. But the truth is the exact opposite. I
was afraid—I am still afraid—that when you hear my story, the story of
Romeo Marescotti, you will wish you had never met me."

I opened my mouth to protest, but he did not let me. "Those things
your cousin Peppo said about me . . . they are all true. I am sure the psychologists could explain it all with some graphs, but in my family, we
don't listen to psychologists. We don't listen to anybody. We—the
Marescottis—have our own theories, and we are so sure they are right
that—as you say—they become dragons beneath our tower, letting no one
in and no one out." He paused to fill up my glass. "Here, the rest is for
you. I am driving."

"Driving?" I laughed. "That doesn't sound like the Romeo Marescotti that Peppo told me about! I thought you were supposed to be reckless. This is a huge disappointment."

"Don't worry . . ." He pulled me closer. "I will make up for it in other ways."

While I sipped my Prosecco, he told me about his mother, who became pregnant at seventeen and wouldn't say who the father was. Naturally, her own father—old man Marescotti, Alessandro's grandfather—had been furious. He threw her out of the house, and she went to live with her mother's old school friend, Eva Maria Salimbeni. When Alessandro was born, Eva Maria became his godmother, and she was the one who insisted that the boy should be baptized with the traditional family name, Romeo Alessandro Marescotti, even though she knew it would make old man Marescotti foam at the mouth to have a bastard carry his name.

Finally, in 1977, Alessandro's grandmother persuaded his grandfather to allow their daughter and grandson to come back to Siena for the first time after Alessandro was born, and the boy was baptized in the Aquila fountain just before the Palio. But that year, the contrada lost both Palios in terrible ways, and old man Marescotti was looking for someone to blame. When he heard that his daughter had taken her little boy to see the Aquila stable before the race—and had let him touch the horse—he became convinced that this was the reason right there: The little bastard had brought bad luck to the whole contrada.

He had yelled to his daughter to take her boy, go back to Rome, and not come home again before she had found a husband. So, she did. She went back to Rome and found a husband, a very good man who was a Carabinieri officer. This man let Alessandro use his last name, Santini, and brought him up like his own sons, with discipline and love. That was how Romeo Marescotti became Alessandro Santini.

But still, every summer, Alessandro had to spend a month at his grandparents' farm in Siena, to get to know his cousins and get away from the big city. This was not his grandfather's idea, or his mother's; but it was his grandmother who insisted on it. The only thing she could not persuade old man Marescotti to do was to let Alessandro come to the Palio. Everyone would go—cousins, uncles, aunts—but Alessandro had to stay at home, because his grandfather was afraid he would bring bad luck to the Aquila horse. Or so he said. So, Alessandro had stayed behind on the farm all alone, and had made his own Palio riding the old workhorse around. Later, he learned how to fix scooters and motorcycles, and his Palio had been just as dangerous as the real thing.

In the end, he didn't want to go back to Siena at all, for whenever he went, his grandfather would nag him with comments about his mother, who—for good reason—never came to visit. And so Alessandro finished school and joined the Carabinieri like his father and brothers, and did everything to forget that he was Romeo Marescotti. From then on, he only called himself Alessandro Santini, and he traveled as far away as he could from Siena, signing up every time there was a peacekeeping mission in another country. This was how he ended up in Iraq, perfecting his English in yelling arguments with American defense contractors and narrowly avoiding being blown to bits when insurgents ran a truck full of explosives into the Carabinieri headquarters in Nassiriyah.

When he finally visited Siena, he did not tell anyone that he was there, not even his grandmother. But on the night before the Palio, he went to the contrada stable. He didn't plan it; he just couldn't stay away. His uncle was there, guarding the horse, and when Alessandro told him who he was, his uncle was so excited that he let him touch the yellow-and-black Aquila giubbetto—the jacket that the jockey would wear during the race—for good luck.

Unfortunately, during the Palio on the following day, the jockey from Pantera—the rival contrada—got hold of that very giubbetto, and was able to slow down the Aquila jockey and horse so much that they lost the race.

At this point in the story, I could not help but twist around and look at Alessandro. "Don't tell me you thought it was your fault."

He shrugged. "What could I think? I had brought bad luck to our giubbetto, and we lost. Even my uncle said so. And we haven't won a Palio since."

"Honestly—!" I began.

"Shh!" He put his hand over my mouth lightly. "Just listen. After that, I was gone for a long period, and I only came back to Siena a few years ago. Just in time. My grandfather was very tired. I remember he was sitting on a bench, looking out over the vineyard, and he didn't hear me until I put my hand on his shoulder. Then he turned his head and took one look at my face, and started crying, he was so happy. That was a good day. We had a big dinner, and my uncle said they would never let me leave again. At first, I wasn't sure I wanted to stay. I had never lived in Siena before, and I had many bad memories. Also, I knew that people would gossip about me if they knew who I was. People don't forget the past, you know. So, I started by just taking a leave. But then something happened. Aquila ran in the July Palio, and for us, it was the worst race of all times. In the whole history of the Palio, I don't think any contrada has ever lost in such a bad way before. We were leading the whole race, but then in the very last curve, Pantera passes us and wins instead." He sighed, reliving the moment. "There is no worse way to lose a Palio. It was a shock to us. And then later, we had to defend our honor in the August Palio, and our fantino—our jockey—was punished. We were all punished. We had no right to run the next year, and the year after that: We were sanctioned. Call it politics if you like, but in my family, we felt it was more than that.

"My grandfather was so upset, he had a heart attack when he realized that it could be two years before Aquila would run in the Palio again. He was eighty-seven. Three days later, he died." Alessandro paused and looked away. "I sat with him those three days. He was so angry with himself for wasting all this time; now he wanted to look at my face as much as possible. At first, I thought he was upset with me for bringing bad luck again, but then he told me that it was not my fault. It was his fault for not understanding earlier."

I had to ask. "Understanding what exactly?"

"My mother. He understood that what had happened to her *had* to happen. My uncle has five girls, no boys. I am the only grandchild who carries the family name. Because my mother was not married when I was born, and I was baptized with her name. You see?"

I sat up straight. "What kind of sick, chauvinist—"

"Giulietta, please!" He pulled me back to lean against his shoulder again. "You will never understand this if you don't listen. What my grandfather realized was that there was an old evil that had woken up after many generations, and it had chosen me, because of my name."

I felt the little hairs on my arms stand up. "Chosen you . . . for what?"

"This . . ." said Alessandro, filling my glass again, "is when we get to Charlemagne."

The ape is dead and I must conjure him.
I conjure thee by Rosaline's bright eyes,
By her high forehead and her scarlet lip

...

THE PLAGUE AND THE RING

Siena, A.D. 1340–1370

THE MARESCOTTIS ARE ONE of the oldest noble families in Siena. It is believed that the name was derived from Marius Scotus, a Scottish general in Charlemagne's army. Most of the Marescottis settled in Bologna, but the family spread its wings far and wide, and the Siena branch was particularly renowned for courage and leadership in times of crisis.

But, as we know, nothing great is great forever, and the fame of the Marescottis is no exception. Hardly anyone remembers their glorious past in Siena nowadays, but then history was always more concerned with those who live to destroy than with those devoted to protection and preservation.

Romeo was born when the family was still illustrious. His father, Comandante Marescotti, was much admired for his moderation and decorum, and his deposits on that account were so plentiful that not even his son—whose greed and sloth were always outstanding—could squander his savings.

However, even the Comandante's virtues were taxed to the bone when, early in the year 1340, Romeo encountered the woman Rosalina. She was the wife of a butcher, but everyone knew they were not happy to-

gether. In Shakespeare's version, Rosalina is a young beauty who tor-
ments Romeo with her vow of chastity; the truth is quite the opposite.
Rosalina was ten years older than he, and she became his mistress. For
months, Romeo tried to persuade her to run away with him, but she was
too wise to trust him.

Just after Christmas of 1340—not long after Romeo and Giulietta died
here at Rocca di Tentennano—Rosalina gave birth to a son, and everyone
could see the butcher was not the father. It was a great scandal, and Rosalina was afraid her husband would learn the truth and kill the baby. So,
she took the newborn to Comandante Marescotti and asked if he would
raise the boy in his own house.

But the Comandante said no. He did not believe her story, and turned
her away. Before she left, however, Rosalina said to him, "One day you
will be sorry for what you have done to me and to this child. One day, God
will punish you for the justice you are denying me!"

The Comandante forgot all about this until, in 1348, the Black Death
came through Siena. More than a third of the population died within
months, and the mortality was worst inside the city. Bodies were piled in
the streets, sons abandoned fathers, wives abandoned husbands; everyone was too afraid to remember what it means to be a human and not an
animal.

In one week, Comandante Marescotti lost his mother, his wife, and all
his five children; only he alone was left to survive. He washed them and
dressed them, and he put them all on a cart and brought them to the
cathedral to find a priest who could perform a funeral. But there were no
priests. Those priests who were still alive were too busy taking care of the
sick in the hospital next to the cathedral, the Santa Maria della Scala. Even
there, they had too many dead bodies to be able to bury them all, and
what they did was build a hollow wall inside the hospital and put all the
bodies inside and seal it off.

When the Comandante arrived at the Siena Cathedral, there were
Misericordia Brothers outside in the piazza digging a big hole for a mass
grave, and he bribed them to admit his family into this holy ground. He
told them that this was his mother, and his wife, and he told them the
names and ages of all his children, and explained that they were dressed
in their finest church clothes. But the men didn't care. They took his gold
and tipped the cart, and the Comandante saw all his loved ones—his

future—tumble into the hole with no prayers, no blessings, and no sper-anza . . . no hope.

When he walked back through town, he did not know where he went. He did not see anything around him. To him, it was the end of the world, and he began yelling at God, asking why he had been left alive to witness this misery, and to bury his own children. He even fell to his knees, and scooped up the dirty water from the gutter running with rot and death, and poured it over himself, and drank it, hoping to finally get sick and die like everyone else.

While he was there, kneeling in the mud, he suddenly heard the voice of a boy say to him, "I've tried that. It doesn't work."

The Comandante looked up at the boy, thinking he was looking at a ghost. "Romeo!" he said. "Romeo? Is it you?"

But it was not Romeo, just a boy of eight or so, very dirty and dressed in rags. "My name is Romanino," said the boy. "I can pull that cart for you."

"Why do you want to pull my cart?" asked the Comandante.

"Because I am hungry," said Romanino.

"Here—" The Comandante took out the rest of his money. "Go buy some food."

But the boy pushed his hand away and said, "I am not a beggar."

So, the Comandante let the boy struggle to pull the cart all the way back to Palazzo Marescotti—occasionally, he helped him and gave the cart a little push—and when they arrived at the gate, the boy looked up at the eagle ornaments on the wall and said, "This is where my father was born."

You can imagine what a shock it was to the Comandante to hear this, and he asked the boy, "How do you know that?"

"Mother used to tell me stories," replied the boy. "She said my father was very brave. He was a great knight with arms this big. But he had to go and fight with the Emperor in the Holy Land, and he never returned. She used to say that maybe, one day, he would come back and look for me. And if he did, I had to tell him something, and then he would know who I was."

"What did you have to tell him?"

The boy grinned, and just then, in that smile, the Comandante knew the truth before he even heard the words: "That I am a little eagle, an aquilino."

That same night, Comandante Marescotti found himself sitting at the empty servants' table in the kitchen, eating food for the first time in days. Across from him, Romanino was gnawing at a chicken bone, too busy to ask questions.

"Tell me," said the Comandante, "when did your mother Rosalina die?"

"Long ago," replied the boy. "Before all this. He beat her, you know. And one day, she didn't get up. He yelled at her, and pulled at her hair, but she didn't move. She didn't move at all. Then he started crying. And I went up to her and talked to her, but she didn't open her eyes. She was cold. I put my hand on her face—that was when I knew he had beat her too hard, and I told him so, and he kicked me, and then he tried to catch me, but I ran . . . out the door. And I just kept running. Even though he yelled after me, I just kept running, and running, until I was at my aunt's, and she took me in, and I stayed there. I worked, you know. I did my bit. And I took care of the baby when it came, and helped her to put food on the table. And they liked me, I think they really liked having me around to take care of the baby, until . . . until everyone started dying. The baker died, and the butcher, and the farmer who sold us fruit, and we did not have enough food. But she kept giving me the same as the others, even though they were still hungry, so . . . I ran away."

The boy looked at him with wise green eyes, and the Comandante thought to himself how strange it was that this boy, a skinny little eight-year-old, could have more integrity than he had ever seen in a man. "How did you survive," he had to ask, "through all this?"

"I don't know"—Romanino shrugged—"but Mother always told me I was different. Stronger. That I wouldn't get sick and stupid like the others. She said that I had a different kind of head on my shoulders. And that's why they didn't like me. Because they knew I was better than them. That was how I survived. By thinking of what she said. About me. And them. She said I would survive. And that's what I did."

"Do you know who I am?" asked the Comandante at last.

The boy looked at him. "You're a great man, I think."

"I don't know about that."

"But you are," insisted Romanino. "You're a great man. You have a big kitchen. And a chicken. And you let me pull your cart all the way. And now you're sharing your chicken with me."

"That doesn't make me a great man."

"You were drinking sewer water when I found you," observed the boy. "Now you are drinking wine. To me, that makes you the greatest man I've ever met."

THE NEXT MORNING, Comandante Marescotti took Romanino back to the boy's aunt and uncle. As they walked together down the steep streets towards Fontebranda, weaving their way through garbage and gore, the sun came out for the first time in days. Or perhaps it had been shining every day, but the Comandante had spent all his time in the darkness of his home, pouring water to lips that were beyond drinking.

"What is your uncle's name?" asked the Comandante, realizing that he had forgotten to ask that most obvious question.

"Benincasa," replied the boy. "He makes colors. I like the blue, but it is expensive." He glanced up at the Comandante. "My father always wore nice colors, you know. Yellow mostly, with a black cape that looked like wings when he was riding fast. When you are rich you can do that."

"I suppose," said the Comandante.

Romanino stopped at a gate of tall iron bars and looked glumly into the courtyard. "This is it. That is Monna Lappa, my aunt. Or . . . she is not really my aunt, but she wanted me to call her that anyway."

Comandante Marescotti was surprised at the size of the place; he had imagined something far more humble. Inside the courtyard, three children were helping their mother spread out laundry, while a tiny girl crawled around on her hands and knees, picking up grains laid out for the geese.

"Romanino!" The woman jumped to her feet when she saw the boy through the gate, and as soon as the bar had been lifted off the hook and the door opened, she pulled him inside and embraced him with tears and kisses. "We thought you were dead, you silly boy!"

In the commotion, nobody took any notice of the baby girl, and the Comandante—who had been just about to back away from the happy family reunion—was the only person with the presence of mind to see her crawling towards the open gate and to bend over and pick her up with awkward hands.

It was an uncommonly pretty little girl, thought Comandante

Marescotti, and much more charming than one would expect from someone that size. In fact, despite his lack of experience with such tiny personnel, he found himself almost unwilling to hand the baby back to Monna Lappa, and he simply stood there, looking at the little face, feeling something stirring inside his chest, like a small spring flower forcing its way up through the frozen soil.

The fascination was equal on both sides; soon, the baby began slapping and pulling at the Comandante's features with all signs of delight.

"Caterina!" cried her mother, quickly liberating the distinguished visitor by snatching away the girl. "I beg your pardon, Messere!"

"No need, no need," said the Comandante. "God has kept his hand over you and yours, Monna Lappa. Your house is blessed, I think."

The woman looked at him for a long time. Then she bent her head. "Thank you, Messere."

The Comandante turned to go, but hesitated. Turning again, he looked at Romanino. The boy was standing straight, like a young tree braced against the wind, and yet his eyes had lost their courage.

"Monna Lappa," said Comandante Marescotti, "I want—I would like—I wonder if you might consider giving up this boy. To me."

The woman's expression was mostly one of disbelief.

"You see," the Comandante quickly added, "I believe he is my grandson."

The words came as a surprise to everyone, including the Comandante. While Monna Lappa looked almost frightened at the confession, Romanino was positively cock-a-hoop, and the boy's glee nearly made the Comandante burst out laughing despite himself.

"You are Comandante Marescotti?" exclaimed the woman, her cheeks flushed with excitement. "Then it was true! Oh, the poor girl! I never—" Too shocked to know how to behave, Monna Lappa grabbed Romanino by the shoulder and pushed him towards the Comandante. "Go! Go, you silly boy! And . . . don't forget to thank the Lord!"

She did not have to say it twice, and before the Comandante even had a visual confirmation of the advance, Romanino's arms were already wrapped around his midsection, a snotty nose burrowing into the embroidered velvet.

"Come now," he said, patting the dirty head, "we need to find you a pair of shoes. And other things. So, stop crying."

"I know," sniffled the boy, wiping away his tears, "knights don't cry."

"They certainly do," said the Comandante, taking the boy's hand, "but only when they are clean and dressed, and wearing shoes. Do you think you can wait that long?"

"I'll do my best."

When they walked away down the street together, hand in hand, Comandante Marescotti found himself struggling against an onslaught of shame. How was it possible that he, a man sick with grief, who had lost everything save his own heartbeat, could find so much comfort in the presence of a small, sticky fist tucked firmly inside his own?

IT WAS MANY YEARS later when, one day, a traveling monk came to Palazzo Marescotti and asked to speak with the head of the family. The monk explained that he had come from a monastery in Viterbo, and that he had been instructed by his abbot to return a great treasure to its proper owner.

Romanino, who was now a grown man of thirty years, invited the monk inside and sent his daughters upstairs to see if their great-grandfather, the old Comandante, had the strength to meet with the guest. While they waited for the Comandante to come down, Romanino made sure the monk had food and drink, and his curiosity was so great that he asked the stranger about the nature of the treasure.

"I know little about its origins," replied the monk between mouthfuls, "but I do know that I cannot take it back with me."

"Why not?" inquired Romanino.

"Because it has a great, destructive power," said the monk, helping himself to more bread. "Everyone who opens the box falls ill."

Romanino sat back on his chair. "I thought you said it was a treasure? Now you tell me it is evil!"

"Pardon me, Messere," the monk corrected him, "but I never said it was evil. I just said that it has great powers. For protection, but also for destruction. And therefore, it must be returned to the hands that can control those powers. It must be returned to its proper owner. That is all I know."

"And that owner is Comandante Marescotti?"

The monk nodded again, but this time with less conviction. "We believe so."

"Because if it is not," Romanino pointed out, "you have brought a demon into my house, you realize."

The monk looked sheepish. "Messere," he said, urgingly, "please believe that I had no intention of harming you or your family. I am only doing what I have been instructed to do. This box"—he reached into his satchel and took out a small and very simple wooden box which he put gently down on the table—"was given to us by the priests of San Lorenzo, our cathedral, and I believe that maybe—but I am not sure—it contains a relic of a saint that was recently sent to Viterbo by its noble patron in Siena."

"I have heard of no such saint!" exclaimed Romanino, eyeing the box with apprehension. "Who was the noble patron?"

The monk folded his hands in respect. "The pious and modest Monna Mina of the Salimbeni, Messere."

"Huh." Romanino fell silent for a while. He had heard of the lady, certainly—who had not heard of the young bride's madness and the alleged curse on the basement wall?—but what kind of saint would befriend the Salimbenis? "Then may I ask why you are not returning this so-called treasure to her?"

"Oh!" The monk was horrified at the idea. "No! The treasure doesn't like the Salimbenis! One of my poor brethren, a Salimbeni by birth, died in his sleep after touching the box—"

"God damn you, monk!" barked Romanino, and stood up. "Take your cursed box and leave my house at once!"

"But then, he was a hundred and two years old!" the monk hastened to add. "And other people who touched it have had miraculous recoveries from long-term ailments!"

Just then, Comandante Marescotti entered the dining hall with great dignity, his proud bearing suported by a cane. Instead of shooing the monk out the door with a broom—as he was just about to do—Romanino calmed himself and made sure his grandfather was seated comfortably at the table end, before he explained the circumstances of the unexpected visit.

"Viterbo?" The Comandante frowned. "How would they know my name?"

The monk stood awkwardly, not knowing whether he should stay up or sit down, and whether he or Romanino was expected to answer the question. "Here . . ." he said instead, placing the box in front of the old man, "this, I was told, must be returned to its proper owner."

"Grandfather, be careful!" exclaimed Romanino as the Comandante reached out to open the box. "We do not know what demons it contains!"

"No, my son," replied the Comandante, "but we intend to find out."

There was a moment's dreadful silence while the Comandante slowly lifted the lid and peeked into the box. Seeing that his grandfather did not immediately fall to the floor in convulsions, Romanino stepped closer and looked, too.

In the box lay a ring.

"I wouldn't . . ." began the monk, but Comandante Marescotti had already taken out the ring and was staring at it in disbelief.

"Who," he said, his hand shaking, "did you say gave you this?"

"My abbot," replied the monk, backing up in fear. "He told me that the men who found it had spoken the name Marescotti before they died of a ghastly fever, three days after receiving the saint's coffin."

Romanino looked at his grandfather, anxious that he should put down the ring. But the Comandante was in another world, touching the ring's eagle signet without any fear and mumbling to himself an old family motto, "Faithful through the centuries," engraved on the inside of the band in tiny letters. "Come, my son," he finally said, reaching out for Romanino. "This was your father's ring. Now it is yours."

Romanino didn't know what to do. On the one hand, he wanted to obey his grandfather; on the other, he was afraid of the ring, and he was not so sure that he was its rightful owner, even if it had belonged to his father. When Comandante Marescotti saw him hesitating, the old man was filled with anger, explosive anger, and he began to yell that Romanino was a coward, and to demand that he take the ring. But just as Romanino stepped forward, the Comandante fell back in his chair in a seizure, dropping the ring on the floor.

When he saw that the old man had fallen prey to the ring's evil, the monk screamed in horror and fled from the room, leaving Romanino to throw himself at his grandfather and beseech his soul to remain in the body for the last sacrament. "Monk!" he bellowed, cradling the Comandante's head, "come back here and do your job, you rat, or I swear I'll bring the devil to Viterbo and we'll eat you all alive!"

Hearing the threat, the monk came back into the kitchen, and he found in his satchel the small vial of consecrated oil that his abbot had given him for the journey. So, the Comandante received the extreme unction, and he lay very peacefully for a moment, looking at Romanino. His last words before he died were, "Shine on high, my son."

Understandably, Romanino did not know what to think about that damned ring. It was obviously evil and had killed his grandfather, but at the same time, it had belonged to his father, Romeo. In the end Romanino decided to keep it, but to put the box in a place where no one but he could find it. And so he went down into the basement and into the Bottini, to put the box away in a dark corner where nobody ever came. He never told his children about it for fear that their curiosity would make them unleash its demons once again, but he wrote down the whole story, sealed the paper, and kept it with the rest of the family records.

It is doubtful whether Romanino ever discovered the truth about the ring in his lifetime and, for many generations, the box remained hidden in the Bottini underneath the house, untouched and unclaimed. But even so, there was a feeling among the Marescottis that an old evil was somehow imbedded in the house, and the family eventually decided to sell the building in 1506. Needless to say, the box with the ring stayed where it was.

NOW, MANY HUNDRED years later, another grandfather, old man Marescotti, was walking through his vineyard one summer day when he suddenly looked down and saw a little girl standing at his feet. He asked her, in Italian, who she was, and she replied, also in Italian, that her name was Giulietta, and that she was almost three years old. He was very surprised, because usually little children were afraid of him, but this one kept talking to him as if they were old friends, and when they started walking, she put her hand in his.

Back at the house, he found that a beautiful young woman was having coffee with his wife. And there was another little girl there, too, stuffing herself with biscotti. His wife explained to him that the young woman was Diane Tolomei, the widow of old Professor Tolomei, and that she had come to ask some questions about the Marescotti family.

Grandfather Marescotti treated Diane Tolomei very well and answered all her questions. She asked him if it was true that his line was descended directly from Romeo Marescotti, through the boy Romanino, and he said yes. She also asked him if he was aware that Romeo Marescotti was the Romeo from Shakespeare's *Romeo and Juliet,* and he said yes, he was aware of that, too. Then she asked if he knew that her line came straight from Juliet, and he said yes, he suspected as much, seeing that she was a Tolomei, and that she had called one of her daughters Giulietta. But when she asked him if he could guess the reason for her visit, he said no, not at all.

Now Diane Tolomei asked him if his family still had in their possession Romeo's ring. Grandfather Marescotti said that he had no idea what she meant by that. She also asked him if he had ever seen a small wooden box that supposedly contained an evil treasure, or if he had ever heard his parents or grandparents mention such a box. He said no, he had never heard anything about it from anyone. She seemed a little disappointed, and when he asked her what this was all about, she said that maybe it was better this way, maybe she should not bring these old things back to life.

You can imagine what Grandfather Marescotti said to that. He told Diane that she had already asked too many questions, and he had answered every one of them, so now it was time she answered some of his. What kind of ring was she talking about, and why did she think he would know anything about it?

What Diane Tolomei told him first was the story of Romanino and the monk from Viterbo. She explained that her husband had been researching these issues all his life, and that he was the one who had found the Marescotti family records in the city archive and discovered Romanino's notes about the box. It was a good thing, she said, that Romanino had been too wise to wear the ring, for he was not its rightful owner, and it was possible that it would have done him much harm.

Before she could continue with her explanations, the old man's grandson, Alessandro—or, as they called him, Romeo—came to the table to steal a biscotto. When Diane realized that he was Romeo, she got very excited, and said, "It is a great honor to meet you, young man. Now, here is someone very special that I want you to meet." And she pulled one of the little girls into her lap, and said, as if she was presenting a wonder of the world, "This is Giulietta."

Romeo stuck the biscotto in his pocket. "I don't think so," he said. "She's wearing a diaper."

"No!" protested Diane Tolomei, pulling down the girl's dress. "Those are fancy pants. She is a big girl. Aren't you, Jules?"

Now, Romeo started backing up, hoping he could sneak away, but his grandfather stopped him and told him to take the two little girls and play with them while the adults had coffee. So, he did.

Meanwhile, Diane Tolomei told Grandfather Marescotti and his wife about Romeo's ring; she explained that it had been his signet ring, and that he had given it to Giulietta Tolomei in a secret marriage ritual performed by their friend, Friar Lorenzo. Therefore, she claimed, the ring's rightful heir was Giulietta, her daughter, and she went on to explain that it must be recovered for the curse on the Tolomeis to finally end.

Grandfather Marescotti was fascinated by Diane Tolomei's story, mostly because she was obviously not an Italian, and yet she was so very passionate about the events of the past. It amazed him that this modern woman from America seemed to believe there was a curse on her family—an ancient curse from the Middle Ages, no less—and that she even thought her husband had died as a result of this. It made sense, he supposed, that she should be eager to somehow try and stop it, so that her little girls could grow up without it hanging over their heads. For some reason, she seemed to think that her daughters were particularly exposed to the curse, maybe because both their parents had been Tolomeis.

Obviously, Grandfather Marescotti was sorry that he could not help this poor young widow, but Diane interrupted him as soon as he started to apologize. "From what you have told me, Signore," she said, "I believe the box with the ring is still there, hidden in the Bottini underneath Palazzo Marescotti, untouched since Romanino put it there more than six hundred years ago."

Grandfather Marescotti could not help laughing and slapping his knees. "That is too fantastic!" he said. "I cannot imagine it would still be there. And if it is, the reason must be that it is hidden so well that no one can find it. Including me."

To persuade him to go looking for the ring, Diane told him that if he were able to find it and give it to her, she would give him something in return that the Marescotti family must be equally keen to recover, and which had been in Tolomei possession for far too long. She asked him if he had any idea what sort of treasure she was talking about, but he did not.

Now, Diane Tolomei took a photo out of her purse and put it on the table in front of him. And Grandfather Marescotti crossed himself when he saw that not only was it an old cencio spread out on a table, but it was a cencio he had heard described many times by his own grandfather; a cencio which he had never imagined he would ever see, or touch, because it could no longer possibly exist.

"How long," he said, his voice shaking, "has your family kept this hidden from us?"

"For as long," replied Diane Tolomei, "as your family has kept the ring hidden from us, Signore. And now, I think, you will agree that it is time we return these treasures to their proper owners, and put an end to the evil that has left us both in this sad state."

Naturally, Grandfather Marescotti was insulted by the suggestion that he was in a sad state, and he said as much, loudly listing all the blessings surrounding him on all sides.

"Are you telling me," said Diane Tolomei, leaning over the table and touching his hands, "that there are not days when you feel a mighty power watching you with impatient eyes, an ancient ally who is waiting for you to do the one thing you *have* to do?"

Her words made a great impression on her two hosts, and they all sat in silence for a moment, until suddenly they heard a terrible noise from the barn, and they saw Romeo come running, trying to carry one of his screaming and kicking guests. It was the girl Giulietta, who had cut herself on a hayfork, and Romeo's grandmother had to stitch her up on the kitchen table.

Romeo's grandparents were not actually angry with him for what had happened. It was much worse. They were simply terrified to see that their grandson was causing pain and destruction wherever he went. And now, after listening to Diane Tolomei's stories, they began to worry that he truly did have evil hands . . . that some old demon lived on inside his body, and that, just like his ancestor Romeo, he would live a life—a short life—of violence and sorrow.

Grandfather Marescotti felt so bad about what had happened to the little girl that he promised Diane he would do everything in his power to find the ring. And she thanked him and said that, regardless of his success, she would return soon with the cencio, so that at least Romeo could get what belonged to him. For some reason, it was very important to her that Romeo still be there when she came back, because she wanted to try something with him. She did not say what it was, and no one dared to ask.

They agreed that Diane Tolomei would return in two weeks, which would give Grandfather Marescotti time to investigate the matter of the ring, and they all parted as friends. Before she drove away, however, Diane said one last thing to him. She told him that if he was successful in his search for the ring, he must be very careful and open the box as little as possible. And under no circumstances must he touch the ring itself. It had, she reminded him, a history of hurting people.

Grandfather Marescotti drove into town the very next day, determined to find the ring. For days and days he went all over the Bottini underneath Palazzo Marescotti to find Romanino's secret hiding place. When he finally found it—he had to borrow a metal detector—he could see why no one else had stumbled across it before; the box had been pushed deep inside a narrow crack in the wall, and was covered with crumbled sandstone.

As he pulled it out, he remembered what Diane Tolomei had said about not opening the lid more than necessary, but after six centuries in dust and gravel, the wood had become so dry and fragile that even his careful touch was too much for the box. And so the wood fell apart like a lump of sawdust, and within a moment, he found himself standing with the ring right in his hand.

He decided not to give in to irrational fears, and instead of putting the ring in another box, he put it in his trouser pocket and drove back to his villa outside of town. After that drive, with the ring in his pocket, no other male was ever born in his family to carry the name Romeo Marescotti— much to his frustration, everyone kept having girls, girls, girls. There would only ever be Romeo, his grandson, and he very much doubted this restless boy would ever marry and have sons of his own.

Of course, Grandfather Marescotti did not realize all this at the time; he was just happy that he had found the ring for Diane Tolomei, and he was anxious to finally get his hands on the old cencio from 1340 and show it around the contrada. He was already planning to donate it to the Eagle Museum, and imagined that it would bring much good luck in the next Palio.

But it was not going to be that way. On the day when Diane Tolomei was supposed to come back and visit them, he had gathered the whole family for a big party, and his wife had been cooking for several days. He had put the ring in a new box, and she had tied a red ribbon around it. They had even taken Romeo into town—despite the fact that it was just before the Palio—to get him a real haircut, not just the gnocchi pot and the scissors. Now, all they had to do was wait.

And so they waited. And waited. But Diane Tolomei did not come. Normally, Grandfather Marescotti would have been furious, but this time, he was afraid. He could not explain it. He felt as if he had a fever, and he could not eat. That same evening he heard the terrible news. His cousin called to tell him that there had been a car accident, and that Professor Tolomei's widow and two little daughters had died. Imagine how he felt. He and his wife were crying for Diane Tolomei and the little girls, and the very next day, he sat down and wrote a letter to his daughter in Rome, asking her to forgive him, and to come home. But she never wrote back, and she never came.

O, I have bought the mansion of a love
But not possess'd it, and though I am sold,
Not yet enjoy'd

...

WHEN ALESSANDRO FINALLY FINISHED his story, we were lying side by side on the wild thyme, holding hands.

"I still remember that day," he added, "when we heard about the car accident. I was only thirteen, but I understood how terrible it was. And I thought of the little girl—you—who was supposed to be Giulietta. Of course, I always knew I was Romeo, but I had never thought much about Giulietta before. Now I started thinking about her, and I realized that it was a very strange thing to be Romeo, when there is no Giulietta in the world. Strange and lonely."

"Oh, come now!" I rolled up on one elbow, poking at his gravity with a nodding violet. "I'm sure there has been no scarcity of women willing to keep you company."

He grinned and brushed the violet away. "I thought you were dead! What could I do?"

I sighed and shook my head. "So much for the engraving on Romeo's ring, Faithful through the centuries."

"Hey!" Alessandro rolled us both over and looked down at me with a frown. "Romeo gave the ring to Giulietta, remember—?"

"Wise of him."

"All right—" He looked into my eyes, not happy about the path of our conversation. "So tell me, Giulietta from America . . . have *you* been faithful through the centuries?"

He was half joking, but it was no joke to me. Instead of answering, I met his stare with resolution and asked him straight out, "Why did you break into my hotel room?"

Although he was already braced for the worst, I could not have shocked him more. Groaning, he rolled over and clutched his face, not even trying to pretend there had been a mistake. "Porca vacca!"

"I'm assuming," I said, staying where I was, squinting at the sky, "you have a really good explanation. If I didn't, I wouldn't be here."

He groaned again. "I do. But I can't tell you."

"I'm sorry?" I sat up abruptly. "You trashed my room, but you won't tell me why?"

"What? No!" Alessandro sat up, too. "I didn't do that! It was already like that—I thought you had messed it up yourself!" Seeing my expression, he threw up his arms. "Look, it's true. That night, after we argued and you left the restaurant, I went over to your hotel to—I don't know. But when I arrived, I saw you climb down from your balcony and sneak off—"

"No way!" I exclaimed. "Why on earth would I do that?"

"Okay, so, it wasn't you," said Alessandro, very uncomfortable with the subject, "but it was a woman. Who looked like you. And she was the one who trashed your room. When I went in, your balcony door was already open, and the whole place was a mess. I hope you believe me."

I clutched my head. "How do you expect me to believe you when you won't even tell me why you did it?"

"I'm sorry." He reached out to pull a twig of thyme from my hair. "I wish I could. But it is not my story to tell. Hopefully, you will hear it soon."

"From whom? Or is that a secret, too?"

"I'm afraid so." He dared to smile. "But I hope you believe me when I say that I had good intentions."

I shook my head, upset with myself for being so easy. "I must be insane."

His smile broadened. "Is that English for *yes*?"

I got up, brushing off my skirt with brisk strokes, still a little angry. "I don't know why I let you get away with this—"

"Come here—" He took my hand and pulled me back down. "You know me. You know I could never hurt you."

"Wrong," I said, turning my head away. "You are Romeo. You are the one who can really, really hurt me."

But when he pulled me into his arms, I did not resist. It was as if a barrier inside me was collapsing—it had been collapsing all afternoon—leaving me soft and pliable, barely able to think beyond the moment.

"Do you really believe in curses?" I whispered, nested in his embrace.

"I believe in blessings," he replied, against my temple, "I believe that for every curse, there is a blessing."

"Do you know where the cencio is?"

I felt his arms tighten. "I wish I did. I want it back just as much as you do."

I looked up at him, trying to figure out if he was lying. "Why?"

"Because"—he met my suspicious stare with convincing calm—"wherever it is, it is meaningless without you."

WHEN WE FINALLY strolled back to the car, our shadows were stretched out before us on the path, and there was a touch of evening in the air. Just as I began wondering if perhaps we were running late for Eva Maria's party, Alessandro's phone rang, and he let me put the glasses and the empty bottle back in the trunk, while he wandered away from the car, trying to explain our mysterious delay to his godmother.

Looking around for a safe place to put the glasses, I noticed a wooden wine case in the far corner of the trunk with the label Castello Salimbeni printed on the side. When I lifted the lid to peek inside, I saw that there were no wine bottles in the box, just wood shavings, and I suspected this was how Alessandro had transported the glasses and the Prosecco. Just to make sure that I could safely stick the glasses back in the box, I dug my hand into the wood shavings and rummaged around a bit. As I did so, I felt something hard against my fingertips, and when I pulled it out, I saw that it was an old box, about the size of a cigar case.

As I stood there, holding the box, I was suddenly back in the Bottini with Janice the day before, watching Alessandro take a similar box out of a safe in the tufa wall. Unable to resist the temptation, I pulled the lid off the box with the trembling urgency of the trespasser; it never even occurred to me that I already knew its contents. Only when I ran my fingers over it—the golden signet ring cushioned in blue velvet—did the truth come crashing down from above, pulverizing all my romantic musings for a second or two.

Because of the shock of discovering that we were, in fact, driving around with an object that had—directly or indirectly—killed a heck of a lot of people, I had barely managed to stuff everything back in the wine case before Alessandro stood next to me, the phone closed in his hand.

"What are you looking for?" he asked, his eyes narrow.

"My skin lotion," I said lightly, unzipping my weekend bag. "The sun here is . . . murderous."

As we drove on, I had a hard time calming myself. Not only had he broken into my room and lied to me about his name, but even now, after everything that had happened between us—the kisses, the confessions, the disclosure of family secrets—he was still not telling me the truth. Sure, he had told me some of the truth, and I had chosen to believe him, but I was not fooled into thinking that he had told me everything there was to know. He had even admitted as much by refusing to explain why he had entered my hotel room. Yes, he might have put a few token cards on the table for me to see, but he was clearly still holding the major part of his hand close to his chest.

And so, I suppose, was I.

"Are you okay?" he asked after a while. "You are very quiet."

"I'm fine!" I wiped a drop of sweat from my nose and noticed that my hand was shaking. "Just hot."

He gave my knee a squeeze. "You will feel much better once we get there. Eva Maria has a swimming pool."

"Of course she does." I took a deep breath and exhaled slowly. My hand felt strangely numb, right where the old ring had touched my skin, and I discreetly wiped my fingers on my clothes. It was definitely not my style to give in to superstitious fears, and yet here they were, bouncing around in my belly like popcorn in a pot. Closing my eyes, I told myself that this was not the time for a panic attack, and that the tightness in my chest was nothing more than my brain trying to throw a monkey wrench into my happiness, the way it always did. But this time, I wouldn't let it.

"I think what you need . . ." Alessandro slowed down to turn into a gravel driveway. "Cazzo!"

A monumental iron gate barred the way. Judging from his reaction, this was not how Eva Maria usually greeted her godson, and it took a diplomatic exchange with an intercom before the magic cave opened and we could start up a long driveway flanked by spiral cypresses. As soon as we were safely inside the property, the tall doors of the gate swung back to close effortlessly behind us, the click of the lock barely audible through the softly crunching gravel and birdsong of late afternoon.

EVA MARIA SALIMBENI lived in something very near a dream. Her majestic farmhouse—or rather, castello—was perched on a hill not far from the village of Castiglione, and fields and vineyards fell around the property to all sides, like the skirt of a maid sitting in a meadow. It was the sort of place one would come across in an unwieldy coffee-table book, but never actually manage to pin down in reality, and, as we approached the house, I silently congratulated myself on my decision to ignore all warnings and come.

Ever since Janice had told me that cousin Peppo suspected Eva Maria of being a mobster queen, I had been swinging back and forth between lip-biting worry and head-shaking disbelief, but now that I was finally here, in broad daylight, the whole idea seemed ridiculous. Surely, if Eva Maria was really pulling the strings of something shady, she would never host a party at her house and invite a stranger like me.

Even the threat of the evil signet ring seemed to fade as Castello Salimbeni rose ahead, and by the time we pulled up beside the central fountain, whatever worries might still be kicking around the pit of my stomach were soon drowned out by the turquoise water that fell in cascades from three cornucopias held high by nude nymphs astride marble griffins.

A catering van was parked in front of a side entrance, and two men in leather aprons were unloading boxes while Eva Maria stood by, hands clasped, overseeing the procedure. As soon as she caught sight of our car, she rushed towards us, waving excitedly, gesturing for us to park and make it snappy. "Benvenuti!" she chirped, coming towards us with open arms. "I am so happy you are both here!"

As always, Eva Maria's exuberance left me too stumped to react in a normal way; all that went through my head was, *If I can wear those pants when I'm her age, I'll be beyond happy.*

She kissed me vigorously, as if she had feared for my safety until this very moment, then turned towards Alessandro—her smile turning coy as they exchanged kisses—and wrapped her fingers around his biceps. "You have been a bad boy, I think! I was expecting you hours ago!"

"I thought," he said, displaying no guilt whatsoever, "I would show Giulietta Rocca di Tentennano."

"Oh no!" exclaimed Eva Maria, all but slapping him. "Not that terrible place! Poor Giulietta!" She turned towards me with an expression of the utmost sympathy. "I am sorry you had to see that ugly building. What did you think of it?"

"Actually," I said, glancing at Alessandro, "I thought it was quite . . . idyllic."

For some inexplicable reason, my answer pleased Eva Maria so much that she kissed me on the forehead before marching into the house ahead of us both. "This way!" She flagged us through a back door, into the kitchen, and around a gigantic table piled with food. "I hope you don't mind, my dear, that we are going this way . . . Marcello! Dio Santo!" She threw up her hands at one of the caterers and said something that made him pick up the box he had just put down and place it very gently somewhere else. "I have to keep an eye on these people, they are hopeless! . . . Bless their hearts! And—oh! Sandro!"

"Pronto!"

"What are you doing?" Eva Maria shooed him impatiently. "Go get the bags! Giulietta will want her things!"

"But—" Alessandro was not too happy to leave me alone with his god-mother, and his helpless expression almost made me laugh.

"We can take care of ourselves!" Eva Maria went on. "We want to talk girl talk! Go! Get the bags!"

Despite the chaos and Eva Maria's energetic gait, I was able to appreciate the dramatic proportions of the kitchen on my way through. I had never seen pots and pans that big before, nor had I ever seen a fireplace with the square footage of my college dorm room; it was the kind of rustic country cuisine most people claim they dream about, but—when the rubber hit the road—would have no clue how to use.

From the kitchen we came out into a grand hall that was clearly the official entrance to Castello Salimbeni. It was a square, ostentatious space with a fifty-foot ceiling and a first-floor loggia going all the way around, not unlike, in fact, the Library of Congress in Washington where Aunt Rose had once taken me and Janice—for educational purposes and to avoid cooking—while Umberto was away on his annual vacation.

"This is where we will have our party tonight!" said Eva Maria, pausing briefly to make sure I was impressed.

"It is . . . breathtaking," was all I could think of saying, my words disappearing under the high ceiling.

The guest rooms were upstairs, off the loggia, and my hostess had very kindly put me in a room with a balcony overlooking a swimming pool, an orchard, and, beyond the orchard wall, Val d'Orcia bathed in gold. It looked like happy hour in Paradise.

"No apple trees?" I joked, leaning out from the balcony and admiring the old vines growing on the wall. "Or snakes?"

"In all my years," said Eva Maria, taking me seriously, "I have never seen a snake here. And I walk in the orchard every night. But if I saw one, I would crush it with a rock, like this." She showed me.

"Yup, he's toast," I said.

"But if you're afraid, Sandro is right in there—" She nodded at the French door next to mine. "Your rooms share this balcony." She elbowed me conspiratorially. "I thought I would make it easy for you two."

Somewhat stunned, I followed her back into my room. It was dominated by a colossal four-poster bed made up with white linen, and when she noticed my awe, Eva Maria wiggled her eyebrows exactly the way Janice would have done. "Nice bed, no? . . . Homeric!"

"You know," I said, my cheeks heating up, "I don't want you to get the wrong idea about me and . . . your godson."

She looked at me with something that looked an awful lot like disappointment. "No?"

"No. I'm not that kind of person." Seeing that I had failed to impress her with my chastity, I added, "I've only known him for a week. Or so."

Now at last, Eva Maria smiled and patted me on the cheek.

"You're a good girl. I like that. Come, now I will demonstrate to you the bathroom—"

When Eva Maria finally left me alone—after pointing out that there was a bikini my size in the bedside drawer and a kimono in the wardrobe—I collapsed, spread-eagled, on the bed. There was something wonderfully relaxing about her lavish hospitality; if I wanted to, I could

undoubtedly stay on for the rest of my life, living the picture-perfect sea-
sons of a Tuscany wall calendar, dressed to fit right in. But at the same
time, the whole scenario was mildly troubling. It seemed to me there was
something terribly important I had to grasp about Eva Maria—not the
Mafia thing, but something else—and it didn't help that the clues I
needed were somehow bobbing around aloft, like newborn balloons
trapped by a ceiling high, high over my head. Nor did it help my focus, I
had to admit, that I had consumed half a bottle of Prosecco on an empty
stomach, and that I, too, was bobbing around in seventh heaven from my
afternoon with Alessandro.

Just as I was drifting off, I heard a loud splash of water from somewhere outside and, seconds later, a voice calling me. After peeling my
limbs off the bed one by one, I staggered out onto the balcony to find
Alessandro waving at me from the swimming pool below, looking excep-
tionally frisky.

"What are you doing up there?" he yelled. "The water is perfect!"

"Why," I yelled back, "does it always have to be water with you?"

He looked perplexed, but it only added to his charms. "What's wrong
with water?"

ALESSANDRO BURST INTO laughter when I joined him by the swimming pool, wrapped in Eva Maria's kimono. "I thought you were hot," he
said, sitting on the edge with his feet in the water, enjoying the last bright
rays of sun.

"I was," I said, standing around awkwardly, playing with the kimono
belt, "but I'm feeling better. And, to be honest, I'm not a great swimmer."

"You don't have to swim," he pointed out. "The pool is not very deep.
And besides"—he gave me the eye—"I am here to protect you."

I looked around at everything but him. He was wearing one of those
skimpy European bathing suits, but that was the only skimpy thing about
him. Sitting there in the light of late afternoon, he looked as if he was made
of bronze; his body was practically glowing, and had clearly been
sculpted by someone intimately familiar with the ideal proportions of the
human physique.

"Come on!" he said, sliding back into the water as if it was his true element. "I promise, you'll love it."

"I'm not kidding," I said, staying where I was, "I'm not good with water."

Not quite believing me, Alessandro swam over to where I was standing, resting his arms on the edge of the pool. "What does that mean? Do you dissolve?"

"I tend to drown," I replied, perhaps more sharply than necessary, "and panic. In reverse order." Seeing his disbelief, I sighed and added, "When I was ten, my sister pushed me off a dock to impress her friends. I hit my head on a mooring line and nearly drowned. Even now, I can't be in deep water without panicking. So, there you have it. Giulietta is a wimp."

"This sister of yours—" Alessandro shook his head.

"Actually," I said, "she's okay. I tried to push her off the dock first."

He laughed. "So, you got what you deserved. Come on. You're too far away." He patted the gray slate. "Sit here."

Now at last, I reluctantly shed the kimono to reveal Eva Maria's minuscule bikini, and walked over to sit down next to him, my feet in the water. "Ow, the stone is hot!"

"Then come down here!" he urged me. "Put your arms around my neck. I'll hold you."

I shook my head. "No. Sorry."

"Yes, come on. We can't live like this, you up there, me down here." He reached out and grabbed me by the waist. "How am I going to teach our children to swim, when they see that you are afraid of the water?"

"Oh, you are priceless!" I sneered, putting my hands on his shoulders. "If I drown, I'm gonna sue you!"

"Yes, sue me," he said, lifting me off the edge and into the water. "Whatever you do, don't take responsibility for anything."

It was probably fortunate that I was too irritated by his remark to pay much attention to the water. Before I knew it, I was in up to my chest, my legs wrapped around his naked waist. And I felt fine.

"See?" He smiled triumphantly. "Not as bad as you think."

I glanced down at the water and saw my own distorted reflection. "Don't even think about letting go of me!"

He took a firm grip of Eva Maria's bikini bottoms. "I'm never letting go of you. You are stuck with me, in this pool, forever."

As my nerves about the water slowly subsided, I began to appreciate the feeling of his body against mine, and, judging by the look in his eyes among other things, the sentiment was mutual. " 'Though his face,' " I said, " 'be better than any man's, yet his leg excels all men's, and for a hand and a foot and a body, though they are not to be talked on, yet they are past compare. He is not the flower of courtesy, but I'll warrant him as gentle as a lamb.' "

Alessandro was clearly trying hard to ignore the engineering feat of my bikini top. "See, that is where Shakespeare is right about Romeo—for a change."

"Let me guess . . . you're not the flower of courtesy?"

He pulled me even closer. "But gentle as a lamb."

I put a hand on his chest. "More like a wolf in lamb's clothing."

"Wolves," he replied, lowering my body until our faces were only inches apart, "are very gentle animals."

When he kissed me, I didn't care who might be watching. It was what I had been longing for ever since Rocca di Tentennano, and I kissed him back without reserve. Only when I felt him testing the flexibility of Eva Maria's bikini did I gasp and say, "What happened to Columbus and exploring the coastline?"

"Columbus," Alessandro replied, pushing me up against the side of the pool and closing my mouth with another kiss, "never met you." He would have said more than that, and I would most likely have responded favorably, had we not been interrupted by a voice calling from a balcony.

"Sandro!" yelled Eva Maria, waving to get his attention, "I need you inside, now!"

Although she disappeared again right away, Eva Maria's sudden manifestation made us both jump with surprise, and, without thinking, I let go of Alessandro and nearly went under. Fortunately, he did not let go of me.

"Thanks!" I gasped, clinging to him. "It seems you don't have evil hands after all."

"See, I told you?" He brushed aside a few wisps of hair that were stuck to my face like wet spaghetti. "For every curse there is a blessing."

I looked into his eyes and was startled by his sudden seriousness. "Well, in my opinion"—I put a hand on his cheek—"curses only work if you believe in them."

...

WHEN I FINALLY RETURNED to my guest room, I sat down in the middle of the floor, laughing. It was such a Janice thing to do—making out in a swimming pool—and I couldn't wait to tell her about it. Although . . . it would not please her one bit to hear that I was exercising so little restraint when it came to Alessandro, and that I paid no attention to her warnings whatsoever. In a way it was very sweet to see her so jealous of him—if that was what was going on. She had never explicitly said so, but I could tell that she had been seriously disappointed that I didn't want to drive to Montepulciano with her, and go hunting for Mom's house together.

Only now, with a twinge of guilt stirring me from my giddy reverie, did I notice a smoky smell—of incense?—that might or might not have been in my room before. Stepping out on the balcony in my wet kimono for a mouthful of fresh air, I saw the sun disappearing behind distant mountains in a feast of gold and blood, and everywhere around me, the sky was turning into deeper shades of blue. With the daylight gone, there was a touch of dew in the air that brought with it a promise of all the smells, all the passions, and all the ghostly chills, of night.

Going back into my room and turning on a lamp, I saw that a dress had been laid out on the bed for me with a handwritten note saying, "Wear this for the party." I picked it up in disbelief; not only was Eva Maria once again dictating my apparel, but this time she had set me up to look ridiculous. It was a floor-length contraption in dark red velvet with a severe, angular neckline and flared sleeves; Janice would have called it the latest scream for the undead and tossed it aside with a scornful laughter. I was tempted to do the same.

But when I took out my own dress and compared the two, it occurred to me that, maybe, flitting downstairs in my itsy black novelty on this particular evening would turn out to be the biggest faux pas of my career. For all Eva Maria's plunging necklines and risqué comments it was entirely possible that the crowd she was hosting tonight was a bunch of prudes who would judge me by my spaghetti straps and find me wanting.

Once dressed—obediently—in Eva Maria's medieval outfit, and with my hair piled on top of my head in an attempt at a festive do, I stood for a moment at my door, listening to the sounds of guests arriving below. There was laughter and music, and in between the popping corks I could hear my hostess greeting not only darling friends and family, but darling clergy and nobility as well. Not sure I had enough backbone to dive into the fun on my own, I tiptoed down the corridor to knock discreetly on Alessandro's door. But he wasn't there. And just as I reached out to try the door handle, someone put a claw on my shoulder.

"Giulietta!" Eva Maria had a way of sneaking up on me that was deeply unsettling. "Are you ready to come downstairs?"

I gasped and spun around, embarrassed to have been caught where I was, almost trespassing into her godson's room. "I was looking for Alessandro!" I blurted out, shocked to see her standing right behind me, somehow taller than I remembered, wearing a golden tiara and—even for her—unusually dramatic makeup.

"He had to run an errand," she said, dismissively. "He will be back. Come—"

Walking back down the loggia with her, it was hard not to stare at Eva Maria's dress. If I had toyed with the idea that my own attire made me look like the heroine of a stage play, I now realized that, at best, I had a supporting role. Dressed in a vision of golden taffeta, Eva Maria shone more brightly than any sun, and as we sashayed down the broad staircase together—her hand clasped tightly above my elbow—the guests gathered below were helpless to ignore her.

At least a hundred people were standing around in the great hall, and they looked up in silent wonder as their hostess descended in all her splendor, graciously escorting me into their circle with the gestures of a flower fairy spreading rose petals before woodland royalty. Eva Maria had clearly planned this drama well in advance, for the whole place was lit exclusively by tall candles in chandeliers and candelabra, and the flickering flames made her dress come alive as if it, too, was on fire. For a while, all I could hear was music; not the classical favorites you would expect, but live music with medieval instruments coming from a small group of musicians at the far end of the hall.

Looking out over the silent crowd, I was relieved at having chosen the red velvet dress over my own. To suggest that Eva Maria's guests this evening were a bunch of prudes would have been a phenomenal understatement; it would be more accurate to say they looked as if they belonged in another world. At first glance, there was not a person in the room under seventy; at second glance, it was more like eighty. Someone charitable might have said that they were all dear old souls who only went to parties every twenty years or so, and that none of them had opened a fashion magazine since World War II . . . but I had lived too long with Janice for that kind of generosity. Had my sister been there with me and seen what I saw, she would have made a scary face and licked her fangs suggestively. The only upside was that if indeed they were all vampires, they looked so fragile that I could probably outrun them.

As we reached the bottom of the stairs, a whole swarm of them approached me, all talking to me in rapid Italian and poking me with bloodless fingers to make sure I was for real. Their amazement in seeing me suggested that—in their minds—it was I, and not they, who had risen from the grave for the occasion.

Seeing my confusion and discomfort, Eva Maria soon began shooing them off, and we were eventually left with the two women who actually had something to say to me.

"This is Monna Teresa," explained Eva Maria, "and Monna Chiara. Monna Teresa is a descendant of Giannozza Tolomei—just like you—and Monna Chiara is descended from Monna Mina of the Salimbeni. They are very excited that you are here, because for many years they thought you were dead. They are both knowledgeable about the past, and know much about the woman whose name you have inherited, Giulietta Tolomei."

I looked at the two old women. It seemed perfectly reasonable that they should know everything about my ancestors and the events of 1340, for they looked as if they had taken a horse-drawn carriage right out of the Middle Ages to attend Eva Maria's party. They both appeared to be held upright exclusively by corsets and the lace ruffs around their necks; one of them, though, kept smiling coyly behind a black fan, while the other looked at me with a bit more reserve, her hair done up in a way I had only ever seen in old paintings, with a peacock feather sticking out. Next to their antiquated forms Eva Maria seemed positively juvenile, and I was happy that she stayed right beside me, on tiptoes with excitement, to translate everything they said to me.

"Monna Teresa," she began, referring to the woman with the fan, "wants to know if you have a twin sister, Giannozza? For hundreds of years it has been tradition in the family to call twin girls Giulietta and Giannozza."

"As a matter of fact, I do," I said. "I wish she was here tonight. She"— I looked around at the candlelit hall and all the bizarre people, swallowing a smile—"would have loved it."

The old woman erupted in a wrinkly smile when she heard that there were two of us, and she made me promise that, next time I came to visit, I would bring along my sister.

"But if those names are a family tradition," I said, "then there must be hundreds—thousands—of Giulietta Tolomeis out there apart from me!"

"No-no-no!" exclaimed Eva Maria. "Remember that we are talking about a tradition in the female line, and that women take their husbands' names when they marry. To Monna Teresa's knowledge, in all these years, no one else was ever baptized Giulietta and Giannozza *Tolomei*. But your mother was stubborn—" Eva Maria shook her head with reluctant admiration. "She wanted desperately to get that name, so she married Professor Tolomei. And what do you know, she had twin girls!" She looked at Monna Teresa for confirmation. "As far as we know, you are the only Giulietta Tolomei in the world. That makes you very special."

They all looked at me expectantly, and I did my best to appear grateful and interested. Obviously, I was delighted to learn more about my family, and to meet distant relatives, but the timing could have been better. There are evenings when one is perfectly content talking to elderly ladies with lace ruffs, and evenings when one would rather be doing something else. On this particular occasion, in all honesty, I was longing to be alone with Alessandro—where on earth was he?—and although I had happily spent many wee hours absorbed in the tragic events of 1340, family lore was not what I felt most like exploring on this particular night.

But now it was Monna Chiara's turn to grab my arm and talk to me intently about the past. Her voice was as crisp and frail as tissue paper, and I leaned as close as I could to hear her and avoid the peacock feather.

"Monna Chiara invites you to come and visit her," translated Eva Maria, "so you can see her archive of family documents. Her ancestor, Monna Mina, was the first woman who tried to unravel the story of Giulietta, Romeo, and Friar Lorenzo. She was the one who found most of the old papers; she found the trial proceedings against Friar Lorenzo—with his confession—in a hidden archive in the old torture chamber in Palazzo Salimbeni, and she also found Giulietta's letters to Giannozza tucked away in many places. Some were under a floor in Palazzo Tolomei, others were hidden in Palazzo Salimbeni, and she even found one—the very last—at Rocca di Tentennano."

"I would love to see those letters," I said, meaning it. "I've seen some fragments, but—"

"When Monna Mina found them," Eva Maria interrupted me, urged on by Monna Chiara, whose eyes were aglow in the candlelight, yet strangely distant, "she traveled a long way to visit Giulietta's sister, Giannozza, and to give her the letters at last. This was around the year 1372, and Giannozza was now a grandmother—a happy grandmother—living with her second husband, Mariotto. But you can imagine what a shock it was for Giannozza to read what her sister had written to her so many years earlier, before she took her own life. Together those two women—Mina and Giannozza—talked about everything that had happened, and they swore that they would do everything in their power to keep the story alive for future generations."

Pausing, Eva Maria smiled and put a gentle arm around the two old women, squeezing them in appreciation, and they both giggled girlishly at her gesture.

"So," she said, looking at me meaningfully, "this is why we are gathered here tonight: to remember what happened, and make sure it never happens again. Monna Mina was the first one to do this, more than six hundred years ago. Every year on the anniversary of her wedding night, for as long as she lived, she would go down into the basement of Palazzo Salimbeni—into that dreadful room—and light candles for Friar Lorenzo. And when her daughters were old enough, she would bring them, too, so they could learn to respect the past and carry on the tradition after her. For many generations, this custom was kept alive by the women of both families. But now, to most people, all those events are very distant. And I'll tell you"—she winked at me, revealing a sliver of her usual self—"big modern banks don't like nightly processions with candles and old women in blue nightgowns walking around in their vaults. Just ask Sandro. So, nowadays we have our meetings here, at Castello Salimbeni, and we light our candles upstairs, not in the basement. We are civilized, you see, and not so young anymore. Therefore, carissima, we are happy to have you here with us tonight, on Mina's wedding night, and to welcome you to our circle."

I FIRST REALIZED something was wrong at the buffet table. Just as I was trying to pry a drumstick off a roasted duck that was sitting very elegantly in the middle of a silver platter, a wave of warm oblivion rolled onto the shore of my consciousness, gently rocking me. It was nothing dramatic, but the serving spoon fell right out of my hand, as if the muscles suddenly all went limp.

After a few deep breaths, I was able to look up and focus on my surroundings. Eva Maria's spectacular buffet had been set up on the terrace off the great hall, underneath the rising moon, and out here, tall torches defied the darkness with concentric semicircles of fire. Behind me, the house shone brilliantly with dozens of lit windows and external spotlights; it was a beacon that stubbornly held the night at bay, one last, refined bastion of Salimbeni pride, and if I was not mistaken, the laws of the world stopped at the gate.

Picking up the serving spoon once more, I tried to shake my sudden wooziness. I had only had one glass of wine—poured for me personally by Eva Maria, who wanted to know what I thought of her new-growth sangiovese—but I had tossed half of it into a potted plant because I did not want to insult her wine-making skills by not finishing my glass. That said, considering everything that had happened that day, it would be odd if I did not, at this point, feel mildly unhinged.

Only then did I see Alessandro. He had emerged from the dark garden to stand between the torches, looking straight at me, and although I was relieved and excited to have him back at last, I instantly knew something was wrong. It was not that he seemed angry; rather, his expression was one of concern, perhaps even condolence, as if he had come to knock on my door and inform me that there had been a terrible accident.

Filled with foreboding, I put down my plate and walked towards him. " 'In a minute,' " I said, attempting a smile, " 'there are many days. O by this count I shall be much in years ere I again behold my Romeo.' " I stopped right in front of him, trying to read his thoughts. But by now, his face was—as it had been the very first time I met him—completely void of emotion.

"Shakespeare, Shakespeare," he said, not appreciating my poetry, "why does he always come between us?"

I dared to reach out to him. "But he is our friend."

"Is he?" Alessandro took my hand and kissed it, then turned it over and kissed my wrist, his eyes never letting go of mine. "Is he really? Then tell me, what would our friend have us do now?" When he read the answer in my eyes, he nodded slowly. "And after that?"

It took me a moment to grasp what he meant. After love came separation, and after separation death . . . according to my friend, Mr. Shakespeare. But before I could remind Alessandro that we were in the process of writing our own happy end—were we not?—Eva Maria came flapping towards us like a magnificent golden swan, her dress ablaze in the torchlight.

"Sandro! Giulietta! Grazie a Dio!" She waved for us both to follow her. "Come! Come quickly!"

There was nothing else to do but obey, and we walked back to the house in Eva Maria's shimmering wake, neither of us bothering to ask her what could possibly be so urgent. Or perhaps Alessandro already knew where we were headed and why; judging by his glower we were once again at the mercy of the Bard, or fickle fortune, or whichever other power commandeered our destinies tonight.

Back in the great hall, Eva Maria led us straight through the crowd, out a side door, down a corridor, and into a smaller, formal dining room that was remarkarbly dark and quiet considering the party going on right around the corner. Only now, crossing the threshold, did she briefly pause and make a face at us—her eyes wide with agitation—to make sure we stayed right behind her and remained quiet.

At first glance, the room had seemed empty, but Eva Maria's theatrics made me look again. And now I saw them. Two candelabra with burning candles stood at either end of the long table, and in each of the twelve tall dining room chairs sat a man wearing the monochrome garb of the clergy. Off to a side, veiled in shadows, stood a younger man in a cowl, discreetly swinging a bowl of incense.

My pulse quickened when I saw these men, and I was suddenly reminded of Janice's warning from the day before. Eva Maria, she had said—bursting with sensational headlines after talking to cousin Peppo—was a mobster queen rumored to dabble in the occult, and out here, at her remote castle, a secret society supposedly met to perform gory blood rituals to conjure the spirits of the dead.

Even in my woozy state, I would have stepped right back out the door, had not Alessandro put a possessive arm around my waist.

"These men," whispered Eva Maria, her voice trembling slightly, "are members of the Lorenzo Brotherhood. They have come all the way from Viterbo to meet you."

"Me?" I looked at the stern dozen. "But why?"

"Shh!" She escorted me up to the head of the table with great circumstance, in order to introduce me to the elderly monk slumped in the thronelike chair at the table end. "He does not speak English, so I will translate." She curtsied before the monk, whose eyes were fixed on me, or, more accurately, on the crucifix hanging around my neck. "Giulietta, this is a very special moment. I would like you to meet Friar Lorenzo."

O blessed blessed night, I am afeard,
Being in night, all this is but a dream,
Too flattering sweet to be substantial

· · ·

"GIULIETTA TOLOMEI!" THE OLD MONK rose from the chair to frame my head with his hands and look deeply into my eyes. Only then did he touch the crucifix hanging around my neck, not with suspicion, but with reverence. When he had seen enough, he leaned forward to kiss my forehead with lips as dry as wood.

"Friar Lorenzo," explained Eva Maria, "is the leader of the Lorenzo Brotherhood. The leader always assumes the name of Lorenzo in remembrance of your ancestor's friend. It is a great honor that these men have agreed to be here tonight and give you something that belongs to you. For many hundreds of years, the men of the Lorenzo Brotherhood have been looking forward to this moment!"

When Eva Maria stopped talking, Friar Lorenzo gestured for the other monks to rise, too, and they all did so, without a word. One of them leaned forward to take a small box that had been sitting in the middle of the dining room table, and it was passed from hand to hand with great ceremony until it finally reached Friar Lorenzo.

As soon as I recognized the box as the one I had found in Alessandro's trunk earlier that day, I took a step back, but when she felt me moving, Eva Maria dug her fingers into my shoulder to make me stay where I was. And when Friar Lorenzo embarked upon a lengthy explanation in Italian, she translated every word he said with breathless urgency. "This is a treasure that has been guarded by the Virgin Mary for many centuries, and only you must wear it. For many years, it was buried under a floor with the original Friar Lorenzo, but when his body was moved from Palazzo Salimbeni in Siena to holy ground in Viterbo, the monks discovered it within his remains. They believe he must have kept it hidden somewhere on his body to keep it from falling into the wrong hands. Since then, it disappeared for many, many years, but finally it is here, and it can be blessed again."

Now, at last, Friar Lorenzo opened the box to reveal Romeo's signet ring that was nested inside in royal blue velvet, and we all—even I—leaned forward to look.

"Dio!" whispered Eva Maria, admiring the wonder. "This is Giulietta's wedding band. It is a miracle that Friar Lorenzo was able to save it."

I stole a glance at Alessandro, expecting him to look at least slightly guilty about driving around with the damned thing in the trunk all day and only telling me part of the story. But his expression was perfectly serene; either he felt no guilt at all, or he was frighteningly good at masking it. Meanwhile, Friar Lorenzo gave the ring an elaborate blessing before taking it out of the box with trembling fingers and handing it not to me, but to Alessandro. "Romeo Marescotti . . . per favore."

Alessandro hesitated before taking the ring, and when I looked up at his face I saw him exchanging a stare with Eva Maria, a dark, unsmiling stare that marked some symbolic point of no return between the two of them and went on to close around my heart like the grip of a butcher before the blow.

Just then—perhaps understandably—a second wave of oblivion blurred my vision, and I swayed briefly as the room took a turn about me and never came to a complete halt. Grabbing Alessandro's arm for support, I blinked a few times, struggling to recover; amazingly, neither he nor Eva Maria allowed my sudden discomposure to interrupt the moment.

"In the Middle Ages," said Alessandro, translating what Friar Lorenzo was telling him, "it was very simple. The groom would say, 'I give you this ring,' and that was it. That was the wedding." He took my hand and let the ring slide onto my finger. "No diamonds. Just the eagle."

It was fortunate for the two of them that I was too groggy to voice my opinion about having an evil ring from a dead man's coffin forced onto my finger without my consent. As it was, some foreign element—not wine, but something else—kept jiggling my consciousness, and all my rational faculties were by now buried under a mudslide of tipsy fatalism. And so I simply stood there, docile as a cow, while Friar Lorenzo sent up a prayer to the powers above and went on to demand yet another object from the table.

It was Romeo's dagger.

"This dagger is polluted," explained Alessandro, his voice low, "but Friar Lorenzo will take care of it and make sure it does not cause any more harm—"

Even in my haze I was able to think, *How nice of him! And how nice of you to ask before you gave this guy an heirloom that my parents left for me!* But I did not say it.

"Shh!" Eva Maria evidently did not care whether I understood what was going on. "Your right hands!"

Both Alessandro and I looked at her, puzzled, as she reached out and placed her own right hand on top of the dagger, which Friar Lorenzo was holding towards us. "Come!" she urged me. "Put your hand on top of mine."

And so I did. I put my hand on top of hers like a child playing a game, and after I had done that, Alessandro put his right hand on top of mine. To close the circle, Friar Lorenzo put his free hand on top of Alessandro's, while he mumbled a prayer that sounded like an invocation to the powers below.

"No more," whispered Alessandro, ignoring Eva Maria's warning glare, "will this dagger harm a Salimbeni, or a Tolomei, or a Marescotti. The circle of violence is ended. No more will we be able to hurt each other with any weapon. Now peace has finally come, and this dagger must be returned to where it came from, poured back into the veins of the earth."

When Friar Lorenzo had finished the prayer, he put the dagger very carefully into an oblong metal box with a lock. And only now, handing off the box to one of his brothers, did the old monk look up and smile at us, as if this was a completely normal social gathering, and we had not just taken part in a medieval wedding ritual and an act of exorcism.

"And now," said Eva Maria, no less exalted than he, "one last thing. A letter—" She waited until Friar Lorenzo had taken a small, yellowed roll of parchment out of a pocket in his cowl. If it was really a letter, it was very old and had never been opened, for it was still sealed with a red wax stamp. "This," Eva Maria explained, "is a letter which Giannozza sent to her sister Giulietta in 1340, while she was living in Palazzo Tolomei. But Friar Lorenzo never managed to give it to Giulietta, because of everything that happened at the Palio. The Lorenzo Brothers only found it recently, in the archives of the monastery where Friar Lorenzo took Romeo to recover after saving his life. It is now yours."

"Uh, thanks," I said, watching as Friar Lorenzo put the letter back in his pocket.

"And now—" Eva Maria snapped her fingers in the air, and within the blink of an eye a waiter had materialized right next to us carrying a tray with antique wine goblets. "Prego—" Eva Maria handed the largest vessel to Friar Lorenzo before serving the rest of us and raising her own goblet in a ceremonial toast. "Oh, and Giulietta . . . Friar Lorenzo says that when you have—when all this is over, you must come to Viterbo and give the crucifix back to its true owner. In return, he will give you Giannozza's letter."

"What crucifix?" I asked, only too aware that my words were slurred.

"That one—" She pointed at the crucifix hanging around my neck. "It belonged to Friar Lorenzo. He wants it back."

Despite the bouquet of dust and metal polish, I drank with a vengeance. There is nothing quite like the presence of ghostly monks in embroidered capes to make a girl need a drink. To say nothing of my recurring wooziness and Romeo's ring, which was now stuck—completely stuck—on my finger. But then, at least I had finally found something that actually belonged to me. As for the dagger—presently locked away in a metal box before its journey back to the crucible—it was probably time for me to acknowledge that it had, in fact, never been mine.

"And now," said Eva Maria, putting down her goblet, "it is time for our procession."

WHEN I WAS LITTLE, curled up on the bench in the kitchen and watching him work, Umberto had sometimes told me stories of religious processions in Italy in the Middle Ages. He had told me about priests carrying the relics of dead saints through the streets, and of torches, palm leaves, and sacred statues on poles. Occasionally he had ended a tale by saying, "and it is still going on, even now," but I had always interpreted that the way one interprets the "happily ever after" at the end of fairy tales: as wishful thinking, and nothing more.

I had certainly never imagined that I would one day take part in a procession of my own, especially not one that seemed to have been put on partly in my honor, and which took twelve austere monks and a small glass case with a relic through the whole house—including my bedroom—followed by the better part of Eva Maria's party guests, carrying tall candles.

As we moved slowly along the upstairs loggia, dutifully following the path of the incense and Friar Lorenzo's Latin chant, I looked around for Alessandro, but could not see him anywhere in the procession. Seeing my distraction, Eva Maria took me by the arm and whispered, "I know you are tired. Why don't you go to bed? This procession will go on for a long time. We will talk tomorrow, you and I, when all this is over."

I did not even try to protest. The truth was that I wanted nothing more than to crawl into my Homeric bed and curl up in a tight ball, even if it meant missing the rest of Eva Maria's strange party. And so, when we passed by my door next, I discreetly extricated myself from the group and stole inside.

My bed was still moist from Friar Lorenzo's holy-water sprinkles, but I didn't care. Without stopping to take off my shoes, I collapsed—facedown—on top of the bedspread, certain that I would be asleep within a minute. I could still taste Eva Maria's bitter sangiovese in my mouth, but didn't even have the energy to go out and brush my teeth.

As I lay there, however, waiting for oblivion, I felt my dizziness receding to a point where everything suddenly became perfectly clear again. The room stopped rotating around me, and I was able to focus on the ring on my finger, which I still could not get off, and which seemed to emanate an energy all its own. At first, the sensation had filled me with fear, but now—seeing that I was still alive and had not been harmed by its destructive powers—the fear gave way to tingling anticipation. Of what, I was not entirely sure, but I suddenly knew that I would not be able to relax until I had talked to Alessandro. Hopefully, he would be able to give me a calm interpretation of the evening's events; failing that, I would be quite content if he simply took me in his arms and let me hide there for a while.

Taking off my shoes, I slipped out onto our shared balcony in the hopes of catching a glimpse of him in his room. Surely, he had not yet gone to bed, and surely—despite everything that had happened this evening—he would be more than ready to continue where we had left off this afternoon.

As it turned out, he was standing right there on the balcony, fully dressed, hands on the railing, looking despondently into the night.

Even though he heard my French door open and knew I was there, he did not turn around, just sighed deeply and said, "You must think we're insane."

"Did you know about all this?" I asked. "That they would be here tonight . . . Friar Lorenzo and the monks?"

Now, finally, Alessandro turned to look at me with eyes that were darker than the star-spangled sky behind him. "If I had known, I wouldn't have brought you here." He paused, then said plainly, "I'm sorry."

"Don't be sorry," I said, hoping to soften his frown. "I'm having the time of my life. Who wouldn't? These people . . . Friar Lorenzo . . . Monna Chiara . . . chasing ghosts around—this is the stuff that dreams are made of."

Alessandro shook his head, but just once. "Not my dreams."

"And look!" I held up my hand. "I got my ring back."

He still did not smile. "But that is not what you were looking for. You came to Siena to find a treasure. Didn't you?"

"Maybe an end to Friar Lorenzo's curse is the most valuable thing I could possibly find," I countered. "I suspect gold and jewelry don't count for much at the bottom of a grave."

"So, is that what you want to do?" He studied my face, clearly wondering what I was trying to say. "End the curse?"

"Isn't that what we're doing tonight?" I stepped closer. "Undoing the evils of the past? Writing a happy end? Correct me if I am wrong, but we just got married . . . or something very like it."

"Oh, God!" He ran both hands through his hair. "I'm so sorry about that!"

Seeing his embarrassment, I couldn't help giggling. "Well, since this is supposed to be our wedding night, shame on you for not bursting into my room and slapping me around in a medieval manner! In fact, I'm going down to complain to Friar Lorenzo right now—" I made a move to go, but he caught my wrist and held me back.

"You're not going anywhere," he said, playing along at last. "Come here, woman—" And he pulled me into his arms and kissed me until I stopped laughing.

Only when I began unbuttoning his shirt did he speak again. "Do you," he asked, briefly stopping my hands, "believe in *forever*?"

I met his eyes, surprised at his sincerity. Holding up the eagle ring between us, I simply said, "Forever started a long time ago."

"If you want, I can take you back to Siena and . . . leave you alone. Right now."

"And then what?"

He buried his face in my hair. "No more chasing ghosts around."

"If you let go of me now," I whispered, stretching against him, "it could be another six hundred years before you find me again. Are you willing to take that risk?"

I WOKE UP when it was not yet day, to find myself alone in a nest of tousled sheets. From the garden outside came a persistent, haunting birdcall, and that was most likely what had pierced my dreams and stirred me from sleep. According to my watch it was three in the morning, and our candles were long since burnt out. By now, the only light in the room was the raw shine from a full moon coming through the French doors.

Perhaps I was being naïve, but it shocked me that Alessandro had left my bed like this, on our first night together. The way he had held me before we fell asleep had made me think he would never let go of me again.

Yet here I was, alone and wondering why, feeling parched and hungover from whatever it was that had hit me earlier. It did not help my confusion that Alessandro's clothes were—as were mine—still lying on the floor beside the bed. Switching on a lamp, I checked the bedside table and found that he had even left behind the leather string with the bullet, which I had personally pulled over his head a few hours ago.

Wrapping myself in one of the sheets from the bed, I winced when I saw the mess we had made of Eva Maria's vintage linen. And not only that, but entangled in the white sheets lay a bundle of frail, blue silk, which I had not even noticed until now. Strangely, as I began unfolding it, it took me a while to recognize it for what it was, probably because I had never expected to see it again. And most definitely not in my bed.

It was the cencio from 1340.

Judging by the fact that I had not noticed it until now, this invaluable artifact had been hidden among the sheets by someone who was determined to have me sleep on it. But who? And why?

Twenty years ago, my mother had gone to extremes to protect this cencio and pass it on to me; I in turn had found it, but quickly lost it, and yet here it was again, right beneath me, like a shadow I couldn't shake. Only the day before, at Rocca di Tentennano, I had asked Alessandro point-blank if he knew where the cencio was. His cryptic response had been that, wherever it was, it was meaningless without me. And now, suddenly, as I sat there holding it in my hands, everything fell into place.

According to Maestro Ambrogio's journal, Romeo Marescotti had vowed that, if he won the Palio of 1340, he would use the cencio as his wedding-sheet. But the evil Salimbeni had done everything in his power to prevent Romeo and Giulietta from ever spending a night together, and he had succeeded.

Until now.

So maybe this, I thought to myself, startled that I was able to make sense of it all at three in the morning, was why there had already been a smell of incense in my room when I came back from the swimming pool the day before; perhaps Friar Lorenzo and the monks had wanted to personally ensure that the cencio was where it belonged . . . in the bed they assumed I would be sharing with Alessandro.

Seen in a flattering light it was all very romantic. The Lorenzo Brotherhood clearly considered it their life mission to help the Tolomeis and the Salimbenis "undo" their sins of old, so that Friar Lorenzo's curse could finally be broken—hence the ceremony this evening to put Romeo's ring back on Giulietta's finger and to discharge the eagle dagger of all its evil. I could even be convinced to look favorably on the placing of the cencio in my bed; if Maestro Ambrogio's version of the story was really true, and Shakespeare's wrong, then Romeo and Giulietta had been waiting to consummate their marriage for a long, long time. Who could possibly object to a little ceremony?

But that was not the issue. The issue was that whoever had placed the cencio in my bed must have been in cahoots with the late Bruno Carrera, and thus—directly or indirectly—been responsible for the break-in at the Owl Museum, which had sent my poor cousin Peppo to the hospital. In other words, it was no mere romantic whim that saw me sitting here tonight with the cencio in my hands; something bigger and more sinister was clearly at stake.

Suddenly afraid that something bad had happened to Alessandro, I got out of bed at last. Rather than scrambling around for new clothes, I simply slipped back into the red velvet dress lying on the floor and went over to open the French doors. Stepping out onto the balcony, I filled my lungs with the soothing sanity of a cool night before stretching to look into Alessandro's room.

I didn't see him. However, all his lights were on, and it looked as if he had left in a hurry, without closing the door behind him.

It took me a second or two to gather courage to push open his balcony door and step inside. Although I now felt closer to him than to any other man I had ever met, there was still a little voice in my head saying that— physiognomy and sweet words aside—I did not know him at all.

I stood for a moment in the middle of the floor of his room, looking at the décor. This was clearly not just another guest room, but *his* room, and if things had been different, I would have loved to poke around and look at the photos on the walls, and all the little jars full of strange knickknacks.

Just as I was about to peek into the bathroom, I became aware of distant voices coming from somewhere beyond the half-open door to the interior loggia. Sticking my head through the doorway, however, I saw no one on the loggia or in the great hall below; the party had clearly wrapped up hours ago, and the whole house lay in darkness, except for the odd wall sconce flickering in a corner.

Stepping out into the loggia, I tried to determine where the voices were coming from, and concluded that the people I could hear were in another guest room a bit farther down the hallway. Despite the scattered disembodiment of the voices—to say nothing of my own state of mind—I was sure I heard Alessandro talking. Alessandro and someone else. The sound of his voice made me nervous and warm at the same time, and I knew I would not be able to go back to sleep unless I saw who it was that had managed to lure him from my side tonight.

The door to the room was ajar, and as I tiptoed closer, I carefully avoided stepping into the light spilling out onto the marble floor. Stretching to see inside the room, I was able to make out two men and even pick up fragments of their conversation, though I did not understand what they were saying. Alessandro was indeed there, sitting on top of a desk in nothing but a pair of jeans, looking remarkably tense compared to the last time I had seen him. But as soon as the other man turned to face him, I understood why.

It was Umberto.

O serpent heart, hid with a flowering face.
Did ever dragon keep so fair a cave?

...

ANICE HAD ALWAYS CLAIMED that you have to get your heart broken at least once in order to grow up and figure out who you really are. To me, this harsh doctrine had never been more than yet another excellent reason for not falling in love. Until now. As I stood there on the loggia that night, watching Alessandro and Umberto conspire against me, I finally knew precisely who I was. I was Shakespeare's fool.

For despite everything I had learned about Umberto over the past week, the first thing I felt when I saw him was joy. A ridiculous, bubbling, nonsensical joy that it took me a few moments to quell. Two weeks ago, after Aunt Rose's funeral, I had felt that he was the only person in the world left for me to love, and when I had taken off on my Italian adventure I had felt guilty about leaving him behind. Now, of course, everything was different, but that didn't mean—I now realized—that I had stopped loving him.

It was a shock to see him, but I knew right away that it ought not have been. As soon as Janice had sprung the news on me—that Umberto was, in fact, Luciano Salimbeni—I had known that, for all his dorky questions over the phone, pretending to misunderstand everything I told him about Mom's box, he had been several steps ahead of me all the time. And because I loved him and had kept defending him to Janice—insisting that she had somehow misunderstood the police, or that it was simply a case of mistaken identity—his betrayal of me was so much more excruciating.

No matter how I tried to explain his presence here, tonight, there could no longer be any doubt that Umberto was really Luciano Salimbeni. He had been the one siccing Bruno Carrera on me in order to get his hands on the cencio. And considering his track record—people had tended to die when Luciano was around—he had most likely been the one who had helped Bruno tie his shoelaces one last time.

The odd thing was that Umberto still looked precisely the way he always had. Even the expression on his face was exactly as I remembered it: a little arrogant, a little amused, and never betraying his innermost thoughts.

The one who had changed was me.

Now I could finally see that Janice had been right about him all these years; he was a psychopath waiting to snap. And as for Alessandro, sadly, she had been right about him, too. She had said that he didn't give a hoot about me, and that it was all just a big charade to get his hands on the treasure. Well, I should have listened to her. But that was all too late now. Here I was, stupid me, feeling as if someone had taken a sledgehammer to my future.

This, I thought to myself as I stood there looking at them through the door, *would be a natural time for me to cry.* But I couldn't. Too much had happened this night—I had no emotions left in store, save a lump in my throat that was part disbelief, part fear.

Meanwhile, inside the room, Alessandro got off the desk and said something to Umberto that involved the familiar concepts, *Friar Lorenzo, Giulietta,* and *cencio.* In response, Umberto reached into his pocket and took out a small, green vial, said something I couldn't understand, and gave it a vigorous shake before handing it to Alessandro.

Breathless and on tiptoes, all I could see was green glass and a cork stopper. What was it? Poison? Sleeping potion? And for what? Me? Did Umberto want Alessandro to kill me? Never had I needed Italian more than now.

Whatever was in the vial, it was a complete surprise to its recipient, and as he turned it over in his hand, his eyes became practically demonic. Handing it back to Umberto, he sneered something dismissive, and for the briefest of moments I dared to believe that, whatever Umberto's wicked plans, Alessandro would have nothing to do with them.

Umberto merely shrugged and put the vial gently down on a table. Then he held out his hand, clearly expecting something in return, and Alessandro frowned and handed him a book.

I recognized it right away. It was my mother's volume of *Romeo and Juliet*, which had disappeared from the box of papers the day before, while Janice and I were out spelunking in the Bottini . . . or maybe later, when we were swapping ghost stories in Maestro Lippi's workshop. No wonder Alessandro had kept calling the hotel over and over; he had obviously wanted to make sure I was out before he broke in and took it.

Without a word of thanks, Umberto started riffling through the book with self-congratulatory greed, while Alessandro stuck his hands in his pockets and walked over to look out the window.

Swallowing hard to keep my heart from popping right out of my throat, I looked at the man whose last words to me, spoken only a few hours ago, had been that he felt reborn and cleansed of all his sins. Here he was, already betraying me, not just with anyone, but with the only other man I had ever trusted.

Just as I decided that I had seen enough, Umberto slammed the book shut and threw it dismissively on the table next to the vial, sneering something I didn't need to know Italian to understand. Like Janice and me, Umberto had come to the frustrating conclusion that the book in itself did not contain any clues to the whereabouts of Romeo and Giulietta's grave, and that some other vital piece of evidence was clearly missing.

Without much of a warning, he came over to the door, and I barely had time to dart off into the shadows before Umberto stepped out onto the loggia, impatiently waving Alessandro along. Pressed against a recess in the wall, I saw them both walking off down the hallway and disappearing quietly down the stairs into the great hall.

Now, finally, I could feel the tears coming, but I held them in, deciding that I was more angry than sad. Fine. So Alessandro had been in it for the money, just as Janice had divined. That being the case, he could at least have had the decency to keep his hands to himself and not make things worse. As for Umberto, there were not enough words in Aunt Rose's big dictionary to describe my fury at his being here tonight and doing this to me. It was obviously he who had manipulated Alessandro, telling him to keep an eye—and two hands, and a mouth, and so forth—on me at all times.

My body executed the only logical game plan before my brain had even approved it. Rushing into the room they had just left, I picked up the book and the vial—the latter exclusively out of spite. Then I ran back to Alessandro's room and bundled up my loot in a shirt lying on his bed.

Looking around the room for other items that could be construed as relevant to my victimhood, it occurred to me that the most useful object I could possibly steal would be the keys to the Alfa Romeo. Ripping open the drawer in Alessandro's bedstand, however, all I found were a handful of foreign change, a rosary, and a pocketknife. Not even bothering to close the drawer, I scanned the room for other possible locations, trying to put myself in Alessandro's place. "Romeo, Romeo," I mumbled, peeking under this and that, "where dost thou keep thine car keys?"

When it finally occurred to me to look under the bed pillows, I was rewarded with the discovery of not only the car keys, but a handgun as well. Without allowing myself time for second thoughts, I grabbed both, and was astounded by the weight of the weapon. If I had not been so upset, I would have laughed at myself. Look at the pacifist now—gone were all my rosy dreams of a world with perfect equality and without guns. To me now, Alessandro's handgun was exactly the kind of equalizer I needed.

Back in my own room, I quickly tossed everything into my weekend bag. As I started to zip it up, my eyes fell on the ring on my finger. Yes, it was mine, and yes, it was solid gold, but it symbolized my spiritual—and now also physical—symbiosis with the man who had broken into my hotel room twice and stolen half of my treasure map in order to give it to the two-faced bastard who had very possibly murdered my parents. So I pulled and pulled until the ring finally came off, and left it on one of the bed pillows as one last, melodramatic goodbye to Alessandro.

Mostly as an afterthought, I grabbed the cencio from the bed and folded it gingerly before putting it into the bag with the rest of my stuff. It wasn't that I had any use for it whatsoever, nor did I think I could ever go out and sell it to anyone—especially in its current condition. No, I simply didn't want *them* to have it.

Whereupon I picked up my loot and slipped right back out the balcony door without waiting for applause.

THE OLD VINES GROWING on the wall were just strong enough to carry my weight as I began my descent from the balcony. I had dropped the bag first, aiming for a spongy bush, and after seeing that it had landed safely, I had embarked on my own laborious escape.

Inching along on the wall, my hands and arms throbbing, I passed closely by a window that was still illuminated despite the late hour. Stretching to make sure there was no one in the room who might wonder about the scratching sounds, I was astounded to see Friar Lorenzo and three of his fellow monks sitting very quietly, hands folded, in four armchairs facing a fireplace full of fresh flowers. Two of the monks were clearly nodding off, but Friar Lorenzo looked as if nothing and no one could compel him to close his eyes until this night was over.

At one point while I was hanging there, panting and desperate, I heard agitated voices coming from my room above, and the sound of someone stepping angrily out onto my balcony. Holding my breath, I hung as still as I possibly could, until I was sure the person had gone back inside. The prolonged strain, however, was too much for the vine. Just as I dared to move again, it snapped and started peeling off the wall, sending me into a headlong plunge to the greenery below.

Fortunately, the drop was no more than ten feet or so. Less fortunate was my landing in a bed of roses. But I was too frantic to feel any real pain as I extracted myself from the thorny branches and picked up my bag; the scratches on my arms and legs were nothing compared to the pangs of defeat I couldn't block out as I limped away from the best of nights and the worst of nights all at once.

Picking my way through the dewy darkness of the garden I eventually emerged from a clingy shrubbery into the dimly lit circle of the driveway. Standing there, clutching the bag against my chest, I now realized that there was no way I could get the Alfa Romeo out; it was trapped behind several black limos which could only belong to the Lorenzo Brotherhood. However little I liked the idea, it was beginning to look as if I would be walking all the way back to Siena.

While I stood there, smarting from my bad luck, I suddenly heard dogs barking madly somewhere behind me. Unzipping the bag, I quickly took out the gun—just in case—and began running down the gravel driveway, sending up gasping prayers to whatever guardian angel was on duty in the area that night. If I was lucky, I could make it out to the main road before they caught up with me, and hitch a ride with a passing car. Surely, if the driver thought my romantic dress-up was meant as an invitation, the gun would quickly set him straight.

The tall gate at the end of Castello Salimbeni's driveway was, of course, closed, and I did not waste my time pressing the buttons to the intercom. Sticking my arm through the iron bars, I put down the gun carefully in the gravel on the other side, before throwing my bag over the gate. Only when it came down with a thud on the other side did it occur to me that the impact might have crushed the vial inside. But that should hardly be a concern; trapped between barking dogs and a tall gate, I was lucky if the vial was all that ended up in pieces tonight.

Then, finally, I grabbed the iron bars and began climbing. Not even halfway to the top, however, I heard running feet in the gravel behind me, and frantically tried to speed up my progress. But the metal was cold and slippery, and before I could pull myself up and out of reach, a hand closed firmly around my ankle. "Giulietta! Wait!" It was Alessandro.

I glared down at him, nearly blinded by fear and fury. "Let me go!" I cried, trying as hard as I could to kick his hand away. "You bastard! I hope you burn in hell! You and your bloody godmother!"

"Come down!" Alessandro was not open for negotiation. "Before you hurt yourself!"

I finally managed to get my foot free, and to hoist myself out of reach. "Yeah right! You asshole! I'd rather break my neck than play your sick games anymore!"

"Come down, now!" He climbed up behind me, this time to grab hold of my skirt. "And let me explain! Please!"

I groaned with frustration. I was frantic to get away, and what more could he possibly tell me now? But with him stubbornly holding on to the fabric of my dress, there was nothing I could do but hang there, fuming with desperation, while my arms and hands slowly started giving way.

"Giulietta. Please listen. I can explain everything—"

I suppose we were so focused on each other that neither of us noticed a third person emerging from the darkness on the other side of the gate, until she spoke. "Okay, Romeo, get your hands off my sister!"

"Janice!" I was so surprised to see her that I very nearly lost my grip.

"Just keep climbing!" Janice knelt down to pick up the gun in the gravel. "And you, mister, let's see your flippers!"

She pointed the gun at Alessandro through the gate, and he let go of me right away. Janice had always been pretty forceful regardless of her accessories; with a gun in her hand she was the very embodiment of "No means no."

"Careful!" Alessandro jumped off the gate and backed up a few steps, "That gun is loaded . . ."

"Of course it's loaded!" snapped Janice. "Put your paws up, lover-boy!"

". . . and it has a very light trigger pull."

"Oh yeah? Well, so do I! But you know what? That's your problem! You're on the smoking end!"

Meanwhile, I was able to painfully work my way over the top of the gate, and as soon as I could, I let myself drop to the ground next to Janice with a howl of pain.

"Jesus, Jules! Are you okay? Here, take this—" Janice handed me the gun. "I'm gonna get our ride—no, you idiot! Point it at *him*!"

We stood there for only a few seconds, but it felt like time had stopped. Alessandro looked at me glumly through the gate while I did my best to point the gun at him, tears of confusion fogging my scope.

"Give me the book," was all he said. "It's what they want. They won't let you go until they have it. Trust me. Please don't—"

"Come on!" cried Janice, pulling up next to me on her motorcycle, gravel flying. "Get the bag and hop on!" Seeing my hesitation, she revved the engine impatiently. "Get your ass in gear, Miss Juliet, the party's over!"

Moments later, we zoomed into the darkness on the Ducati Monster, and when I turned around to look one last time, Alessandro just stood there, leaning on the gate, like a man who has missed the most important flight of his life because of a silly miscalculation.

Death lies on her like an untimely frost
Upon the sweetest flower of all the field

...

WE DROVE FOR AN ETERNITY along dark country roads, up hills and down hills, through valleys and sleeping villages. Janice never stopped to tell me where we were headed, and I didn't care. It was enough that we were moving, and that I wouldn't have to make any decisions for a while.

When we finally pulled into a bumpy driveway at the edge of a village, I was so tired I felt like curling up in the nearest flower bed and sleeping for a month. With nothing but the headlamp of the bike to guide us, we wound our way through a wilderness of shrubs and tall weeds before finally pulling up in front of a completely dark house.

Killing the engine, Janice took off her helmet, shook out her hair, and looked at me over her shoulder. "This is Mom's house. Actually, now it's ours." She pulled a small flashlight out of her pocket. "There's no power, so I got this." Walking ahead of me up to a side door, she unlocked it and held it open for me. "Welcome home."

A narrow hallway took us directly into a room that could only be a kitchen. Even in the darkness, the dirt and dust were tangible, and the air smelled musty, like wet clothes festering in a hamper. "I say we camp out here tonight," Janice went on, lighting a few candles. "There's no water, and everything is kinda dirty, but the upstairs is even worse. And the front door is totally stuck."

"How on earth," I said, briefly forgetting how tired and cold I was, "did you find this place?"

"It wasn't easy." Janice unzipped another pocket and took out a folded-up map. "After you and what's-his-face took off yesterday, I went and bought this. Of course, try to find a street address in this country—" When I didn't take the map to see for myself, she pointed the torch right at my face and shook her head. "Look at you, you're a mess. And you know what? I knew this would happen! And I told you so! But you wouldn't listen! It's always like this—"

"Excuse me!" I glared at her, in no mood for her gloating. "You knew what, exactly, O crystal ball? That some esoteric cult would . . . drug me and—?"

Instead of shouting back at me as she was undoubtedly dying to do, Janice merely tapped my nose with the map and said, seriously, "I knew the Italian Stallion was bad news. And I told you so. Jules, I said, this guy—"

I pushed the map away and covered my face with my hands. "Please! I don't want to talk about it. Right now." When she kept pointing the flashlight at me, I reached out and pushed that away, too. "Stop it! I have a splitting headache!"

"Oh dear," said Janice, in the sarcastic voice I knew so well. "Disaster narrowly avoided tonight in Tuscany . . . American virgitarian saved by sister . . . but suffers severe headache."

"Yeah, go ahead," I muttered, "just laugh at me. I deserve it."

Expecting her to carry on, I was puzzled when she didn't. Uncovering my face at last I found her staring at me, quizzically. Then her mouth fell open, and her eyes turned perfectly circular. "No! You *slept* with him, didn't you?"

When there was no rebuttal, just tears, she sighed deeply and put her arms around me. "Well, you did say you would rather be screwed by him than by me." She kissed me on the hair. "I hope it was worth it."

CAMPING OUT ON moth-eaten coats and cushions on the kitchen floor, way too wound up to sleep, we lay for hours in the dwindling darkness, dissecting my escapade at Castello Salimbeni. Although Janice's comments were peppered with the odd, knee-jerk buffoonery, we ended up agreeing on most things, except the issue of whether or not I should have—as Janice phrased it—made whoopee with the eagle boy.

"Well, that's your opinion," I had finally said, turning my back to her in an attempt at closing the subject, "but even if I had known everything I know now, I would still have done it."

Janice's only response had been a sour "Hallelujah! I'm glad you got *something* for our money."

A little while later, still lying there with our backs turned to each other in stubborn silence, she suddenly sighed and muttered, "I miss Aunt Rose."

Not really sure what she meant—these kinds of exclamations were completely unlike her—I very nearly made some snarky remark about her missing Aunt Rose because Aunt Rose would have agreed with her, and not with me, on the issue of me being a sap for accepting Eva Maria's invitation. But instead, I heard myself simply saying, "Me, too."

And that was it. Minutes later, her breathing slowed, and I knew she was asleep. As for me, alone with my thoughts at last, I wished more than ever that I could conk out just like her and fly away in a hazelnut shell, leaving behind my heavy heart.

THE NEXT MORNING—or rather, well past noon—we shared a bottle of water and a granola bar outside in the sun, sitting on the crumbly front step of the house, occasionally pinching each other to make sure we weren't dreaming. Janice had had a hard time finding the house in the first place, she told me, and had it not been for friendly locals pointing her in the right direction, she might never have noticed the sleeping beauty of a building hiding in the wilderness that was once a driveway and front yard.

"I had a heck of a time just opening the gate," she told me. "It was rusted shut. To say nothing of the door. I can't believe that a house can sit like this, completely empty, for twenty years, without anybody moving in or taking over the property."

"It's Italy," I said, shrugging. "Twenty years is nothing. Age is not an issue here. How can it be, when you're surrounded by immortal spirits? We're just lucky they let us hang around for a while, pretending we belong here."

Janice snorted. "I bet immortality sucks. That's why they like to play with juicy little mortals"—she grinned and ran her tongue suggestively along her upper lip—"like you."

Seeing that I still couldn't laugh, her smile became more sympathetic, almost genuine. "Look at you, you got away! Imagine what would have happened if they had caught you. They would have—I don't know—" Even Janice had a hard time imagining the horror I would have been put through. "Just be happy your ol' sis found you in time."

Seeing her hopeful expression, I threw my arms around her and gave her a squeeze. "I am! Trust me. I just don't understand—why did you come? It's a hell of a drive to Castello Salimbeni from here. Why didn't you just let me—"

Janice looked at me with raised eyebrows. "Are you kidding me? Those rat-bastards stole our book! It's payback time! If you hadn't come running out the driveway the way you did, ass on fire, I would have broken in and searched the whole goddamn castello."

"Well, it's your lucky day!" I got up and went into the kitchen to grab my overnight bag. "Voilà!" I threw the bag at Janice's feet. "Don't say I wasn't working for the team."

"You're kidding!" She unzipped the bag eagerly, and started rifling through it. But after only a few seconds she recoiled in disgust. "Eew! What the hell is this?"

We both stared at her hands. They were smeared in blood or something very like it. "Jesus, Jules!" gasped Janice. "Did you murder someone? Eek! What *is* this?" She smelled her hands with great apprehension. "It's blood, all right. Please don't tell me it's yours, because if it is, I'm gonna go back right now and turn that guy into a piece of modern art!"

For some reason, her belligerent grimace made me laugh, maybe because I was still so unused to her standing up for me like this.

"There we go!" she said, forgetting her anger as soon as she saw me smiling at last. "You had me scared there for a while. Don't ever do that again."

Together, we took my bag and turned it upside down. Out tumbled my clothes, as well as the volume of *Romeo and Juliet,* which had—fortunately—not suffered too much damage. The mysterious green vial, however, had been completely crushed, probably when I threw the bag over the gate during my escape.

"What is this?" Janice picked up a piece of the shattered glass and turned it over in her hand.

"That's the vial," I said, "that I told you about; the one Umberto gave to Alessandro, and which really pissed him off."

"Huh." Janice wiped her hands on the grass. "Well, at least now we know what was in it. Blood. Go figure. Maybe you were right and they were really all vampires. Maybe this was some kind of mid-morning snack—"

We sat for a moment, pondering the possibilities. At one point I gathered up the cencio and looked at it with regret. "Such a shame. How do you get blood off old silk?"

Janice picked up a corner, and we held out the cencio between us, looking at the damage. Admittedly, the vial was not the sole culprit, but I knew better than to tell her that.

"Holy Mary, Mother of God!" said Janice suddenly. "That's the whole point: You don't get the blood out. This is exactly what they wanted the cencio to look like. Don't you see?"

She stared at me eagerly, but I must have looked blank. "It's just like the old days," she explained, "when the women would inspect the bridal sheet on the morning after the wedding! And I'll bet you a kangaroo"— she picked up a couple pieces of the broken vial, including the cork stopper—"this is—or *was*—what we in the matchmaking community refer to as an *insta-virgin*. Not just blood, but blood mixed with other stuff. It's a science, believe me."

Seeing my expression, Janice burst out laughing. "Oh yes, it's still going on. You don't believe me? You think people only looked at sheets in the Middle Ages? Wrong! Lest we forget, some cultures still live in the Middle Ages. Think about it: If you're going back to The-Middle-of-Nowherestan to be married off to some goatherd cousin, but—oops— you've already been fooling around with Tom, Harry, and Dick . . . what do you do? Chances are, your goatherd groom plus in-laws are not gonna be happy that someone else ate the cheese. Solution: You can get fixed in a private clinic. Get everything reinstalled and go through the whole goddamn thing once more, just to please the audience. *Or* you can simply bring a sneaky little bottle of *this* to the party. Much cheaper."

"That," I protested, "is so far out—"

"You know what I think?" Janice went on, eyes gleaming. "I think they set you up big-time. I think they drugged you—or at least tried to—

and were hoping you would be totally out after tripping the light fantastic with Friar Lorenzo and the dream team, *so that* they could go ahead and fish out the cencio and smear it with this stuff, making it look like good old Romeo had been driving the love-bus into cherry-town."

I winced, but Janice didn't seem to notice. "The irony is, of course," she continued, too absorbed in her own lewd logic to notice my extreme discomfort with the subject and her choice of words, "that they could have saved themselves the whole friggin' trouble. 'Cause you two went ahead and stuffed the cannelloni anyway. Just like Romeo and Juliet. Shazam! From the ballroom to the balcony to the bed in fifty pages. Tell me, were you trying to break their record?"

She looked at me enthusiastically, clearly hoping for a pat on the head and a cookie for being such a clever girl.

"Is it humanly possible," I moaned, "to be any more crass than you?"

Janice grinned as if this was the highest praise possible. "Probably not. If it's poetry you want, crawl back to your bird man."

I leaned back against the door frame and closed my eyes. Every time Janice referred to Alessandro, even in her unspeakably vulgar way, I had little flashbacks to the night before—some painful, some not—and they kept distracting me from present reality. But if I asked her to stop, she would most certainly do the exact opposite.

"What I don't understand," I said, determined to have us both move on and catch up with the big picture, "is why they had the vial in the first place. I mean, if they really wanted to end the curse on the Tolomeis and the Salimbenis, then presumably the last thing they would do would be to *fake* Romeo and Giulietta's wedding night. Did they actually think they could fool the Virgin Mary?"

Janice pursed her lips. "You're right. It doesn't make sense."

"As far as I can see," I went on, "the only one who got fooled—apart from me—was Friar Lorenzo. Or rather, he *would* have been fooled, *if* they had used the stuff in the vial."

"But why the hell would they want to dupe Friar Lorenzo?" Janice threw up her hands. "He's just an old relic. Unless"—she looked at me, eyebrows raised—"Friar Lorenzo has access to something that they don't. Something important. Something they want. Such as—?"

I snapped upright. "Romeo and Giulietta's grave?"

We stared at each other. "I think," said Janice, nodding slowly, "that's the connection right there. When we talked about it that night at Maestro Lippi's, I thought you were crazy. But maybe you're right. Maybe part of the whole undo-your-sins thing involves the actual grave and the actual statue. How about this . . . after making sure Romeo and Giulietta *finally* get together, the Tolomeis and the Salimbenis have to go to the grave and kneel before the statue?"

"But the curse said *kneel before the Virgin.*"

"So?" Janice shrugged. "Obviously the statue is somewhere close to a statue of the Virgin Mary—the problem is that *they* don't know the exact location. Only Friar Lorenzo does. And that's why they need him."

We sat for a while in silence, running through the math.

"You know," I eventually said, fondling the cencio, "I don't think he knew."

"Who?"

I glanced at her, heat rising in my cheeks. "You know . . . *him.*"

"Oh, come on, Jules!" moaned Janice. "Stop defending the creep. You saw him with Umberto, and"—she tried to soften the edge in her voice, but this was new to her, and she wasn't very good at it—"he *did* chase you out the driveway and tell you to give him the book. Of course he knew."

"But if you are right," I said, feeling an absurd urge to push back and defend Alessandro, "about all this, then he would have followed the plan and not—you know."

"Engaged in physical relations?" Janice suggested primly.

"Exactly," I nodded. "Plus, he would not have been so surprised when Umberto gave him the vial. In fact, he would already have *had* the vial."

"Honey!" Janice looked at me over the rim of imaginary glasses, "he broke into your hotel room, he lied to you, and he stole Mom's book and gave it to Umberto. The guy is scum. And I don't care if he has all the balls and whistles and knows how to use them, he's still—excuse my French— a shyster. And as for your oh-so-friendly mobster queen—"

"Speaking of lying to me and breaking into my hotel room," I said, staring right back at her, "why did you tell me he had trashed my hotel room when it was you all along?"

Janice gasped. *"What?"*

"Are you going to deny it?" I went on. "That you broke into my room and blamed Alessandro?"

"Hey!" she cried. "He broke in, too, okay! I am your sister! I have a right to know what's going on—" She stopped herself and looked sheepish. "How did you know?"

"Because he saw you. He thought you were me, crawling down from my own balcony."

"He thought—?" Janice gaped in disbelief. "*Now* I'm insulted! Honestly!"

"Janice," I sighed, frustrated with her for sliding right back into her old sassiness, pulling me along. "You lied to me. Why? After everything that has happened, I would totally understand if you had broken into my room. You thought I was scamming you out of a fortune."

"Really?" Janice looked at me with budding hope.

I shrugged. "Why don't we try honesty for a change?"

Swift recoveries were my sister's specialty. "Excellent," she smirked, "honesty it is. And now, if you don't mind"—she wiggled her eyebrows— "I have a few more questions about last night."

AFTER GETTING SOME provisions from the village store, we spent the rest of the afternoon poking around in the house trying to recognize our childhood things. But it didn't help that everything was covered in dust and mold, that every piece of textile had holes from some kind of animal, and that there was mouse shit in every possible—and impossible— crevice. Upstairs, the cobwebs were as thick as shower curtains, and when we opened the second-floor shutters to let in some light, more than half of them fell right off their hinges.

"Whoops!" said Janice when a shutter came crashing down on the front step, two feet from the Ducati. "I guess it's time to date a carpenter."

"How about a plumber?" I proposed, peeling spiderwebs from my hair. "Or an electrician?"

"You date the electrician," she shot back. "You need some wiring done."

The high point came when we discovered the wobbly chess table, hidden in a corner behind a mangy sofa.

"I told you, didn't I?" Janice beamed, rocking it gently, just to make sure. "It was right here all along."

By sunset, we had made so much progress mucking out that we decided to move our camp upstairs to what had once been an office. Sitting across from each other at an old writing desk, we had a candlelit dinner consisting of bread, cheese, and red wine, while we tried to figure out what to do next. Neither of us had any desire to return to Siena just yet, but at the same time, we both knew that our current situation was not sustainable. In order to get the house back in some kind of livable shape, we would need to invest a lot of time and money in red tape and handymen, and even if we succeeded, how would we live? We would be like fugitives, digging ourselves further and further into debt, and we would always be wondering when our past would catch up with us.

"The way I see it," said Janice, pouring more wine, "we either stay here—which we can't—or we go back to the States—which would be pathetic—or we go treasure hunting and see what happens."

"I think you're forgetting that the book in itself is useless," I pointed out. "We need Mom's sketchbook to figure out the secret code."

"Which is precisely," said Janice, reaching into her handbag, "why I brought it. Ta-daa!" She put the sketchbook on the desk in front of me. "Any further questions?"

I laughed out loud. "You know, I think I love you."

Janice worked hard not to smile. "Easy now. We don't want you to pull something."

Once we had the two books side by side, it did not take us long to crack the code, which was, in fact, not even really a code, merely a cunningly hidden list of page, line, and word numbers. While Janice read out the numbers scribbled in the margins of the sketchbook, I leafed through the volume of *Romeo and Juliet* and read out the bits and pieces of the message our mother had wanted us to find. It went like this:

MY LOVE

THIS PRECIOUS BOOK

LOCKS IN THE GOLDEN STORY

    OF

THE DEAREST

STONE

AS FAR AS THE VAST SHORE WASH'D WITH THE FARTHEST SEA

    I SHOULD ADVENTURE FOR SUCH MERCHANDISE

GO WITH

ROMEO'S

GHOSTLY CONFESSOR

SACRIFIC'D SOME HOUR BEFORE HIS TIME

SEARCH, SEEK

WITH INSTRUMENTS

FIT TO OPEN THESE DEAD MEN'S TOMBS

IT NEEDS MUST BE BY STEALTH

HERE LIES JULIET

LIKE A POOR PRISONER

MANY HUNDRED YEARS

UNDER

QUEEN

MARIA

WHERE

LITTLE STARS

MAKE THE FACE OF HEAVEN SO FINE

GET THEE HENCE TO

SAINT

MARIA

LADDER

AMONG A SISTERHOOD OF HOLY NUNS

A HOUSE WHERE THE INFECTIOUS PESTILENCE DID REIGN
    SEAL'D UP THE DOORS

MISTRESS

SAINT

GOOSE

VISITING THE SICK

CHAMBER

BED

THIS HOLY SHRINE

IS

THE STONY ENTRANCE

TO THE

ANCIENT VAULT

O LET US HENCE

GET ME AN IRON CROW
    AWAY WITH THE
    CROSS
    AND FOOT IT GIRLS!

When we had come to the end of the long message, we sat back and looked at each other in bewilderment, our initial enthusiasm on hold.

"Okay, so I have two questions," said Janice. "One: Why the hell didn't we do this before? And two: What was Mom smoking?" She glared at me and reached out for her wineglass. "Sure, I get that she hid her secret code in 'this precious book,' and that it is somehow a treasure map to find Juliet's grave and 'the dearest stone,' but . . . where are we supposed to go digging? What's up with the pestilence and the crowbar?"

"I have a feeling," I said, leafing back and forth to reread a few passages, "that she is talking about the Siena Cathedral. 'Queen Maria' . . . that can only mean the Virgin Mary. And the bit about the little stars making the face of heaven so fine sounds to me like the inside of the cathedral dome. It is painted blue with little golden stars on it." I looked up at her, suddenly excited. "Suppose that's where the grave is? Remember, Maestro Lippi said that Salimbeni buried Romeo and Giulietta in a 'most holy place'; what could be more holy than a cathedral?"

"Makes sense to me," agreed Janice, "but what about the whole pestilence thing and the 'sisterhood of holy nuns'? That doesn't sound like it has anything to do with the cathedral."

" 'Saint Maria, ladder'—" I mumbled, riffling through the book once more, " 'a house where the infectious pestilence did reign . . . seal'd up the doors . . . mistress saint . . . goose . . . visiting the sick' . . . and blah-blah-blah." I let the book fall shut and leaned back on the chair, trying to remember the story Alessandro had told me about Comandante Marescotti and the Plague. "Okay, I know it sounds crazy, but"—I hesitated and looked at Janice, whose eyes were wide and full of faith in my riddle-solving skills—"during the bubonic plague, which was only a few years after Romeo and Giulietta died, they had so many corpses lying around that they couldn't bury them all. So, in Santa Maria della Scala—I think *scala* means ladder—the enormous hospital facing the cathedral, where 'a sisterhood of holy nuns' took care of the sick during the 'infectious pestilence' . . . well, they simply stuffed the dead into a wall and sealed it off."

Janice made a face. "Eek."

"So," I went on, "it seems to me that we're looking for a 'chamber' with a 'bed' inside that hospital, Santa Maria della Scala—"

". . . in which slept the 'mistress' of the 'saint' of geese," proposed Janice. "Whoever he is."

"Or," I said, "the 'mistress saint' of Siena, born in the contrada of the 'goose,' Saint Catherine—"

Janice whistled. "Go, girl!"

". . . who, incidentally, had a bedroom in Santa Maria della Scala, where she slept when she worked late hours 'visiting the sick.' Don't you remember? It was in the story Maestro Lippi read to us. I'll bet you a sapphire and an emerald that this is where we'll find the 'stony entrance to the ancient vault.' "

"Whoa, wait!" said Janice. "Now I'm confused. First, it's the cathedral, then it's Saint Catherine's room at the hospital, but now it's an 'ancient vault'? Which is it?"

I pondered the question for a moment, trying to recall the voice of the sensationalist British tour guide I had overheard in the Siena Cathedral a few days earlier. "Apparently," I finally said, "in the Middle Ages there used to be a crypt underneath the cathedral. But it disappeared during the time of the Plague, and they've never been able to find it since. Of course, it's hard for the archaeologists to do anything around here, since all the buildings are protected. Anyway, some people think it's just a legend—"

"I don't!" said Janice, jumping at the idea. "This has to be it. Romeo and Giulietta are buried in the crypt underneath the cathedral. It makes sense. If you were Salimbeni, isn't that exactly where you would have put the shrine? And since the whole place—I assume—is consecrated to the Virgin Mary . . . Voilà!"

"Voilà what?"

Janice held out her arms as if she was going to bless me. "If you kneel in the cathedral crypt, you 'kneel before the Virgin,' just like the curse says! Don't you see? It has to be the place!"

"But if that's the case," I said, "we'll need to do a lot of digging to get there. People have been looking everywhere for this crypt."

"Not," said Janice, pushing the book towards me again, "if Mom has found a secret entrance from that old hospital, Santa Maria della Scala. Read it again, I'm sure I'm right."

We went through the message once more, and this time, the whole thing suddenly made sense. Yes, we were definitely talking about an 'ancient vault' underneath the cathedral, and yes, the 'stony entrance' was to be found in Saint Catherine's room at Santa Maria della Scala, right across the piazza from the church.

"Holy crap!" Janice sat back, overwhelmed. "If it's this easy, then why didn't Mom go tomb raiding herself?"

Just then, one of our candle stumps extinguished itself with a small puff, and although we still had other candles left, the shadows of the room suddenly seemed to close in on us from all sides.

"She knew she was in danger," I replied, my voice oddly hollow in the darkness, "and that's why she did what she did, and put the code in the book, the book in the box, and the box in the bank."

"So," said Janice, trying to hit a bushy-tailed note, "now that we've solved the riddle, what's preventing us from—"

"Breaking into a protected building and wrecking Saint Catherine's cell with a crowbar?" I made a face. "Gee, I don't know!"

"Seriously. It's what Mom would want us to do. Isn't it?"

"It's not that simple." I poked at the book, trying to remember the exact words in the message. "Mom tells us to 'go with Romeo's ghostly confessor . . . sacrificed before his time.' Who is that? That's Friar Lorenzo. Obviously not the real one, but maybe his new . . . incarnation. And I bet that means we were right: The old guy knows something about the location of the crypt and the grave—something crucial, which even Mom couldn't figure out."

"So, what are you suggesting?" Janice wanted to know. "That we kidnap Friar Lorenzo and interrogate him under a hundred-watt bulb? Look, maybe you got it wrong. Let's do this one more time, separately, and see if we get the same result—" She began opening the drawers in the desk one by one. "Come on! There's gotta be some pens kicking around here somewhere! . . . Wait! Hang on!" She stuck her whole head into the bottom drawer, struggling to liberate something that was trapped in the woodwork. When she finally got it loose, she sat up triumphantly, her hair tumbling over her face. "Will you look at that! A letter!"

But it was not a letter. It was a blank envelope full of photographs.

...

BY THE TIME we had finished looking at Mom's photographs, Janice declared that we needed at least one more bottle of vino to get through the night without going totally insane. While she went downstairs to get it, I turned to the photos again, putting them out on the desk side by side, my hands still shaking from the shock, hoping I could somehow make them tell a different story.

But there could only be one interpretation of Mom's exploits in Italy; no matter how we sliced it, the main characters and the conclusion remained the same: Diane Lloyd had gone to Italy, had started working for Professor Tolomei, had met a young playboy in a yellow Ferrari, had become pregnant, had married Professor Tolomei, had given birth to twin girls, had survived a house fire that had killed her elderly husband, and had proceeded to hook up once again with the young playboy, who, in every single photo, looked so happy with the twins—that is, with *us*—that we both agreed he must be our real father.

That playboy was Umberto.

"This is so unreal!" wheezed Janice, returning with bottle and corkscrew. "All these years. Pretending to be a butler and never saying a word. It's too friggin' weird."

"Although," I said, picking up one of the photos of him with us, "he always *was* our dad. Even if we didn't call him that. He was always—" But I couldn't go on.

Only now did I look up and see that Janice was crying, too, although she was wiping away her tears angrily, not wanting Umberto to have that satisfaction. "What a scumbag!" she said. "Forcing us to live his lie all these years. And now suddenly—" She broke off with a grunt, as the wine cork broke in half.

"Well," I said, "at least it explains why he knew about the golden statue. He obviously got all that from Mom. And if they really were . . . you know, *together,* he must have known about the box of papers in the bank as well. Which explains why he would write a fake letter to me from Aunt Rose, telling me to go to Siena and speak to Presidente Maconi in Palazzo Tolomei in the first place. He obviously got that name from Mom."

"But all this time!" Janice spilled some wine on the table as she hurriedly filled up our glasses, and a few drops fell on the photos. "Why didn't he do it years ago? Why didn't he explain all this to Aunt Rose while she was still alive—?"

"Yeah right!" I quickly wiped the wine from the photos. "Of course he couldn't tell her the truth. She would have called the police right away." Pretending to be Umberto, I said in a deep voice, "By the way, Rosie-doll, my real name is Luciano Salimbeni—yes, the man who killed Diane and who is wanted by the Italian authorities. If you had ever bothered to visit Diane in Italy—bless her heart—you'd have met me a hundred times."

"But what a life!" Janice interjected. "Look at this—" She pointed at the photos of Umberto and the Ferrari, parked on some scenic spot overlooking a Tuscan valley and smiling into the camera with the eyes of a lover. "He had it all. And then . . . he becomes a *servant* in Aunt Rose's house."

"Mind you," I said, "he was a fugitive. Aless—someone told me he was one of the most wanted criminals in Italy. Lucky for him he wasn't in jail. Or dead. At least, working for Aunt Rose, he could watch us growing up in some kind of freedom."

"I still don't believe it!" Janice shook her head dismissively. "Yes, Mom is pregnant in her wedding photo, but that happens to a lot of women. And it doesn't necessarily mean that the groom is not the father."

"Jan!" I pushed a few of the wedding photos towards her. "Professor Tolomei was old enough to be her grandfather. Put yourself in Mom's shoes for a second." Seeing that she was determined to disagree with me, I grabbed her by the arm and pulled her closer. "Come on, it's the only explanation. Look at him—" I picked up one of many photos of Umberto lying on a blanket in the grass with Janice and me crawling all over him. "He loves us." As soon as I said the words, I felt a lump in my throat and had to swallow to keep down the tears. "Crap!" I whimpered, "I don't think I can take much more of this."

We sat for a moment in unhappy silence. Then Janice put down her wineglass and picked up a group photo taken in front of Castello Salimbeni. "So," she said, at last, "does this mean your mobster queen is our . . . grandmother?" The photo showed Eva Maria juggling a large hat and two small dogs on a leash, Mom looking efficient with white slacks and a clipboard, Professor Tolomei frowning and saying something to the photographer, and a young Umberto off to a side, leaning against his Ferrari, arms crossed. "Whatever the hell it means," she went on, before I could answer, "I hope I'll never meet him again."

We probably should have seen it coming, but didn't. Too busy unraveling the knot that our lives had become, we had forgotten to pay attention to things that go bump in the night, or even to sit back and use our common sense for a moment.

Not until a voice spoke to us from the door to the office did we realize how moronic we had been, seeking refuge in Mom's house.

"What a nice little family reunion," said Umberto, stepping into the room ahead of two other men I'd never seen before. "Sorry to keep you waiting."

"Umberto!" I exclaimed, jumping from the chair. "What on earth—"

"Julie! No!" Janice grabbed my arm and pulled me back down, her face contorted with fear.

Only now did I see it. Umberto's hands were tied in the back, and one of the men was holding a gun to his head.

"My friend Cocco here," said Umberto, able to maintain his cool despite the muzzle burrowing into his neck, "would like to know if you ladies are going to be of use to him, or not."

Her body sleeps in Capel's monument,
And her immortal part with angels lives

...

WHEN I HAD LEFT SIENA with Alessandro the day before, I had not imagined I would be returning so soon, so dirty, and with my hands cuffed. And I had certainly not anticipated being accompanied by my sister, my father, and three thugs who looked as if they had been sprung from death row, not by paperwork, but by dynamite.

It was clear that, even though he knew them by name, Umberto was as much a hostage to these men as we were. They tossed him into the back of their van—a small flower delivery truck, most likely stolen—just as they did Janice and me, and we all fell hard on the metal floor. With our arms tied, there was little but a potpourri of rotting flower cuttings to block the fall.

"Hey!" protested Janice, "we're your daughters, right? Tell them they can't treat us like this. Honestly—Jules, say something to him."

But I couldn't think of anything to say. I felt as if the whole world had turned upside down around me—or maybe the world was right side up, and I was the one who had completely keeled over. Still struggling to process Umberto's transformation from hero to villain, I now had to accept the fact that he was my father as well, which almost took me full circle and back to square one: I loved him, but I really shouldn't.

Just as the villains pulled the doors closed behind us, I caught a glimpse of another victim they had already picked up somewhere en route. The man was propped up in a corner, gagged and blindfolded; had it not been for his clothes, I would never have recognized him. Now at last, the words came to me spontaneously. "Friar Lorenzo!" I cried. "My God! They've kidnapped *Friar Lorenzo!*"

Just then, the van jolted into action, and we spent the next few minutes sliding back and forth on the ridged floor, while the driver took us through the wilderness of Mom's driveway.

As soon as things were smoother, Janice let out a deep, unhappy sigh. "Okay," she said, loudly, into the darkness, "you win. The gems are yours . . . or, *theirs.* We don't want them anyway. And we'll help you. We'll do anything. Anything they want. You're our dad, right? We gotta stick together! There's no need to . . . kill us. Is there?"

Her question was met by silence.

"Look," Janice went on, her voice shaky with fear, "I hope they know they'll never find that statue without us—"

Umberto still didn't answer. He didn't have to. Even though we had already told the bandits about the supposed secret entrance in Santa Maria della Scala, they clearly thought they might still need us to help them find the gems, or they surely wouldn't have brought us along for the ride.

"What about Friar Lorenzo?" I asked.

Now at last, Umberto spoke. "What about him?"

"Come on," said Janice, recovering some of her spirit, "do you really think the poor guy is going to be of any help whatsoever?"

"Oh, he'll sing."

When Umberto heard us both gasp at his indifference, he made a sound that could have been laughter, but probably wasn't. "What the hell did you expect?" he grunted. "That they'd just . . . give up? You're lucky we tried it the nice way first—"

"The *nice* way—?" cried Janice, but I managed to poke her with my knee and shut her up.

"Unfortunately," Umberto went on, "our little Julie didn't play her role."

"It might have helped if I knew I *had* a role!" I pointed out, my throat so tight I could barely get the words out. "Why didn't you tell me? Why did it have to be like this? We could have gone treasure hunting years ago, together. It could have been . . . fun."

"Oh, I see!" Umberto shifted around in the darkness, clearly as uncomfortable as we were. "You think this is what I want? Come back here, risk everything, play charades with old monks and get kicked around by these assholes, all to search for a couple rocks that probably disappeared hundreds of years ago? I don't think you realize—" He sighed. "Of course you don't. Why do you think I let Aunt Rose take you away and bring you up in the States? Huh? I'll tell you why. Because *they* would have used you against me . . . to make me work for them again. There was only one solution: We had to disappear."

"Are you talking about . . . the Mafia?" asked Janice.

Umberto laughed scornfully. "The Mafia! These people make the Mafia look like the Salvation Army. They recruited me when I needed money, and once you're on the hook, you don't get off. If you wiggle, the hook just goes deeper."

I heard Janice take in air for a bitchy comment, but somehow managed to elbow her in the darkness and silence her yet again. Provoking Umberto and starting an argument was not the way to prepare for whatever lay ahead, I was sure of that much.

"So, let me guess," I said, as calmly as I could, "the moment they don't need us anymore . . . it's over?"

Umberto hesitated. "Cocco owes me a favor. I spared his life once. I'm hoping he'll return the favor."

"So," said Janice, "he'll spare you. What about us?"

There was a long silence, or at least, it felt long. Only now, mixed in with the engine noise and general rattle, did I pick up the sound of someone praying. "And what," I quickly added, "about Friar Lorenzo?"

"Let's just hope," replied Umberto at last, "that Cocco is feeling generous."

"I don't get it," grumbled Janice. "Who are these guys anyway, and why are you letting them do this to us?"

"That," said Umberto wearily, "is not exactly a bedtime story."

"Well, this is not exactly a bedside," Janice pointed out. "So, why don't you tell us, dear father, what the hell went wrong in fairyland?"

Once he started talking, Umberto could not stop. It was as if he had been waiting to tell us his story all these years, and yet, now that he finally did, he clearly did not feel much relief, for his voice kept getting more and more bitter as he spoke.

His father, he told us, who had been known as Count Salimbeni, had always lamented the fact that his wife, Eva Maria, only ever bore him one child, and had set out to make sure the boy was never spoiled and always disciplined. Enrolled in a military academy against his will, Umberto had eventually run away to Naples to find a job and maybe go to university and study music, but he had quickly run out of money. So, he had started doing jobs that other people were afraid to do, and he was good at it. Somehow, breaking the law came naturally to him, and it was not long before he owned ten tailored suits, a Ferrari, and a patrician apartment with no furniture. It was paradise.

When he finally went back to visit his parents at Castello Salimbeni, he pretended that he had become a stockbroker, and managed to persuade his father to forgive him for dropping out of the military academy. A few days later his parents hosted a big party, and among the guests were Professor Tolomei and his young American assistant, Diane.

Stealing her right off the dance floor, Umberto took Diane for a drive under the full moon, and that was the beginning of a long, beautiful summer. Soon, they were spending every weekend together, driving around Tuscany, and when he finally invited her to visit him in Naples, she said yes. There, over a bottle of wine in the best restaurant in town, he dared to tell her the truth about what he did for a living.

Diane was horrified. She did not want to listen to his explanations, or his apologies, and as soon as she was back in Siena she returned everything he had given her—jewelry, clothes, letters—and told him she never wanted to hear from him again.

After that, he did not see her for over a year, and when he did, he had a shock. Diane was walking across the Campo in Siena, pushing a stroller with twins, and someone told him she was now married to old Professor Tolomei. Umberto knew right away that he was the father of the twins, and when he walked up to Diane, she went pale and said, yes, he was their father, but she did not want her girls to be raised by a criminal.

Now Umberto did something horrible. He remembered that Diane had told him about Professor Tolomei's research and a statue with gemstone eyes, and, because he was sick with jealousy, Umberto told the story to some people back in Naples. It was not long before his boss heard about it, too, and pressured him to look up Professor Tolomei and find out more, and so he did, with two other men. They waited until Diane and the twins were away from home before knocking on the door. The professor was very polite and invited them inside, but he soon turned hostile when he discovered why they had come.

Seeing that the professor was unwilling to speak, Umberto's two partners began putting pressure on the old man, and he ended up having a heart attack and dying. Umberto, of course, was terrified about this, and tried to revive the professor, but it was all in vain. He now told the others he would meet them back in Naples, and as soon as they had left, he set fire to the house, hoping to burn all the professor's research together with the body and put an end to the story of the golden statue.

After this tragedy, Umberto decided to break with his evil past, and to move back to Tuscany, living on the money he had made. Some months after the fire he looked up Diane and told her that he was now an honest man. At first, she didn't believe him, and accused him of having had a hand in the suspicious fire that killed her husband. But Umberto was determined to win her over, and she eventually came around, even though she never fully believed in his innocence.

They lived together for two years, almost like a family, and Umberto even took Diane back to visit Castello Salimbeni. Of course, he never told his parents the truth about the twins, and his father was furious with him for not getting married and having children of his own. For who would inherit Castello Salimbeni, if Umberto did not have children?

It would have been a happy time, had not Diane become increasingly obsessed with what she called "the curse on both our houses." She had told him about it when they first met, but he had not taken it seriously at the time. Now he had to finally accept the fact that this beautiful woman— the mother of his children—was by nature a very nervous and compulsive person, and that the pressure of motherhood only made it worse. Instead of children's books, she would read Shakespeare's *Romeo and Juliet* to the little girls, over and over, until Umberto would come and gently take the book away. But no matter where he hid it, she would always find it again.

And when the twins were asleep, she would spend hours in solitude, trying to re-create Professor Tolomei's research into family treasures and the location of Romeo and Giulietta's grave. She was not interested in the gems; all she wanted was to save her daughters. She was convinced that, because the little girls had a Tolomei mother and a Salimbeni father, they would be doubly vulnerable to Friar Lorenzo's curse.

Umberto did not even realize how close Diane was to figuring out the location of the grave when, one day, some of his old buddies from Naples showed up at the house and started asking questions. Knowing that these men were pure evil, Umberto told Diane to take the twins out back and hide, while he did his best to explain to the men that neither he nor she knew anything.

But when Diane heard them beating him up, she came back with a gun and told them to leave her family alone. Seeing that they did not listen, she tried to shoot them, but she was not used to the gun, and she missed. Instead, they shot and killed her. After that, the men told Umberto it was just the beginning; if he did not give them the four gemstones, they would come for his daughters next.

At this point in the story, Janice and I both burst out, simultaneously, "So, you didn't kill Mom?"

"Of course not!" Umberto snapped. "How could you think that?"

"Maybe," said Janice, all choked up, "because you've lied about everything else until now."

Umberto sighed deeply and shifted around again, unable to find comfort. Frustrated and tired, he resumed his story and told us that, after the men had killed Diane and left the house, he was heartbroken and didn't know what to do. The last thing he wanted was to call the police, or the priest, and risk some bureaucrats taking the girls away. So, he took Diane's body and drove it to a deserted place, where he could push the car from a cliff to make it look as if she had died in a car accident. He even put some of the girls' things in the car to make people think they had died, too. Then he took the girls and left them with their godparents, Peppo and Pia Tolomei, but drove away before they could ask him any questions.

"Wait!" exclaimed Janice. "What about the bullet wound? Wouldn't the police notice that she was dead before the car crash?"

Umberto hesitated, then said reluctantly, "I torched the car. I didn't think they would dig into it that much. Why would they? They get their paycheck anyway. But some smart-ass journalist started asking questions, and before I knew it they had me framed for all of it—the professor, the fire, your mother . . . even you two, for God's sake."

That same night, Umberto went on to tell us, he had called Aunt Rose in the States and pretended to be a police officer from Siena. He told her that her niece had died, and that the little girls were left with family, and he also told her they were not safe in Italy, and that she had better come and get them right away. After the phone call, he drove down to Naples and paid a visit to the men who had killed Diane, and to most of the other people who knew about the treasure. He did not even try to hide his identity. He wanted it to be a warning. The only one he didn't kill was Cocco. He couldn't bring himself to kill a boy of nineteen.

After that, he disappeared for many months, while the police were looking for him everywhere. In the end, he went to the States to find the girls and see that they were well. He did not have any specific plans; once he found out where they lived, he just hung around waiting for something to happen. A few days later he saw a woman walking about in the garden, trimming roses. Assuming it was Aunt Rose, he approached her and asked if she needed someone to help her with yard work. That was how it started. Six months later Umberto moved in full-time, agreeing to work for little more than house and board.

"I don't believe it!" I burst out. "Did she never wonder how you just . . . happened to be in the neighborhood?"

"She was lonely," Umberto muttered, clearly not proud of himself. "Too young to be a widow, but too old to be a mother. She was ready to believe anything."

"And what about Eva Maria? Did she know where you were?"

"I stayed in touch with her, but I never said where I was over the phone. And I never told her about you two."

Umberto went on to explain that he had been afraid that if Eva Maria found out she had two granddaughters, she would insist they all move back to Italy again. He knew very well that *he* could never go back; people would recognize him, and the police would undoubtedly be on to him right away, despite his false name and passport. And even if she didn't insist, he knew his mother well enough to fear that she would somehow contrive a way to see the girls, thereby compromising their safety. Failing that, Eva Maria would most certainly spend the rest of her life pining for the granddaughters she had never met, eventually die of a broken heart, and undoubtedly blame Umberto. So, for all those excellent reasons, he never told her.

As time went by, however, Umberto began to believe his evil past in Naples was buried for good. But that ended abruptly when, one day, he noticed a limousine coming up Aunt Rose's driveway and stopping in front of the door. There were four men in the car, and he immediately recognized Cocco among them. He never found out how they had located him after all those years, but suspected they had bribed people in the intelligence community to trace Eva Maria's phone calls.

The men told Umberto he still owed them something, and that he had to repay them, or they would track down his daughters and do unspeakable things to them. Umberto told them he had no money, but they just laughed at him and reminded him of the statue with the four gemstones that he had promised them a long time ago. When he tried to explain that it was impossible, and that he couldn't go back to Italy, they just shrugged and said that it was too bad, because now they had to go looking for his daughters. So, in the end, Umberto agreed to try and find the gems, and they gave him three weeks to do it.

Before they left, they wanted to make sure he knew they were serious, and so they took him into the hall and started beating him up. While they were doing that, they knocked over the Venetian vase standing on the table beneath the chandelier, and it fell to the floor and smashed into pieces. The noise woke Aunt Rose from her nap, and she came out of her bedroom and—when she saw what was going on—started screaming from the top of the staircase. One of the men pulled out a gun and was going to shoot her, but Umberto managed to push the gun aside. Unfortunately, Aunt Rose was so frightened she lost her balance and fell halfway down the staircase. When the men had left and Umberto was finally able to get to her, she was already dead.

"Poor Aunt Rose!" I exclaimed. "You told me she died peacefully, in her sleep."

"Well, I lied," said Umberto, his voice thick. "The truth is, she died because of me. Would you have liked me to say that?"

"I would have liked," I replied, "for you to tell us the truth. If you had only done that years ago"—I paused to take a deep breath, my throat still tight with emotion—"perhaps we could have avoided all this."

"Maybe. But that's too late now. I didn't want you to know—I wanted you to be happy . . . to live the way normal people do."

Umberto went on to tell us that on the night after Aunt Rose died, he had called Eva Maria in Italy and told her everything. He even told her she had two granddaughters. He also asked her if there was any chance she could help him pay off the thugs. But she told him she could not liquidate that much money in three weeks. At first, she wanted to involve the police and her godson, Alessandro, but Umberto knew better. There was only one way out of this squeeze: Do as the assholes said and find the bloody rocks.

In the end, Eva Maria agreed to help him, and promised that she would try to trick the Lorenzo Brotherhood in Viterbo into helping her. Her only condition was that, when it was all over, she could finally get to know her granddaughters, and that they would never know about their father's crimes. With this, Umberto agreed. He had never wanted the girls to know about his evil past, and for that reason he did not even want them to know who he really was. He was sure that if they learned he was their father, they would discover everything else, too.

"But that's ridiculous!" I protested. "If you had told us the truth, we would have understood."

"Would you?" said Umberto. "I'm not so sure."

"Well," Janice cut in, "we'll never know now, will we?"

Ignoring her comment, Umberto told us that, on the very next day, Eva Maria had gone to Viterbo to talk to Friar Lorenzo, and through this conversation she had found out what was needed in order for the monks to help her find Romeo and Giulietta's grave. Friar Lorenzo had told her she must host a ceremony to "undo the sins" of the Salimbenis and the Tolomeis, and had promised that, once she had done this, he would take her and the other penitents to the grave, to kneel before the mercy of the Virgin.

The only problem was that Friar Lorenzo was not entirely sure how to find the place. He knew there was a secret entrance somewhere in Siena, and he knew where to go from there, but he didn't know where exactly that entrance was located. Once, he told Eva Maria, a young woman by the name of Diane Tolomei had visited him and told him she had figured out where the entrance was, but she wouldn't tell him, because she was afraid the wrong people might find the statue and ruin it.

She had also told him she had found the cencio from 1340, and that she was going to do an experiment. She wanted to have her little girl, Giulietta, lie down on it together with a boy named Romeo, and she very much hoped this would somehow help undo the sins of the past. Friar Lorenzo was not so sure it would really work, but he was ready to give it a try. They agreed that Diane should come back a few weeks later, so they could set out to find the grave together. But sadly, she never came.

When Eva Maria told Umberto all this, he began to hope their plan could really work. For he knew Diane had kept a box of important documents in the bank in Palazzo Tolomei, and he was sure that among the papers would be a clue to the secret entrance to the grave.

"Believe me," said Umberto, perhaps feeling my bad vibes, "the last thing I wanted was to involve you in all this. But with only two weeks left—"

"And so you set me up," I concluded, feeling a whole new kind of anger towards him, "and let me think this was all Aunt Rose's doing."

"What about me?" Janice chimed in. "He let me think I'd inherited a fortune!"

"Tough shit!" Umberto shot back. "Be happy you're still alive!"

"I suppose I wasn't any good in your little scheme," Janice went on, in her most cranky voice. "Jules was always the brainy one."

"Oh, would you stop it!" I cried. "*I* am Giulietta, and *I* am the one who was in danger—"

"Enough!" barked Umberto. "Trust me, I would have liked nothing more than to keep you both out of this. But there was no other way. So, I had an old pal keep an eye on Julie to make sure she was safe—"

"You mean Bruno?" I gasped. "I thought he was trying to kill me!"

"He was there to protect you," Umberto contradicted me. "Unfortunately, he thought he could make a quick buck on the side." He sighed. "Bruno was a mistake."

"So you had him . . . silenced?" I wanted to know.

"No need. Bruno knew too much about too many. People like that don't last long in the clink." Not at all comfortable with the issue, Umberto went on to conclude that, on the whole, everything had gone according to plan once Eva Maria had been convinced I was really her granddaughter and not just some actress he had hired for the job, to lure her into helping him. She was so suspicious she even had Alessandro break into my hotel room to get a DNA sample. But once she had the proof she wanted, she immediately set about planning the party.

Remembering everything Friar Lorenzo had told her, Eva Maria asked Alessandro to bring Romeo's dagger and Giulietta's ring to Castello Salimbeni, but she didn't tell him why. She knew that if he had the smallest inkling of what was going on, he would ruin everything by bringing in the Carabinieri. In fact, Eva Maria would have liked nothing more than to keep her godson out of her plans entirely, but since he was, in fact, Romeo Marescotti, she needed him to—unwittingly—play his part in front of Friar Lorenzo.

In hindsight, admitted Umberto, it would have been better if Eva Maria had let me in on her plans, or at least part of them. But that was only because things went wrong. If I had done what I was supposed to do— drink her wine, go to bed, and fall asleep—everything would have been so smooth.

"Wait!" I said. "Are you saying she drugged me?"

Umberto hesitated. "Just a little bit. For your own safety."

"I can't believe it! She is my grandmother!"

"If it's any consolation, she wasn't happy about it. But I told her it was the only way we could avoid getting you involved. You and Alessandro. Unfortunately, it looks like he didn't drink it either."

"But wait a minute!" I objected. "He stole Mom's book from my hotel room and gave it to you last night! I saw it with my own eyes!"

"You're wrong!" Umberto was clearly annoyed with me for contradicting him, and possibly a little shocked that I had witnessed his secret meeting with Alessandro. "He was only a courier. Someone in Siena gave him the book yesterday morning and asked him to pass it on to Eva Maria. He obviously didn't know it was stolen, or he would have—"

"Wait!" said Janice. "This is too stupid. Whoever the thief was, why the heck didn't he steal the whole box? Why just the paperback?"

Umberto hesitated, then said, quietly, "Because your mother told me the code was in the book. She told me that if anything happened to her—" He couldn't go on.

We were all silent for a while, until Janice sighed and said, "Well, I think you owe Jules an apology—"

"Jan!" I interrupted her. "Let's not go there."

"But look what happened to you—" she insisted.

"That was my own fault!" I shot back. "I was the one who—" But I barely knew how to go on.

Umberto grunted. "I can't believe the two of you! Did I teach you nothing? You have known him for a week—but there you were! And weren't you two cute!"

"You spied on us?" I felt an explosion of embarrassment. "That is just so—"

"I needed to get the cencio!" Umberto pointed out. "Everything would have been so easy, if it hadn't been for you two—"

"While we're on the subject," Janice cut him off, "how much did Alessandro know about all this?"

Umberto snorted. "Clearly, he knew enough! He knew that Julie was Eva Maria's granddaughter, but that Eva Maria wanted to tell her in person. That's it. As I said, we couldn't risk getting the police involved. And so Eva Maria didn't tell him about the ceremony with the ring and the dagger until just before it took place, and, believe me, he was not happy to have been kept in the dark. But he agreed to do it anyway, because she told him it was important for her, and for you, to have a ceremony that would—supposedly—end the family curse." Umberto paused, then said, more gently, "It's too bad things had to end like this."

"Who says this is the end?" snapped Janice.

Umberto didn't say it, but I am sure we both knew what he was thinking: *Oh it's the end, all right.*

As we lay there in bitter silence, I could feel the blackness closing in on me from all sides, seeping into my body through countless little wounds and filling me to the brim with despair. The fear I had known before, when Bruno Carrera was chasing me, or when Janice and I had been trapped in the Bottini, had been nothing compared to what I felt now, torn by regret and knowing that it was far too late for me to set things straight.

"Just out of curiosity," muttered Janice, her mind clearly wandering along different paths than mine, although perhaps just as desolate, "did you ever actually love her? Mom, I mean?"

When Umberto didn't answer right away, she added, more hesitantly, "And did she . . . love you?"

Umberto sighed. "She loved to hate me. That was her greatest thrill. She said it was in our genes to fight, and that she wouldn't have it otherwise. She used to call me . . ." He paused to steady his voice. "Nino."

...

WHEN THE VAN finally stopped, I had almost forgotten where we were going, and why. But as soon as the doors swung open to reveal the silhouettes of Cocco and his cronies against the backdrop of a moonlit Siena Cathedral, it all came back to me like a kick to the stomach.

The men pulled us out of the truck by the ankles as if we were nothing but luggage, before climbing in to get Friar Lorenzo. It happened so fast that I barely registered the pain of banging along over the ridged floor, and both Janice and I staggered when they put us down, neither of us quite ready to stand upright after lying so long in the darkness.

"Hey look!" hissed Janice, a spark of hope in her voice. "Musicians!"

She was right. Three other cars were parked a stone's throw from the van, and half a dozen men wearing tuxedos were standing around with cello and violin cases, smoking and joking. I felt a twitch of relief at the sight, but as soon as Cocco walked towards them, hand raised in a greeting, I understood that these men had not come to play music; they were part of his gang from Naples.

When the men caught sight of Janice and me, they were quick to show their appreciation. Not the least bit concerned about the noise they were making, they began catcalling and whistling, trying to make us look at them. Umberto did not even try to shut down the fun; there was no question that he—and we—were simply lucky to still be alive. Only when the men saw Friar Lorenzo emerging from the van did their glee give way to something resembling uneasiness, and they all bent over to pick up their instrument cases the way schoolboys grab their bags at the arrival of a teacher.

To everyone else in the piazza that night—and there were quite a few, mostly tourists and teenagers—we must have looked like your average group of locals returning from some festivity to do with the Palio. Cocco's men never stopped chatting and laughing, and in the center of the group Janice and I walked obediently along, each of us draped with a large contrada flag that elegantly concealed the ropes and the switchblade knives pressed against our ribs.

As we approached the main entrance of Santa Maria della Scala, I suddenly caught sight of Maestro Lippi, walking along carrying an easel, undoubtedly preoccupied with otherworldly matters. Not daring to call out and get his attention, I stared at him with as much intensity as I could muster, hoping to reach him in some spiritual way. But when the artist finally glanced in our direction, his eyes merely brushed over us without any recognition, and I deflated with disappointment.

Just then, the bells of the cathedral rang midnight. It had been a hot night so far, still and muggy, and somewhere in the distance, a thunderstorm was brewing. As we came up to the forbidding front door of the old hospital, the first gusts of wind came sweeping across the piazza, turning up every piece of garbage in their way, like invisible demons searching for something, or someone.

Wasting no time, Cocco broke out a cell phone and made a call; seconds later, the two small lights on either side of the door went out, and it was as if the entire building complex exhaled with a deep sigh. With no further ado, he proceeded to take a large, cast-iron key out of his pocket, stick it into the keyhole beneath the massive door handle, and unlock the whole thing with a loud clang.

Only now, as we were about to enter the building, did it occur to me that Santa Maria della Scala was one of the last places in Siena I felt like exploring in the middle of the night, knife against my ribs or no. Although the building had, according to Umberto, been turned into a museum many years ago, it still had a history of sickness and death. Even to someone who didn't want to believe in ghosts, there were plenty of other things to worry about, starting with dormant plague germs. But it didn't really matter what I felt like; I had long since lost control over my own fate.

When Cocco opened the door, I was half expecting a rush of fleeting shadows and a smell of decay, but there was nothing but cool darkness on the other side. Even so, both Janice and I hesitated on the threshold, and only when the men yanked at us did we reluctantly stumble forward, into the unknown.

Once everyone was inside and the door securely closed behind us, a host of small lights came on as the men put on headlamps and clicked open their musical instrument cases. Nested in the foam were torchlights, weapons, and power tools, and as soon as everything was assembled, the cases were kicked aside.

"Andiamo!" said Cocco, waving with a submachine gun to make us all straddle the thigh-high security gate. Our hands still tied in the back, Janice and I had a hard time getting over it, and the men eventually grabbed us by the arms and hauled us over, ignoring our cries of pain as our shins scraped against the metal bars.

Now for the first time, Umberto dared to speak out against their brutality, saying something to Cocco that could only mean, *come on, go easy on the girls,* but all he got for his trouble was an elbow in the chest that made him double over coughing. And when I paused to see if he was okay, two of Cocco's henchmen took me by the shoulders and thrust me forward impatiently, their stony faces betraying no emotions whatsoever.

The only one they treated with any kind of respect was Friar Lorenzo, who was allowed to take his time and climb the gate with whatever dignity he had left.

"Why is he still blindfolded?" I whispered to Janice, as soon as the men let go of me.

"Because they're going to let him live," was her dismal reply.

"Shh!" hushed Umberto, making a face at us. "The less attention you two draw to yourselves, the better."

Everything considered, that was a tall order. Neither Janice nor I had showered since the day before, let alone washed our hands, and I was still wearing the long, red dress from Eva Maria's party, although, by now, it was a sorry sight. Earlier that day, Janice had suggested I put on some of the clothes from Mom's wardrobe and lose the bodice-ripper look. Once I did, however, we had both found the smell of mothballs unbearable. And so here I was, trying to blend in, barefoot and grimy but still dressed for a ball.

We walked for a while in silence, following the bouncing headlamps as they ricocheted along black corridors and down several different staircases, led on by Cocco and one of his lackeys—a tall, jaundiced fellow whose gaunt face and hunched shoulders made me think of a turkey vulture. Every now and then the two of them would stop and orient themselves according to a large piece of paper, which I assumed was a map of the building. And whenever they did, someone would pull hard at my hair or my arm to make sure I stopped, too.

There were five men in front of us and five men behind us at all times, and if I tried to exchange glances with either Janice or Umberto, the guy behind me would dig the muzzle of his gun in between my shoulder blades until I yelped with pain. Right next to me, Janice was getting the exact same treatment and, although I couldn't look at her, I knew she was just as scared and furious as I was, and just as helpless to fight back.

Despite their tuxedos and gelled hair, there was a sharp, almost rancid odor about the men, which suggested that they, too, felt under pressure. Or maybe it was the building I could smell; the farther into the underground we went, the worse it became. To the eye, the whole place appeared very clean, even sterile, but as we descended into the network of narrow corridors beneath the basement, I couldn't shake a feeling that— just on the other side of those dry, well-sealed walls—something putrid was slowly eating its way through the plaster.

When the men finally stopped, I had long since lost my sense of direction. It seemed to me that we must be at least fifty feet underground, but I was no longer sure we were directly beneath Santa Maria della Scala. Shivering now with cold, I picked up my frozen feet one by one, to press them briefly against my calves in an attempt at getting the blood flowing.

"Jules!" said Janice suddenly, interrupting my gymnastics. "Come on!"

I half expected someone to hit us both over the head to stop us from talking, but instead, the men pushed us forward until we were face-to-face with Cocco and the turkey vulture.

"E ora, ragazze?" said Cocco, blinding us both with his headlamp.

"What did he say?" hissed Janice, turning her head to avoid the beam.

"Something *girlfriend,*" I replied under my breath, not at all happy to have recognized the word.

"He said, 'What now, ladies?' " interjected Umberto. "This is Santa Caterina's room—where do we go from here?"

Only then did we notice that the turkey vulture was pointing a flashlight through a lattice gate in the wall, illuminating a small, monastic cell with a narrow bed and an altar. On the bed lay a recumbent statue of a woman—presumably Saint Catherine—and the wall behind her bed was painted blue and studded with golden stars.

"Uh," said Janice, clearly as awestruck as I was to discover that we were actually here, by the chamber mentioned in Mom's riddle, " 'hand me an iron crow.' "

"And then what?" asked Umberto, anxious to demonstrate to Cocco how useful we were.

Janice and I looked at each other, only too aware that Mom's directions had ended just about there, with a merry, "and foot it girls!"

"Wait—" I suddenly remembered another little snippet. "Oh yes . . . 'away with the cross'—"

"The cross?" Umberto looked mystified. "La croce—"

We all stretched to look into the chamber again, and just as Cocco was shoving us aside to see for himself, Janice nodded vigorously, trying to point with her nose. "There! Look! Under the altar!"

And indeed, beneath the altar was a large marble tile with a black cross on it, looking much like the door to a grave. Not wasting a moment, Cocco took a step back and aimed the submachine gun at the padlock that held the lattice door in place. Before anyone had time to run for cover, he blasted the whole thing open with a deafening salvo that took the gate right off its hinges.

"Oh, *Jesus!*" cried Janice, grimacing with pain. "I think that blew my eardrums. This guy is a total nutcase!"

Without a word, Cocco spun around and took her by the throat, squeezing so hard she nearly choked. It was all so fast that I hardly even saw what happened, until he suddenly let go of her and she dropped to her knees, gasping for air.

"Oh, Jan!" I cried, kneeling down next to her. "Are you okay?"

It took her a moment to find air for an answer. And when she finally did, her voice was trembling. "Note to self . . ." she muttered, blinking to clear her eyes, "the little charmer understands English."

Moments later, the men were going at the cross under the altar with crowbars and drills, and when the tile finally came loose and fell out on the stone floor with a thud that threw up a cloud of dust, none of us was surprised to see that behind it was the entrance to a tunnel.

WHEN JANICE AND I had crawled out of the sewer in the Campo three days earlier, we had promised each other never to go spelunking in the Bottini again. Yet here we were, making our way through a passage that was little more than a wormhole, in near darkness and without a blue sky beckoning us at the other end.

Before pushing us into the hole, Cocco had cut our hands free—not out of kindness, but because it was the only way of bringing us along. Fortunately, he was still under the impression that he needed us in order to find Romeo and Giulietta's grave; he didn't know that the cross under the altar in Saint Catherine's room had been the very last clue in Mom's directions.

Inching along behind Janice, seeing nothing but her jeans and the random flicker of headlamps against the jagged surface of the tunnel, I wished I had been wearing pants, too. I kept getting caught in the long skirt of the dress, and the thin velvet did nothing to protect my scabby knees from the uneven sandstone. The only upside was that I was so numb with cold I could barely feel the pain.

When we finally came to the end of the tunnel, I was as relieved as the men to find that there was no boulder or pile of rubble blocking our way and forcing us to backtrack. Instead we came out into a wide-open cave, about twenty feet across and tall enough for everyone to stand upright.

"E ora?" said Cocco as soon as Janice and I were within earshot, and this time we did not need Umberto to translate. *What now?* was indeed the question.

"Oh, no!" Janice whispered, but only to me, "It's a dead end!"

Behind us, the rest of the men were emerging from the tunnel, too, and one of them was Friar Lorenzo, who was eased out by the turkey vulture and some other guy with a ponytail, as if he were a prince being delivered by royal midwives. Someone had mercifully removed the blindfold before shoving the old monk into the hole, and now Friar Lorenzo stepped forward eagerly, eyes wide with amazement, as if he had completely forgotten the violent circumstances that had brought him here.

"What do we do?" Janice hissed, trying to catch Umberto's eye. But he was busy brushing dust off his pants and didn't pick up on the sudden tension. "How do you say *dead end* in Italian?"

Fortunately for us, Janice was wrong. As I looked around more carefully I saw that there were, in fact, two other exits to the cave, apart from the wormhole we had used to get in. One was in the ceiling, but it was a long, dark shaft, blocked at the top by what looked like a slab of concrete; even with a ladder it would have been impossible to reach. Most of all, it resembled an ancient garbage chute, and this impression was supported by the fact that the other exit was in the floor right beneath it. Or, at least, I assumed there was an opening beneath the rusty metal plate lying on the floor of the cave, well covered in dust and rubble. Anything dropped from aloft would in theory—if both holes had been open—be able to plunge right through the cave without even pausing in between.

Seeing that Cocco was still looking at Janice and me for directions, I did the only logical thing, which was to point at the metal plate on the floor. "Search, seek," I said, trying to fabricate a sufficiently oracular instruction, "look beneath your feet. For here lies Juliet."

"Yes!" nodded Janice, tugging nervously at my arm. "Here lies Juliet."

After glaring at Umberto for confirmation, Cocco had the men start working on the metal plate with crowbars, trying to loosen it and push it aside, and they went at it with so much vengeance that Friar Lorenzo retreated into a corner and began going through his rosary.

"Poor guy," said Janice, biting her lip, "he's totally off his rocker. I just hope—" She didn't say it, but I knew what she was thinking, because I had long been thinking the same. It was only a matter of time before Cocco would realize that the old monk was nothing but deadweight. And when that happened, we would be helpless to save him.

Yes, our hands were now free, but we both knew that we were just as trapped as we had been before. As soon as the last man had come out of the tunnel, the guy with the ponytail had positioned himself right in front of the opening, making sure no one was stupid enough to try to leave. And so there was really only one way out of this cave for Janice and me—with or without Umberto and Friar Lorenzo—and that was down the drain with everybody else.

When the metal cover finally came off, it did indeed reveal an opening in the floor, big enough for a man to climb through. Stepping forward, Cocco pointed a torchlight into the hole, and after the briefest hesitation the other men did the same, mumbling among themselves with half-hearted enthusiasm. The smell coming from the blackness below was definitely foul, and Janice and I were not the only ones to hold our noses at first, but then, after a few moments, it was no longer unbearable. We were clearly getting a bit too familiar with the smell of rot.

Whatever Cocco saw down there, it merely made him shrug and say, "Un bel niente."

"He says there is nothing," translated Umberto, frowning.

"Well, what the hell did he expect?" sneered Janice. "A neon sign saying, *grave robbers this way?*"

Her comment made me cringe, and when I saw the provoking glare she shot Cocco, I was sure he would jump right over the hole in the floor and take her, once again, by the throat.

But he didn't. Instead he looked at her in an uncanny, calculating way, and I suddenly understood that my clever sister had been feeling him out from the very beginning, trying to figure out how to bait and hook him. Why? Because he was our only ride out of there.

"Dai, dai!" was all he said, gesturing at his men to jump into the hole one after the other. Judging from the way they all braced themselves before doing so, and from the faint yelps coming from below as they hit the floor of the other cave, the drop was big enough to be a challenge, if not quite big enough to justify a rope.

When it became our turn, Janice stepped forward immediately, probably to demonstrate to Cocco that we were not afraid. And when he held out a hand to help her—maybe for the first time in his career—she spat in his palm before pushing off and disappearing through the hole. Amazingly, all he did was bare his teeth in a smile and say something to Umberto that I was happy not to understand.

Seeing that Janice was already waving at me from the cave below, and that the drop was no more than eight or nine feet, I, too, let myself fall into the forest of arms waiting to receive me. As they caught me and put me down on the floor, however, one of the men seemed to think he had now earned the right to grope me, and I struggled in vain to fight him off.

Laughing, he caught both my wrists and tried to engage the others in the fun, but just as I was beginning to panic, Janice came blasting to my rescue, cutting through the hands and arms and positioning herself between the men and me.

"You want some fun?" she asked them, her grimace one of disgust. "Is that what you want? Huh? Then why don't you have some fun with me—" She started ripping open her own shirt with such fury that the men barely knew what to do. Transfixed by the sight of her bra they all started backing away, except the guy who had started it all. Still smirking, he reached out brazenly to touch her breasts, but was stopped by an earsplitting burst of gunshots that had us all jump with fear and bewilderment.

A split-second later, a rattling shower of crumbling sandstone threw everyone down on the floor, and as my head hit the ground and my mouth and nostrils filled with dirt, I had a dizzying flashback to choking on tear gas in Rome and thinking I was going to die. For several minutes I was coughing so hard I nearly threw up, and I was not the only one. All around me, the men were down for the count, and so was Janice. The only consolation was that the floor of the cave was not hard at all, but oddly springy; had it been solid rock it might have knocked me out.

Eventually looking up through a haze of dust, I saw Cocco standing there, submachine gun in hand, waiting to see if anyone else felt like having fun. But no one did. It seemed his warning salvo had sent a vibration through the cave that had made parts of the ceiling fall down, and the men were too busy brushing rubble from their hair and clothes to challenge his resolve.

Apparently satisfied with the effect, Cocco pointed two fingers at Janice and said, in a tone no one could ignore, "La stronza è mia!" Not entirely sure what a stronza was, I was nevertheless fairly certain of the general message: No one was to ravage my sister, except him.

Getting back on my feet I noticed that I was trembling all over, unable to control my nerves. And when Janice came up to me, throwing her arms around my neck, I could feel her shaking, too.

"You're crazy," I said, squeezing her hard. "These guys are not like the dupes you usually operate. Evil doesn't come with a manual."

Janice snorted. "All men come with a manual. Just give me time. Little Cocco-nut is going to fly us out of here first class."

"I'm not so sure about that," I muttered, watching as the men lowered a very nervous Friar Lorenzo from the cave above. "I think our lives are pretty cheap to these people."

"Then why," said Janice, disentangling herself, "don't you just lie down and die right now? It's much easier that way, right?"

"I'm just trying to be rational—" I began, but she wouldn't let me go on.

"You've never done a rational thing in your life!" She closed her ripped shirt with a tight knot. "Why start now?"

As she stomped away from me, I very nearly did sit down and give up. To think it was all my own doing—this whole nightmare of a treasure hunt—and that it could have been avoided, had I trusted Alessandro and not run away from Castello Salimbeni the way I did. If only I had stayed where I was, hearing nothing, seeing nothing, and, most important, *doing* nothing, I might still have been there now, once again asleep in my canopy bed with his arms around me.

But my destiny had demanded otherwise. And so here I was instead, in the bowels of nowhere, filthy beyond recognition and watching passively while a homicidal freak with a submachine gun was screaming at my father and my sister to tell him where to go next in this cave with no exits.

Knowing very well that I couldn't just stand there doing nothing when they so desperately needed my help, I reached down to pick up a flashlight that had been dropped on the floor. Only then did I notice something sticking out of the dirt right in front of me. In the pale light of the beam it looked like a large, cracked seashell but, obviously, it couldn't be. The ocean was nearly fifty miles away. I knelt down to take a closer look, and my pulse quickened when I realized that I was looking at part of a human skull.

After the initial fright, I was surprised the discovery did not upset me more than it did. But then, I thought, considering Mom's directions, the sight of human remains was merely to be expected; we were, after all, looking for a grave. And so I began digging into the porous floor with my hands to see if the rest of the skeleton was there, and it did not take me long to determine that, indeed, it was. But it was not alone.

Right beneath the surface—a mix of earth and ashes, by the feel of it— the bottom of the cave was filled with tightly packed, randomly interlocking human bones.

A grave? O no, a lantern, slaughter'd youth.
For here lies Juliet, and her beauty makes
This vault a feasting presence, full of light

...

MY MACABRE DISCOVERY HAD everyone recoiling in revulsion, and Janice nearly threw up when she saw what I had found.

"Oh, my God!" she gagged. "It's a mass grave!" Stumbling backwards, she pressed her sleeve tightly against her mouth and nose. "Of all the disgusting places—we're in a plague pit! Full of microbes. We're all going to die!"

Her panic sent a ripple of fear through the men as well, and Cocco had to yell at the top of his lungs to calm everybody down. The only one who did not appear too frazzled was Friar Lorenzo, who merely bent his head and started praying, presumably for the souls of the departed, of whom—depending on the actual depth of the cave—there must be hundreds, if not thousands.

But Cocco was in no mood for prayers. Forcing the monk aside with the butt of his gun, he pointed straight at me and barked something nasty.

"He wants to know where to go from here," Umberto translated, his voice a calm counterweight to Cocco's hysteria. "He says you told him Giulietta was buried in this cave."

"I didn't say that—" I protested, knowing full well that it was precisely what I had said. "Mom says . . . go through the door, and here lies Juliet."

"Where door?" Cocco wanted to know, glaring demonstratively this way and that. "Me, I see no door!"

"You know," I lied, "the door that is here. Somewhere."

Cocco rolled his eyes and growled something dismissive before stomping off.

"He doesn't believe it," said Umberto, grimly. "He thinks you set him up. Now he is going to talk to Friar Lorenzo."

Janice and I watched with growing alarm as the men surrounded the monk and started bombarding him with questions. Dumbstruck with fear, he tried to listen to them all at once, but after a while he simply closed his eyes and covered his ears.

"Stupido!" sneered Cocco, reaching out for the old man.

"No!" exclaimed Janice, rushing forward and grabbing Cocco by the elbow to prevent him from hurting Friar Lorenzo. "Let me try! Please!"

For a few chilling seconds, it looked as if my sister had overestimated her own power over the crook. Judging by the way Cocco stared at his own elbow—still with her hands wrapped around it—he could barely fathom that she had actually had the gall to restrain him.

Probably realizing her own mistake, Janice quickly let go of Cocco's arm and dropped to her knees to hug his legs in submission, and after another few baffled moments Cocco finally threw up his hands with a grin and said something to his comrades that sounded like, *Women! What is a man to do?*

And so, thanks to Janice, we were allowed to talk to Friar Lorenzo without interference, while Cocco and his men fired up a pack of cigarettes and started kicking around a human skull as if it were a soccer ball.

Positioning ourselves so that Friar Lorenzo couldn't see their obscene game, we asked him—through Umberto—if he had any idea how to get to Romeo and Giulietta's grave from where we were. But as soon as he understood the question, the monk gave a brisk answer and shook his head dismissively.

"He says," translated Umberto, "that he does not want to show these evil men where the grave is. He knows they will desecrate it. And he says he is not afraid of dying."

"God help us!" muttered Janice under her breath. Then she put a hand on Friar Lorenzo's arm and said, "We understand. But you see, they will kill us, too. And then they will go back up there, and kidnap more people, and kill them as well. Priests, women, innocent people. It will never end, until someone takes them to that grave."

Friar Lorenzo pondered Umberto's translation for a while. Then he pointed at me and asked a question that sounded strangely accusatory.

"He asks if your husband knows where you are," said Umberto, looking almost bemused despite the circumstances. "He thinks you are very foolish to be here, surrounded by these bad men, when you should be at home, doing your duty."

I more felt than saw Janice rolling her eyes, ready to give up on the whole thing. But there was something incredibly sincere about Friar Lorenzo that resonated inside me in a way my sister would never be able to understand.

"I know," I said, meeting the monk's eyes. "But my most important duty is to end the curse. You know that. And I can't do it without your help."

After hearing Umberto's translation of my answer, Friar Lorenzo frowned slightly and reached out to touch my neck.

"He asks where the crucifix is," says Umberto. "The crucifix will protect you from the demons."

"I . . . don't know where it is," I stammered, thinking back to Alessandro removing it from my neck—mostly to tease—and putting it on the bedstand right where I had put his bullet. After that I had forgotten all about it.

Friar Lorenzo was clearly not happy with my answer, nor was he pleased to discover that I was no longer wearing the eagle ring.

"He says it would be very dangerous for you to approach the grave like this," said Umberto, wiping a drop of sweat from his forehead, "and he wants you to reconsider."

I swallowed a few times, trying to calm my galloping heart. Then I said, before I could convince myself otherwise, "Tell him that there is nothing for me to consider. I have no choice. We must find that grave tonight." I nodded at the men behind us. "Those are the real demons. Only the Virgin Mary can protect us from them. But I know their punishment will find them."

Now at last, Friar Lorenzo nodded. But instead of speaking, he closed his eyes and started humming a little tune, head rocking back and forth as if he was trying to remember the lyrics to a song. Glancing at Janice I saw her making a face at Umberto, but just as she opened her mouth to comment on my progress—or lack thereof—the monk stopped humming, opened his eyes, and recited what sounded like a short poem.

" 'Black plague guards the Virgin's door,' " translated Umberto, "that is what the book says."

"What book?" Janice wanted to know.

" 'Look at them now,' " Umberto went on, ignoring her, " 'the godless men and women, prostrate before her door, which remains forever closed.' Friar Lorenzo says this cave must be the old antechamber to the crypt. The question is—" Umberto broke off when the monk suddenly started walking towards the nearest wall, muttering to himself.

Not quite sure what we were supposed to do, we dutifully followed Friar Lorenzo as he walked slowly around the cave with a hand to the wall. Now that we knew what we were walking on, I felt a little shiver for every step I took, and the wafts of cigarette smoke were almost welcome, for they drowned out the other smell in the cave, which I now knew was the smell of death.

Only when we had come full circle and were back where we started— all the while trying to ignore the rude gibes from Cocco's men, who were watching us with contemptuous amusement—did Friar Lorenzo finally stop and speak to us again.

"The Siena Cathedral is oriented east-west," Umberto explained, "with the entrance facing west. That is normal for cathedrals. And so you'd think it would be the same with the crypt. However, the book says—"

"What book?" Janice asked again.

"For crap's sake," I snapped. "Some book that monks read in Viterbo, okay?"

"The book says," Umberto continued, looking daggers at us both, "that 'the Virgin's black part is the mirror image of her white part,' which could mean that the crypt—being the black part, that is, the one below-ground—is in fact oriented west-east, with the entrance in the east, in which case the door leading to it from *this* room would be facing west. Don't you agree?"

Janice and I exchanged glances; she looked precisely as dazed as I felt. "We have no idea," I said to Umberto, "how he got to that conclusion, but at this point, we'll believe anything."

When Cocco heard the news, he flicked away his cigarette butt and pushed up his sleeve to set the compass on his wristwatch. And as soon as he was confident which way was west, he began yelling instructions to the men.

Minutes later, they were all busy breaking up the floor in the western-most part of the cave, ripping out dismembered skeletons with their bare hands and tossing them aside as if they were nothing but the branches off a dead tree. It was an odd sight, the men crawling around in their tuxedos and shiny shoes, headlamps on, not the least bit worried about breathing in the dust from the disintegrating bones.

Almost sick to my stomach, I turned to Janice, who seemed com-pletely mesmerized by the excavation. When she saw me looking at her, she shuddered slightly and said, " 'Lady, come from that nest of death, contagion, and unnatural sleep. A greater power than we can contradict hath thwarted our intents.' "

I put an arm around her, trying to shield us both from the horrendous sight. "And I who thought you'd never learn those damn lines."

"It wasn't the lines," she said. "It was the role. I was never Juliet." She wrapped my arm more tightly around her. "I could never die for love."

I tried to read her face in the wavering light. "How do you know?"

She didn't answer, but it didn't matter. For just then, one of the men yelled out from the hole they were making, and we both stepped forward to see what had happened.

"They found the top of something," said Umberto, pointing. "It looks like Friar Lorenzo was right."

We both stretched to see what he was pointing at, but in the sporadic light of the headlamps it was nearly impossible to make out anything other than the men themselves, bustling around in the hole like frenzied beetles.

Only later, when they all climbed out to get their power tools, did I dare point my flashlight into the crater to see what they had found. "Look!" I grabbed Janice by the arm. "It's a sealed-up door!"

In reality, it was no more than the pointy top of a white structure in the cave wall—barely three feet high—but there was no question it had once been a door frame, or at least the upper part of one, and it even had a five-petal rose carved at the very top. The door opening, however, had been sealed off with a jumble of brown brick and fragments of marble décor; whoever had overseen the work—presumably sometime in the dreadful year 1348—had clearly been in too much of a hurry to care about the building materials or the pattern.

When the men returned with their tools and started drilling into the brick, Janice and I took cover behind Umberto and Friar Lorenzo. Soon, the cave was vibrating with the mayhem of demolition, and chunks of tufa began falling like hail from the ceiling, covering us all—once more—in rubble.

No less than four layers of brick separated the mass grave from what lay beyond, and as soon as the men with the drills saw that they were through the final one, they stepped back and started kicking at the remainder to bring it down. It didn't take them long to make a big, jagged hole, and before the dust had even settled, Cocco pushed them all aside in order to be the first man to point his torch through the opening.

In the silence following the bedlam, we very clearly heard him whistling in wonder, and the sound created an eerie, hollow echo.

"La cripta!" whispered Friar Lorenzo, crossing himself.

"Here we go," muttered Janice. "I hope you brought garlic."

IT TOOK COCCO'S MEN about half an hour to prepare our descent into the crypt. Digging further into the interlaced bones, and drilling out the brick in the wall as they went, they were clearly trying to bring us down to floor level. In the end, however, they got tired of the dusty job and began tossing bones and rubble through the hole, trying to create a heap that could serve as a ramp on the other side. In the beginning, the bricks came down with loud thuds on what sounded like a stone floor, but as the pile started growing, the noise became more faint.

When Cocco finally sent us through the opening, Janice and I descended into the crypt hand in hand with Friar Lorenzo, carefully making our way down the sloping pile of brick and bones, feeling not unlike air-raid survivors clambering down a shattered staircase, wondering if this was the end—or the beginning—of the world.

The air was much cooler in the crypt than it had been in the cave behind us, and definitely cleaner. Looking around in the light of a dozen swaying searchlights, I half expected to see a long, narrow room with rows of grim sarcophagi and sinister Latin inscriptions on the walls, but much to my surprise it was a beautiful, even majestic space with a vaulted ceiling and tall, supporting pillars. Here and there stood a number of stone tables that might originally have been altars, but which were now stripped of all sacred objects. Apart from that, there was not much left in the crypt but shadows and silence.

"Oh, my God!" whispered Janice, pointing my torchlight at the walls around us, "Look at those frescoes! We're the first people to see them since—"

"The Plague," I said. "And this is probably bad for them . . . all this air and light."

She giggled, but it sounded more like a sob. "That should be the very least of our concerns right now, if you don't mind."

Walking along the wall, looking at the frescoes, we passed by a doorway that was covered by a cast-iron gate with golden filigree. Pointing the flashlight through the bars we could see a small side chapel with graves that made me think of the village cemetery with the Tolomei sepulchre, which I had visited with cousin Peppo a lifetime ago.

Janice and I were not the only ones interested in the side chapels. All around us, Cocco's men were systematically checking each and every door, obviously looking for Romeo and Giulietta's grave.

"What if it isn't here?" whispered Janice, glancing nervously at Cocco, who was becoming more and more frustrated as the search continued without result. "Or what if they're buried here all right, but the statue is somewhere else? . . . Jules?"

But I was only listening to her with half an ear. After stepping on several chunks of what looked like crumbled plaster, I had pointed my flashlight upwards and discovered that the whole place was far more dilapidated than I had first assumed. Here and there, parts of the vaulted ceiling had come down, and a couple of the supporting pillars were leaning, ominously, under the burden of the modern world.

"Oh, boy," I said, suddenly realizing that Cocco and his men were no longer our only enemies, "this whole place is just waiting to collapse."

Looking over my shoulder at the jagged opening leading to the antechamber with the mass grave, I knew that, even if we were able to sneak back there unseen, we would never get up through the hole in the ceiling, where the men had helped us down. Using all my strength, I might be able to lift up Janice, but then what about me? And what about Friar Lorenzo? In theory, Umberto could lift all three of us one by one, but then what about him? Would we just leave him there?

My speculations were interrupted when Cocco summoned us both with a sharp whistle and ordered Umberto to ask us if we had any more clues as to where the damned statue could be.

"Oh, it's here!" Janice blurted out. "The question is where they hid it."

When she saw that Cocco wasn't following, she tried to laugh. "Did you really think," she went on, her voice beginning to shake, "they would put something so valuable in a place where everyone would see it?"

"What did Friar Lorenzo say?" I asked Umberto, mostly to get everyone's attention off Janice, who looked as if she might burst into tears at any moment. "He must have some idea."

We all looked at the monk, who was wandering about on his own, gazing at the golden stars on the ceiling.

" 'And he put a dragon there to guard their eyes,' " recited Umberto. "That's all. But there's no dragon here. Not a single statue anywhere."

"What's odd," I said, looking from one side of the crypt to the other, "is that over there on the left we have five side chapels at regular intervals, but over here we only have four. Look. The middle one is missing. There's just wall."

Before Umberto had even finished translating what I said, Cocco marched us all over to the place where the fifth doorway should have been, in order to take a closer look.

"Not just wall," observed Janice, pointing at a colorful fresco, "but a landscape with a big, red, flying . . . snake."

"Looks like a dragon to me," I said, taking a step back. "You know what I think? I think the grave is behind this wall. See . . ." I pointed at a long crack in the fresco betraying the shape of a door frame beneath the plaster. "This was obviously a side chapel, just like the others, but I bet Salimbeni got tired of posting guards here twenty-four seven. And so he simply walled it up. It makes sense."

Cocco did not need any more proof that this was, indeed, the location of the grave, and within minutes the power tools were going again, the roar of metal against stone reverberating through the crypt as the men drilled into the dragon fresco to get access to the presumed hidden niche. This time it was not just dust and rubble that fell on us as we stood there, watching the destruction with our fingers in our ears, but big chunks of the vaulted ceiling, including several golden stars that fell around us with fateful clangs, as if the very cogwheels of the universe were coming off.

...

WHEN THE DRILLS FINALLY stopped, the opening in the wall was just large enough for a person to walk through, and it did indeed reveal a hidden niche. One by one, the men disappeared through the improvised doorway, and in the end neither Janice nor I could resist the temptation to follow, even though nobody told us to.

Ducking through the hole, we emerged into a small, dimly lit side chapel, nearly bumping into the others, who were all standing still. Stretching to see what they were looking at, I merely caught a glimpse of something shiny, before one of the men finally had the presence of mind to point his torch directly at the massive object that seemed to be hovering in the air before us.

"Holy shit!" said someone with perfect pronunciation, and for once even Janice was dumbstruck.

There it was, the statue of Romeo and Giulietta, far bigger and much more spectacular than I had ever imagined—in fact, its proportions made it almost threatening. It was as if its creator had wanted the beholders to fall to their knees spontaneously, begging for forgiveness. And I almost did.

Even as it stood there, set on top of a large marble sarcophagus and covered in six hundred years of dust, it had a golden glow about it that no span of time could take away. And in the dim light of the chapel the four gemstone eyes—two blue sapphires and two green emeralds—shone with an almost supernatural brilliance.

To someone who did not know its story, the statue spoke not of grief, but of love. Romeo was kneeling on the sarcophagus, picking up Giulietta in his arms, and they were looking at each other with an intensity that found its way into the dark cranny where my heart was hiding, reminding me of my own fresh sorrows. The drawings in Mom's sketchbook had clearly been nothing more than guesswork; even her most loving portraits of these two figures, Romeo and Giulietta, did not begin to do them justice.

Standing there, choking back my regrets, it was hard for me to accept that I had originally come to Siena to find this statue and these four gemstones. Now they were right here in front of me, but I no longer felt the slightest desire to own them. And even if they had been mine, I would happily have given them away a thousand times to be back in the real world, safe from the likes of Cocco, or even just to see Alessandro one more time.

"Do you think they put them both in the same coffin?" whispered Janice, interrupting my thoughts. "Come—" She elbowed her way through the men, pulling me along, and when we were right next to the sarcophagus, she took my flashlight and pointed it at an inscription that was carved into the stone. "Look! Remember this from the story? Do you think it's the one?"

We both leaned closer to look, but could not make out the Italian.

"What was it now?" Janice frowned, trying to remember the English translation. "Oh yes! 'Here sleeps true and faithful Giulietta . . . By the love and mercy of God'—" She paused, forgetting the rest.

" 'To be woken by Romeo, her rightful spouse,' " I went on quietly, mesmerized by the golden face of Romeo, looking right down at me, " 'in an hour of perfect grace.' "

If the story Maestro Lippi had translated to us was true—and it was certainly beginning to look that way—then old Maestro Ambrogio had personally overseen the creation of this statue back in 1341. Surely he, being Romeo and Giulietta's friend, would have been adamant about getting it right; surely this was a faithful representation of what they had really looked like.

But Cocco and his men had not come all the way from Naples to be lost in reverie, and two of them were already climbing around on top of the sarcophagus, trying to figure out what tools were needed to gouge out the eyes of the statue. In the end they decided that a special kind of drill was necessary, and once the tools had been assembled and handed to them, they each turned to a figure—one to Giulietta, one to Romeo— ready to go ahead.

When he saw what they were about to do, Friar Lorenzo—who had been perfectly calm until this very moment—burst forward and tried to stop the men, pleading with them not to ruin the statue. It was not just a matter of desecrating a piece of art; the monk was clearly convinced that stealing its eyes would trigger some unspeakable evil that would undo us all. But Cocco had no further need for Friar Lorenzo's superstitious riddles; he pushed the monk brusquely aside and ordered the men to proceed.

As if the racket from tearing down the wall had not been bad enough, the noise from the metal drills was absolutely hellish. Backing away from the mayhem, hands flat against our ears, Janice and I were only too aware that we were rapidly approaching the bitter end of our quest.

Ducking through the hole in the wall and returning to the main part of the crypt—a visibly distressed Friar Lorenzo in tow—we saw right away that the whole place was, quite literally, falling apart. Large cracks were traveling along the plaster walls and up the vaulted ceiling, creating cobweb patterns that needed no more than the tiniest vibration to spread further in all directions.

"I say we make a run for it," said Janice, looking around nervously. "At least back in the other cave we only have dead people to deal with."

"And then what?" I asked. "Sit around underneath the hole in the ceiling, waiting for these . . . gentlemen to come and help us out?"

"No," she replied, rubbing her arm where a star had strafed her, "but one of us could help the other get out, and then that other could crawl back through the tunnel and get help."

I stared at her, realizing she was right, and that I was an idiot for not thinking of this approach before. "So," I said, hesitantly, "who gets to go?"

Janice smiled wryly. "You go. You're the one who has something to lose—" Then she added, more smugly, "Besides, I'm the one who knows how to deal with the Cocco-Nut."

We stood like that for a moment, just looking at each other. Then I caught sight of Friar Lorenzo out of the corner of my eye; he was kneeling in front of one of the stripped stone tables, praying to a God who was no longer there.

"I can't do it," I whispered. "I can't leave you here."

"You have to," said Janice, firmly. "If you won't, I will."

"Fine," I said, "then go. Please."

"Oh, Jules!" She threw her arms around me. "Why do you always have to be the hero?"

We could have saved ourselves the emotional turmoil of fighting over martyrdom, for by now the metal drills had stopped, and the men came pouring out of the side chapel, laughing and joking about their exploits and throwing the four walnut-sized gemstones back and forth. The last person to emerge was Umberto, and I could see he was thinking exactly the same as we: Did this finally conclude our business with Cocco and the gang from Naples, or would they decide they wanted more?

As if they had read our thoughts, the men now stopped in the middle of their merriment and took a good solid look at Janice and me, standing as we were, huddled against each other. Cocco in particular seemed to take pleasure in the sight of us, and the smirk on his face told me that he knew exactly how we might still add value to his enterprise. But then, after undressing Janice with his eyes and concluding that, regardless of her nasty attitude, she was just another scared little girl, his calculating eyes turned cold, and he said something to his men that made Umberto jump forward, arms wide, to position himself between them and us.

"No!" he begged, "Ti prego!"

"Vaffanculo!" sneered Cocco, pointing the submachine gun at him.

By the sound of it, the two of them went on to exchange a legion of pleas and obscenities before finally, Umberto switched into English.

"My friend," he said, all but dropping to his knees, "I know you are a generous man. And a father, too. Be merciful. I promise, you will not regret it."

Cocco did not reply right away. His squint suggested that he was not happy to be reminded of his own humanity.

"Please," Umberto went on, "the girls will never speak to anybody. I swear to you."

Now, finally, Cocco grimaced and said, in his halting English, "Girls always talk. Talk-talk-talk."

Behind my back Janice squeezed my hand so hard that it hurt. She knew, as well as I did, that there was no earthly reason why Cocco should let us walk away from this place alive. He had his gems now, and that was all he wanted. What he most certainly did *not* need were eyewitnesses. Even so, I had a hard time understanding that this was really it; after all our crawling around and helping him find the statue, he would really kill us? Instead of fear I felt fury—fury that Cocco was the cold bastard he was, and that the only man to step forward and defend us was our father.

Even Friar Lorenzo stood idly by, going through his rosary with closed eyes, as if none of what was going on had anything to do with him. But then, how could he possibly know? He understood neither evil nor English.

"My friend," said Umberto again, doing his best to speak calmly, perhaps hoping it would rub off on Cocco, "I spared your life once. Remember? Does that count for nothing?"

Cocco pretended to think about it for a moment. Then he replied, with a contemptuous grimace, "Okay. You spared my life once. So, I will spare a life for you." He nodded at Janice and me. "Who you like most? The stronza or the angelo?"

"Oh, Jules!" whimpered Janice, hugging me so hard I couldn't breathe. "I love you! No matter what happens, I love you!"

"Please don't make me choose," said Umberto in a voice I could barely recognize. "Cocco. I know your mother. She is a good woman. She wouldn't like this."

"My mother," sneered Cocco, "she will spit in your grave! Last chance: the stronza or the angelo? Choose now, or I kill both two."

When Umberto didn't answer, Cocco walked right up to him. "You," he said slowly, placing the muzzle of the submachine gun against Umberto's chest, "are a stupid man."

In our panic, both Janice and I were too frozen to leap forward and try to prevent Cocco from pulling the trigger, and one second later, an ear-piercing gunshot sent a tremor through the whole cave.

Certain that he had been shot, we both screamed and ran up to Umberto, expecting him to fall over, already dead. But amazingly, when we reached him he was still standing, stiff with shock. The one who was lying on the floor, grotesquely sprawled, was Cocco. Something—a thunderbolt from heaven?—had gone right through his skull, taking off the back of his head on the way.

"Jesus Christ!" whimpered Janice, white as a ghost, "what was *that*?"

"Get down!" cried Umberto, pulling fiercely at us both. "And cover your heads!"

Everywhere around us, Cocco's men began scrambling for cover as a series of gunshots rang out, and those who paused to return the fire were taken down instantly, with startling accuracy. Lying flat on my stomach on the floor, I turned my head to see who was firing the shots, and for the first time in my life, the sight of advancing police officers in combat gear was not unwelcome. Pouring into the crypt through the hole we had made, they took up position behind the nearest pillars and yelled at the remaining bandits to—I assumed—drop their weapons and surrender.

My relief at seeing the police and realizing that our nightmare was over, made me want to laugh and cry at the same time. If they had arrived one minute later than they did, everything would have been different. Or maybe they had in fact been there for a while, just watching us, waiting for an excuse to drop the hammer on Cocco without a trial. Whatever the details, as I lay there on the stone floor, my head still spinning from the horror we had been through, I was quite ready to believe they had been sent by the Virgin Mary, to punish those who had violated her shrine.

Faced with hopeless odds, the few surviving mobsters eventually emerged from behind the columns, hands in the air. When one of them was stupid enough to bend over and reach for something on the floor—most likely a gemstone—he was shot immediately. It took me a few seconds to realize that he was the one who had groped me and Janice back in the cave, but even more important, that the man who shot him was Alessandro.

As soon as I recognized him, I was filled by an intense, giddy joy. But before I could share my discovery with Janice, there was an ominous rumble somewhere above us, which rose to a maddening crescendo as one of the pillars supporting the vaulted ceiling came crashing down, right on top of the surviving bandits, slamming them with several tons of stone.

The trembling echoes of the collapsing column spread through the entire web of Bottini caves surrounding us on all sides. It seemed the chaos in the crypt had set off a vibration in the underground that felt very much like an earthquake, and I saw Umberto jumping to his feet, waving at Janice and me to get up, too.

"Come on!" he urged us, looking nervously at the pillars around us. "I don't think we have much time."

Scurrying across the floor, we narrowly missed a shower of rubble spilling out of the ruptured ceiling, and when a falling star hit me right on the temple, I very nearly blacked out. Pausing briefly to regain my balance, I saw Alessandro coming towards me, striding over the debris and ignoring the warning remarks from the other police officers. He didn't say anything, but then, he didn't have to. His eyes said everything I could ever hope to hear.

I would have walked right into his embrace had I not, just then, heard a faint cry behind me.

"Friar Lorenzo!" I gasped, suddenly realizing that we had forgotten all about the monk. Spinning around, I caught sight of his crouched form somewhere in the middle of the devastation, and before Alessandro could prevent me, I ran back the way I had come, anxious to get to the old man before some flying chunk of masonry beat me to it.

Alessandro would most certainly have stopped me, had not another column come crashing down between us in a cloud of dust, immediately followed by a downpour of crumbled plaster. And this time, the impact of the pillar broke open the floor right next to me, revealing that, beneath the stone tiles, there were no wooden rafters, no slab of concrete, just a big, dark void.

Petrified at the sight, I stopped right there, afraid to go on. Behind me I heard Alessandro yelling at me to come back, but before I could even turn around, the part of the floor on which I was standing began to separate from the surrounding structure. The next thing I knew, the floor was no longer there, and I plunged straight into nothingness, too stunned to scream, feeling as if the very glue of the world had evaporated, and all that was left in this new chaos were bits and pieces, me, and gravity.

How far did I fall? I feel like saying that I fell through time itself, through lives, deaths, and centuries past, but in terms of actual measurement the drop was no more than twenty feet. At least, that is what they say. They also say that, fortunately for me, it was neither rocks nor demons that caught me as I came tumbling into the underworld. It was the ancient river that wakes you from dreams, and which few people have ever been allowed to find.

Her name is Diana.

THEY SAY THAT AS soon as I fell over the edge of the crumbling floor, Alessandro jumped in after me, not even stopping to take off his gear. When he plunged into the cool water he was dragged down by the weight of it all—the vest, the boots, the gun—and it took him a moment to come up for air. Struggling against the swift current, he managed to pull out a flashlight and eventually find my limp body stuck on a protruding rock.

Yelling at the other police officers to hurry, Alessandro had them lower a rope and haul us both back up to the cathedral crypt. Deaf to everybody and everything, he put me down on the floor in the middle of the debris, forced the water from my lungs, and began reviving me.

Standing there, watching his efforts, Janice did not fully understand the seriousness of the situation until she looked up and saw the other men exchanging grim glances. They all knew what Alessandro would not yet accept: that I was dead. Only then did she feel the tears coming, and once they had started, there was no stopping them.

In the end Alessandro gave up trying to revive me and merely held me, as if he would never let go of me again. He stroked my cheek and talked to me, saying things he should have said while I was still alive, not caring who could hear him. At that moment, Janice says, we looked very much like the statue of Romeo and Giulietta, except that my eyes were closed, and Alessandro's face was torn with grief.

Seeing that even he had lost hope, my sister pulled away from the police officers holding her and ran over to Friar Lorenzo, grabbing the monk by the shoulders.

"Why are you not praying?" she cried, shaking the old man. "Pray to the Virgin Mary, and tell her—" Realizing that he didn't understand her, Janice stepped away from the monk, looked up at the shattered ceiling, and screamed at the top of her lungs, "Make her live! I know you can do it! Let her live!"

When there was no answer, my sister sank to her knees at last, crying hysterically. And there was not a man in the crowd who dared to touch her.

Just then, Alessandro felt something. It was no more than a quiver, and maybe it was him and not me, but it was enough to give him hope. Cradling my head in his hands he spoke to me again, tenderly at first, then impatiently.

"Look at me!" he begged. "Look at me, Giulietta!"

They say that when I finally heard him, I did not cough, or gasp, or groan. I just opened my eyes and looked at him. And once I began to understand what was going on around me, apparently I smiled and whispered, "Shakespeare won't like it."

All this was told to me later; I remember almost none of it. I don't even remember Friar Lorenzo kneeling down to kiss me on the forehead, or Janice dancing around like a whirling dervish, kissing all the laughing police officers in turn. All I remember are the eyes of the man who had refused to lose me again, and who had wrested me from the clutches of the Bard so we could finally write our own happy end.

[x]

. . . and all these woes shall serve
For sweet discourses in our times to come

. . .

MAESTRO LIPPI WAS AT A loss to understand why I could not sit still. Here we were at last, he behind an easel and me looking my very best, framed by wildflowers and bathed in the golden light of a late summer sun. All he needed was ten more minutes, and the portrait would be done.

"Please!" he said, waving the palette. "Don't move!"

"But Maestro," I protested, "I really, really have to go."

"Bah!" He disappeared once more behind the canvas. "These things never start on time."

Behind me, from the monastery on the hilltop, the bells had long since stopped ringing, and when I twisted around to look one more time, I saw a figure in a fluttering dress come running down the sloping lawn towards us.

"Jesus, Jules!" gasped Janice, too out of breath to give me the full brunt of her disapproval. "Someone's gonna blow a fuse if you don't get your ass up there *right now!*"

"I know, but—" I glanced at Maestro Lippi, loath to disrupt his work. After all, Janice and I both owed him our lives.

There was no getting around the fact that our ordeal in the cathedral crypt might have ended very differently, had not the Maestro—in a moment of uncharacteristic clarity—recognized the two of us as we walked across Piazza del Duomo that night, surrounded by musicians and wrapped in contrada flags. He had seen us before we saw him, but as soon as he realized that we were wearing flags from the contrada of the Unicorn—the great rival of our own contrada, the Owl—he had known something was horribly wrong.

Rushing back to his workshop, he had called the police right away. As it turned out, Alessandro was already at the police station, interrogating two ne'er-do-wells from Naples who had tried to kill him and broken their arms in the process.

And so had it not been for Maestro Lippi, the police might never have followed us into the crypt, and Alessandro might never have saved me from the river Diana . . . and I might not have been here today, at Friar Lorenzo's monastery in Viterbo, looking my very best.

"I'm sorry, Maestro," I said, getting up, "but we'll have to finish this some other time."

Running up the hill with my sister, I couldn't help laughing. She was wearing one of Eva Maria's tailored dresses, and, of course, it fit her perfectly.

"What's so funny?" she snapped, still annoyed with me for being late.

"You," I chuckled. "I can't believe it never occurred to me how much you look like Eva Maria. And *sound* like her."

"Thanks a lot!" she said. "I guess it's better than sounding like Umberto—" But as soon as the words were out of her mouth, she winced. "I'm sorry."

"Don't be sorry. I'm sure he's here in spirit."

The truth was, we had no idea what had become of Umberto. Neither of us had seen him since the shoot-out in the cathedral crypt. In all likelihood, he had disappeared into the underground when the floor broke up, but then, nobody had actually seen it happen. They had been too busy looking for me.

Nor were the four gemstones ever found. Personally, I suspected Earth had taken back her treasures, assuming Romeo's and Giulietta's eyes back into her womb the way she had demanded the return of the eagle dagger.

Janice, on the other hand, was convinced Umberto had pocketed the sparkle and escaped through the Bottini caves to live the sweet life in the slicked-back tango parlors of Buenos Aires . . . or wherever else gentleman gangsters go when they retire. And after a few poolside chocolate martinis at Castello Salimbeni, Eva Maria began to agree with her. Umberto, she told us, adjusting her sunglasses under her large, floppy sunhat, had always had a habit of disappearing, sometimes for years, and then suddenly calling her out of the blue. Besides, she was confident that, even if her son had really fallen through the floor and into the river Diana, he would have kept his head above water and simply followed the current until it spat him out in a lake somewhere. How could it possibly be otherwise?

TO GET TO THE sanctuary we had to run past an olive grove and an herb nursery with beehives. Friar Lorenzo had walked us through the grounds that same morning, and we had eventually ended up in a secluded rose garden dominated by an open marble rotunda.

In the middle of the little temple stood a life-size bronze statue of a monk, arms open in a gesture of friendship. Friar Lorenzo had explained that this was what the brothers liked to imagine the original Friar Lorenzo had looked like, and that his remains were buried under the floor. It was supposed to be a place of peace and contemplation, he had told us, but because we were who we were, he would make an exception.

Approaching the sanctuary now, with Janice in tow, I stopped briefly to catch my breath. They were all there, waiting for us—Eva Maria, Malèna, cousin Peppo with his leg in a cast, plus a couple dozen other people whose names I was only starting to learn—and next to Friar Lorenzo stood Alessandro, tense and to-die-for, frowning at his wristwatch.

When he saw us walking towards him, he shook his head and sent me a smile that was part reproach, part relief. And as soon as I was within reach, he pulled me close to kiss my cheek and whisper into my ear, "I think maybe I *will* have to chain you in the dungeon."

"How medieval of you," I replied, disentangling myself with feigned modesty, seeing that we had an audience.

"You bring it out in me."

"Scusi?" Friar Lorenzo looked at us both with raised eyebrows, clearly eager to get on with the ceremony, and I dutifully turned my attention to the monk, postponing my rebuttal until later.

We were not getting married because we felt we had to. This wedding ceremony in the Lorenzo sanctuary was not only for us, it was also a way of proving to everyone else that we were serious when we said we belonged together—something Alessandro and I had known for a long, long time. Besides, Eva Maria had demanded an opportunity to celebrate the return of her long-lost granddaughters, and it would have broken Janice's heart had she not been given a glamorous part to play. And so the two of them had spent an entire evening going through Eva Maria's wardrobe, looking for the perfect bridesmaid's dress, while Alessandro and I had continued my swimming lessons in the pool.

But even if our wedding today felt like little more than a confirmation of vows we had already exchanged, I was still moved by Friar Lorenzo's sincerity, and by the sight of Alessandro right next to me, listening intently to the monk's speech.

Standing there with my hand in his, I suddenly understood why—all my life—I had been haunted by the fear of dying young. Whenever I had tried to envision my future beyond the age that my mother had been when she died, I had seen nothing but darkness. Only now did it make sense. The darkness had not been death, but blindness; how could I possibly have known that I was going to wake up—as from a dream—to a life I never knew existed?

The ceremony went on in Italian with great solemnity until the best man—Malèna's husband, Vincenzo—handed Friar Lorenzo the rings. Recognizing the eagle signet ring, Friar Lorenzo grimaced with exasperation and said something that made everyone laugh.

"What did he say?" I whispered under my breath.

Seizing the opportunity to kiss my neck, Alessandro whispered back, "He said, *Holy Mother of God, how many times do I have to do this?*"

WE HAD DINNER in the inner courtyard of the monastery, under a trellis overgrown with grapevines. As twilight turned to darkness, the Lorenzo brothers went inside to fetch oil lamps and beeswax candles in handblown glasses, and before long the golden light from our tables drowned out the cold glimmer from the starry sky above.

It was gratifying to sit there next to Alessandro, surrounded by people who would never have been brought together otherwise. After some initial apprehensions, Eva Maria, Pia, and cousin Peppo were all getting along famously, chipping away at the old family misunderstandings at last. And what better occasion to do so? They were, after all, our godparents.

The majority of the guests, however, were neither Salimbenis nor Tolomeis, but Alessandro's friends from Siena and members of the Marescotti family. I had already been to dinner with his aunt and uncle several times—not to mention all his cousins living down the street—but it was the first time I met his parents and brothers from Rome.

Alessandro had warned me that his father, Colonel Santini, was not a great fan of metaphysics, and that his mother tended to keep her husband on a need-to-know basis when it came to Marescotti family lore. Personally, I couldn't be more happy that none of them felt a need to dig into the official story of our courtship, and I had just squeezed Alessandro's hand in relief, underneath the table, when his mother leaned over to whisper to me, with a teasing wink, "When you come to visit, you must tell me what really happened, no?"

"Have you ever been to Rome, Giulietta?" Colonel Santini wanted to know, his booming voice briefly extinguishing all other conversation.

"Uh . . . no," I said, digging my nails into Alessandro's thigh. "But I'd love to go."

"It is very strange . . ." The Colonel frowned slightly. "I have a feeling I have seen you before."

"That," said Alessandro, putting an arm around me, "is exactly how I felt when we met the first time." And then he kissed me, right on the mouth, until they all started laughing and rapping at the table, and the conversation turned—thankfully—to the Palio.

Two days after the drama in the cathedral crypt Aquila had finally won the race after almost twenty years of disappointment. Despite the doctor's recommendation that I take it easy for a while, we had been right there in the fray, Alessandro and I, celebrating the rebirth of our destinies. Afterwards, we had flocked with Malèna and Vincenzo and all the other aquilini to the Siena Cathedral for the victory mass in celebration of the Virgin Mary and the cencio she had so graciously bestowed on Contrada dell'Aquila despite Alessandro being in town.

As I had stood there in the church, singing along to a hymn I didn't know, I thought of the crypt that was somewhere below us, and the golden statue that no one knew of but us. Maybe one day the crypt would be safe enough for visitors, and maybe Maestro Lippi would restore the statue and give it new eyes, but until then, it was our secret. And perhaps it ought to remain that way. The Virgin had allowed us to find her shrine, but everyone who had entered it with evil intent had died. Not exactly a great pitch for group tours.

As for the old cencio, it had been returned to the Virgin Mary just as Romeo Marescotti had vowed it would be. We had taken it to Florence to get it professionally cleaned and preserved, and now it hung in a glass casing in the small chapel at the Eagle Museum, looking surprisingly pristine considering its recent trials. Everyone in the contrada was, of course, euphoric that we had managed to track down this important piece of history, and no one seemed to find it the least bit odd that the subject of its recovery and fine condition always gave me rosy cheeks.

OVER DESSERT—A GRANDIOSE wedding cake personally designed by Eva Maria—Janice leaned over to put a yellowed roll of parchment on the table in front of me. I recognized it right away; it was the letter from Giannozza to Giulietta that Friar Lorenzo had shown me at Castello Salimbeni. The only change was that, by now, the seal had been broken.

"Here is a little present," said Janice, handing me a folded-up sheet of paper. "This is the English version. I got the letter from Friar Lorenzo, and Eva Maria helped me translate it."

I could see that she was eager for me to read it right away, and so I did. This is what it said:

> *My darling sister,*
>
> *I cannot tell you how happy I was to receive a letter from you after this long silence. And I cannot tell you how I grieved when I read its news. Mother and Father dead, and Mino and Jacopo and little Benni—I do not know how to put words on my sorrow. It has taken me many days to be able to write you a reply.*
>
> *If Friar Lorenzo was here, he would tell me that it is all part of the grand design of Heaven, and that I should not cry for dear souls that are now safely in Paradise. But he is not here, and nor are you. I am all alone in a barbarous land.*
>
> *How I wish I could travel to see you, my dearest, or you to see*

me, that we might console each other in these dark times. But I am here as always, a prisoner in my husband's home, and although he is mostly in bed, getting weaker every day, I fear he might live on forever. Occasionally I venture outside at night, to lie in the grass and look at the stars, but from tomorrow, meddlesome strangers from Rome will fill the house—trade connections from some obscure Gambacorta family—and my freedom will, once again, be cut off at the windowsill. But I am determined not to fatigue you with my sorrows. They are negligible compared to yours.

It grieves me to hear that our uncle keeps you imprisoned, and that you are consumed by thoughts of vengeance on that evil man, S———. My dearest sister, I know it is near impossible, but I beg you to rid yourself of these destructive thoughts. Put your faith in Heaven to punish that man in due course. As for me, I have spent many hours in the chapel, giving thanks for your own deliverance from the villains. Your description of that young man, Romeo, makes me certain he is the true knight you were so patiently waiting for.

Now I am once again glad that it was I who entered into this wretched marriage and not you—write me more often, my dearest, and spare me no detail so that, through you, I may live the love that was denied me.

I pray this letter finds you smiling, and in good health, freed from the demons that were haunting you. God willing I shall see you again soon, and we will lie together in the daisies and laugh away past sorrows as if they never were. In this bright future awaiting us, you shall be wed to your Romeo, and I shall be free of my bonds at last—pray with me, my love, that it may be so.

Yours in eternity—G

When I stopped reading, both Janice and I were crying. Only too aware that everyone at the table was mystified at this outbreak of emotion, I threw my arms around her and thanked her for the perfect present. It was doubtful how many of the other guests would have understood the significance of the letter; even those who knew the sad story of the original Giulietta and Giannozza could not possibly have understood what it meant to my sister and me.

IT WAS NEAR MIDNIGHT when I was finally able to tiptoe back into the garden, pulling along a rather unenthusiastic Alessandro. By now everyone had gone to bed, and it was time to carry out something I had been meaning to do for a while. Opening the squeaky gate to the Lorenzo sanctuary, I looked at my grudging companion and put a finger on my lips. "We're not supposed to be here now."

"I agree," said Alessandro, trying to draw me into his arms. "Let me tell you where we're supposed to be—"

"Shh!" I put a hand over his mouth. "I really have to do this."

"What's wrong with tomorrow?"

I removed my hand and kissed him quickly. "I wasn't planning on getting out of bed tomorrow."

Now at last, Alessandro let me pull him into the sanctuary and up to the marble rotunda that held the bronze statue of Friar Lorenzo. In the light of the rising moon, the statue looked almost like a real person, standing there with his arms open, waiting for us. Needless to say, the chances that his features resembled the original in any way were slim, but that did not matter. What mattered was that thoughtful people had recognized this man's sacrifice, and had made it possible for us to find him again, and thank him.

Taking off the crucifix, which I had been wearing ever since Alessandro gave it back to me, I reached up to hang it around the statue's neck where it belonged. "Monna Mina kept this as a token of their connection," I said, mostly to myself. "I don't need it to remember what he did for Romeo and Giulietta." I paused. "Who knows, maybe there never was a curse. Maybe it was just us—all of us—thinking that we deserved one."

Alessandro did not say anything. Instead, he reached out and touched my cheek the way he had done that day at Fontebranda and, this time, I knew exactly what he meant. Whether or not we had truly been cursed, and whether or not we had now paid our dues, he was my blessing, and I was his, and that was enough to disarm any missile that fate—or Shakespeare—might still be foolish enough to hurl our way.

...

W HILE *JULIET* IS A WORK OF FICTION, it is steeped in historical fact. The earliest version of *Romeo and Juliet* was indeed set in Siena, and once you start digging into local history, you begin to understand why the story originated precisely where it did.

Perhaps more than any other Tuscan city, Siena was torn by fierce family feuds all through the Middle Ages, and the Tolomeis and the Salimbenis were famously pitted against each other in a manner that very much resembles the bloody rivalry between the Capulets and the Montagues in Shakespeare's play.

That said, I have taken a few liberties in portraying Messer Salimbeni as an evil wife-beater, and I am not sure Dr. Antonio Tasso at Monte dei Paschi di Siena—who was kind enough to show my mother around Palazzo Salimbeni and tell her about its remarkable history—would appreciate the idea of a torture chamber in the basement of his venerable institution.

Nor will my friends Gian Paolo Ricchi, Dario Colombo, Alex Baldi, Patrizio Pugliese, and Cristian Cipo Riccardi be happy that I made the ancient Palio such a violent affair, but since we know so very little about the medieval version of the race, I hope they will give me the benefit of the doubt.

I also hope Saint Catherine of Siena will forgive me for involving her in the legend of Monna Mina and the curse on the wall, as well as in the story of Comandante Marescotti and the boy Romanino, where she appears as a baby in the Benincasa household. Both scenarios are my invention, and yet I have tried to remain faithful to the spirit of Saint

Catherine's early life in Siena, her remarkable personality, and the miracles attributed to her.

Archaeologist Antonella Rossi Pugliese was kind enough to take me on a walking tour of Siena's most ancient parts, and it was she who inspired me to delve into the mysteries of the Siena underground, such as the Bottini caves, the lost cathedral crypt, and the remnants of the bubonic plague of 1348. However, it was my mother who discovered Santa Caterina's room in the old hospital, Santa Maria della Scala, and who—on the same occasion—managed to convince a kind custodian to show her the entrance to a medieval plague pit.

The less macabre parts of my mother's research on Sienese history were primarily made possible by the Biblioteca Comunale degli Intronati, Archivio dello Stato, and Libreria Ancilli—which, by the way, is where Julie goes to have the index card that was hidden in her mother's box deciphered—but we are also grateful for the illuminating insights of Professor Paolo Nardi; Padre Alfred White, OP; and John W. Peck, SJ, as well as the literary legacy of the late Johannes Jørgensen, a Danish poet and journalist whose biography of Saint Catherine offers a spellbinding insight into Siena in the fourteenth century. Furthermore, the Museo della Contrada della Civetta and the Siena municipal police have been tremendously helpful, the latter primarily for not arresting my mother during her many clandestine investigations into bank security systems and the like.

While on the issue of suspicious activities, I hasten to apologize to Direttor Rosi at Hotel Chiusarelli for staging a break-in at his beautiful establishment. As far as I know, there has never been a breach of security at the hotel, nor would the director and his staff ever interfere with the movements of their guests or remove personal belongings from their rooms.

I also need to emphasize that the artist Maestro Lippi—who is a real person—is not quite as eccentric as I have laid him out to be. Nor does he have a messy workshop in downtown Siena, but rather a breathtaking atelier in an old Tolomei castle in the countryside. I hope the Maestro will forgive me these artistic liberties.

Two friends from Siena have been particularly helpful and generous with their local knowledge: Avv. Alessio Piscini has been an inexhaustible resource of everything related to Contrada dell'Aquila and the Palio tradition, and author Simone Berni has patiently suffered a barrage of questions regarding Italian usage and Sienese logistics. I owe it to them both to say that, if any factual errors managed to sneak into the book, they are my own fault, not theirs.

I would also like to extend my very special thanks to the following people outside Siena: My friend and fellow freedom-fighter from the Institute for Humane Studies, Elisabeth McCaffrey, and my book-club sisters, Jo Austin, Maureen Fontaine, Dara Jane Loomis, Mia Pascale, Tamie Salter, Monica Stinson, and Alma Valevicius, who kindly critiqued an early draft.

Two people have been key in helping me turn story into book: My agent, Dan Lazar, whose enthusiasm, diligence, and savvy made it all possible, and my editor, Susanna Porter, whose keen eyes and expert touch helped to trim and tighten the book without getting me all tangled up. It has been an honor and a privilege to work with them both.

Needless to say, I am deeply grateful for the tremendous help and encouragement from all the wonderful people at Writers House and Random House, two households (dare I say) both alike in dignity. Maja Nikolic, Stephen Barr, Jillian Quint, Kim Hovey, Vincent La Scala, Lisa Barnes, Theresa Zoro, and Libby McGuire in particular have been instrumental in realizing this book. And a thank-you also to Iris Tupholme at HarperCollins Canada for her constructive advice about the work.

And finally, I owe so much more than thanks to my husband, Jonathan Fortier, without whose love, support, and humor I could never have written this book, and without whom I would still be asleep, not even knowing it.

I have dedicated *Juliet* to my amazing mother, Birgit Malling Eriksen, whose generosity and devotion are boundless, and who spent almost as much time doing research for the story as I spent writing it. I hope the book is everything she prayed it would be.

ABOUT THE AUTHOR

...

ANNE FORTIER grew up in Denmark and emigrated to the United States in 2002 to work in film. She co-produced the Emmy-winning documentary *Fire and Ice: The Winter War of Finland and Russia* and holds a Ph.D. in the history of ideas from Aarhus University, Denmark. The story of *Juliet* was inspired by Anne Fortier's mother, who always considered Verona her true home . . . until she discovered Siena.

ABOUT THE TYPE

...

This book was set in Bulmer, a typeface designed in the late eighteenth century by the London type-cutter William Martin. The typeface was created especially for the Shakespeare Press, directed by William Bulmer; hence, the font's name. Bulmer is considered to be a transitional typeface, containing characteristics of old-style and modern designs. It is recognized for its elegantly proportioned letters, with their long ascenders and descenders.